THE CARRINGTON PROPHECY

Other novels in the series from R. Lawson:

Cabo Caper
Killing Time
Retribution
Existential Threats

For more information, please visit www.RLawsonAuthor.com

THE CARRINGTON PROPHECY

R. LAWSON

ISBN-13: 9780989891646

DEDICATION

To Uncle Mike

EPIGRAPH

AUDENTES FORTUNA IUVAT - Fortune favors the bold.
- Virgil's Aeneid X, 284

TABLE OF CONTENTS

CHAPTER ONE

THE CARRINGTON PROPHECY

Andrews AFB

After brief conversation, considerable reflection, and two bottles of vintage champagne, Biff Roberts and the other members of the CIA's counterterrorism team finally slept for the remainder of the flight from San Francisco back to Andrews Air Force Base. It had been a long, harrowing week that thankfully had ended in averting a national disaster. They had successfully aborted an Iranian terror plot, one potentially of 9/11 dimensions that could have killed thousands.

Upon arrival at Andrews Air Force Base, Biff noticed the CIA's DCI Admiral Delaney, his attaché, and an entourage of Langley officials and security guards were waiting to greet them on the tarmac. As the CIA G-4 taxied to its designated parking spot, many in the crowd waved excitedly. Biff also noticed the DCI had a large dossier under his arm.

That's usually not a good sign, Biff thought. *Something's brewing — something big.*

Biff and his team descended from the plane into the smiling crowd. They received a combination of applause, thumbs up, and salutes as acknowledgement of their lead role in thwarting the terrorist plot in San Francisco.

"Fine job, Biff," the admiral said. "Welcome back." They shook hands and exchanged pats on the back.

Admiral Delaney was sincere in his admiration of his top field operative, recently promoted to Director of the Counterterrorism division. Even after all the long hours and stress of his work in San Francisco, Biff seemed as sharp as ever. His energy and appearance were the envy of many younger men. His six-foot-four athletic frame was still packed with muscle well into middle age, and his thick, wavy blond hair belied his age.

"Extraordinary how you pulled it off, Biff. Impressive tactics," Delaney said as they walked toward a line of waiting cars. "You never cease to amaze me. That Switchblade drone/flash bang caper will become a classic in our CIA annals."

"Thank you, sir. I had some good help."

"Word is Javari will talk at GITMO," Delaney said. "They're confident they'll break him. Another good move, whisking him offshore as an enemy combatant. We're sure to get some blowback, but what the hell. I'm certain we'll get valuable intelligence from him that will outweigh any misguided liberal bellyaching about enhanced interrogation." The admiral shook his head. "They can't fathom the distinction between harsh interrogation and torture. They should take a sabbatical in the Middle East and observe the prisons there. Their methods are torture. And when they're finished with you, they cut your head off."

"Jihadists and terrorists don't fall under Geneva conventions," Biff said. "The treatment at GITMO is harsh, but humane. I've personally observed the methodology."

"Enough of this interrogation method talk," Delaney said. "I'll manage the blowback… Back to your San Francisco exploit. Job well done, my good man, glad I made you a director. You're making me look good. After that Snowden NSA fiasco, we needed to score some points. Our NSA colleagues over in Fort Meade caught a lot of flak over that security lapse."

"They sure did," Biff said. "I appreciate your comments, sir."

Biff and the admiral reached the line of cars, pausing in front of a limo.

"I want you to spend a week at Rose Hill with Patricia. You deserve a good rest." The admiral gestured toward the vehicle beside them. "Our limo will drop you off."

"Thank you again, sir. Glad to be home."

"I bet. Listen, when you get a chance, please review this information carefully and let me know your thoughts. It's very important to get your input before I advise the Chiefs of Staff next month with our intelligence estimate about how we should manage this grave situation."

The DCI handed the dossier to Biff like a hot potato, as if he couldn't wait to get it out of his hands. This was more than a homecoming reception. As Biff had anticipated, something big was brewing, and Biff sensed he'd soon be in the middle of it.

Biff noted the thick folder was marked *CARRINGTON EVENT – Classified: Top Secret – B.C. ROBERTS V's copy (# 2 of 5)*

"Know anything about this subject?" The DCI asked as Biff looked at the cover title.

"The Carrington Event?" Biff said. He paused, probing his memory. The subject did ring a bell, setting off his remarkable recall, a trait that had distinguished him at Yale and contributed to his successful CIA career.

Biff nodded. "A cosmic event involving the sun's electromagnetic pulses, a flare or burst of gamma rays. A major solar storm occurred in the mid-1800s. The Carrington Prophecy says that the event may recur every 150 to 180 years or so, as a natural catastrophic event."

"Your recall is remarkable, Biff. Actually it was September 1, 1859. A solar super storm hit the earth with the flare power of a billion atomic bombs exploding. Night became day. Telegraph systems went down worldwide and electrical outages occurred nearly everywhere, resulting in general chaos. That geomagnetic interruption was like a dirt road compared to today's information superhighway. Our almost total dependency on electronics in modern life makes us frighteningly vulnerable to another solar storm of that magnitude.

"Think about the ramifications of a foreign attack generating a massive electromagnetic pulse," the admiral added, "a form of sabotage that would elicit a similar catastrophe."

"It's a scary scenario, Admiral, very threatening. Not sure I want to go there."

"I like your choice of words, Biff. But I'm concerned we will have to go there. Consider a nuclear device detonated in the stratosphere over the U.S. That scenario would make the Carrington Prophesy come true, maybe much sooner than a natural occurrence. It would paralyze all of our power grids, bringing all electronic communication and basic functions to a halt. It would pitch our IT-based society into perpetual night, vulnerable to attack."

The admiral's expression was grim. "That's our next existential threat, Biff. It's essential for us to avert such a doomsday scenario."

"You're thinking of an ICBM attack?" Biff asked. "Iran? China? North Korea?"

"Who's got the craziest leader, the loose cannon?"

Biff didn't have to think long about that one. "Kim Jong-un."

"Precisely. Come up with a plan. You're our Counterterrorism Director."

Chapter Two

THE TASK

Rose Hill Farm, Virginia

Biff awoke to the sunrise, the light seeping through the plantation shutters, creating a laddered pattern across the hardwood floor of the historic farmhouse. The upstairs bedroom faced east across the hillsides. Outside acres of cornfields and pine trees rolled down to the Potomac River, providing a lovely view. The filtered light announced it was time to rise and shine. He was ready.

He loved the early sunrises at this time of year, late May, when the days became longer approaching the summer solstice. After a hectic week, it felt good to be home. He glanced at his watch — 5:40. Time to get to work on the task the DCI assigned him yesterday upon his arrival at Andrews.

As he slipped out of bed to shower, he stepped onto one of Patricia's antique Persian throw rugs. Biff found it irritating that she had purchased the rugs for their new home. Why patronize Iranians whose leaders had issued a *fatwa* on him?

The *fatwa*, an ancient Islamic religious decree, had been issued to exact retribution for his perceived crimes against the Islamic Republic. Listed as their most wanted man, assassins had pursued him worldwide for three years for his suspected CIA role in an ingenious cyber-attack on their key nuclear facility, and targeted assassinations of strategic Iranian nuclear scientists.

They sought revenge for his collaboration in thwarting Iran's nuclear ambitions with their archenemy, Mossad, Israel's secret service, an unforgivable sin that increased their passion in pursuing him. As the CIA's top operative in the Special Activity Division, he'd collaborated with Israel's expert hackers and Mossad to devise an ingenious malware scheme that had destroyed the Natanz uranium enrichment centrifuges and sabotaged the Iranian nuclear installation's computerized command and control system. The cyber-attack had set back Iran's nuclear ambitions for almost three years.

They had murdered his first wife, Mary Beth, two years ago on Easter Sunday. And they'd finally caught up to him last New Year's Day while he was on a ski holiday in Cortina, Italy, to meet Patricia's family, wounding him in the shoulder.

Now they'd sought revenge by trying to strike his hometown, San Francisco, in the terror plot he and his team had just foiled this past week. With the choice of location, Iran's Revolutionary Guards intended to send a powerful message that they would continue to hunt him down until they succeeded in killing him.

The Persian rugs struck him as incongruous in his home, a reminder of the evil empire out to get him. The association set him off, but he didn't want to hurt Patricia's feelings by criticizing her choice of rugs.

Patricia was still sleeping soundly. Judging from their relations last night, she was glad to have him home. Yet even her wonderful, intimate welcome, an expression of love, had failed to relieve all his tension. Afterward, she had slept soundly, while he tossed and turned. He studied her for a moment as she rested peacefully. She was a strikingly beautiful woman, still stunning in her fifties. He considered himself a lucky guy.

He still harbored some guilt for marrying Patricia so soon after Mary Beth's murder, but Patricia had rescued him from the depths of despair. He had been consumed by overwhelming grief over the tragedy and Patricia had helped him move on with his life and resume his work. Her support and empathy, having survived a similar tragic experience herself years before, had made her a lifeline for Biff during that horrific time.

Her first husband, Italy's ambassador to Israel, had been assassinated by Hamas while on a peacekeeping mission in Gaza. That experience had given her insight that enabled her to help Biff through his own grief over Mary Beth. Consequently, he healed quicker than most confronting such dire circumstances. As a kindred spirit, Patricia guided him through the emotional quagmire, her intuition getting him back on track.

But he never fully recovered from that traumatic episode in his life. He planned more than just getting even with the Iranian radicals who killed Mary Beth. He planned proactive retaliation to cripple Iran's quest for a nuclear weapon and to thwart the terrorism they exported through the Quds division of the Revolutionary Guards.

Madmen like Javari, the leader of the terror plot they'd just foiled in San Francisco, represented this evil force that had hijacked a religion. The ruling theocracy in Tehran used Islam as a masquerade to attempt to impose universal Sharia law. Mullahs converted Islam into a jihadist movement along with Arabic Muslims who shared their beliefs. They exported terrorism, killing innocents in the name of Allah. Biff would not let that state of circumstances stand in his new job as Counterterrorism Director.

Biff tiptoed to the bathroom, hoping a refreshing shower would clear his mind. He had a lot of work to do.

As the hot water pounded his tired body, he realized he was pushing himself hard, too hard, but his job demanded it. Little things like Persian rugs set him off. But worrying about the government's ambiguous response to the threat of radical Islam went with his job. He was particularly concerned about the exportation of state-sponsored terrorism by Iran, allowing them to play games with the U.S., stalling negotiations, killing time while they enriched uranium to weapons-grade. The list of Iran's transgressions included nuclear collaboration with North Korea, that alliance complicating his current task.

Clearly, a change in national strategy was indicated, something more definitive. The enemy respected action, not political rhetoric, imaginary red lines drawn in the shifting geopolitical sands, and empty warnings. Islamist extremists were existential threats, and North Korea was another danger looming on the horizon, adding to the list.

He reflected on the menacing dimension the radical Islamists had introduced into his life, adding another challenge to his demanding job at Langley. Just staying alive had become a daring feat.

Recalling the intense drama of the past week filled him with anxiety. Usually calm and collected, it was time for serious self-assessment. They had come way too close to disaster in San Francisco.

As the CIA's new Counterterrorism Director, failure was not an option. He bore ultimate responsibility when national security was at stake. He replayed the events in his mind, analyzing the options, considering other actions they might have taken to avert the attack.

Should he have ordered a different course of action, another set of countermeasures? What if he'd ordered the FBI to be more aggressive in their surveillance? Yet he knew that "what ifs" could drive him crazy, like a Monday morning quarterback knowing he could have performed much better, critical even though his team won the game. Fortunately, they had prevented the well-conceived act of terror, one so horrendous that the resulting national outrage from the attack likely would have triggered another war in the Middle East.

Not a textbook operation for the CIA or the FBI, the operation had been poorly coordinated in many aspects, but it had been clever in the aspects that counted. Bottom line, they achieved an impressive outcome. Style points didn't count in the CIA, only positive results. Biff had become accustomed to success, having been on a roll controlling Black Swan events like the recent San Francisco plot. Protecting national security was his job. He recognized he was tightly wound up and must pull it together, learn to command close encounters like this even more effectively if he was to succeed in his new CT Director's role at Langley.

The faceless global enemy, many without uniforms or a national flag, continued to raise the ante in a high-stakes, asymmetric war game. Facing a jihad that permitted no backing down, he was committed to confronting these apocalyptic terror groups. Better now than later, and better on their turf than in the U.S.

Regrouping, he analyzed the terror threat, seeking solutions to avoid another near miss or, much worse, failing to prevent a major disaster. What should he do in his new position about the escalating global threat posed by terrorists, foreign and homegrown? Since 2010 jihadist groups had increased worldwide by almost sixty percent. Driven by a radical ideology, Islamic fanatics were launching a virtual Crusade of their own, the tables reversed almost a millennium later. How many times could the U.S. prevent these attacks?

The Mexican border was porous, and had allowed Javari to sneak across. Others would predictably follow, presenting imminent threats to the homeland by slipping through the cracks in the national border security. Was it simply a matter of time before they succeeded in launching a successful major terror attack, another 9/11? Over a thousand Middle Easterners were apprehended last year by the southern Border Patrol. They were mingled among the flood of hundreds of thousands of illegal aliens apprehended annually. How many made it across to become sleeper cells? There were no stats on that, but clearly the U.S. was vulnerable. Without a serious change in national strategy and commitment, increased acts of terrorism loomed as lethal threats.

Much as the recent San Francisco plot had been a close call, not only had they foiled the plot in the end, they had also captured the Iranian perpetrator, the infamous Revolutionary Guard Colonel, Mahmoud Abu Javari, a man who personified evil. When Javari was finally captured, Biff would never forget Javari's hateful stare. He was a man without a soul, a man who got his kicks by blowing up people he considered infidels because of his extremist Islamic beliefs. He had a long history of violence and mass murder. He was known to supply IEDs to Shiite insurgents in Iraq, weapons that killed and maimed American soldiers.

And last week the saboteur had plotted to blow up the Golden Gate Bridge and the BART tunnel under San Francisco Bay with stolen military-grade Semtex. Javari had recruited the assistance of homegrown jihadists to pull off the terror attack.

That was what they were up against, confronting violent religious fanatics — impassioned zealots like Javari. And now they were increasingly using homegrown jihadists, a new facet of the emerging global threat.

Despite the pounding of the shower's pulsating jets, Biff's back remained tense as he thought about the enormity of the problems confronting him. The still-healing wound in his left shoulder throbbed, adding to his angst regarding jihadists. The ache made him recall the nightmare of the gunshot wound inflicted by would-be assassins in Cortina five months ago. He adjusted the showerhead to massage his shoulder.

He already had enough on his plate dealing with the Middle Eastern terrorist problems, and now he faced a mindboggling threat from North Korea. He was approaching overload.

A Carrington Event triggered by an enemy ICBM exploding a nuclear bomb a hundred fifty miles above the stratosphere over the States would be a nightmare scenario with devastating consequences. Despite being a CIA veteran with years of exposure to unthinkable events and heinous crimes, the deliberation troubled him. The EMP weapon concept seemed like sci-fi that Hollywood dreamed up. To Biff, the concept hadn't seemed feasible, much less an impending reality.

After all these years in his risky profession as a CIA operative, he thought he'd seen everything. The possibility of a paralyzing Carrington Event challenged him to come up with a counterplan to a threat he unfortunately knew little about.

The admiral's latest "existential threat" disturbed Biff deeply. But how credible a threat did it represent? How imminent? Was it even technically possible at this stage? North Korea had a nuclear device, but could they deliver it? They had tested intermediate range missiles during the last year, even managed to launch a satellite, but did they possess a long-range ICBM with enough accuracy to explode it above the atmosphere of the U.S. to create a crippling EMP event?

The subject required research on his part to address these critical questions. He lacked a thorough background on the subject of an EMP created by a high-altitude nuclear explosion. He realized terrorism took no holidays, and he needed to formulate a comprehensive plan, soon.

Still perturbed, he toweled off, dressed, and quietly went downstairs to his study.

***

Later that morning Biff was still sorting through the Carrington documents in his study when Patricia called out, "Biff, I'll have our breakfast ready in fifteen minutes. Then I'd like to take a nice long walk with you down to our pier. It's a lovely morning to sit and chat, catch up. Are you up for that?"

What could he say? "Sure, dear, sounds like a plan."

Biff was three hours into reviewing the top-secret documents in the Carrington file the NSA had compiled. He was far enough along to discern the admiral's level of apprehension was justified.

Biff had lost track of the recent technological advances in this fast-developing field. Rocket science had taken a quantum leap since he last reviewed the topic at the U.S. Naval War College in Rhode Island over two years ago. Admiral Delaney wasn't crying wolf. The rapid progress of the technology had brought Star Wars reality to their doorstep. It was alarming to contemplate being thrust suddenly into a Dark Age by an EMP attack. Biff thought that a break to spend time with Patricia might help him to come up with some ideas. Besides, he'd just arrived home yesterday and couldn't ignore her. He'd revisit the topic later, he decided.

He put the documents in his safe and joined her in the kitchen.

"Give Jerry a heads up regarding our walk following breakfast, okay?" Biff said. Jerry was their body guard today, filling in for Tim, who was taking a few days off. "I assume the grounds are secure with a team?"

"You got it, big fella," she said. The endearment was one she had used since the shootout in Tel Aviv last year when Biff had saved her life. "An entire detail is scattered around the farm. Your boss is looking out for us. No surprises lurking.

"Too nice a day for anyone to try shooting you, anyway," she added, smiling.

Patricia embodied *joie de vivre*. He considered himself fortunate. She was the light of his new life and had pulled out him of a virtual Dante's Inferno to Purgatory's mountaintop. Like Beatrice, Patricia lifted him to a pinnacle where he could see Paradise ahead, happiness replacing despair, hope and meaning restored in his life.

"Thank you, Patricia. Be right there, dear."

As he locked up the classified material, he thought how the country was incredibly vulnerable to an EMP attack. The realization had continued to disconcert and preoccupy him since Admiral Delaney handed him the manila folder yesterday. He did not know how much sand was left in the hourglass. He needed time to come up with and implement a defensive plan. Maybe devise an offensive strategy.

But first, he needed factual data and more information, lots more.

***

Two hours later, Biff and Patricia sat on the pier, chatting and enjoying the view.

"So have you made peace with Reza? Is he back in your good graces?" Patricia asked abruptly, jumping from a pleasant discussion of grandchildren to a touchy subject, surprising Biff.

"How'd you know about that?" he asked.

"Tim told me before he took some time off. We'd discussed your conspiracy theory regarding Reza on prior occasions." Patricia referred to Biff's past suspicion that his colleague Reza was an Iranian triple agent setting up the CIA, waiting for the opportunity to strike. Tim and others at Langley thought it a baseless hang up of his, but no one could convince him otherwise. "Tim wanted my take on the situation, the 'inside story,' he said."

"Really?"

"I told him you marched to your own drummer and I just follow along without being too analytical, much less judgmental. Told him you'd been burned and swore never again to be betrayed, but that you'd figure it out with time."

Biff grinned. "You never cease to amaze me." Biff knew her experience working with Mossad had made her an astute observer of human behavior. Betrayal was a recurring theme in the spy world. One could never be too careful in this business. Reza had mastered the fine art of deception by surviving fifteen years undercover as a double agent in Tehran. Espionage annals were filled with duplicity that compromised covert operations, and got folks killed. Betrayals blew entire networks, revealed sources and methods.

"But yes," Biff continued, "I confess I was wrong about Reza. He proved himself in the San Francisco operation last week. He was in position to compromise our mission and cause a disaster if he really was a traitor. It turned out not to be the case."

She squeezed his hand gently. "That's good to hear."

"Tim and I were prepared to knock him off at the slightest misstep. The stakes were that high. Sorry to say I treated him unfairly." Biff had been suspicious of Reza for over a year, but he now saw his reasoning was biased. "I told him I misjudged him and apologized. He was good with that, and we moved on. It's yesterday's news."

"I'm pleased that uncomfortable situation is resolved, Biff. Reza's a good man; he's been through a lot."

"You're right."

She glanced at him, hesitating before finally asking, "Will you be able to forgive Enzo for his mistake?" Enzo was her son, who had unintentionally revealed their New Year's plans to go skiing in Italy. His innocent slip of the tongue had led to the assassination attempt on Biff. "I assure you, he was mortified."

Patricia was obviously trying to clear the air, leaving no lingering misunderstandings, Biff surmised.

"Nothing to forgive, Enzo had no prior knowledge of that banker, al-Laqis', connection to Hezbollah. Like you say, it was an innocent mistake. Enzo's a financier, not some agent moving in clandestine circles." Biff smiled at her. "No worries. I'll call Enzo and tell him not to sweat it. No hard feelings, life's too short."

Patricia nodded. She agreed life was too short, especially in Biff's line of work, but she thought better of voicing it. It did little good to worry constantly about the danger he was in, and the *fatwa* hanging over his head. She would cherish whatever amount of time they had together.

It appeared to him she intended to clear the air so they could take advantage of the lovely May morning. Relaxing on the farm's pier overlooking the Potomac River was conducive to conversation. She preferred an upfront relationship, no harboring grudges, hurt feelings, or misunderstandings. It was one of the many qualities he admired about her.

When she didn't answer right away, he wondered if she had more to get off her chest.

"I like the way you think, Biff," she finally responded. "I love you."

She wasn't surprised by his reaction to her questions. Biff possessed a strong character that she loved, always meeting life's challenges head on. They were both well acquainted with adversity and tragedy.

"I've arranged for a picnic lunch down here at noon," she said. "I've chilled a bottle of Mer Soleil. Will that fit into your schedule? I'm aware Admiral Delaney gave you a new assignment."

"I'll make it fit."

"I'm so happy you have a week off to spend with me."

"Listen, Patricia, I'm sorry, but I'll have to cut our week short to attend to some pressing company business. I need to make a couple of urgent trips."

"Where?"

"Fullerton, California, and Seoul, Korea."

"An unusual combination. Regarding the new assignment?"

He noted the disappointment on her face, and her attempt to disguise her distress in the tone of her voice. But he also knew she understood his commitment. Counterterrorism was not a nine-to-five job at Langley. As CIA's CT Director he had pressing responsibilities. Biff knew she accepted that.

"Yes, another 'need to know' thing. Can't discuss it. It's a serious threat I must address. Sorry, I'm really disappointed to leave you again so soon."

She nodded. "When do you leave?"

"Tomorrow morning, unfortunately."

"Shall I leave a light on?"

"I should wrap up my business in a week. I'll stay in touch."

"In that case, can I offer you a glass of your favorite Chardonnay as a sendoff, my love?" As always, her tone was supportive.

"Sure, why not? It's five o'clock somewhere." He grinned and hugged her.

Chapter Three

ROCKET SCIENCE

HTMS Headquarters – Fullerton, California
The next day

As Biff entered Professor Siegel's office, the aroma of strong coffee greeted him. The smell permeated the spacious, well-lit room, emanating from a small kitchenette in the far corner. Judging from Jonas Siegel's liveliness, he wasn't brewing decaf. He sparkled with energy as he sprung from his desk to welcome Biff, offering his hand with a wide smile.

As they shook hands, Jonas peered over the steel-rimmed bifocals balanced on the tip of his ample Roman nose. "Know anything about rockets, Mr. Roberts?" he asked.

"A very rudimentary knowledge, I must confess," Biff said. "That's why I'm here. I appreciate that you interrupted your busy schedule on such short notice to accommodate me, Professor Siegel."

"Jonas is fine with me. Not every day a CIA Director drops by my office." He chuckled.

"Make it Biff then, Professor." Biff came right to the point. "I need to pick your brain. Bring me up to speed."

It was immediately apparent to Biff that he'd arrived in the right place to learn about rocket and missile technology. Jonas' office was a rocket science academy. Biff thought Jonas looked the part, although he was younger than Biff anticipated. He projected the enthusiasm of a young professor eager to imbue his new student with knowledge of rockets.

Biff observed his surroundings, taking the details in quickly, an irrepressible habit in the espionage business.

Jonas' fourth floor office overlooked a pleasant, tree-lined park visible through a large window behind the scientist's desk. A huge table piled high with paperwork, both the inbox and outbox full to the brim, indicated Jonas operated on overload. The office was cluttered with rocket blueprints. A sizeable whiteboard on the wall was filled with equations, diagrams, and formulas. Science journals and math books stacked everywhere added to the jumble. On another wall, a floor-to-ceiling bookcase packed with even more books, journals, and binders of government regulations looked like it might topple over under their weight. Diplomas, citations, and framed photos of Jonas with famous people covered another wall.

It was as if Biff had stumbled into Einstein's office, legendarily messy, but organized to its occupant. Biff bet Jonas knew the location of everything and could lay a hand on any document without a moment's pause.

Biff stood in front of Jonas' desk, looking across at him as the aerospace engineer took a quick sip from his mug with the Raytheon company logo.

Biff had reviewed Siegel's credentials on the flight out from Andrews. It was an impressive bio: Princeton BS in physics, MIT masters in engineering sciences, and a PhD in aeronautical engineering from Cal Tech, where he'd taught for many years before landing part-time consulting jobs with Boeing and Thiokol. He'd built his reputation and burnished his résumé along the way. That experience eventually led to a lucrative, full-time job at Raytheon pursuing his lifelong interest, rocket science. They offered him a deal he couldn't refuse, luring him from the ivory tower to run their missile development program.

The man was well cast for his lofty position, looking and acting the part of a busy scientist with an inventive mind. His manicured, salt and pepper beard matched his hair and went well with his intense stare, now fully focused on his visitor. To Biff, the man's countenance announced that he'd likely cancelled his calendar to accommodate Biff and was eager to get on with it.

Jonas wore a wrinkled, blue button-down shirt, the collar open with no tie, and his shirt sleeves rolled up. His baggy, khaki cargo pants were also un-ironed. Unlike his neat beard, his hair appeared a bit disheveled, probably from running his fingers through it.

Maybe a nervous habit, Biff assessed. Despite appearing casual and relaxed, maybe he was the high-strung sort.

"Coffee, Biff?" Jonas seemed oblivious that Biff was evaluating him and meticulously surveying his office.

"Sure, thank you, Jonas."

Biff settled into a plush leather chair across from his host's huge wooden desk. The professor delivered a small tray of coffee, accompanied by sugar and low fat milk, to a side table within easy reach. Biff helped himself to a cup.

Without preamble Jonas launched into an overview of ballistics involved in ICBM technology, as if he couldn't wait to share his wealth of experience with his illustrious visitor. Biff was unaware that Raytheon's president had requested Siegel brief the CIA Counterterrorism Director following an urgent phone call from Admiral Delaney.

Jonas launched into his spiel like a recording, assuming his visitor knew little or nothing about the subject. Biff appreciated that he wasn't trying to impress him with his vast knowledge, instead keeping it straightforward and not overly didactic, difficult as it was.

"Consider rocket ballistics first of all," Jonas said. "The Tsiolkovsky rocket equation explains the relationship between mass and weight, the key problem for ballistic missiles."

"How do you spell that?" Biff asked, taking notes on his iPad.

After spelling it for Biff, Jonas continued, "To use a baseball analogy of a fellow scientist, David Wright, a baseball accelerates with the force of the throw, a quick power burst, then it freefalls, pulled by gravity. That's simply the nature of ballistics that after launch a missile's trajectory is controlled by gravity, friction, and other laws of classical mechanics. The faster the pitch, the farther the ball goes. To launch a missile, higher speeds are required, which means more fuel, which requires a bigger rocket to carry the fuel. With me, so far?"

"Got it. Pitched at Yale, I understand the metaphor." Biff had been the Ivy League's top pitcher, leading Yale to a championship.

Jonas pressed on without comment, moving into his professorial lecture mode.

"The basic problem in delivering big and heavy payloads is you need bigger and heavier rockets. Eventually you arrive at a point where the rocket is unable to lift off the pad because of its enormous weight. The way around this problem is to scale the missile to hold more propellant so the fuel represents a smaller fraction of the total mass. Relative to the amount of propellant the missile requires, the need goes up exponentially with the speed you desire to achieve in flight. Eventually you get into the realm of diminishing returns. Not a big surprise, right?"

"I'll take your word for it."

"Higher speeds require more fuel, which means a bigger rocket to carry the fuel, which means more fuel to launch the rocket. That's the essence of the problem."

"Take our ICBMs, what are their specs?" Biff asked. "They tested well, seemed to have solved that problem, so why wouldn't that be a benchmark, a reference point?" Biff was fascinated by the complexity of rocket science.

Jonas smiled. "Good question, astute, in fact. Let me explain it in layman's terms. In general, a long-range ballistic missile weighs eighty to one hundred tons. Only about one percent is the actual payload, the nuclear warhead. The rocket's basic structure accounts for about ten percent; the remaining eighty-nine percent is all fuel."

"Interesting facts, Professor. Never would have guessed those proportions, those weight distributions."

"No one would expect you to be familiar with those pivotal considerations. There are ways around the problem, however." Jonas ran his fingers through his hair absentmindedly as he contemplated how to present this concept simply to the CIA CT Director, confirming Biff's earlier suspicion of the habit.

Jonas continued, "As missiles increase in size they become more complex, a linear relationship. Therefore it becomes more efficient to employ several stages of thrusters and boosters, jettisoning a detachable section of the rocket once that part's fuel is spent. This lightens the remaining load, negating the construction of one giant, single-frame rocket. Staging allows rockets to drop dead weight once that section's fuel is consumed, but that requires complex components that must work in perfect harmony. While it may appear straightforward, I assure you, it's not. That's where rocket science comes in. The process involves complex formulas and execution. Follow me?"

Biff nodded. "So far. My big question, does North Korea possess this long-range ICBM capability? That's my concern from a national security position, and why I'm here on such short notice."

"Several North Korean multistage rocket launches failed miserably," Jonas said. "Last summer one blew up following launch. Finally, last December they managed to successfully send a weather satellite into orbit on a multistage Unha-3 rocket, but that doesn't necessarily guarantee future success."

"Explain that. Suppose they attempt the same launch tomorrow, can they pull off a repeat performance? How proficient are they?"

Jonas leaned back in his chair. "I'd say the probability of success is well under ten percent, based on the number of complex functions required to make all things go right."

"How'd you derive that calculation? That's a low probability; not a good performance record."

"Another good question," Jonas replied. "I understand why the CIA made you a director." He smiled. "You zero in on the basic considerations."

"Thank you," Biff said. "There's a lot at stake. I need to get my head around these principles."

"You're very thorough. I predict you will." Jonas leaned forward, resting his arms on his desk. "The odds are based on previous launch failures. Accomplishing the task once only means you have the components and basic technology, but the essential factor for repeat success is getting everything working at the same time in proper sequence consistently, time after time. The North Koreans still have work to do to get it right. Timing is key in computerized missile technology."

"As in life," Biff added.

"I wouldn't disagree with that observation," the professor said before pressing on, not interested in a philosophical digression. "Only a missile's launch energy and initial trajectory can be controlled. As soon as the rocket runs out of fuel, gravity and other forces take over. A ballistic missile burns only three to five minutes then coasts for about a half hour. In contrast, a satellite launcher needs to burn fuel for a longer period to reach higher speeds and altitude. While an ICBM sends a projectile into a parabolic arc back to earth, a satellite launcher must accelerate the satellite to orbital speeds."

Jonas added, "A satellite launcher conceivably could loft a missile, but bombs are considerably heavier than satellites. That's a major unknown in North Korea's case, but it's extremely doubtful that the same rocket could launch an eighty to one-hundred-megaton nuclear warhead over 3,500 miles. Virtually impossible, I'd be inclined to predict. A satellite averages around one ton or less. That would represent a very small warhead payload, not a smart proposition to risk war with a superior force to deliver a rather puny payload."

"Will there be a bluebook quiz later?" Biff jested.

"Possibly, but there's another issue to cover in my rocket science 101 briefing, it involves accuracy, so hang on." Smiling again, Jonas continued his overview.

"After its initial boost, an ICBM coasts through suborbital space for around five minutes, as I mentioned, reaching altitudes of two hundred to seven hundred miles above the Earth's surface. The payload is subjected to continually thickening air, changing atmospheric densities, winds, and other forces as it reenters the atmosphere. If the warhead is not perfectly symmetrical, it will tumble, be thrown off balance."

"Not a good thing, I suppose," Biff interjected.

"Correct. All these factors can widen the missile's range of accuracy. Or conversely, increase its inaccuracy, I should say. Presently, I estimate that North Korea has a medium range target accuracy of about five kilometers. By that I mean if a warhead is aimed at precise target, it could be reasonably expected to land within five kilometers of it, an area of nearly eighty square kilometers. Not very effective in a military system, but operational as a terror attack on a large population center.

"But," he hastened to add, "an ICBM attack is not very useful unless you use a highly explosive warhead. If your point is to launch a missile in the first place, then you want to put something with a dramatic impact on it, something in the order of eighty to one hundred megatons of nuclear explosive capacity."

"Got it, Professor. That's an attention getter for sure." Biff paused to take a sip of coffee. "Recently, Pyongyang released video of the pudgy boy leader, Kim Jong-un, reviewing a military parade of six ICBMs. It was a comical, like something out of an Austin Powers movie, celebrating a display of military might. That wacko has delusions of adequacy. Makes me wonder, were those six missiles fake?"

"Maybe, maybe not. We know from Japan's seismic data that North Korea has tested nuclear devices underground. But how far they're along with a reliable delivery system and warhead is open to speculation."

"What's your best guess?" Biff asked.

"Two years at the earliest, twenty years in the longest scenario, depending on multivariate developments. You're aware that they're collaborating with Russia and Iran?"

"I am. I'm trying to get a good fix on that."

"Stay for a late lunch downstairs in our corporate suite," Jonas offered. "We have an excellent chef. We can discuss that subject this afternoon."

"Thanks. I'd like to, but I'm meeting up with colleagues in L.A. this afternoon; I'm heading to Seoul tonight."

Jonas nodded. "Their NIS will have the latest data on the North's current progress and a projection of the imminent threat. And more detail than I have regarding the Iran and Russian connection," Jonas predicted. "See what they think regarding your question of timing."

"I'm counting on it. Thank you for your briefing, very helpful." Biff rose to shake hands.

"I have a suggestion you may find quite useful," Jonas said as he grasped Biff's hand. "Stop by Boeing in Seattle on your return flight and check out their Phantom Division's new CHAMP technology. We recently collaborated with them, the USAF, and K Tech on a successful missile project in the Utah desert. I'm certain the project will interest you. It's sci-fi becoming reality."

"CHAMP?"

"It's an acronym for Counter-electronics High-powered Advanced Missile Project. I promise you," Jonas added, grinning, "the project will blow your mind."

Chapter Four

SEOUL – NIS

The next day

"Got visitors, Ed," Tom, the pilot of the long-range G-5, said. "Off the right wing, check it out."

"Yeah," his copilot answered, "looks like a couple of South Korean F-15 K Eagles, how 'bout that? Look, dipping their wings to welcome us." Ed gave them a thumbs up to show that the CIA pilots recognized them as friendlies.

"Guess NIS requested them to escort us to Gimpo International. Nice looking aircraft, huh?"

"Yeah, nifty birds; check out the missiles," Ed answered. "The NIS obviously doesn't want to run the risk of a rogue encounter with enemy MiG intercepts." They were currently 150 miles offshore the Korean peninsula, and the North Koreans were known to sometimes act without provocation.

Their CIA aircraft was equipped with Elbit just in case MiGs strayed into their flight path. Elbit was a top-notch Israeli defense electronics company that had fitted the G-5 with a music system that incorporated an ingenious feature—sensors that could detect an incoming SAM or any missile and counter it with a deflecting laser beam, sending it off course. Because Israel was under constant threat from hostile surface-to-air missiles from Gaza, they installed it on all their commercial airliners. Necessity was the mother of invention, and Elbit limited the chances of an aircraft disaster.

"Since we're transporting such high profile passengers," Tom said, "I suppose Langley's taking no chances. Probably the admiral also arranged the fighter escorts with NIS. We don't need an international incident with North Korea."

"You can take that to the bank," Ed agreed, thinking of their passengers, Biff Roberts and his colleagues, sitting in their plush seats in the passenger cabin. Admiral Delaney didn't want to lose them and start a war in the process. Both pilots knew there was a lot at stake with this upcoming meeting with NIS, and they had to make certain their passengers arrived safely.

"Heard Biff pulled off another stunner in San Francisco last week," Tom said. "Hear about it? Off the charts, man."

Ed nodded. "All they could talk about at Langley. You'd have to be on another planet not to know about it. The guy's phenomenal." And now Biff was on his way to Seoul for a high-level intel meeting with the NIS honchos. "Never know he's in his sixties with his whirlwind schedule. The man never tires out."

They'd flown all night on short notice from L.A. in the company G-5, crossing the International Date Line. Biff had told them something very important had come up requiring immediate attention. No need to stop in Guam to refuel, either; the Gulfstream jet had a range of 6,500 nautical miles. They'd soon land at Gimpo International after a pleasant 6,000 mile trip in a little over thirteen hours.

"Contacted the tower," Ed said. "We're cleared to land on runway 14/32 L."

"Weather's pretty good," Tom replied, "request a visual."

"Okay ... Gimpo tower, come in. This is N49982 requesting a VFR approach on 14/32L."

"Copy that," the reply came immediately. "Request granted to N49982 for VFR approach on runway 14/32L. Ceiling is 15,500 feet, scattered clouds, visibility forty miles with light haze. Wind ten knots at 270. Adjust glide path as flight manual advises for Gimpo International approach from the east over the Sea of Japan. We will monitor your glide path and advise accordingly." The air traffic controller's Korean accent was barely perceptible.

"Roger that," Ed answered.

"After landing," the controller added, "take exit Alpha Romeo to your reserved chocks."

"Thank you. See you soon, Gimpo, over and out."

"Guess he didn't pick up on our call number," Tom said.

Ed frowned. "How's that? Why should he?"

"This plane used to be a rendition aircraft. That call number was famous, or infamous, depending on how you looked at it. It was in the news for weeks several years ago, the subject of multiple investigations into our black site activities. Investigations kept checking the flight records of this plane's number. The *New York Times* wrote a big exposé on CIA renditions based on leaked information from an anonymous source. Published our call number in the newspaper, noting the aircraft's unusual patterns and destinations; can you fucking believe that?"

"No way," Ed said.

"All that bullshit happened probably before your time with us, years ago. The incident caused quite an uproar back then, even triggered an internal review with polygraphs at Langley to avoid more leaks of our black site activity. A lot of pissing and moaning, accusations and denials going on; believe me, it was a nightmare. CIA publically maintained plausible deniability, of course. This plane's been reconfigured and refurbished for more conventional business trips like this, after some time off the circuit, but still has the same tail number, same call sign."

"Why didn't they just change the number?" Ed asked.

Tom grinned. "The DCI kept the call number as an 'in your face' symbol to the assholes on the hill. The shit had really hit the fan, with the liberals screaming like banshees, going nuts, congressional investigations, the whole nine yards. You'd have thought we were the friggin' enemy!"

"You fly some of those missions?"

"Yep. Worried like hell I'd be called to testify before Congress. Almost developed an ulcer from the stress."

"What were the missions like?"

"If I tell you," Tom said quietly, "I'd have to kill you."

"Ha! You're starting to sound like Biff."

Both pilots laughed at the old CIA joke, but Tom Wilson was a veteran CIA pilot who knew top secret things that if he ever divulged would get him thirty years in Leavenworth. He was privy to highly confidential information about the post 9/11 CIA program for enhanced interrogation in remote sites offshore, the so-called black sites. He was part of rendition, a collaborator in what many progressives viewed as war crimes. He'd landed at all of the black sites under the cover of night, filed incorrect flight plans to remote spots where his aircraft never arrived, and taken other intricate precautions against detection, leaving no trail to trace.

He acted without reservations or moral qualms. In his worldview, after 9/11, it was no holds barred. He saw it as his duty to his country as a patriot. To him, the jihadist bastards were enemy combatants, not POWs who should be afforded Geneva rights.

He often wondered what the bleeding hearts were thinking.

Even if he'd wanted to breathe a word as a whistle blower, it was possible someone would simply kill him in order to silence him. But Tom Wilson was a dedicated 'company' man who loved to fly, anywhere, and, he particularly enjoyed his lifestyle. Most of all, he wanted to live, period. His lips were sealed, and it would take an enhanced interrogation to get it out of him. Maybe not even that would get him to tell what he knew.

***

Upon arrival, an entourage of NIS and military security greeted Biff and his group on the tarmac of the airport's private terminal. Formerly Kimpo AB, K-14, home of F-86 Saber fighter jet squadrons in years past, the airbase had been converted to an international airport now known as Gimpo. Located just thirty-five miles south of the DMZ, the military airbase was considered dangerously close to North Korea. Their hosts explained that was the reason the squadrons were moved farther south down the South Korean peninsula in recent years.

As if North Korean missiles couldn't reach them there, Biff mused, and as if North Korea wouldn't target a civilian airport. He refrained from commenting aloud. Pointing out the obvious wasn't a good way to start a trip to a foreign country.

After hasty introductions, their National Intelligence Service hosts whisked them to NIS headquarters in the Naegok-dong district of central Seoul, a little over nine miles south on a congested highway surrounded by rice paddies, shanties, and scattered industrial buildings, some in disrepair, some under construction. The repulsive fecal smell of the fertilizer on the rice paddies was inescapable, dominating Biff's initial impression of Korea until the limo's air conditioning kicked in.

The roads were jammed with traffic, bicycles, scooters, horse carts, pedestrians, and all sorts of animals coming and going, so the short trip took some time. The limo was forced to stop frequently. The crowds of people seemed oblivious to the danger of being run over by a vehicle. People seemed focused on their mundane quest to survive another day in East Asia by any means possible, many toting heavy loads on their backs and heads as they trudged to and from market.

Biff took in the sight, similar to scenes from his three-year tour of duty in Vietnam as Deputy Station Manager in Saigon. Korea evoked memories of that stint with its overwhelming masses of humanity struggling to survive amidst congestion, poverty, and war.

Kim Min-Jun, Deputy Director of NIS, sat in the back seat of the bullet and bombproof Hyundai limo chatting amicably with Biff. Kim wasn't bothered in the least by the congestion. It allowed him time to converse and demonstrate his perfect English to his esteemed guest. Four years at UCLA had acquainted him with American colloquial expressions and customs, and he strove to appear relaxed in the company of the internationally admired CIA Director. Kim was honored to be in Biff's presence, not wasting a moment to bask in the experience. He sensed the man was in a serious mood as he gazed out the tinted windows, or maybe just suffering jet lag. Nevertheless, Kim felt compelled to strike up a conversation with his guest.

"Seoul lives on the edge," Kim said, "much like Tel Aviv, with the persistent threat of hostilities by unfriendly neighbors. We live in constant fear of a North Korean attack. Kim Jong-un is unstable and unpredictable. A nuclear attack would kill an estimated eleven million citizens in Seoul alone. Many of the thirty-six thousand American troops stationed in South Korea remain at risk."

"I share your concern," Biff said, turning away from the limousine window to look at his host. "I hope to address that common threat on this trip. But first I need to acquire some factual data, more background information, and your sense of how imminent the threat is."

Kim nodded. "Our NIS director, Nam Jae-Joon, awaits our arrival at headquarters. He's looking forward to your visit. We'll discuss those issues and the ramifications. We have much to accomplish, many shared concerns, but I don't want to preempt him."

***

An hour after leaving the airport, the limo pulled into the fortified checkpoint at the gate of NIS headquarters, manned by heavily armed guards outfitted in Kevlar. After checking their credentials, the guards saluted and waved them through. They drove up a long road to the ultra-modern main building, placed well back from the main road and surrounded by a sprawling front lawn, a security consideration. The spacious lawn surprised Biff; it was something he'd expect to see on the way to Dulles International Airport in the rolling Virginia countryside, not in South Korea.

He was impressed with the futuristic architecture of the five-story, pristine white building. It was modern and distinctly non-Asian in every respect. They parked in the underground bomb shelter and took the elevator to the director's conference room on the fourth floor. There, two more military guards checked their credentials as they got off the lift.

Biff wasn't surprised by the tight security.

Kim escorted them down a long hallway and into a large conference room with floor-to-ceiling bulletproof windows. More guards stationed outside the door appraised them as closely as they could without staring, which was considered impolite in Asian society. Discerning no threat, the guards beckoned them to pass by, saluting and nodding their heads in respect.

Their host, Nam Jae-Joon, the NIS Director, rushed over to graciously welcome them. "Nice to have you visit us here, Director Roberts. We patterned our NIS after the CIA. You should feel at home." Nam was a spry, middle-aged man dressed in a dark business suit accented by an Oxford club tie. Biff towered over him, but Nam seemed not the least bit intimidated, gregariously ignoring the height disparity as he shook Biff's hand.

Nam possessed a self-confidence that made him a mover and shaker in Seoul politics. He enjoyed his reputation and his job. He was anxious to see what this CIA Counterterrorism Director had to say and to learn the purpose of his ad hoc visit.

Biff introduced his select team of five, all dressed casually in contrast to their host. First was his special consultant, Dr. Peter Vincent, Director of the Homeland Security task force, congressional consultant, and renowned expert on nuclear threats, specifically EMPs.

Next Biff introduced Reza Tehrani, a senior CIA operative with few peers in covert ops. Reza was a former CIA double agent imbedded fifteen years in Tehran's Revolutionary Guards who had been privy to Iran's scientific research. Reza added the rare perspective of a North Korean ally, a collaborator in North Korea's nuclear program.

NSA expert in ciphers and cyber warfare, Rokman Behrouz, had also come along from Langley to offer his hacking expertise. Rokman knew both sides of the cyber equation — offense and defense. South Korea's computers were assaulted daily by hackers operating in North Korea, although fortunately rarely successfully. Rokman had some clever ideas to offer on exploiting the enemy's IT network to get inside their nuclear operations.

Biff's attaché, Tyler DuBain, was a former Navy SEAL and counterinsurgency expert who offered extensive field experience in special ops should they attempt to infiltrate a spy above the DMZ. That was a risky plan, but on the table for discussion. CIA needed more inside information, no matter the risks.

Biff's bodyguard rounded out the select group. Tim Cochran, a CIA operative, was in charge of Biff's security, requiring that he stay up to speed on the fast moving events in his boss' life. Yet even Tim found it difficult to keep pace with Biff, a man twenty years his senior. Tim also found it increasingly challenging to protect Biff from danger since the *fatwa* had been issued on him by Iranian mullahs.

After introductions, Nam offered them traditional Korean presents before he led them to a lavish buffet of tea, sweets, and rice cakes that had been set out in the soundproof conference room that was used for top secret discussions.

"We have much to discuss," Nam said, "but first some refreshments after your long journey." In Biff's experience, Nam's politeness was typical of Asian hospitality. Nam engaged them enthusiastically, clearly delighted to have the opportunity to align their mission with the Americans over their common threat.

Tyler immediately attacked the buffet, apparently famished, loading his fine china plate to the edges. The others hesitated until Nam poured tea for Biff, who signaled to his group to dig in. Protocol was obviously relaxed in this group, and Tyler's faux pas not an issue.

Nam smiled at Biff. "The man's hungry."

"Can't hold him back from a buffet table, Director," Biff joked.

All of the South Koreans were extremely polite and cordial, their affection for Americans obvious. Biff came right to the point of his impromptu visit, not observing protocol.

"What does North Korea have, Director Nam?" Biff asked. Korean names, like many Asian names, were the reverse order of American names. The surname came first, and thus Nam Jae-Joon was referred to as Director Nam. Biff had learned that the second and third names usually indicated the month and date of birth.

Biff looked his counterpart directly in the eye and spoke as if he expected an enemy attack tomorrow, maybe even tonight. There was no mistaking Biff's sense of urgency.

"This nuclear EMP topic has been sitting on the back burner too long," Biff added. "We need to coordinate our strategy."

The threat scared the bejesus out of Biff. It was time to get their act together and formulate a plan, but he worried about the timeline. He needed the South Koreans to share their intelligence estimates, and they needed to bounce questions off each other. This communication demanded personal interaction, hence his quick trip. Biff wanted face-to-face interaction, which so often provided valuable input not possible in encrypted communication channels from afar.

For his part, Nam thought how Americans were always in a hurry, pressing a sense of urgency. Familiar with the foreign habit, Nam obliged. He'd presented the overview countless times to numerous audiences with top-secret clearances.

"North Korea has just two missile launchers tested and operational that we can confirm," Nam began. "We'd categorize the threat level range as intermediate. The Hwasong, a Scud-like missile, ranges up to 500 kilometers carrying a 700 to 1,000 kilogram warhead. The Nodong is more worrisome. It can carry the same size warhead farther, 1,000 to 1,300 kilometers, allowing it to strike most of Japan. South Korea and your troops stationed here are vulnerable to both missiles, of course."

Nam continued, "The Musudan missile hypothetically has a range of 3,000 kilometers, but has not been tested, nor can we confirm it is even operational. The North Korean's fourth missile, the Taepo-Dong-2, is based on the technology used in the Unha satellite launcher, but is neither tested or considered operational. Basically, as far as we know at this point in time, they lack ICBM capability to reach the U.S. And it could be years before they develop that level of technical expertise, even with outside help from Iran and Russia.

"They lack reliability and have experienced multiple problems and failures. The design system for ICBMs is different from launching satellites into orbit. Satellites do not require sophisticated reentry technology like ICBMs with the two-second stages designed to work as a ballistic missile. Furthermore, satellites do not require reentry heat shields. According to our aeronautical engineers and ballistic consultants, what North Korea launched last December is not indicative of how you would construct a ballistic missile."

"Maybe that wasn't their intention," Dr. Vincent interjected.

Nam Jae-Joon frowned, puzzled by the comment, but pressed on. Nam had his presentation down pat.

"They've tested three nuclear devices underground," Nam continued, "all low yields in the seven kiloton explosive range, plus or minus a kiloton."

"That small yield may be adequate for their intended purpose," Dr. Vincent added politely, hoping for a response.

Biff spoke up, hoping to clarify that Dr. Vincent's remarks were offered constructively and not intended to offend the NIS Director.

"Dr. Vincent is suggesting North Korea is involved in an elaborate disinformation scheme, a false flag of sorts, designed to delude Western nations and allies regarding the true nature of its nuclear and ballistic programs. They intend that we underestimate the sophistication and strategic implications of both their programs, missile and nuclear. Our facts do not support the viewpoint that they are years away as a nuclear threat. Our current intelligence indicates North Korea is a clear and present danger, a near-term existential threat engaged in misdirecting us to gain a strategic advantage."

"Kindly share the data supporting your position, Mr. Roberts," Nam said evenly. "Explain how we've been deluded." Nam was not the least bit insulted, but he was not convinced about a false flag or any sort of *ruse de guerre* perpetrated by North Korea. In his opinion they were not that sophisticated or clever. He felt Biff's assertion of subterfuge was likely fictional, merely a conspiracy theory popular in some intelligence agencies. He wondered where this was leading, although he had an educated guess. He'd learned a lot about the real world since Oxford.

One thing he was certain of was that they were in this together. The U.S. had always been a staunch supporter of South Korea, a trusted advisor in these matters, stationing a serious number of U.S. troops in his country for the past sixty years. Nam knew being offended would be counterproductive. He would listen carefully to what they had to say.

"I'll defer to Dr. Peter Vincent to elaborate, Director," Biff said. "Peter has been on top of this conundrum for some time, but we've been remiss in taking definitive action, as have other agencies and government departments who should have acknowledged his warnings and taken action sooner. We're all late to the party and playing catch up. Dr. Vincent saw the big picture and warned of their deception. Now the time has arrived to heed his warnings. I need to get my ducks in a row, get your input, and enlist your assistance."

Nam raised an eyebrow. "Ducks in a row?"

"It's an idiom, Director," NIS Deputy Director Kim Min-Jun explained in English, then swiftly again in Korean. "It means insuring all the small details and elements are accounted for before taking action."

"Ah, I see," Nam said. "You mean taking a logical approach to the problem, conducting a judicious deliberation before acting. Interesting metaphor, 'ducks in a row.'"

That moment of confusion settled, Dr. Vincent carefully explained his analysis of the situation.

"Many decision makers in Washington D.C. and the press have bought into this act of deception by North Korea, Director. They have failed to recognize North Korea's clever misdirection and artful deceit."

Dr. Vincent had everyone's full attention. Even Tyler had stopped eating to listen.

"Allow me elaborate on how they have misled us and concealed the true status of their programs," Dr. Vincent continued. "Common wisdom is that they are pursuing development of miniaturized nuclear warheads for missile delivery and that the three nuclear tests over the last two and a half years were for that purpose alone. This claim is merely disinformation designed to conceal the fact that North Korea's nuclear program is far advanced beyond miniaturization, a process that is not difficult, and in fact can be accomplished without nuclear testing. So what's their motive?"

He paused, but no one said a word, waiting for his explanation.

"North Korea and Iran have strategic reasons to mislead and conceal the true status and purpose of their missile and nuclear pursuits. The end game is to create confusion so we underestimate the sophistication of their plans and fail to act in time to stop them before they achieve superpower nuclear status. Their ultimate goal is to become progenitors of a dystopian new world order by spawning chaos beyond imagination."

"How do they propose to achieve that goal, Doctor?" Nam asked, anxious for his answer. Nam wondered how NIS could have missed this, if it was indeed verifiable. "Our intel indicates that they have no ICBM capability for the foreseeable future," Nam stated emphatically. "So, how will they deliver a devastating attack on the States? Their kilogram payload is puny, even if they managed to get it there."

Dr. Vincent nodded. "That's exactly what they want us to believe, Director Nam. Former DCI Woolsey of the CIA testified before Congress in 1994 that North Korea had enough plutonium for a nuclear bomb. It's a stretch to think that after twenty years, they still haven't figured out how to construct a miniature warhead for missile delivery, especially with technical assistance from Pakistan, Russia, and Iran. Really, it defies logic."

"So what do you propose they're up to, Doctor?" Nam replied.

"A surprise electromagnetic pulse attack, triggered by a nuclear explosion above the stratosphere," Dr. Vincent announced. "An EMP attack in the near future, in fact."

"We're aware that Russia has supplied them with EMP weapons and technology, and that they're working on their own DPRK version," Nam said.

"DPRK?"

"Democratic People's Republic of Korea, an oxymoron," Nam quipped, eliciting smiles all around and a few guffaws.

"Tell them how you see it coming down, Doc," Biff urged, anxious to get all the cards on the table. Biff was enjoying this exchange and carefully watching Nam's reaction.

"Note that all their missile tests all were aimed over the South China Sea toward the South Pole," Dr. Vincent said. "Same with last December's satellite launch, which tracked an orbital path over the South Pole, progressing back north over Mexico's Yucatan peninsula, passing closely to the U.S. This is not a mere coincidence, I assure you."

"And that is because?" Nam interposed, impressed with this consultant's knowledge.

"Our enemies know our BMEWs, ballistic missile early warning systems, all point north, toward the North Pole. Only two U.S. PAVE PAWS Large Phased Array Radars face south for early alert from that direction. There's a gap between the two fields, a hole in the coverage larger than the Yucatan peninsula and in that general location. These two radar arrays on the east and west coasts were designed to spot missiles launched from submarines or Cuba, but may not detect a missile or satellite incoming from the South Pole through that particularly vulnerable spot."

Dr. Vincent paused. "A simple course correction of an orbiting North Korean satellite carrying a nuclear device of low-kiloton fission material, plutonium and uranium, would bring them through that critical, strategic location undetected, then into space over the United States. I believe they plan to explode a nuclear bomb in space, somewhere around 150 miles above the earth's surface. The explosion would release a mass of gamma rays, inciting a devastating EMP, frying all electronics in the States, creating instant Armageddon. Modern life would screech to a halt, destroying the most civilized, innovative nation on Earth, leaving those surviving defenseless and in a state of chaos, susceptible to follow up conventional attacks and domination."

There was a brief silence while everyone listening seemed to consider the magnitude of what he was saying.

"A frightening concept," Nam finally said. "We must pursue our discussion of this alarming scenario. Will you be staying a few days, Mr. Roberts? We need to get both our countries' 'ducks in a row.'"

"We'll be staying at our embassy for forty-eight hours," Biff said. "In the morning I need to meet with Colonel Logan Scott, our chief of military intelligence here in South Korea, and our station manager and his intel officers at our embassy. Perhaps we can continue our discussion tomorrow afternoon."

"I deem it imperative," Nam declared. "May we pick you up at the embassy at noon?"

"That would work," Biff said.

Unbeknownst to them, someone in the conference room carefully noted the precise time of their travel arrangements.

CHAPTER FIVE

TROUBLE FOLLOWS HIM

Tehran, Iran – IRGC Headquarters
Later that day

"We have confirmed that our nemesis, the CIA operative Roberts, thwarted Abu Javari's plot in San Francisco last week, General," Colonel Ali Shirazi said. "They captured him, flew him to Cuba, and incarcerated him at Guantanamo for interrogation."

"Will he talk?" asked the Quds Force General, Haj Qassem. He was still furious at the failure of the terrorist plot, and that an entire year's planning had been foiled. That Javari had been taken alive only added insult to injury.

"Most likely. I fear he will crack over time, even with what they call their 'enhanced' methods of interrogation." The colonel's disdain for the CIA's methods was clear.

General Qassem silently agreed. What the CIA called enhanced interrogation—water boarding, sleep deprivation, being forced to stand for long periods in uncomfortable positions—were not methods that qualified as torture in the Middle East. Such treatments were more like a harsh form of persuasion, and generally not even a starting point for the ruthless interrogations that took place at Evin prison's torture chamber a short distance away in Tehran. The General thought such restraint a pointless waste of time, but he knew that eventually, even such softer methods were often successful.

"Will Javari divulge our plans with North Korea?" the General asked.

"Over time he could answer all their questions," the colonel acknowledged. "Most likely, they will eventually wear him down and squeeze it out of him."

General Qassem scowled. Javari knew a great deal about their sources, methods, and planned operations, including Iran's nuclear progress and intentions.

"We're so close to achieving our ultimate goal, the eradication of Israel from the face of the Earth," the General said in a tone somewhere between annoyance and frustration. Since the '79 Revolution and overthrow of the Shah, Iran had spent billions and suffered the targeted assassinations of four key nuclear scientists as well as high-ranking Revolutionary Guard officers by the Americans and Israelis. Iran had endured their Stuxnet cyber warfare that disrupted their uranium centrifuges and endured severe economic sanctions. "We're too close to fail now. We must prevail, Ali."

"I share your aggravation, General. Too often, they seem somehow to anticipate our plans and disrupt them."

"We cannot stop short of the finish line. We must sustain our efforts. If Javari is broken and reveals our plans, the Americans will inform Israel regarding our timetable and our progress. That will prompt them to mount a preemptive strike, ruining our grand scheme. We need more time to accomplish our plans. We need to stall. Tell me, how does this Roberts manage to thwart us time after time?"

"That's a big question. For him to predict and forestall so many of our classified operations over the last three years would require an army of spies with many well-placed moles."

"All moles are spies, but not all spies are moles. There must be another explanation. Maybe one or two sleeper cells could penetrate our inner network to steal our vital intelligence, but multiple agents would be required to do this much damage. It doesn't seem possible in the system of checks and balances we've set up to ferret out such deception. We've never discovered even a single double agent in our midst."

"Some say kismet embraces Roberts' life," Colonel Shirazi said. "He's dodged the mullahs' *fatwa* for three years. Our Hezbollah team shot him early this year in Cortina, but he survived. He's back on the job, actively interfering with our extension of jihad in Africa, dismantling our affiliate operations there. No doubt he's scheming with Mossad to launch another covert attack against us."

General Qassem drummed his pen on his desk, gazing at the ceiling, searching for a rational explanation for the series of frustrating events surrounding his paramilitary unit's hit squads' repeated failures to take out the CIA operative Roberts. IRGC and contracted assassination jobs all failed in their attempts. Kismet, a belief of the supernatural pervasive in the Middle East, remained prevalent in the General's mindset, but were they missing something else? He couldn't bring himself to attribute this persistent CIA problem to destiny. No one controlled fate, not even this legendary operative, Biff Roberts.

Colonel Ali Shirazi knew better than to interrupt. Not when the commander was venting or deliberating. He waited patiently for instructions.

"Where is Roberts now?" General Qassem asked. "Sequestered in Langley where we can't get to him? Retribution is long overdue in his case."

"Actually, our North Korean contact in Pyongyang informed us he arrived in Seoul with a delegation this morning. He's staying at the U.S. embassy, conferring with the South Korean intelligence service."

The general's gaze snapped back to the colonel. "How did they learn that?"

"They have a well-placed spy in Seoul who informed us that a top CIA official was visiting NIS. The informant goes by the code name Jin-Ju. DPRK infiltrated him years ago. He has contacts in NIS posts, none high-ranking, but he's in a position to glean snippets of valuable information. Jin-Ju forwarded the information to his superior who was aware of our interest in Roberts."

"I assume by superior you imply Jin-Ju informed the Dragon Lady?"

The colonel nodded. "He does indeed answer to her, and acts only with her approval. The Dragon Lady keeps a tight rein on her network. She vouches for Jin-Ju's reliability according to our Pyongyang associates in RGB. She notified DPRK's security agency, which relayed the information to us, thinking it may present an opportunity."

"Then we must mount a hasty operation to eliminate Roberts and catch him off guard in South Korea," General Qassem said. "I don't care how many men it takes, just kill him."

"Jin-Ju is a spy, not an operative capable of mounting a major assault, General. But I'm certain he has valuable contacts that could arrange

Roberts' assassination. I know North Korea maintains a special capability for contingency missions like this within Seoul. Not topnotch special ops or military personnel like ours, but a paramilitary criminal element experienced in firearms that can be contracted for jobs like this. I'll contact Pyongyang to arrange it."

"Tell them to hire a lot of men. I don't want him to get away again. I'm losing track of how many times he's escaped us."

"Consider it done, sir."

General Qassem nodded, his bad mood dissipating. Hopefully, this time Roberts' luck would finally run out.

***

Kismet played no little or no role in Iran's failure to eliminate Biff Roberts over the last three years. The Revolutionary Guard remained unaware that their headquarters were cleverly compromised and their plans routinely telegraphed. Quds Force special ops, tasked with coordinating with proxy terror groups Hezbollah and Hamas, ran their international operations from this location.

The Quds officers' private conversations were recorded by a nearby office computer infiltrated by a malware Flame virus capable of screen shots and eavesdropping. CIA assets had exploited IRGC's intranet over a year ago by cleverly hacking the system through a payroll vulnerability. Despite IRGC's conversion from the Internet to an intranet for increased cybersecurity, they were seriously compromised. Huawei telecommunication experts who installed the latest Chinese system had assured the IRGC it would not be possible, and no one inside of IRGC had yet discovered the penetration of their new in-house security system. They assumed discussions of classified information were protected. A supernatural event did not explain Biff Roberts 'uncanny' performance, but modern, crafty cyber spying that gave the CIA a leg up on Iranian operation plans did. Knowledge was the ultimate power play in the intelligence game of espionage. The CIA remained "man up" on Iran through covert human intelligence operations and cyber espionage.

A clique of dissident Iranian Green Party twenty-somethings took responsibility for this shrewd deception. Five highly intelligent CIA assets, designated as the "cousins" had exploited the IRGC computers. Bluetooth wireless technology relayed the pilfered discussions to a pomegranate stand on the sidewalk outside the Revolutionary Guards' headquarters, ironically the former U.S. embassy. No one suspected the fruit stand operator's covert role. The ruse had gone on undetected for well over two years, first exploiting IRGC's Internet, and now infiltrating the Guards' newly established intranet. The cousins' ingenuity knew no bounds when it came to cyber spying, and their brilliant exploits were financed by the CIA, who also supplied technical assistance and malware.

From the fruit stand, the secret information was relayed across Tehran by hi-tech electronics concealed inside the portable stand's construction. The penthouse apartment of the covert group's ringleader received the purloined transmissions and encrypted them for satellite uplink to the NSA 'monastery' inside Langley for analysis. A distant "cousin," Rokman Behrouz, an Iranian refugee from the early 1980s, handled and correlated the forwarded information. A valuable chain of intelligence data streamed daily from Tehran, insuring the CIA maintained the upper hand in their covert war with Iran.

It was a clever, ongoing operation not involving drop boxes, invisible ink, Minox cameras, or old-fashioned listening devices. No secret conversations were required between shady "cold war" characters lurking in trench coats in the shadows of a park or back alley. All these historic methods risked exposing covert agents or networks.

Deniable plausibility, paramount in the CIA, was assured with the modern methods. Cyber surveillance had arrived, becoming the ultimate clandestine modus operandi. Anonymous malware left no trace to its perpetrator unless the penetrated party possessed sophisticated analytics. IRGC had no clue their computers were exploited, much less possessed the complex diagnostic technology to figure out who hacked in and how.

***

RGB Headquarters – Pyongyang, North Korea

General Pak Jin-Se carefully studied the cryptogram from Tehran. The security agent major who had decoded it for him stood respectfully in front of his desk, awaiting orders. The communication was quite detailed. Pak reread it several times before making a decision.

"Copy this communiqué immediately to the Dragon Lady," Pak finally said. "Have her covert agent Jin-Ju organize the hit using local contractors. I don't want North Korea implicated in case things don't go as planned. We owe the Iranians this favor for their assistance. The Revolutionary Guard informs me that this CIA operative Roberts seems to have an uncanny knack for escaping assassination."

"Yes, sir," the major said. "I'll get our ciphers right on it. She'll receive it in less than an hour."

"We're not certain why Roberts arrived in Seoul, but we can't afford to have the CIA discover our plans." General Pak looked the major in the eye. "You understand what's at stake?"

"Our plans to cripple the U.S., sir."

"That's correct. Without electronics America is defenseless."

Defenseless and ready to be taken down at last.

General Pak had convinced Kim Jong-un that the bold plan presented a method to neutralize America. He'd promoted this daring project to the supreme leader, who was seeking a method to punish America. Despite dissenting opinions from other generals, General Pak had prevailed, spiriting the venture through the bureaucracy and military.

And when they struck, Pak would be revered as a hero.

***

CHAPTER SIX

U.S. EMBASSY – SEOUL

The next morning

"The leadership maintains a counterinsurgency mindset," said Colonel Logan Scott, the U.S. Chief of Military Intelligence in South Korea. "North Korea is smaller than Mississippi but armed to its teeth. They have more military personnel in that small country than are in all the domestic bases in the U.S. I'm not counting our overseas deployments. All military units combined, the Korean Peoples' Army, the KPA, is estimated to have close to one million in various units, about forty percent of the adult population."

"That's the fourth largest standing army in the world, right?" Biff interjected. "My understanding is their active military forces are twice those of South Korea."

Colonel Scott nodded. "Correct. North Korea's population stands at twenty-five million, half that of South Korea, but their army is twice as big."

Biff and his counterterrorism team were meeting with the military's top intel officer stationed in ROK on the top floor of the U.S. embassy. The former chancery building, located in the busy Jongno-Gu district near the Kyonbok Palace in the heart of downtown Seoul, was the hub of the CIA's station in South Korea. The embassy provided the diplomatic cover for America's sixty plus years of clandestine commitment to South Korea's security following the partition of Korea after the war along the 38th parallel, the demilitarized zone.

The DMZ divided two distinctly different nations: one democratic and defensive, the other totalitarian and bellicose. South Korea had become modern and progressive, while the North seemed caught in a time warp reminiscent of the 1950s, the time of the original conflict, and remained aggressively militaristic decades later.

Now the two close allies, South Korea and the USA, faced a mutual grave concern. They were confronting an alarming, imminent threat — North Korea with a lethal, nuclear EMP weapon. The threat level was heightened by the realization that the North was led by a deranged, unpredictable dictator who could quickly thrust the world into another major war.

Seoul lived on the edge of a DEFCON environment, a defense readiness condition not conducive to a relaxed lifestyle even before this most recent threat. The North and South jockeyed to achieve hegemony, while the public remained unaware of the new, imminent threat of a surprise EMP attack on both South Korea and the U.S. that could leave them immobilized and at risk of conventional warfare.

"Suspicious to their core," Colonel Scott continued, "the North Koreans shoot first and ask questions later. They live in a state of paranoia. The regime holds one hundred thousand political prisoners captive under gruesome conditions in what they call 'reeducation camps.'"

"Basically gulags or concentration camps," Biff commented.

"Yes, essentially. They survive under primitive conditions. Many other citizens starve thanks to a government dedicated to spending on the military over providing the basics for its people. Under the totalitarian rule of Kim Jong-un, the grandson of Kim Il-sung, things continue to go downhill. He's a ruthless lunatic who had his uncle shot to solidify his power, to give you the idea of the loony toon environment up there. The family has ruled the Hermit Kingdom for over sixty years. Needless to say, it's a primal, insular society. Most of the population lives in abject poverty with limited refrigeration, sanitation, and access to communication. Without modern electronics, email, Google, or even telephones for the vast majority, they have no means of contact with the outside world, no way to know what's going on."

"Or any means to mount a rebellion against the oppression," Biff added.

"Right, Kim Jong-un has the populace securely under his thumb," Colonel Scott said. "Summary executions are not uncommon on specious grounds or accusations without a trial. No one really has a day in court. The OGD, the secretive Organization and Guidance Department, maintains surveillance much like the SS and KGB. Their intelligence service is more powerful politically than the military or the RGB. It's unimaginable totalitarianism up there."

"At Langley," Biff said, "it's our belief that OGD actually runs the country. It's a powerful old boys club of Kim Jong-Il's university pals. His son, Jong-un, acts merely as a figurehead."

"That's an accurate assessment. OGD ensures that no one steps out of line. General Pak heads up the RGB and is the one exception to the rule. After forty years in the spy business, he's probably the number two man in the country and enjoys autonomy."

"I find it hard to envision that degree of cruel subjugation and total mind control," Biff said. "I understand the living conditions rival the lowest in the world."

"It's a deplorable situation. DPRK spends their limited resources building up military might, not to benefit the populace, as I mentioned. They spend billions on armaments. At night, our satellites show South Korea lit up while the North remains in darkness. That's how bad it is up there; there's virtually no electricity."

"We need more human intelligence," Biff said. "What are the chances of infiltrating a South Korean spy above the DMZ?"

"Slim to none. Extremely risky at best, and likely suicidal," Colonel Scott said without hesitation.

"So it's doable," Biff responded to the bird colonel without blinking an eye. He was deadly serious.

The irony of his unexpected comeback was not lost on Biff's select staff listening to the colonel's briefing. The room was silent as they watched for his response to Biff's comment.

Colonel Scott's jaw dropped. He was momentarily speechless at the CIA's Director of Counterterrorism's preposterous proposal of infiltrating a spy.

This was Biff Roberts at his best, demonstrating his patented self-confidence that no task was impossible in his covert world. To him the destination was paramount, not the journey. The journey involved intricate planning and building a conspiracy of lies and deception, an undertaking in which he thrived.

Biff's team observed Colonel Scott's response to his remark with amusement. Jon Gunderson, the CIA's station manager under diplomatic cover in Seoul, caught Tyler DuBain's eye and winked. Tyler grinned in response.

"Gunner" was a former Marine NCO. He had immediately bonded with Tyler, a former SEAL. They shared a distinguished military special ops background, both decorated for service in Iraq and Afghanistan. Gunner respected his military liaison in Seoul, Colonel Scott, but realized the colonel underestimated Biff Roberts' boldness. Obviously, the Colonel didn't know Biff's rep or his indomitable will. Or maybe he thought Biff had misunderstood his pessimistic appraisal of the chances of sneaking a spy into North Korea of "slim to none."

Actually, Colonel Scott had never met Biff and didn't know if he was kidding or not. The CIA director hadn't cracked a smile, adding to Scott's confusion.

Affectionately known at Langley as the "Big Kahuna," Biff Roberts had established a reputation for pulling off the impossible. If the colonel had been able to read Biff's résumé closely, he would have learned that fundamental fact, but he'd been assigned this briefing on short notice and much to his disadvantage, he was unacquainted with the CIA CT Director's background and accomplishments.

But astutely he recognized the man he was briefing was not the average spymaster. His visitor had a commanding presence, projecting an aura of authority that strongly suggested no one blew smoke up his ass. He'd expected an older person, someone out of touch with the situation in South Korea, a policy wonk. Instead, this man came across as vigorous, undaunted, ageless, and well informed about the imminent threat North Korea represented.

Caught off guard, Colonel Scott recalled the commanding General of USFK at Yongsan garrison in Seoul had described Biff as "a wizard of sorts" when he assigned Scott to the briefing.

Still, Scott was stunned that he suggested infiltrating a spy into North Korea after he presented his pessimistic overview of the situation up there.

Biff's suggestion was like throwing a cat in the middle of a pack of mad dogs. Had the man lost it?

The CIA had a reputation of a cowboy attitude, a tendency to take reckless action on occasion. Biff's suggestion, if he was serious, seemed to confirm that.

When he noted the colonel's obvious surprise and hesitation, Biff hastened to clarify how it was "doable." He had no intent to embarrass the man, or indulge in a contentious discussion. In his complex world, obstacles were viewed as challenges, not impediments. He realized that his particular worldview was not shared by others, and his proposal might appear rash. Opinionated in some respects, he tolerated opposing views but only if supported by factual data or if they did not compromise the mission. He never lost sight of the primary objective and was not easily dissuaded by naysayers.

Experience had taught him how to manage adversity, sometimes by simply defying the odds, toughing it out, and not being afraid to fail. He found that persevering often rewarded bold decisions and actions despite contrary conventional wisdom. Dwelling on the downside wasn't his bag, and herd mentality turned him off. He followed his instincts. His capacity to read his enemy helped to secure positive outcomes, and his success bred confidence.

"'You can't win if you don't play', as they say in Vegas," Biff informed the colonel with a grin, hoping to sway him by lightening the tense mood.

Not sure how to respond, Colonel Scott thought of the Air Force adage, "There are old pilots and bold pilots, but not many old, bold pilots."

This CIA officer definitely fell in the "bold" category, but the colonel politely refrained from comment. He'd met some colorful characters in his twenty-year career since graduating West Point, but he realized Biff Roberts fell in the iconic category, part of a special breed of spies. You don't argue with men of renowned stature in a command position, and a CIA director carried the weight of a general. Colonel Scott resigned himself to listen to Biff's wild plan.

As a young Special Activity Division officer performing dangerous paramilitary tasks, many "off the books" in Vietnam and Central America, Biff Roberts had learned his life lessons well. Some lessons learned the hard way were indelibly imprinted on his mind, resolutely engrained in his character. This mission relied on that vast experience.

"Here's my plan," Biff said politely, hoping to convince the skeptical colonel. "The proposal may strike you as off the wall, but bear with me. It's worth the chance since so much is at stake. Our dilemma calls for clandestine action, not a military confrontation."

Colonel Scott leaned forward in his chair. "Okay, please go on."

"South Korea's NIS recently caught and is about to convict a North Korean of spying. After his cover was blown, NIS determined the spy was a top notch IT expert working for Samsung as a cybersecurity specialist. He conducted his business undetected for twenty years, but slipped up. Only takes one slip up sometimes to get caught, right? Name is Kwon do-Hyun."

The colonel nodded. "I'm familiar with that case; he's awaiting trial in a Seoul jail. He did considerable damage, facilitating North Korea's hacking into our security systems as well as South Korea's. In fact, they still attempt to hack in daily."

"Perfect set up for us," Biff said. "While he's awaiting trial, why not turn him and return him back up north?"

"How do you propose to accomplish that?" Colonel Scott retorted. "These North Korean guys are tough nuts to crack. They're inscrutable, dogged." The colonel was feeling overwhelmed by Biff's aggressive approach. Sending in a double agent seemed too crazy an idea. He struggled to weigh the option fairly, but he feared this D.C. man didn't understand North Koreans. There was no way such a scheme would work.

"Here's how we do it, Colonel," Biff said, sensing his lack of enthusiasm. "Set up a speedy kangaroo court to sentence him to death by firing squad. Make it happen in record time. Say by the first of next month. Publicize the trial big time on TV, and give it front-page newspaper spreads. Make it the talk of the town. Then offer Kwon the choice, death by firing squad, or spying for us as a double agent."

"We could make that speedy trail happen," Scott replied. "No problem. Public sentiment is against him. But, how do we convince him to play along with us? What leverage do we have? Turning him would be quite a trick, maybe impossible in that time frame. He's a hardcore spy, committed to North Korea."

"Hear me out, it's a complicated scheme. We'll set up a clever disinformation program to cover our tracks, muddy the water. As a ruse we'll arrange for his escape from jail."

"No disrespect, but how in the hell are you going to do that?" the colonel asked.

"You'll see. It will be spectacular, sell a lot of newspapers, glue folks to the TV."

The colonel frowned. "I worry about us getting involved in local politics and law enforcement in a foreign country. That's kryptonite."

"I'll be collaborating with NIS, don't worry; we've got cover and plausible deniability."

"Their director, Nam, is a tough sell. How're you going to manage that aspect?'

"Trust me, I'll handle Nam. It's not my first rodeo."

"Tell me more."

"While the manhunt is going on for the decoy we arrange, we'll train Kwon in a safe house. Then we'll set up an escape plan to sneak him into North Korea."

"I'm following you. Again, don't get me wrong, no disrespect intended, but that's an enormous challenge."

"If we pull this mission off, you'll get your star, Colonel. Bear with me." Biff continued, "Nam will have to sell it, publicize his escape and him eluding authorities despite an APB for him and our decoy. Widely flash the headlines across the media as an embarrassing security failure. Have someone sacked as a consequence to make it look authentic. Rig up something with consequences, responding to public outrage at the bungling, letting him and our red herring decoy escape. We hype it, play it up big so the North will get the message through their channels and be on alert in case he tries to return home somehow."

"I'm following you. The disinformation campaign sounds good. But how can you manage to smuggle him in?"

"We've got a clever plan for that also, one with a high probability of success. I can't overemphasize how important it is to disseminate the disinformation widely and convince North Korea that Kwon's the real deal, an escapee, a convicted, desperate spy hiding out to avoid being shot on sight. Then out of the blue we allow him to mysteriously show up in disguise, secretly making his way home like any good escaped spy."

"It may backfire."

"We'll make it work. Now comes some interesting twists to my plot. After his capture and subsequent interrogation, the DPRK should be convinced he's one of theirs, escaping back home. We'll prep him on polygraphs and interrogation techniques. That's something we do well."

"Interesting gambit," Colonel Scott acknowledged. "But what makes you think they'll take the bait? They're suspicious bastards." Scott was starting to get into the intrigue, but still hesitant to commit to the risk.

"It's highly likely they'll bite if they think he still has something to offer. Even though they may question his loyalty despite all the productive years of spying he's provided them. I predict they will proceed cautiously. That's the natural course in this business."

"It's a tricky business."

"It really depends on Kwon giving a convincing performance and gaining their trust. If he's properly coached to carry out a limited mission, he will succeed. We plan on keeping it simple and straightforward to avoid exposure."

"I still have serious reservations about the plan. His escape and return may be a hard sell under interrogation."

"That's the essence of our job, to prep him properly. We'll fabricate his authenticity. Embellish his credentials."

"What assurance do we have that he wouldn't still bolt, turning his back on his family?"

"We'll sweeten the deal with a reward. The stakes are high; I need to sell that deal to NIS."

Everyone else in the room listened intently as Biff related an overview of the master plan.

Tyler was incredulous, wondering how he came up with these wild, but still plausible schemes.

Tim rolled his eyes. Nothing Biff came up with surprised him anymore. And knowing Biff, no matter how wild the plan, he'd pull it off.

Reza understood the complexity of being a double agent and extractions all too well. Everything had to click. But he thought Biff's plan was feasible. Definitely spy craft at its finest.

Biff hastened to add, "Kwon's simply a means to our end, you'll see. His covert role should remain secure until we choose to extract him."

"Impressive plan—risky, but you guys have obviously thought this out," Colonel Scott said. "It may work if Kwon performs convincingly. That's the key, as you said. And if he does pull it off, he may do well enough to reach hero status. How sure are you that you can convince NIS to collaborate?" Colonel Scott asked.

Still amazed at the grand scope of the plan to groom a double agent and successfully sneak him into North Korea and dubious, Colonel Scott worried about the outcome. A lot of "ifs" were involved in the intricate counterterrorism plan.

"I'll let you know if South Korean intel accepts this proposal. NIS has a big stake in this fight. It's basically a risk-reward decision. North Korea has the capability of destroying their country overnight." Biff glanced at his watch. "We're meeting with them in half an hour, and Director Nam's limo will pick us up on the Embassy Circle soon. Nam strikes me as a rational man, one dedicated to his country who will grasp the significance of the North Korean threat and be willing to take a chance of this magnitude."

Colonel Scott shook his head. "It's a long shot."

"Long shots are my specialty." Biff grinned. "This is what I do."

***

As Biff's group exited later though the embassy security doors, an inconspicuous janitor who had been sweeping the tile floors ducked into an alcove and placed a cell phone call. "They just left and are about to get into the black NIS Hyundai limo …"

***

CHAPTER SEVEN

SEOUL TRAFFIC JAM

As the NIS limo left the U.S. embassy grounds, Biff once again noted the congestion typical of Asian cities. The avenue was choked with traffic of every imaginable description—vehicles, donkeys pulling carts, dogs tagging along with pedestrians, scooters and bikes weaving in and out of lanes—all jockeying for position.

As the limo pulled onto the busy Sejong-Daero Avenue, two large trucks worked their way close to the NIS vehicle in the heavy traffic. As the trucks cut off other vehicles, agitated drivers blared their horns. The trucks suddenly angled sideways, blocking the road in both directions, and screeched to a halt, brakes squealing, causing several rear end collisions. More horns blared, and angry shouts erupted.

With no cross street to escape onto, traffic came to a standstill, and the NIS limo was effectively pinned down.

A dozen men in ragtag outfits and armed with Daewoo K-2 semi-automatic assault rifles swiftly jumped out of the trucks. They immediately opened withering fire on the limo. The bullets ricocheted off the NIS vehicle's special armor, instead shattering windows of nearby vehicles also hemmed in by the sudden ambush. Their occupants screamed, jumped out, and fled for their lives. Some unlucky souls wounded by flying bullet fragments fell onto the pavement moaning. Panic ensued as pedestrians ducked and ran for their lives amid the deafening gunfire.

One of the two NIS armed escorts seated next to the limo driver immediately got on the horn to NIS headquarters, the embassy, and local authorities over the car's emergency channel to call for help.

"We're under attack, taking hostile automatic fire," the escort said. "We are transporting American VIPs in our NIS limo, request emergency military assistance. Our vehicle has GPS locator, zoom in on our signal stat and send help immediately. We're just outside the U.S. embassy on Sejong. We're in big trouble. Repeat, taking heavy fire."

"Deep kimchi," Biff quipped.

It seemed assassination attempts in his life were becoming commonplace.

Tyler and Tim had pulled out their Smith and Wesson .40 mms, ready to jump out and return fire, but Biff restrained them.

"We're safer inside this bulletproof limo, fellas. Don't even think about returning fire at this point. I know it's against your instincts, but we're outgunned. Best to ride it out until help arrives. Seoul is an armed camp. Our embassy guard post will hear the gunfire and send help immediately. Our escorts up front already have radioed for help. Sit tight, and keep down."

"We're toast if they don't show up soon," Tim said, but then quickly wished he hadn't.

"I'm testing my karma, Tim," Biff said in half jest, slipping a .9mm round into his Beretta's chamber, anticipating an "up close and personal" shootout. They'd not go down without a fight.

Next to Biff, Reza slipped the safety off his Glock semiautomatic.

In the far back seat Rokman thought he'd come a long way from home to die. He muttered, "Holy shit, man," while noting Biff remained calm even with bullets flying off the limo. Guess he's accustomed to this crap, Rokman reflected.

Dr. Vincent remained speechless, terrified as he hunkered down. Not what he'd signed on for when he'd joined this trip as a consultant.

Only one hundred yards away, an embassy "ready alert" platoon of Marines rallied from their barracks, running toward the gunfire. The Embassy guard station quickly notified the roof security detail about the surprise assault on their CIA visitors.

Moments later an Apache chopper took off from the embassy roof. A standby crew always on alert for these contingencies piloted the attack helicopter rapidly to the scene. The AH-64 was armed with a Hughes 30 mm chain gun. The attack chopper arrived on scene within two minutes of the alert, and the crew quickly assessed the shootout transpiring two hundred feet below.

"There they are, buddy, three o'clock," Troy, the Apache pilot, said as they closed in on the NIS limo. "Our guys are taking fire from both sides. Bad guys are firing from outside those two white trucks."

"Got 'em," the gunner, Jed, responded as he zoomed in on the shooters with his electronic sights. "It'll be duck soup taking them out."

"It looks like they've got the NIS limo pinned down," Troy said. "Thank God it's the latest bulletproof model."

"I've got a solution to that problem. Watch this, man."

Jed zeroed the chain gun in on the assailants, locked in electronically. He expertly maneuvered the M-230 machine gun, firing six hundred rounds a minute of .30 mm ammo at the assailants, a violent, lethal spray. The hired assassins dropped like flies. It was over faster than it started thanks to the attack's proximity to the embassy and the rapid response teamwork. Preparation and rehearsal for hostile attacks had saved the day.

"How's that grab you?" Jed asked.

"Awesome! Where did you learn to shoot like that?"

"Afghanistan," Jed said, "lots of practice."

"Impressive. I need one of those chain guns for my duck club."

"Ha! Yeah, right."

"Look down there," the pilot said, "the Marines just arrived to mop up and ID those dudes."

"We made their job easy—a little messy, but they can handle a lot of blood and guts."

"Has to be a hired hit squad, they don't look like a paramilitary outfit in those grubby civvies."

"Don't put anything past those wild ass guys from up north."

***

NIS HEADQUARTERS – Two hours later

"I regret the breakdown in security," NIS Director Nam said. "Please accept my apologies. It was a close call."

"No need to apologize," Biff replied. "I've had closer calls, if you can imagine that. Seems it goes with the territory, at least mine."

The two men were meeting privately in Nam's office.

"The question is," Biff continued, "how'd they know my schedule? That attack was too well timed. It suggests you have a mole or informant in your agency, Director."

"Or perhaps you have a leak in your Embassy?" Nam countered.

"Got a point, maybe both of us are compromised. Clearly, someone tipped them off about our plans. But I can attest to your vehicle's protective armor. That and the embassy's rapid response teams saved our butts. The chopper was the big gun we brought to the knife fight."

"Fortunately things worked out," Nam said. "We'll thoroughly investigate the incident, I assure you. That motley squad was comprised of criminals with a history of hit jobs, but nothing on the scale of assassinating a visiting dignitary. Luckily they were amateurs and no match for the embassy security, or ours. Nevertheless, there's no question that some insider informed them. I promise to look closely into the matter."

"Do you think the North had a hand in this?" Biff asked. "Nothing happens by accident. 'If it happens, you can bet someone planned it,' as one of our famous presidents said."

"I believe that was FDR, correct?"

Biff smiled. "You know our history."

"It's beneficial to know the history of your friends as well as your enemies. It would not surprise me if DPRK is involved. Their spies have an underground network here despite our countermeasures." Nam frowned. "But why target you?"

"Mullahs in Iran issued a *fatwa* on me almost three years ago. They've chased me to the ends of the earth. I suspect a spy in your unit or my embassy informed Pyongyang, who relayed the message to Tehran agents, who quickly set up the hit this morning. CIA has documented Iran's collaboration with North Korea." Biff paused. "But that's water over the dam. I've got something to run by you concerning our mutual threat."

Biff dismissed the assassination attempt to move on to a topic of more immediate concern to him. He was upset, but put on a brave face. His professional façade hid his inner feelings about the foiled effort to kill him. He appeared convincingly calm and carried on with his business. Anxious to see Director Nam's response to his scheme to infiltrate North Korea's classified information system, he launched into his presentation.

"You recently captured a North Korean agent working in Samsung's cybersecurity division, named Kwon do-Hyun. He's an IT hacking expert. We want to turn him and return him as a double agent to spy for us."

"Now that's a very bold plan. How do you propose to accomplish this?" Nam asked, sounding skeptical.

Over the next three hours, Biff outlined his intricate plan in expansive detail. Nam listened carefully, taking notes, only interrupting to clarify issues, not to argue a point.

"What do you think, Director?" Biff asked as he concluded his briefing.

"This elaborate proposal requires considerable deliberation and consultation through command channels. You understand I'm not at liberty to make unilateral decisions of this magnitude, considering the consequences of failure, and the limitations of my intelligence service."

"Never fear failure, Director. The potential benefits are worth the risk," Biff reassured him.

"That's one way to put it. Actually, I like your crafty plot," Nam said with a smile. "It's so out of the box it might well succeed. I'll push it through command. There's a lot at stake and success depends on Kwon's sincere cooperation. But, I'm stating the obvious."

"Think he'll play ball?" Biff asked.

"Yes, I do. He won't put his family at risk. Has a lovely wife, and three good children achieving in science prep schools. He enjoys his comfortable lifestyle. He understands NIS plays hardball. There's no way he'd sacrifice his standard of living or them."

"Good to know your perspective," Biff said. "We can help you prep him, if you get your chain of command to concur with the plan."

"Command may be willing to chance it, especially since it doesn't involve a continual stream of communication from Kwon, which would be cumbersome and dangerous for him as a double agent, his handler, and us. Can you stay awhile to discuss the plan with my superiors after I present it?"

Biff shook his head. "I have a week of commitments, a busy schedule to keep. I leave for the West Coast tomorrow to attend to business there, but I promise to keep in touch. And I'll return as soon as you get your command to go along with the plan."

"You move around a lot."

"A moving target keeps the Iranian *fatwa* gang hopping. All part of the challenge in my line of work."

∗∗∗

CHAPTER EIGHT

A FITFUL NIGHT

U.S. Embassy, Seoul

That night

Biff tossed and turned, upset, unable to sleep in the comfortable bed in the embassy's VIP guest suite. The assassination attempt earlier that day deeply troubled him. His stress had been incrementally increasing over the past three years, and threatening events were creating a cumulative effect, gnawing at him.

They just keep coming out of nowhere, he thought.

"They" were the *fatwa*-driven Iranians and their hit contractors out to kill him. They could seemingly track him anywhere on earth, anytime of the day or night, for their deadly purpose. Today was one more failed effort by their agents, and this time a brazen assault in broad daylight in downtown Seoul. The gunshot wound to his shoulder from the prior assassination attempt in Cortina only five months ago hadn't completely healed yet, and here they were, at it again.

Emotionally overloaded with one problem cropping up after another, he knew he must cope. He had a job to do. He came to South Korea seeking solutions to the pressing problem of North Korea, hoping that working with the South Korean intelligence service would be productive. This latest assassination attempt was more than a distraction. It was an alarming trend interfering with his missions, a reminder that there was almost no safe haven for him. His already complicated life was becoming even more complex, and his aggravation was becoming uncontainable.

No fucking let up with these fanatics, he thought. And a shootout in broad daylight in downtown Seoul would bring attention to their presence when the press started snooping around. If this got out, it would send the DCI through the roof.

Admiral Delaney had assigned him to confirm and confront the current national security threat. Biff had arrived in Seoul to research the situation firsthand and document that North Korea was indeed developing an EMP nuclear device and a delivery system. Then he must formulate a plan to counter the threat. Based on actionable CIA intelligence, DPRK was well along with their program, but holes in the intelligence estimates made the timing of their plans unclear. The basic consideration was how soon would North Korea achieve the technical expertise to launch an attack? The DCI had tasked him to fill in the holes in their intelligence.

Now the stress of this latest ambush had interrupted his mission, breaking his primary focus and risking sidetracking him.

Iran had to have a hand in what happened today. That Korean street gang had no bone to pick with him; it had to be a contract hit job. Now they were back in his face with an audacious commando-style attack in midtown Seoul, hiring a rag tag street gang armed with military weapons. Another close call orchestrated by the ruthless bastards.

Someone tipped them off. Set him up. A mole? He considered U.S. embassy and NIS security breaches as he rearranged his pillows, trying to get comfortable and get some rest. He still hadn't fully unwound following the perilous San Francisco counterterrorism operation and now this. Confronting that terrorist Quds Colonel from Tehran hell bent on destruction had taken a lot out of him.

He wondered if this attempt was an early reprisal for the CIA preventing Javari's evil mission. Their spies and assassins seem to be lurking around every corner. In the last three years, assassins attempted hits on him in Tel Aviv, Kuwait, and London before wounding him in Cortina last New Year's Day. Javari had travelled seven thousand miles from Tehran to commit an act of terror in San Francisco only weeks ago. Distance appeared no obstacle to these fanatics. Two Easter Sundays ago, another Quds Colonel had made a similar long trip to San Francisco from Tehran to kill his first wife, Mary Beth. The handler managed a homegrown jihadist sniper who went after her as a soft target after prior attempts to nail him had failed.

Since then, the tyrannical Shiite Iranians topped his short list of bad actors. Retribution drove him on a personal and professional level. As CT Director he was in a unique position, a certified "vigilante" of sorts, authorized to eliminate high-value targets, like the Iranian Colonel who murdered his wife, and terror bombers like Javari. It was a task Biff would not shirk but relish.

They'd picked the wrong guy to mess with.

His CIA position enabled retaliation, the means and opportunity to kill two birds with one stone while diminishing the national threats. Based on actionable intelligence, he had drones, cyber warfare experts, and his Special Operations Division, a covert CIA paramilitary group, at his beck and call. He planned proactive clandestine operations to eliminate high-value terrorist targets in collaboration with Mossad, the acknowledged experts in taking out bad guys. Targeted assassinations would become the norm. He had every intention of implementing all of these elements in his dedicated mission in his new role as Director of Counterterrorism.

His strong personal feelings aside, intellectually Biff viewed Islamist extremists as existential threats to democratic societies. Peace could never coexist with their warped mindset, their commitment to a universal jihad against nonbelievers because of their radical interpretation of the Koran's teachings. It was time to call out their motives and extreme intolerance. To them, the only options were convert to Islam or die. Democratic coexistence with Sharia law was a pipedream. In reality, there was no escaping the fact that their brand of bigotry and terrorism constituted a perpetual, apocalyptic threat to the free world. In Biff's view, they had declared war on the free world, and free societies couldn't afford to be in a state of denial.

This latest assassination attempt brought his frustrations to the surface. The lack of definitive political action to devise constructive policies to confront the jihadists angered him. D.C. was stuck in a reactionary mode and political leaders seemed unable to formulate a constructive strategy.

Biff believed they must take the battle to the terrorists, be proactive. Isolation, reaction, and retaliation didn't cut it. They couldn't afford to wait around for the next disaster. If it seemed so clear to him, why couldn't D.C. get the big picture?

By failing to detect and successfully counter jihadists, more 9/11s could occur, and more attacks like the Boston Marathon bombings.

Homegrown jihadists moved freely about in their liberal society, remaining undetected like a deadly virus. Their presence imposed an alarming element of vulnerability to the naïve, unsuspecting man in the street. And to clueless politicians who should be aware of the imminent danger they posed and should enact countermeasures.

Would profiling diminish the risk? Should they institute a covert program of surveillance of all mosques, potential breeding grounds for those with sick minds and bad intentions? Was political correctness helping to shield the potential menace?

He weighed that thought.

All nineteen 9/11 terrorists were radical Muslims. Was that a warning sign of the dangerous trend in the new millennium? Was this grim form of anarchy spilling over into civilized societies under the guise of Islam an indication for profiling? Free nations' tolerance of religious expression might be exposing them to potential danger. Were basic civil liberties in a free society their Achilles heel?

His mind raced with troubling thoughts. No easy answers came to mind. Personally he'd never bought into the PC social contract. Discrimination was a big part of a spy's life—that is if he intended to stay alive. Maintaining a high index of suspicion of someone's appearance and behavior was essential in the national security business. Evil knew no bounds in his world and no culture had a monopoly on wicked intentions. But radical Islamists seemed to be grabbing the market share at this point in his life, driven by a warped religious passion as addictive as opium. Maybe Karl Marx had a point in his famous observation about religion being the opium of the masses. Radical Islam approached a critical mass, about to explode in its hatred of perceived "non-believers."

Javari was one such radical who, thankfully, they had stopped. He was imprisoned in GITMO where he belonged, spirited off in a CIA jet before someone in the DOJ decided to allow him to lawyer up and try him in the U.S. criminal justice system. Not going to happen on Biff Roberts' watch. Javari was an enemy combatant, a terrorist with no rights, a view Biff did not consider contentious, but remained controversial to the "Kumbaya" crowd in Washington. Javari could rot in Guantanamo after interrogation. Biff didn't give a rat's ass. The SOB intended to blow up San Francisco and kill as many innocents as possible.

Why couldn't the Foggy Bottom politicians get it? What the hell were they thinking?

And the Islamist group demographics were dismal and frightening. The radical element gave the relatively benign ninety plus percent of the brand a bad name. Unfortunately, the peaceful Muslims seemed incapable of controlling the minority's hateful, belligerent behavior. They showed no inclination to eradicate madrassas that indoctrinated children to intolerance of other religions and lifestyles, ingraining hatred at a formative age. No wonder their radical behavior disrupted the world with a malevolent pipeline engendering splinter groups like ISIS, a group so violent that Al Qaeda threw them out of their terrorist ranks.

Were the Muslim masses intimidated? Powerless? Apathetic? Co-dependent? Their lack of responsibility puzzled him. Why couldn't they rein in the radical behavior of the minority? At least protest the brutality of splinter groups like ISIS beheading people and posting the gruesome videos on YouTube?

He flung the covers off and got up. He poured himself a Jack Daniel's on the rocks from the minibar, downed it, and returned to bed.

This malignant minority was spreading like a cancer, incorporating affiliates in Africa and recruiting militant homegrown jihadists worldwide, including the United States. The recent San Francisco episode was a case in point. Twenty percent of the world's Muslims lived in twenty countries and territories in the Middle East and North Africa, and they appeared to be the epicenter of radical Islam.

He must focus on the epicenter, he concluded.

Assuming a ballpark number of about a ten percent radical conversion rate of 320 million Muslims in the Middle East and North Africa, that was a hell of a lot of jihadists to deal with, he calculated. That was thirty-two million radicals. Even if it was only one percent, 3.2 million, it was still a huge problem. The numbers were scary, especially when he factored in the differential birth rate of thirty-two million or lowball estimate of three million plus potential terrorists, reproducing at a seven to two ratio compared to families in Europe and the United States.

The Islamist extremists must be defeated at any cost if democratic, civilized society was to survive, he concluded. The fanatical bastards were obviously coming after them yet to Biff, it was the same old, sad story. Supposedly responsible folks in charge of the country misperceived the threats time and again. Some leaders were so incompetent they couldn't lead a platoon of men with full bladders to the men's room. D.C. was a place where good ideas went to die, but bad ideas seemed to have a life of their own. That summed up his frustration with opportunist politicians and the armchair military commanders who catered to their whims.

It seemed to him the government decision makers, the administrators in charge of the nation's defense, had fallen through a cosmic rabbit hole into a wonderland of cognitive dissonance and indecision. Their inaction compounded the problem by emboldening the enemy. Their policies were inept, and they were prisoners of their rigid ideology. Incapable of adapting to dynamic real world paradigms, they failed to act decisively, always late to the party and missing golden opportunities.

It reminded him of Pogo's declaration in the Peanuts cartoon. "We have met the enemy and he is us."

But the existing situation was not comical. Not the least bit humorous.

He'd put up with Washington D.C.'s fuzzy thinking and misguided strategies since his stint as a very young CIA deputy station manager working under diplomatic cover in Vietnam in the late 1960s. He'd seen plenty of evidence to support the adage that those who never learn the lessons of history are condemned to repeat them.

Instead, Biff followed the timeless maxims that were proven effective. Don't draw red lines in the sand close to an incoming tide if you don't intend to enforce them before they are washed away. The window of opportunity doesn't stay open for prolonged periods. Don't allow the enemy safe sanctuary, limiting your options. Do not fight wars unless you intend to win decisively in the shortest time possible employing maximal force.

No matter the decade, he mused, *those in power have difficulty locating the yellow brick road, the road to success. Why?*

Exhausted, after another Jack Daniel's on the rocks, he finally drifted off. As the soothing spa music from the stereo played softly in the background, he buried his head in a pillow, escaping from the troubled world at least for one more night.

One thought that did bring him comfort — knowing a Marine stood guard outside his door.

CHAPTER NINE

BOEING — PHANTOM WORK TEAM

Seattle, Washington
Two days later

"**W**e've been working with K Tech Corporation and Raytheon on a gangbuster project," the young rocket scientist Adam Kahn announced enthusiastically as he rushed over to greet Biff and his counterterrorism team. "Our preliminary tests are very encouraging. Something I'm sure you'll be really interested in, Director Roberts. The timing of your arrival couldn't be better."

Biff shook his hand. "Call me Biff."

Adam was the senior project manager of Boeing's Phantom Works. His office featured a large window with a spectacular view of Puget Sound. Nothing appeared out of place in the upscale, modern office, a sharp contrast to Biff's visit to Jonas Siegel's jumbled Raytheon office in Fullerton last week.

Different folks, different strokes, same discipline ... rocket science, Biff thought. The bright young engineer was clearly excited to brief Biff's select group on their latest scientific breakthrough. Adam shook hands with everyone vigorously, memorizing their names, asking their roles, and smiling ear to ear as he graciously chatted them up. Prematurely balding gave Adam a somewhat older appearance that didn't jibe with his youthful energy or with his casual attire of tattered jeans, a t-shirt featuring a large cannabis leaf, and worn Nike sneakers. *Must allow him to blend in with Seattle's coffee house crowd,* Biff surmised. He appreciated that Adam wasn't the least bit pretentious about occupying such a high corporate position.

Biff had committed to memory the essential bullet points in Kahn's impressive résumé while on the flight from Seoul to Seattle. The data had been forwarded via satellite from Admiral Delaney. The admiral had made a few critical calls to coordinate this special impromptu briefing on Biff's return trip from Seoul.

Kahn had graduated for the University of Washington, cum laude in engineering, followed by a Masters and PhD from MIT, and then a two-year stint teaching at USAF's School of Aerospace Medicine in San Antonio. Finally, he spent a year at NASA before landing the high post with Boeing. The young man had come a long way in a short time, a rising star in the rocket and missile industry.

Adam motioned for them all to sit at a conference table close to the window.

"Whatcha got for me, Adam?" Biff asked as he took a seat, adapting to Adam's informal attitude. Laid back worked for him. D.C. posturing got a bit old.

"I'll brief you on our sensational joint development with K Tech today. Tomorrow morning we plan to fly to Area 51 for a demonstration."

"Area 51?" Biff perked up at the mention of that name.

Adam smiled. "Familiar with that designation?"

"I am, as a matter of fact, KXTA. Some refer to it as 'Dreamland Resort.'" Biff grinned.

"Say no more. You've obviously got the picture." Adam laughed congenially. "Our preliminary CHAMP test with USAF in the Utah desert last week went well. Tomorrow we'll target multiple sites with our EMP cruise missile in Area 51. Your team will be among the first to witness this stunning development in our LRS program."

"Can't wait, Adam," Biff said. "Clarify LRS for my team, please."

"We use a lot of acronyms, sorry. LRS stands for long-range strike program. CHAMP refers to our Counter-electronics High-powered Microwave Advanced Missile Project, our EMP cruise missile."

"Thank you for bringing us up to speed. We're on the same page now. Please continue."

"You're welcome. Let me share some background with you. Basically we've developed a specialized cruise missile designed with drone programming capability to selectively attack multiple targets. It's equipped with a powerful magnetron that produces a massive pulse of microwave radiation. It has the same effect as an EMP, but the result lacks the intensity of an EMP occurring from a huge solar storm or a high-altitude nuclear explosion. It's a matter of lesser magnitude, but it effectively serves its targeted purpose."

"Sounds very interesting," Biff said. "Tell me about the magnetron."

"The magnetron is a high-powered vacuum tube that generates microwaves that interact and interfere with electrons in a magnetic field. This creates an EMP blast that irreparably destroys electronics but without collateral damage to civilians or buildings. It has the same effect as a MICG bomb, a magnetic flux-compression generator, producing tens of mega joules in tenths of microseconds, but contained in a relatively small package."

Dr. Vincent piped up. "So our preparation for strengthening our national electronic power grids must now include the contingency of an EMP strike from a cruise missile-drone hybrid, as well as from a cosmic event involving the sun, or an EMP attack triggered by a high altitude nuclear blast."

"You got it, Doc," Adam said. "Heads up. We're entering a new era in modern warfare, rendering the enemy's electronic and data systems useless before the first troops arrive. You'll witness its effectiveness firsthand in tomorrow's demonstration in Area 51."

"I find that worrisome, Site M stuff," Dr. Vincent commented.

Adam frowned. "Site M?"

"Fort Meade's top-secret warfare development center for the Pentagon," Biff interjected. "Classified, better leave it there."

"Well. I suppose it depends on who's being attacked or who's attacking," Adam retorted. "Best to be in the driver's seat. Wait 'til you see tomorrow's demo."

Chapter Ten

AREA 51

Nevada, the next morning

Area 51 was part myth, part extraterrestrial fantasy, and part mystique, but in reality a top-secret military base located for decades in a remote Nevada salt flat next to a large dry lake called Groom Lake. As the subject of UFO and alien conspiracy theories, sci-fi films, and the development and test site of military technology such as the atom bomb, U2 surveillance aircraft, and the F-22 Raptor fifth generation stealth fighter, the base was legendary.

Biff knew Area 51 well as KXTA, a CIA "Black Project" test site; clandestine code names Aquatone and Oxcart came to mind. Well suited for secretive activity in its isolated desert spot, it was really out in the middle of nowhere, eighty-five miles north-northwest of Las Vegas.

After they passed through multiple layers of security, Adam greeted Biff and his team and escorted them to the base commander's office for a brief introduction. Biff was amused to note that the commander had a bronze sign on his desk that read: *Real life beats the imaginary lives here.*

Adam then led them to the area where the Phantom team was developing the innovative, top-secret weapons system. They took an elevator several flights down to an underground laboratory complex.

"Like in Vegas," Adam related. "What happens here, stays here." He smiled at his own quip.

"You don't need a library card to educate yourself in EMP technology, gentlemen. Plenty of information is out there on the Internet. The essence is developing EMP waves into a reliable weapons system." He led them through a pair of heavy metal doors into an enormous underground hangar.

"Here's what we've come up with." He pointed proudly to a large rocket on a mobile launch pad.

"That's our CHAMP-EMP cruise missile."

"What's the missile's range?" Biff asked.

"Over six hundred miles, about the same as a Tomahawk missile."

"Size?"

"Slightly bigger than the Tomahawk."

"Which is about twenty feet with a booster," Biff noted, making a mental note of the missile's specs.

"Right on, Director, you know your missiles."

"Thanks. Tell me about the launch protocols."

"Plane, ship, or from a stationary or mobile pad are equally reliable. That gives you a variety of attack options."

"What about from a SSGN's VLS?"

"Now that's an interesting concept, using an attack submarine's vertical launch system. That would enhance the stealth factor and add another element of surprise. I'm certain our CHAMP missile could be modified for a vertical launch system compartmentalized in a guided missile submarine. Got something in mind?"

"Just brainstorming applications, preparing for any contingency."

"Okay, got it. That's an idea worth pursuing. We'll check it out and get back to you."

"I'd appreciate that, Adam. Soon as possible."

"Today's demo is set for noon. Let's get over to our control center to monitor the launch effectiveness. The missile is programmed to target six buildings filled with functioning electronic equipment and test animals in the Tonopah test range seventy miles northwest of here. We can watch the live feed video from drone control and satellite."

***

Two Hours Later

"How's that grab you, fellows?" Adam said. "The CHAMP flyover successfully fried the targets' electronics without harm to the animals or the six structures, hitting the targets' precisely programmed coordinates dead on."

"Impressive demonstration, Adam," Biff acknowledged. "You're convincing me you're on to something with this new EMP weapons system. It seems you've invented a new mousetrap, young man."

Adam chuckled. "Guess the Defense Department will soon be beating down our door." He paused before adding, "Stay for a late lunch? We have time to hit Vegas, just a short hop by plane. I know some great spots."

"Thanks, but we have to get back East. Have another stop on my information tour. Sure appreciate your time and effort in educating us on the new weapon. Super demonstration, spectacular targeting. CHAMP may come in handy. Can you loan me the specs of your new mousetrap?"

"No problem. Got several copies right here, classified, of course," he added, smiling.

"I think I have proper clearance," Biff replied, grinning. "Need my ID?"

CHAPTER ELEVEN

INDIAN HEAD NAVAL WEAPONS CENTER

Charles County, Maryland

The next morning

"Thank you for fitting us into your busy schedule on such short notice, Commander," Biff said after entering Commander Wilbourne's office.

"CIA carries some weight around here," Commander Wilbourne said, shaking Biff's hand. "When Admiral Delaney calls from Langley, we answer."

After quick introductions, the commander gestured for Biff and his team to sit around the conference table in his office. The commander motioned for a corpsman to offer their guests coffee — a strong Navy brew, naturally.

"How can I help you, Director Roberts?" the commander said once they all had coffee.

"Need an update on your sea based anti-ballistic missiles program, a rundown on your BMD protocol."

"We have some interesting developments in our ballistic missile defense systems. I'll gladly give you an overview. Let me pull some things together. It'll take only a minute."

Commander Wilbourne retrieved some diagrams, DVDs, and photos from his worktable to illustrate his points. An Academy officer, he was accustomed to impromptu presentations as a result of being located so close to D.C. and Annapolis. "Need to know" folks with top-secret clearances dropped by frequently. He knew his business and was proud to relate the Navy's progress in their defense system. He gathered his presentation information and spread materials out on the large table for review. A white board was ready nearby for added explanations.

"Our Aegis anti-ballistic missile is based on the RIM 161," he began, showing them photos and a mockup model of the missile.

"That's our mainstay, and it's awesome. We've recently had two successful tests of a Lockheed-Martin intercept missile, code named FTM-22. The trial was performed on a 'no notice' exercise from our ship *Lake Erie*, a Hawaii-based guided missile cruiser now stationed off the coast of North Korea and Vietnam in the South China Sea. She's deployed with a fleet of eight sister ships, all ballistic missile defense, BMD, equipped. Watch this video, gentlemen. You won't be able to look away."

He proceeded to insert a DVD into a computer driven projector, dimmed the lights, and took a swig from his coffee mug. On a large wall screen, a dramatic demonstration followed of an Aegis ship-to-air missile as it downed an intermediate range "enemy" missile, tracking and exploding it on ascent before it reached the stratosphere.

"That was six months ago," the commander said. "Look at this most recent refinement in the next video."

The screen came to life with another impressive shoot down, the explosion of the intercept missile spectacularly captured by satellite and shipboard cameras.

"Did you note the second video showed our missile intercepting and knocking out the enemy missile on early ascent?"

"I did," Biff said. "A very impressive improvement."

"As a matter of fact, it is. That result is attributed to development of earlier detection and tracking systems. This exercise was unannounced, not staged, gentlemen. That's important to note. Our radar and computer tracking has become more refined in our current BMD system. Our enemy does not formally announce their launches, so we must be ever vigilant, always on alert. That's why we practice on a 'no notice' basis. We have to stay sharp."

"Has a certain 'wow' factor," Biff commented, "Exciting display, Commander."

"Most would agree it puts North Korea on warning," Commander Wilbourne proudly responded to the compliment. "They routinely observe our naval exercises from surveillance aircraft. They know we have that intercept capability."

"That's our major concern," Biff said, "the purpose of our visit. Our intel indicates North Korea is cooking up something."

The commander raised an eyebrow. "And that is?"

"We fear a surprise nuclear-induced EMP attack by a North Korean ICBM. That assumes they have developed one with effective range and accurate targeting reliability. Or more likely, that we may suffer a sneak attack from an orbiting rogue satellite carrying a low-yield nuclear device into space. We know they possess that rocket technology, as they recently demonstrated." Biff paused. "Does the Navy have the capacity to thwart either of those wartime scenarios, ICBM or satellite, with your current BMD?"

"Our 'Brilliant Pebble' system is still on the drawing board," Commander Wilbourne said. "That would be the best option to counter both space threats you mention."

"Brilliant Pebble? Catchy name, fill me in on the program."

"It's a great concept involving orbiting multiple 'smart' small satellites. The system is capable of cross linking communications and initiating a kinetic response from the early warning system, BMEWS, to intercept incoming ICBMs. But unfortunately, the ingenious technique is not yet perfected to go into the field. With satellites, that involves more subtle considerations."

"Terrific idea, Commander," Biff said, "keep working on it. What other stopgaps do you have in your arsenal in the meantime?"

"We have operational sophisticated laser battle stations with nuclear pumped X-ray laser systems, but the brunt of our BMD is our Aegis ship-to-air intercept system. Currently we have eighty-four ships completely outfitted. Battle ready destroyers and cruisers, each with sixty-eight intercept missiles to manage the event of multiple enemy missile launches, or dealing with MERV warheads." MERVs were multiple, independently targetable reentry vehicles. Biff had learned the terminology in his research.

"So you're telling me you're capable of addressing the issue of MERVs?" Biff asked.

Wilbourne nodded. "Absolutely. Our next round of live fire testing will concentrate on this challenging issue. The Seventh Fleet is deployed all over the South China Sea, on standby, ready to address the threat level, continually developing and improving our BMD capability."

"Excellent foresight, Commander." Biff was impressed with the judicious implementation in the Pacific trouble spots, a prudent move on the Navy's part.

"Wait until you see this," Commander Wilbourne said. "Here's our latest futuristic weapon, an electromagnetic rail gun. It weighs only twenty-five pounds and can shoot a projectile at Mach seven. That's seven times the speed of sound. Approximately 761 mph equals one Mach, if you're not familiar with that terminology. Unit cost is $25k. Cheap, huh? Projectile can pierce three concrete reinforced walls, and six inches of steel, so taking down missiles is a snap. It can sequentially fire volleys. Look at our latest test video, gentlemen."

The commander fired up the next demo.

"Impressive. Anticipated deployment?" Biff commented after viewing the dazzling display.

"Maybe by early next year, or possibly late this year."

"We might need it sooner."

"We're working hard on the project, top priority in the Navy."

Biff nodded. "Good to know."

"Our Naval BMD doesn't rely solely on intercepts, Director. We have a diversity of options. We have the capability of jamming enemy missiles' terminal guidance systems, or technically blinding the missile before it locks on to its target."

"Good that you have the foresight to employ backup systems in case the intercepts fail."

"Exactly, however, our best strategy is to disable the ICBM on the launch pad, but that entails risks. Therefore, we employ a 'break the kill chain' strategy with the systems I've outlined. If any one step of the enemy's proposed attack fails, the chain breaks and their missile strike misses its target or is destroyed. In summary, our naval defense strategy is to use electronic and cyber warfare to scramble the enemy's entire system, versus bombing the launch site or shooting down the missile. If we can jam or hack their computers or disable them at the launch site, we accomplish our task without risk."

"I find that very interesting. We've been thinking along that line, as a matter of fact." Biff removed a file from his briefcase. "Look at the specs on this experimental cruise missile that I brought with me. It has some drone attributes, sort of a hybrid concept. Can an SSGN sub's VLS be modified to launch it? It's slightly bigger than a Tomahawk missile."

"Hmm." The commander studied the diagrams. "Interesting concept. If you leave this information with me, I'll review it with our engineers and let you know the first of the week. Those guys are hotshots on projects like this."

Biff smiled. "That works for me, Commander."

***

As the meeting continued, Biff took out his iPad. Not trusting this expansive information to recall, Biff entered the pertinent data into his iPad and hit the automatic encryption key, adding it to data previously acquired on his trip. After an exhaustive information gathering tour, he'd started to suffer overload and decided it was time to make electronic "mental" notes.

Now he only needed further background on the vulnerability of the national electronic grid system. His next stop would be FERC headquarters in D.C., nice and close to home after an eventful week of the EMP threat assessment. His knowledge had expanded exponentially.

Chapter Twelve

FERC HEADQUARTERS

Washington, D.C.

"T he short answer to your question, Director, is yes, our electrical grid is vulnerable to sabotage. Targeted attacks on just nine critical electrical transmission substations, out of our 55,000 nationwide, would cause a coast-to-coast blackout if carried out on a scorching hot summer day. With 160,000 miles of transmission lines, the grid is inherently defenseless to even small-scale attacks, especially on the East Coast where targeting specific substations would knock out seventy percent of the grid. A well-organized cyber-attack with zero-day exploits would be devastating."

Biff Roberts logged that critical data into his iPad and sat back in the uncomfortable, government-issued chair at the D.C. headquarters of FERC, the Federal Energy Regulatory Commission.

"I read a short synopsis of that disconcerting fact in the *New York Times*," Biff commented. "In fact, the paper published a map of the grids in case terrorists failed to find sufficient information on Google to conduct an attack," he added sarcastically. He tried shifting his weight to get comfortable in the chair. Not a chance.

"Got to love our journalists," Oliver Rhoads said. "Ran a number of similar articles after some nuts shot up a San Jose transformer with AK-47s out in California. I worry that may have been just a dress rehearsal. Fortunately the damage was limited."

Biff wondered if Oliver's nickname was "Dusty" but refrained from asking. No time for joking and he was certain Rhoads had heard it many times before. The Federal Energy Regulation Commissioner had a handle on the grid situation, a wealth of knowledge that Biff required.

"Please continue your briefing. Sorry to interrupt."

"Not a problem. Other vulnerabilities in the grid are technical obstacles, resulting in limited connections between our substations, preventing efficient cross over to help each other in emergencies when one station goes down. A substation plays a vital role in keeping the electrical grid humming by boosting voltage for long distance travel, then transforming electricity to usable levels upon arrival.

"Terror attacks on multiple line transmission corridors could cause cascading blackouts. An agency study concluded that the systems could go dark if as few as nine critical locations were disabled: four in the East, three in the West, and two in Texas. Big transformers and other equipment are hard to replace. The power grid was constructed many decades ago in a benign environment that now faces a range of threats, both physical and cyber-based attacks."

"So it makes them prime targets for terrorists," Biff noted.

"Precisely. A well-executed, small-scale attack on several critical facilities would be a disaster with weeks, if not months, of interruption of IT business and commerce, resulting in nightmares for those regions. I'd estimate most likely up to eighteen months out of service, especially on the East Coast."

Biff nodded. "Got your point regarding the system's vulnerability to a cyber-attack or local assaults, but I'm thinking in terms of a massive disruption of the entire system."

"How?" Rhoads frowned.

"My concern is something enormous, like a foreign country launching an EMP attack, triggered by a high-altitude nuclear explosion above the stratosphere."

Rhoads eyes widened at the thought. "That would be a major catastrophe with Dark Age repercussions. We depend on electricity for all communication, our computer systems, our defense structures, the commercial and aerospace industry, the pumps at the gas station, the factory command and control systems, ATMs, the lights and machinery in hospitals and businesses. You name it. I could go on ad infinitum regarding our total dependency on electricity."

"No need," Biff said. "I get the big picture. What steps are we taking to harden the grid? To protect the transformers? Are adequate precautions in place to prevent a national disaster?"

"No government agency is designated or accountable for safeguarding the power grid," Rhoads said. "Utility power companies fear legal liability if they change their security systems, even shore up defenses. It's more or less become our job by default.

"Here's the problem as I see it," Rhoads continued, furrowing his brow. "The power grid is especially vulnerable because many substations are located in rural areas protected only by chain link fences. The security of the grid is too important to be left to mere fencing. We need high, reinforced concrete walls with barbed wire plus wireless digital sensors to alert standby security services, and to automatically shut down systems under attack to minimize damage. We also advise surveillance drones over critical substations. We advocate FAA approval of cheap, reliable commercial drones for this safeguarding purpose. Legalization would expedite their development and deployment. This would be an ideal security step to follow."

"That legislation is pending, I understand," Biff said. "What about micro grids for major emergencies?"

"Good point. We advocate wider development and use of micro grids' distributed power generation to complement the main power grid, connecting through a PCC, point of common coupling. The PCC maintains even voltage levels between the main and micro grid to prevent problems like explosions caused by uneven loads or overloads.

"A circuit breaker separates the two systems in case the main system fails. The micro grid's control system balances power needs with capacity. It may tap into alternate and backup systems in an emergency such as natural gas turbines, fuel cell storage batteries, and energy from solar arrays. The Department of Energy has set aside seven million for micro grid design. Several big utilities like Dominion Resources plan to spend $500 million over the next seven years to harden its facilities."

"Congress has bills pending to secure the grids. How's that going?" Biff asked.

"Slowly, in a word. They recognize the EMP threat in the Shield Act introduced by Trent Franks in HR 2417, but it's not passed yet."

Dr. Vincent could not restrain himself and piped up.

"It's imperative Congress acts soon. An EMP attack would change the world as we know it." He was an authority on the subject and spoke with conviction. "Nearly fifty-two years ago a nuclear test in the South Pacific, code named 'Starfish Prime,' disrupted electricity sources as far away as eight hundred miles east of Hawaii. The detonation of 1.4 megaton nuclear weapon 250 miles above the ocean caused an enormous shock wave. We know North Korea possesses a seven to ten megaton bomb, puny by our standards, but exponentially stronger than Starfish, and still capable of massive devastation."

He continued, "Scientists consider electromagnetic forces as one of four fundamental forces in the universe, billions of times stronger than gravity. We narrowly escaped a Carrington Event in 2012. The shockwave of a coronal mass ejection associated with solar flares erupting from the surface of the sun barely missed us in space. The massive solar winds and magnetic energy of gamma rays released would have destroyed us, figuratively speaking.

"We must take steps to protect ourselves from an enemy EMP attack, which is more likely than a natural event. A onetime investment of two billion dollars would provide national grid protection. That's less than what was spent on the 2012 Presidential election. Think about that for a moment."

"That puts priorities in perspective, Doctor," Rhoads said. "You're preaching to the choir. Congress needs to expedite the Shield Act."

"That more or less sums it up, gentlemen," Biff said. "Congress better get humping on that funding problem."

CHAPTER THIRTEEN

THE PLAN

CIA – Langley

The next week

"Y ou did your homework regarding the risks and the enemy's capability," Admiral Delaney said. "The vulnerability of the grid to an EMP attack is very worrisome, Biff, despite our defensive options. I like your concise briefing, well done."

"Thank you, Admiral." Biff sat with Admiral Delaney in the DCI's office.

"What do you propose I advise the Joint Chiefs of Staff next week?" Delaney asked. "What should we do about the situation brewing over there, and how should we counterman a surprise EMP attack?"

"It's a bold plan I've conceived, but I think it will work. We'll beef up our defenses, of course, but go on offense."

"What does that involve?" Admiral Delaney asked.

"It involves a proactive move to preempt the EMP attack. Here's my plan. South Korea recently captured a North Korean spy named Kwon do-Hyun. He was a top notch cybersecurity specialist with Samsung, privy to bits and pieces of critical South Korean classified information that he managed to rip off and pass to the to the North periodically. He conducted his covert business undetected for twenty years, but slipped up and got caught by NIS trying to hack into CENTCOM over there, big mistake.

"Kwon's espionage did some serious damage," Biff added. "He's awaiting trial in Seoul and will likely face a death sentence. I want to turn him, set up a disinformation campaign, and infiltrate him into North Korea as a double agent."

"That's a daunting task. Just how do you plan to pull that off?"

"Hardball."

"Hardball?"

"Yes, we're playing for keeps. Hear me out, Admiral. I've got a game plan. Off the wall, but I believe it will work. There's a lot at stake with the threat of an EMP attack. I'm increasing the ante. I'll be gone awhile, taking my team with me to coordinate the operation with NIS in Seoul. As soon as you push the plan through the Joint Chiefs and get it sanctioned, I'll set my offensive plan in motion."

"Okay, shoot. It better be good if you want me to sell a risky proposal to the Chiefs of Staff. The President's Security Council is big on second guessing our intelligence estimates and the military staff recommendations, so the Chiefs of Staff have become risk adverse, reluctant to go out on a limb fighting city hall."

"Okay, here's how I see it going down. Want to bet they'll buy the plan?"

"I'll never bet against you, Biff." He smiled. "You seem somehow to defy the odds, no matter what. Go ahead; brief me on your wild 'Hardball' plan."

The DCI sat back in his chair, smiled, and lit a cigar.

"Still smoking Cubans, Biff? Have a Cohiba?" Admiral Delaney offered. Biff got special treatment. No need for military protocol with this man. Delaney had the utmost confidence in him. He'd never failed him.

The admiral slid the humidor across the desk and put his feet up, anticipating a comprehensive briefing. Biff was the CIA's best field operative during the admiral's long tenure at Langley, which is why he'd recently promoted Biff to Director of Counterterrorism. The CIA needed innovation in their spy craft, a new direction to confront ever-evolving threats, such as a nuclear-triggered EMP attack. Biff's proposal of going on offense rather than depending on multiple defense systems appealed to Delaney. Biff Roberts was fundamentally a renaissance man, as his track record attested. He represented the CIA's best hope to counter North Korea's imminent threat.

Biff lit his cigar, blew a perfect smoke ring, and grinned before laying out his plan.

"My scheme involves a lot of smoke and mirrors, layers of intrigue and deception, Admiral. It requires perfect planning and flawless execution, but it's feasible…"

Chapter Fourteen

HARDBALL

NIS – Seoul, South Korea
Two weeks later

"**M**r. Kwon, you realize you'll face a firing squad after we sentence you for the state crime of spying for North Korea?" the Director of NIS, Nam Jae-Joon, said. "Conviction for your despicable act is a foregone conclusion. Thought about that? You have done irreparable damage to our country with your subversion."

Kwon made no reply. The prisoner avoided eye contact, looking at the floor. Loosely strapped in a hard wooden chair, Kwon's body language indicated defeat, dejection, and exhaustion. Following five days of practically non-stop questioning, day and night, forced to stand up all night with little chance for sleep, Kwon could barely lift his head.

The interrogation room was humid, poorly ventilated purposely to increase the uncomfortable atmosphere, a psychological tool of intimidation as Nam continued to berate Kwon and wear him down.

"Consequently, you will have a speedy trial followed by a swift execution," his interrogator said caustically. "I promise you will soon face a firing squad, possibly in the public square." At that, Kwon cringed. "Everyone is clamoring for your head. We plan to expedite the proceedings to appease them before they storm the jail and lynch you. That's how much public uproar your treachery has caused." Nam paused to let the threat sink in, observing the prisoner's response.

Kwon briefly lifted his head, blinked, but still said nothing. He slumped back in his chair, drained of color.

One NIS team after another had accused him of high crimes and attempted to trick him into inconsistencies in his confessions of what classified information he had divulged. They had relentlessly hounded him. How did he pass his information to North Korea? Was he networking? Who was his handler? Grueling questions, one after another, asking him to explain his sources and methods in detail.

Despite the hostile atmosphere, Kwon was puzzled that so far no one had laid a hand on him. He'd expected to have been flogged by now. Now he wondered if they hadn't been saving the rough stuff for today, when they brought in the top man, the Director of the National Intelligence Service himself, Nam Jae-Joon, for a personal interrogation.

Kwon had recognized the well-tailored man immediately; Nam was always immaculately groomed, always smiling on TV and in the press photos. But this morning he was not smiling. He was glaring menacingly as he conducted the interrogation.

Kwon had read about this legendary figure in the newspapers, seen his no-nonsense interviews on TV, and was well acquainted with his uncompromising reputation. The Korean spymaster was a celebrated figure—a patriot, a former paratrooper, and now a military hawk known for ruthless treatment of traitors and spies. Nam's reputation included resorting to torture to extract incriminating evidence and confessions in matters of national security. There were no holds barred with this old-school intelligence officer. Kwon braced himself for being hauled over the coals, abused, and possibly mutilated.

After his opening rebuke, Kwon noted Nam continued staring him down, not saying a word, gauging him. The stifling heat in the room prompted Nam to remove his jacket, which he neatly folded and handed to an aide. He didn't loosen his silk club tie, tightly knotted over his starched white shirt. Kwon noted his monogrammed initials on the sleeve's right cuff, a Western affectation among the elite Koreans. He could imagine Nam casually having lunch at a private club shortly after beating him half to death.

Obviously Nam maintained his renowned decorum in any situation, even NIS interrogations, Kwon thought. But Kwon knew Nam's restraint was just a façade. He faced a harsh grilling.

"Do you think for a moment that our overwhelming evidence against you will fail to convince the judge and jury?" Nam continued. "If so, you are deluding yourself. Justice will be swiftly served. Your days are numbered."

Kwon squirmed in his seat, becoming more uncomfortable by the moment. Nam's eyes bored through him as the NIS Director made no attempt to disguise his scorn.

"Think about this serious consideration, Kwon, not your personal fate for a moment. I doubt you have given it much thought, consumed with worry about yourself." Nam's voice was thick with loathing and disdain. "Did you ever think for a moment about what the consequences of your treachery will be for your family?"

Nam paused while Kwon stared at the floor, his head hanging in shame, unable to look Nam in the eye. When he first began spying, he'd been nervous, but his fears had quickly faded. After twenty successful years, he never seriously contemplated getting caught. Occasionally, when such worries seeped into his thoughts, he would quickly push them away. And he could never bring himself to consider there might be consequences to his family. Now the Director was forcing him to face a harsh reality. His gut tightened. His pulse sped up as his mind raced. He was terrified of what might happen to them.

Nam immediately made their fate quite clear, dispelling any confusion he might be experiencing in his enervated state of mind and body entering his sixth day of questioning.

"Your wife and children will become pariahs, living a miserable life of persecution here in Seoul, victimized by angry neighbors during the trial, your kids bullied and shamed." Nam delivered the words in a harsh tone, right in Kwon's face. He took another meaningful pause for that to sink in.

"You have subjected your family to the ultimate loss of face by your disgraceful, treasonous behavior," Nam said. "Was spying on us worth it? Look what harm you've done to them, you self-centered fool!"

Kwon felt like he might pass out following this censure. Guilt consumed him. Nam was correct. He had not factored his family's future into the eventuality he would ever be caught spying. After twenty years he'd become complacent, a fatal flaw, especially in espionage.

"Your execution will not end their grief and mistreatment," Nam continued. "They will continue to be humiliated and then we will expel them, disgraced, to North Korea."

Kwon's head snapped up. *Expel them?* he thought, his mouth too dry to speak.

"You've subjected them to a fate worse than death," Nam said. "They are native born South Koreans who abhor the totalitarian regime up north, where they treat their citizens like animals, perhaps worse."

Kwon had never dreamed South Korea would banish his family to North Korea as punishment for what was solely his crime.

"They are innocent!" Kwon blurted, his first words in over an hour. "That's not fair!"

"Fair?" Nam scowled and leaned closer to him once again. "Do you think their innocence matters to an angry mob who despises traitors? Fair?" His voice rose. "Do you think for a minute they fucking care? You have put our citizens in mortal danger by spying for our enemy. You are a despicable person who betrayed our country. They are guilty by association, a natural reaction by a nation that kindly took you in as a North Korean refugee twenty years ago and gave you freedom, a real life. Some gratitude you've shown. As a consequence of your betrayal, your loved ones will suffer the most."

Nam lowered his voice again, his tone no less menacing. "You will be executed, but they will continue to pay for your crime. No one will sympathize with your family, or really give a damn. It's your fault, Kwon. Don't you understand the enormity of the horror you've created for them?"

He's right, Kwon thought, adding to his misery. Many would never believe they were unaware of his espionage activity.

Nam pressed on with persistent accusations designed to stress the captured spy, using his family as leverage to pile on guilt and disgrace. Nam knew that Kwon's family was the spy's vulnerability. Years of experience told Nam this represented the key to breaking him. Nam increased the pressure, tightening the psychological vise.

"I expect you never considered that outcome of your espionage, correct? Never dreamed we'd catch you spying? Thought you were the smartest man in the room, an IT and cybersecurity expert way too clever to be discovered. Guess what? Now we've got you by the balls. You're a fucking dirtball, Kwon. Scum awaiting execution. You're a dead man walking."

The intense grilling continued only with a brief pause for the words to sink in. Nam whipped him with accusatory and degrading words designed to discredit him, to dehumanize him, and with no let up. Every man had his breaking point. He sensed Kwon was on the brink.

"Death will be swift for you, but your family will be forced to endure a living hell with those savages. How do you think those North Korean barbarians will treat your family when we expel them? Like dogs? Not even that well, I assure you. Your family is South Korean, well born, provincial, have never left the country. Well educated, civilized, how will they cope in an uncultured country indoctrinated to despise South Koreans? There will be no mercy rule to save them."

Kwon found this harangue unbearable. He remained speechless, unable to make eye contact, much less utter a response. Profound despair overwhelmed him.

Noting the captive's body language, Nam proceeded without let up.

"I'll tell you how. The North will hate them and never accept them. Never mind that you came from the North and spied for them. It's irrelevant, as they will be seen as the enemy. Expect no gratitude or leniency for your loved ones. They will be horribly mistreated. Your wife will be gang raped repeatedly by those savages while incarcerated in a reeducation gulag. Got that ugly picture? And your three young boys … They will be sentenced to hard labor—if they are lucky and not sodomized." Nam watched Kwon flinch at that statement.

"Yes, your family will pay dearly for your transgressions, believe me. It will not be a pleasant experience. Did those brutal thoughts ever cross your deceitful mind while you were stealing our State secrets?" Nam hissed.

Kwon knew it was no idle threat; Nam was definitely intending to expel them. What had he done to his family? Overcome by a wave of guilt, he suddenly felt nauseous.

"Kwon, ask yourself a basic question, are you married to your family or your North Korean ideology? Who means the most to you? Where does your ultimate loyalty lie? With your dear family, or with DPRK's subversive objectives? I suggest you seriously consider your priorities. Your family, or allegiance to a crazed North Korean dictator imposing a cruel system of totalitarian government that impoverishes and demeans its citizens?"

Nam continued to grind the prisoner down mercilessly, the psychological impact of his rebuke taking an immense toll on Kwon, whose resistance was visibly waning.

Kwon shifted in the uncomfortable chair. From the stuffy air, and now his intense fear for his family, Kwon sweated profusely. Anxiety set in, his heart raced, and he felt faint.

He was a family man, completely devoted to them. His spying was something he'd compartmentalized, separating it utterly in his mind from his family. It never occurred to him, if he was caught, that they would be part of his punishment. He had committed the state crime of spying, not them. They were unaware of his covert activity, and not remotely involved except unwittingly providing a cover for him as a happily married man working at Samsung.

But it was obvious that didn't matter to his callous interrogator. Nam had him by the balls, as he said. There was no way out.

Kwon let out an audible groan as the reality for his family set in, as if Nam had punched him in the gut. He thought he might vomit as malaise swept over him. He broke into a cold sweat.

Nam, a veteran at this game, could see his methods were working on Kwon. He was getting to him, he observed, and it wouldn't be long now. Kwon was squirming, thinking about the ramifications, and about to capitulate.

Kwon thought once again of the last message he'd sent to Pyongyang, the one that had tripped him up. After years of subterfuge, he'd been caught red-handed. Remorse was useless. They had him and there was no way out.

Director Nam had shown him the communiqué he had encrypted, the one they intercepted and deciphered, the one indicting him beyond a reasonable doubt. Not a chance of dodging the firing squad. After only one single screw up in his successful twenty-year career, now he realized it was time to pay the piper. But, why punish his family? It seemed so unfair. But Nam was correct, no one really cared about the fate of a traitor or his family.

They were out for blood.

***

Biff and his CIA entourage observed through the interrogation room's one-way mirror, listening to Nam increasing the psychological pressure on Kwon. They were witnessing the flip side of the NIS Director's everyday engaging personality. The director's formality and charm vanished as he got down to business.

"He can be a hard ass, don't be fooled," Biff said, grinning. "The man's a pro at this. Take note, gentlemen."

"Big time nasty!" Tyler concurred. "Nam's threat against Kwon's family struck home. He's quaking in his boots, if not peeing his pants."

"Kwon didn't see this coming," Biff observed. "He'll soon fold."

***

As the interrogation was entering its sixth hour, the NIS team still offered no water to the prisoner, although they had refrained from physical persuasion up to this point. On top of being sleep-deprived and having been forced to stand up all night, this was his sixth straight day of questioning. Yesterday he'd come close to hitting the wall. Today he would hit it.

Yesterday he'd began to divulge what intelligence he had passed to North Korea. He was beginning to break, losing his once resolute commitment to his spy mission. He was an IT expert, not a covert agent conditioned and trained to resist coercive measures and the intense stress of skillful interrogation. The nonstop questioning of his motives and his techniques of relaying the pilfered information had started to get results; details dribbled out along with his sources and methods.

Kwon simply couldn't take it anymore. He knew NIS' reputation for getting rough when routine interrogation tactics fell short. Trapped like an animal, he felt desperate, fearing escalation to the next level—torture.

***

Kwon was unaware in his fatigued state of mind that he had inadvertently provided enough information yesterday for NIS to track his North Korean handler. The man was hiding out in a shantytown outside Seoul, down a dirt road between rice paddies, literally the boondocks. NIS had put out a hit job on him last night. They'd dumped Hwan Hyon-Hui's beaten body in a remote rice paddy after a short round of torture. They confiscated his computer and smart phone that were electrically powered by a clever set up. He'd used a propane generator and solar panel wireless communication tower for satellite communication, out in the middle of nowhere. Hwan had run hi tech espionage on a budget. The hit team skillfully bugged the premises with concealed microdot cameras before departing.

As a final insult, they cut off the handler's fingertips and set him on fire so the body could not be easily traced if it was ever found in the abandoned, remote rice paddy, a signature hardball move by the NIS hit squad.

***

Out in the observation room, Biff sensed it was about time for the "good cop, bad cop" routine. The good cop was Kim Min-Jun's assignment in the interrogation plan. As the Deputy Director entered the room, Nam backed off deferentially, as if Kim was a superior officer taking charge. Nam stepped back and observed, crossing his arms, and continuing to glare menacingly at Kwon for good measure. All part of the act.

Kwon pondered what to expect next with this new agent, a person he knew nothing about, and had never seen, but appeared to have a gentle manner. He hoped for better treatment from someone higher in command.

Kim approached Kwon with a look of concern on his face. He wiped the perspiration from Kwon's brow with a cold cloth. He spoke gently, offered him tea, and loosened his restraints.

"Let's take a break, Kwon," Kim said in a friendly manner, pretending he cared. "Seems Nam's been hard on you."

He paused while the man gulped down the tea and asked for another.

"Sure." Kim motioned for an aide to refill the prisoner's cup. "You look thirsty, drink up."

Kwon looked up plaintively, wondering why the sudden kindness from someone he'd never seen before.

"Thank you," he said in a pitiful little voice, his resistance fading.

"Look, you're an intelligent man, Kwon," Kim said. "I've read your résumé. I'm in a position to offer you a deal that will spare your family, maybe even you." He paused artfully. "Interested?"

Kwon hesitated, suspecting a trick.

"You should jump at the opportunity. You have no bargaining chips," Kim said kindly. "These men have little patience with you. Let me help you sort out a solution to your problem."

Kwon remained silent while he processed the possibility of wiggling out of his dilemma. He wondered why the offer was being made, and who this man was in a position to pardon him. Maybe it was just a trick.

"Do you not understand my offer?" Kim asked.

Kwon looked at him silently. Was he about to offer an option to spare his family, maybe even him? Kwon was exhausted after six grueling days and surprised that they were willing to offer a way out of his dilemma. He was processing everything too slowly to reply.

Kim didn't mess around. Impatient that Kwon didn't immediately jump at the opportunity, Kim thought maybe Kwon was tougher than they estimated. Kim decided he should step it up.

"Or," Kim said, "shall we continue on with our little exercise, and progress to the next level of the interrogation? I'll warn you it's very unpleasant."

Unfortunately, the prisoner again did not respond quickly enough to his question, his reaction slowed by duress and fatigue.

Kim's mood abruptly changed again with Kwon's delay, misinterpreted as vacillation.

"Unzip your pants," Kim suddenly commanded, his tone now hostile. Kwon's eyes widened.

Kim motioned to a heavyset man over in one corner.

Kwon glanced in that direction and immediately terror filled him. The Asian man who stepped forward was the size of a sumo wrestler with a pockmarked and scarred face. He looked like a medieval executioner, but lacking the traditional black hood and wearing a tank top. The giant of a man sported a large multicolor Grateful Dead tattoo on his right bicep.

Weird tattoo for an Asian, Kwon thought. *Scary looking guy, looks like a MMA fighter.* He tensed up, anticipating the worst.

"Jung," Kim said, "bring over your equipment and do your thing." The huge man picked up an electrical cord and jumper cables from nearby shelves. He lumbered toward Kwon ominously, sneering at him like a psychopath.

"This man needs to be persuaded we're not fucking around here," Kim added. "No more bullshit."

Kwon flinched, his eyes bulging in terror. "Wait. Please, just a moment." He wet his pants in fear. He did not want the electrical cord clamps attached to his testicles. And, most of all he wanted his family spared.

"Speak up man," Kim said. "Shall we make a deal?"

"Yes, please. Anything but Jung! May I have more tea?" Kwon's mouth was dry, his heart racing, and his crotch wet. Beyond desperate, he'd agree to anything at this point.

***

"Okay, Tyler, here comes the knockout punch. He's cracking." Biff nudged his special ops man to watch through the one-way mirror.

"All the telltale signs are there. Things are going as planned, just as Nam and I discussed."

"He's definitely folding, Biff," Tyler said. "You guys called it. Colonel Scott won't believe it."

"We're not there yet. We've got a ways to go after he folds. Reza will be a busy man."

***

"Of course you may have more." Kim motioned for an aide to offer Kwon more tea.

Kwon looked wasted. He swilled the tea down, his mouth dry as a desert, and held his cup out for more. He was anxious to cut a deal, any deal.

"Listen up," Kim said. "It's a 'take it or leave it' proposition. There will be no negotiations. And it's a onetime offer, got it? No second chances, no bargaining. We're not screwing around with you," he added, his tone hardening, "you worthless piece of dung. We're calling the shots, and you've got only one chance, understand? I suggest you don't fuck it up."

Quivering, overwhelmed, and startled by the swift turn of events, Kwon unraveled before them. "Okay," he finally said.

***

"Here comes the big squeeze, fellows," Biff noted to his team as they watched through the mirror as the gambit played out. "Hardball's about to pay off."

Tyler smiled, enjoying the plan Biff devised. Tim chuckled, knowing his boss wrote the script with Nam.

Gunner was fascinated. He hadn't been sure they would actually pull it off. Watching them break the North Korean spy and watching him fold was almost surreal.

Tyler nudged Gunner, noticing his reaction. "Never seen the boss operate before? Don't be surprised. Biff's a master at this stuff."

Reza listened to the interrogation, knowing what was coming next. Reza had serious reservations about whether the frail Asian computer whiz was up for the task. He didn't inspire confidence. It was one thing to pilfer technology and secretly relay bits and pieces of cybersecurity intelligence, another thing to perform in the field as a double agent. Reza's fifteen years of experience embedded in Tehran's Revolutionary Guards as a double agent made him wary of novices. It wasn't a game for amateurs.

Kwon would require intense indoctrination, iron clad training, and foolproof programming. North Koreans were suspicious of their own mothers. Kwon would need an Oscar performance to not blow the mission. Biff's bold scheme would be difficult enough to pull off even with a more experienced agent. To Reza, there was just too much at stake.

This was no minor op. They were charged with stopping an attack that could potentially cripple the U.S. and send civilization back into the Dark Ages.

Reza forced his doubts away. Biff thought it could be done. If Biff was right and Kwon could be made to pull it off, Reza would make it happen.

***

CHAPTER FIFTEEN

THE DEAL

"**H**ere's the deal. Listen carefully, Kwon," Kim said. "We want you to spy for us. Become a double agent. Got that? We will carefully train you to perform a specific task. Only one mission assignment is required, but it's of vital importance, and it must result in relaying one hundred percent reliable information, accurate and actionable intelligence."

Kwon frowned. He was less dehydrated now, but he still struggled to think clearly. "Spy for you? How?" he stuttered, baffled at the astonishing request. "Become a double agent? Me?"

"We have Americans with special clandestine skills to help us tutor you to become an expert in your new role as a double agent. Teach you the essential spy craft. Then we plan to infiltrate you back into North Korea."

Kwon looked utterly bewildered. "How could you possibly do that?"

Kim cut him off. "Not your concern. It will happen, trust me."

"But…"

"Never mind, just listen carefully. Your survival in North Korea will depend on a flawless performance. You must hone your skills, learn studiously, and ask a lot of questions about how you should behave in your role. While we train you as a double agent, you'll practice twelve hours a day until you master your task. You must have an absolute comprehension of how critical your part is in this undertaking, and be comfortable in your role. It must become second nature, not play-acting. Up there, one awkward moment could get you killed."

"I'm not sure I'll be able to pull that off," Kwon said. "I'm an expert at hacking computers, not performing field assignments. Honestly, I'm not that kind of spy. You should know that from your investigation."

"Field ops will not be your requirement," Kim assured him. "You will maintain your same identity as a cybersecurity expert. We ask you to continue to be the same person you've always been so as not to arouse suspicion. Use your knowledge and experience gained at Samsung. That should be easy, right? We plan to keep it simple."

"It sounds very complicated to me," Kwon said quietly.

"Let me explain our plan further to make it clear what we request of you. All that's required is to just keep your eyes and ears open for one specific piece of evidence, the precise date and a time of a special planned event, a top-secret North Korean operation. It may take some time to discover this information, but we need to know the facts as soon as you find out. That in essence is your major duty, in fact, your only obligation to us. Your sole responsibility is to observe what's going on up there and supply us this one specific bit of information as soon as you know. I reemphasize that point. A limited form of spying is all we ask."

"Really? That's all?"

"Yes, that's it. You won't be required to kill anyone, carry a gun, or sneak around pilfering information. No hacking into computers, no need to relay periodic information to a contact. That would put your discovery as a double agent at risk. They're good at spotting spies, so we want you to maintain a low profile. We'll emboss your credentials and put you in a position to get an IT job up there by offering something they sorely need, so they'll be anxious to use your expertise."

"How exactly?"

"Employ your cybersecurity system experience with Samsung to offer them Singapore contacts to supply them with updated cybersecurity equipment, software and hardware for their rocket programs."

"How can I offer that? How will they verify my credentials?"

"We'll manage those problems and make all the necessary arrangements. We'll explain that part of our plan later."

"If I spy for you, how do I get the messages to you?" Kwon asked. He was worried about the complexity of the deal, even if it ultimately involved only a single task.

"Contact is not required except on one single occasion, as I said. We don't want to hear from you otherwise. As I mentioned, you will not need to make frequent contact with your handler either. In fact, you will speak with him only once, and never meet him in person. On that special occasion, the simple message will be only to make a future lunch reservation at a precise time and date over a Pyongyang payphone, untraceable, of course. We will have you commit the contact's phone number to memory. Do not write it down, got it?"

"You want me to become a double agent just to make contact with my handler only once to make a lunch reservation? Not mention any information about this special event the North is planning, not inform him of the time and date? Take all that risk just to go to lunch?" Now Kwon was really confused. He wondered if they were messing with him.

"The reservation message is a tactic, a code he understands and will relay to us immediately. You won't know the handler's name or location. He's a deep dark agent of ours and NIS, a covert agent in the 'restaurant' business in Pyongyang. He will be awaiting your call 24/7 to a dedicated phone number reserved for that sole purpose. He'll know the coded meaning of your reservation request, the specific time and date, so no further conversation is required by you. You will keep the call short and to the point. No chatting, no names, questions, nothing else should be spoken. Speak in Chinese with a Cantonese dialect. All calls are monitored up there, even from pay phones. This call should take less than a minute. Anything extraneous could possibly compromise the mission. Just give him the time and date we need to know in the guise of a lunch reservation you're requesting, okay?"

"I understand," Kwon said, still nervous and confused at the sudden turn of events after six brutal days of interrogation.

"You look confused," Kim said, realizing Kwon was perhaps overwhelmed. "So I repeat for the third time, you will have only this single task to carry out. Understand?"

"I think so."

Kim repeated the detailed instructions again and added, "At the completion of your training you'll understand what we're up to, why we're infiltrating you. Why we're keeping it simple. It's straight forward, Kwon, not a difficult undertaking. You can do this."

"I suppose so, but I've never done anything like this."

"I understand. That's why we're keeping it simple. I repeat, concentrate on what I'm telling you. I know you're exhausted, confused, so I'll go over it again as many times as necessary..." Kim again went through the details of Kwon's task. "Got it now? Think you can handle that? Do we have a deal?"

"I think so. If I agree, when and how does all this happen?"

"I remind you that you're in no position to bargain. It will take place when we think you are proficiently trained. At that time we'll covertly slip you back into North Korea with specific instructions, understand?"

"I understand your request, but I'm confused. I'm in jail. How do I get out of jail in order to spy for you? How do I get to North Korea? Make the right contacts?"

"We'll manage all those problems and details when the time comes. Don't worry. You will be brought here from jail for daily training until we manage to get you out of jail. Then we'll train you in a safe house until you are good to go."

"What about my family?"

"Oh yes, your family," Kim said. "Let me address that problem and allay your apprehension. In return for your agreement to perform our task, we will spare your life and relocate your family in protective custody. They will live under assumed names with our colleagues in Busan who will care for them and school your boys in a private academy. We assure you nothing will happen to them if you successfully complete your assignment."

Kim lowered his voice menacingly. "But don't even think of bolting, or reneging on our deal once you're back up North. We'll hold your family as hostages, very comfortably, but we will hold them until we verify you've honored our agreement. If you don't run off and you successfully complete your one simple task, we promise to extract you from the North and reunite you with your family to 'live happily ever after,' as they say in the storybooks, under assumed names, of course. We'll fake your death to avoid any reprisals."

The details were spoken with a hint of sarcasm, Kim's contempt once again clear.

After a moment of hesitation, Kwon asked quietly, "If I don't accomplish my task, what happens to my family?"

Kim smiled coldly. "You don't want to know."

* * *

Chapter Sixteen

THE NEWS

Seoul, the next week

T*he Korean Times* headline read SPY TRIAL SET FOR NEXT WEEK. *NIS promises swift conviction for espionage and sentencing of Kwon do-Hyun. Spy expected to face firing squad. See full story below.*

The Korean Herald headline was SAMSUNG CYBER SPY KWON TO FACE SPEEDY TRIAL.

Similar news appeared on TV and the Internet morning, noon, and night. NIS Director Nam held daily update conferences, leaking snippets of Kwon's espionage career, embellishing his spy escapades, and subtly creating a monster. Nam convincingly captured public interest in the national treachery. Soon incensed, the South Koreans clamored for Kwon's head, the effect Nam intended. The man was a master at soundbites, and never passed up a photo op. The press loved him. Nam knew how to work a crowd and whip up support against public enemy number one — Kwon do-Hyun.

Not since NIS tracked the notorious Korean mafia founder, Cho Yang-Eun, to Manila for extradition had there been so much excitement in Seoul. Three months ago, everyone followed the developing news about the mobster. The sensational coverage of his capture had been over the top, linking Cho to the Seven Star mobsters in Busan. Cho also awaited trail while the government tried to replace the star witness against him. The witness mysteriously had gone missing, stalling Cho's conviction and sentencing trial.

The capture of a North Korean spy embedded for years in a critical cybersecurity industry at Samsung rattled the nation. Nam's exposure of Kwon's state crimes cemented his stellar reputation. Kwon's story was destined to soon overshadow Cho's. Both high-profile prisoners were imprisoned in Andong, but only Kwon's case would be expedited for a swift trial. Nam had a good reason for that decision.

***

One week later the *Korean Times* headline read: *KWON CONVICTED AND SENTENCED TO FACE FIRING SQUAD.* The *Korean Herald went with JURY CONVICTS KWON/SPY SENTENCED TO DEATH BY FIRING SQUAD NEXT WEEK.*

***

At NIS headquarters Nam read the stories and smiled at his deputy, Kim. "Our disinformation scheme is underway."

"Looking good," Kim agreed. "They're buying into the misdirection."

CHAPTER SEVENTEEN

ANDONG PRISON

Seoul

Three days later

At dusk the Hyosung motor scooter drove alongside the high, concrete prison wall, which was covered by concertina wire at the top and graffiti at street level. Half way down the potholed road the scooter roared to a stop. There was no traffic on the dead end side street. Other than occasional foot traffic from those who lived nearby, there never was much activity here, which suited the driver's purpose.

Few chose to live next to a prison in the run-down neighborhood. Only those with no other option lived here, the poverty stricken with nowhere else to go.

A haze hung over the few trees lining the street. The late July humidity was stifling; flies and other insects swarmed around the driver. He looked around, finding the street deserted by its residents, with not even a stray dog or cat wandering around. The evening was too hot and muggy for anyone to be outside, even at this late hour when it normally cooled down. The monsoon season was winding down, but it didn't seem like it tonight. The only activity was noise coming from the other side of the prison wall.

Perfect, the scooter rider thought.

He checked his watch. On prior scouting visits, he'd memorized the timing of the prison's perimeter flood lights. He had to move fast. They were scheduled to come on in fifteen minutes, after the exercise yard was cleared of prisoners who were right now catching a few moments of fresh air and stretching their legs before returning to their cramped cells for the night. He could hear their animated chatter over the high wall.

The guards would change shifts following the evening routine that he'd memorized. Precise timing was essential to his task.

The driver removed his helmet, hopped off his scooter, and grabbed his backpack. He wore a gruesome plastic Halloween mask of a circus clown, a strange sight in Asia. He walked briskly over to the two-foot thick cement wall reinforced with rebar, to a point where there was a large crack. The damage was the result of a recent DUI crash publicized in the news. He tried to avoid the surveillance cameras thirty yards to his left and right, but he knew some camera would catch a glimpse of him, his reason for wearing the mask. He'd scouted out the cameras and the weak spot in the wall last week. He knew what he had to do.

He removed C-4 plastic bonded explosive from his backpack and expertly molded the off-white, putty-like material into the crack. Once the C-4 was securely in place, he attached a detonator with a remote control code.

Almost twice as powerful as TNT, he thought it should do the job nicely.

He returned to his scooter and placed a brief cell call.

"You're good to go," he said slowly and distinctly. He wanted to avoid any misunderstanding. Then he sped off, spinning the wheels of the scooter and sending cinders flying. The scooter bumped over the potholes, catching air.

A minute after the scooter departed, a van with a Korean Telecom logo pulled into the dead-end street fifty yards past the spot where the C-4 had been applied to the heavy prison wall. Despite the heat, the van driver and passenger in the front seat wore ski masks.

"Call the designated number," the man in the passenger seat commanded in English. Then he hunkered down.

A few seconds later the detonation blew a five-foot diameter hole in the thick prison wall. The explosion rocked the neighborhood, shaking the van with the massive concussion wave. Debris flew thirty yards through the air, the fragments silhouetted by the explosion's huge flash.

"Holy shit!" the driver exclaimed. "Awesome fireworks!"

"Fourth of July caliber," the man in the passenger seat responded with a guffaw. "Quick. Back up. Let's roll."

The driver quickly backed the van down the street until they were directly across from the hole blasted in the concrete wall. They watched as the smoke and dust started to clear.

"Go!" the man in the passenger seat commanded, turning toward the rear compartment of the van.

Four Korean commandoes wearing ski masks and regulation blue prison uniforms with large numbers on the front jumped out of the back-door of the van. Armed with MP-5 automatic pistols, they scampered through the hole in the wall into the prison exercise yard. The commandoes fanned out, their matching prison uniforms helping them to blend in with the inmates as they searched for two special prisoners.

Following the blast most inmates scattered, but a few unfortunate ones close to the explosion were sprawled on the ground, injured. Mass confusion reigned. Smoke from the massive explosion enveloped much of the area, providing some cover for the commandoes' mission. The pungent smell of oily tar from the C-4 detonation permeated the air, causing many prisoners to cough.

Immediately after entering the prison yard, one of the Korean commandoes launched a flash-bang grenade at the watchtower to distract the guards from figuring out what was happening below. The explosion temporarily blinded and deafened the guards, but it also tripped the siren, which started to blare loudly, adding to the pandemonium.

The rehearsed breakout went as planned. Kwon and Cho were swiftly located by the commandoes and ushered out the gap in the wall to the van without explanation, only the command, "Come quickly with us!" Both obeyed, absolutely astounded at what was transpiring.

As they exited the prison yard, the commandoes fired a few volleys into the air. The shots slowed the stampede of prisoners anxious to take advantage of the opportunity to escape through the hole, all part of the plan to create mass disorder. After leaving the scene, the commandoes had no concern for how many prisoners escaped. A massive jailbreak would provide cover for their own escape.

"Into the back of the van, move!" one commando ordered Kwon and Cho, both still stunned and baffled by the unexpected jailbreak.

The operation went off without a hitch, taking less than ten minutes. As the van exited the dead end street, the van's driver noted the chaotic scene in his rearview mirror. The prison's perimeter lights illuminated the inmates pouring through the wall. The prisoners quickly mixed with crowds of local residents who had rushed out of their homes to see what had happened.

The van driver chuckled to himself, "Beautiful, just fucking beautiful. What a scene. Wish I had a photo."

The van sped off into the approaching night through side streets along a prearranged route. As they departed, one of the commandoes slammed a needle into Cho's shoulder and injected a syringe of ketamine. Cho passed out on the van's floor.

Kwon was blindfolded after witnessing this swift action. He followed the instructions to sit still and stay quiet. Despite the hot interior of the van, he shivered, wondering what would happen next. It had been a tough week. Tried, convicted, sentenced to face a firing squad, incarcerated in a cramped prison cell, and now rescued from jail by armed men blowing a huge hole in the prison wall. It was a lot to assimilate.

He heard the two men joking in the front seat of the van. There was no mistaking their accents. Why were Americans involved in this, he wondered.

Now he was really puzzled.

Chapter Eighteen

NIS SAFE HOUSE

Later that afternoon
Undisclosed Seoul suburb

"Great to be in air conditioning and out of that friggin' heat," Gunner said as he walked into the living room of the safe house. "That ski mask was really bugging me." Gunner felt like a million bucks after a shower and putting on some clean clothes.

"Got that right," Tyler said. He was sprawled on the couch. "It was like a friggin' sauna in Seoul. Thank God the mission didn't take long."

Gunner sat in the comfy recliner beside the couch.

"Sorry 'bout the ski mask," Tyler added, "but there were too many surveillance cameras around to take a chance of being identified as Americans. Don't want to embarrass our company, you know." He chuckled.

"Yeah, no way we'd risk being ID'ed with that disguise," Gunner said. "What about the van?"

"I've got the commandoes removing the logo and repainting it so no one can trace the vehicle to us. I took the plates off beforehand and put on a fake paper temporary license."

"Bet your sweet ass surveillance cameras saw us down that street and maybe our scooter guy too," Gunner said. "Loved Tim's outrageous Halloween mask. Where did he pick that thing up?"

"Army BX, over by the Seoul garrison."

"Wait until the authorities review that surveillance film."

"Guarantee it'll be a 'what the fuck' moment," Tyler said. They both laughed, imagining the authorities' reaction.

"A caricature mask of a circus clown resembling Kim Jong-un? Classic!"

Tim's hilarious rip on the North Korean leader would certainly get a rise out of those reviewing the digital records of the jailbreak from the perimeter cameras. American dark humor at its finest.

"The Halloween comedy might be lost on them considering the seriousness of the massive jailbreak," Tyler said. "And the joke will not go down well in North Korea."

"Yeah, just ask SONY about that. DPRK lacks a sense of humor."

"Tim sure knows how to set up C-4 for remote detonation. Not a hitch blowing a hole in that thick wall."

"Not his first go round that block," Gunner said, "former special ops demolition guy."

Tim was currently soaking in a hot tub, recuperating with some beer.

"Feel like we made the right moves to cover our tracks. I'm sure the authorities are running that video now trying to figure out what the hell happened."

"We'll be hard to track." Even the Korean NIS commandoes had worn ski masks and prison uniforms. "They'll spend weeks trying to figure it out. Like you said, Tim's Halloween mask will confuse the heck out of them. Can't you hear 'em? 'Who were those guys?'"

"Ha! Yeah, just like that scene in *Butch Cassidy and the Sundance Kid.*" Tyler thought it was a good thing they disguised themselves. CIA hated international incidents. Got the politicians riled up, which was why Biff had set this up as an off-the-books operation, financed from their black vault.

The two CIA operatives shared another good laugh, jacked up that the well-planned operation went off without a hitch. The two former Special Forces officers had bonded, used their extensive military experience to attain a remarkable jailbreak in a brief amount of time, directing four Korean commandoes to snatch their targets from the prison's exercise yard.

Tyler and Gunner were part of the CIA's special activity division, SAD. Basically they were paramilitary operatives, performing the same line of work as in their special force experience under a new undercover auspice, the CIA. They loved it, taking pride in pulling off the bold jailbreak so smoothly. Both knew it was not always the case to have an operation go so flawlessly. Good results come from experience, and experience unfortunately often came from bad results. Both had been there, done that. They had learned their lessons well.

Biff had planned the operation down to every detail, even calculated the exact amount of C-4 that would be required to blow a hole that size in the prison wall. This undertaking was the start of Biff using his special activity division more aggressively. Staging a spectacular jailbreak in a foreign country was unheard of in CIA annals, more like the type of daring stunt Mossad would pull off. Biff intended for SAD to be in that same covert op league.

"That was a textbook 'boom, boom, quick in and out.'"

"Sure pulled it off with precision. Love it. Have to give Biff the credit for putting it all together, convincing Nam he'd make it happen. Let's break out the beer. Nam stocked the fridge for us, Coors from our Base Exchange."

"Yeah, man. Guess he's got an ID pass, surprised the hell out of me, American beer. Pretty nice hideout NIS set up for us, huh?" Gunner stood. "I'll go get the beers."

Coming down off an adrenaline high, they fist bumped.

"Right on," Tyler said, "sure could use a cold brew."

Gunner returned with two beers and handed one to Tyler before sitting back down. "Agree, sweet digs, especially the AC. We can finish training Kwon here while we finalize our plan to sneak him back into North Korea. But, what about Cho, what are we going to do with him? He seemed a little dingy before we sedated him, one fry short of a Happy Meal."

"Yeah, he looked out of it. Look at it this way, Cho's an old guy who got worked over by the guards pretty good in prison, judging from his bruises. Obviously took some blows to his head. No love lost when it comes to the Korean mafia. I'm sure the guards kicked the crap outta him. But he'll be okay, don't worry."

"That would explain his behavior," Gunner said, "plus the confusion of the jailbreak."

"Cho's one of the keys to our ruse," Tyler said, "a diversion tactic. We'll hide him out here under guard for a week or so, get him in shape. After that we'll cut him loose, let him run and lead the manhunt chase. The government will blame the breakout on the Kkangpae, the Korean mafia. Cho Yang-Eun was their Godfather, the kingpin of the Yangeuni family. It's a natural assumption that the local mafia orchestrated the jailbreak to get him out. Cho will give 'em a run for their money; he knows Seoul inside out, has a lot of contacts, chips to cash in."

"Is Nam going to hype the chase?" Gunner asked.

"You bet. Nam will encourage the press to play the mafia aspect up. Post BOLOs everywhere to capture him, get the public involved in his search. The media love Nam and he knows the public eats up gangster stories like this, like an action movie. They'll buy into the narrative that Kwon just happened to escape with forty other prisoners. They'll sell the story that Cho's street gang busted him out of jail, and no one will suspect that Kwon was the prime motive of our jailbreak. Nam will manage the disinformation campaign, that's his forte. North Korea will be monitoring the developments down here, I guarantee you. If we play our hand right, we'll convince them Kwon's at large avoiding the BOLO also, and may try to return home to avoid execution."

"Crafty move," Gunner said. "Set up a disinformation campaign to convince the North that Kwon, their fugitive spy, is on the run taking advantage of the mafia jailbreak to escape."

Tyler nodded. "That's a critical part of Biff's game plan, that the North accepts this manufactured account of the breakout."

"Where's Cho now? He's not in his retention room I noticed."

"In the interrogation room, still out cold from the ketamine injection. Seems the commandoes almost OD'ed him. A Korean doc who does classified jobs for NIS is putting a chip in Cho's ass while he's still sedated."

"What's that chip thing all about?" Gunner asked.

"Miniature GPS chip like they insert in dogs so you can find them if they run off. We'll release Cho after our disinformation campaign, while the manhunt is in full force looking for both of these fugitives. Cho will be the target of our diversion scheme while we smuggle Kwon back into North Korea. After we get our double agent back in up there, we'll anonymously tip off the authorities regarding Cho's whereabouts. We'll be tracking his GPS locator, not them, so our tip will allow the authorities to capture Cho. They'll get all the praise — regain some public approval. It's important in Asian society to save face, get some positive press. The public will eat up Cho's capture. After that, NIS will hype up press releases that Kwon's still at large despite a massive manhunt."

"Cool idea. That move adds credibility to cover Kwon's infiltration into North Korea."

"Precisely the big picture," Tyler said, "another of Biff's objectives. He's thought all of this through. While everyone thinks Kwon's still at large, police and NIS searching all over for him, we'll arrange to get him into North Korea by a roundabout route. All the while we'll be playing up his manhunt big time in the news. You know, APB, dangerous spy stuff; shoot him on sight, that sort of disinformation."

"Sounds good to me, create a distraction, whip up the crowd."

"Also, we plan to play up the angle that Kwon should have been in solitary confinement, not in an exercise yard. Allude to poor management, complacency at the prison. 'What were they thinking?' accusations. Get the media to stir things up. Since North Korea monitors the news down here, it will lend authenticity to Kwon's fugitive story when he arrives up there. That's the game plan."

Gunner smiled. "Got it now, pretty slick. Think the fat boy's regime will buy it?"

"We've got to sell it. Biff and Reza will be over in the morning to get started on the final phases of Kwon's prep. Kwon knows Kim's playing hardball, so he's jacked up. He fears for his family if he screws up."

"Strong incentive for him to produce, I'd say."

"You bet," Tyler said. "Put yourself in his place."

"Like between a rock and hard spot?"

"You got it. And for sure, he gets it."

***

The next morning *the Korean Times* headline was *SPECTACULAR JAILBREAK — KKANGPAE SUSPECTED IN ESCAPE OF MAFIA KINGPIN CHO/ SAMSUNG CYBER SPY KWON ALSO ESCAPES — See full story and details below. Full coverage continued on page two with photos*

*of bomb blast tearing huge hole in Andong prison wall. Forty prisoners
escape through gap.*

The Korean Herald went with *KKANGPAE SPRING GODFATHER
CHO BY BLOWING HOLE IN PRISON WALL/ NOTORIOUS SPY
KWON ALSO ESCAPES WITH FORTY OTHER PRISONERS* – *See full
story on pages one and two.*

In his NIS office in downtown Seoul, Director Nam read the headlines, put the papers down, and smiled at his Deputy Chief Kim. "Game
on."

"Going according to the American's bold strategy, got to give Biff
Roberts his due for pulling off stage one of our game plan, Director," Kim
remarked.

"I agree. It was ingenious."

"That out-of-the-box strategy worked to perfection. But the American
sense of humor …" Kim shook his head. "Can you believe the mask on the
scooter guy?"

"I can, that's typical of their kind of humor. Kim Jong-un will be
pissed. Biff has a reputation for accomplishing the outrageous. So far, he
is living up to it," Nam added. "Let's get over to our safe house to get the
next stage in our plan underway."

Chapter Nineteen

PYONGYANG RGB HEADQUARTERS

The following day

General Pak laid the copies of the *Korean Times* and the *Korean Herald* on his desk. The headlines and photos of the spectacular Andong jail break stunned him. One of DPRK's cyber spies was on the run just weeks after being captured by NIS.

"See these headlines, major?" the general asked. "Our agent escaped thanks to a lucky break. Someone blew a huge hole in the prison wall."

"I did, sir, leading to an incredible escape. Kwon's not one of our field agents, general. He'll not survive long."

"I agree. Cyber agents don't do well in the field. He was scheduled for execution as a traitor, so he has an incentive to run and hide. Maybe he'll luck out. NIS may lose their propaganda tool if we're also lucky. Kwon caused them great embarrassment by getting caught spying on ROK intelligence."

"Did you see the photo of the scooter driver who blew the hole in the prison wall?" The major asked.

"I did. Our beloved leader will go ballistic when he sees it. Where did the bomber get that mask?" From what the general had seen of the media coverage, the caricature mask of Kim Jong-un had captured the attention of all of South Korea.

"I don't know, but it will not go down well, sir. There will be reprisals."

"I suspect that will be the case," General Pak said. "Kim Jong-un will not see any humor in it ... We're fortunate that Kwon had no information regarding our plans to divulge under interrogation. So far our damage control has been successful."

The general knew that the Dragon Lady was a master at that sort of thing. She had carefully protected her network in layers of command so that only she and Jin-Ju knew the vertical structure of the organization. Should Kwon be captured, he would not be able to give up any information on their agents operating in South Korea beyond a few details about his handler.

Kwon certainly had no knowledge of their EMP attack plans. That plot was moving ahead as scheduled, and Pak would make sure nothing interfered with its success.

***

Chapter Twenty

FINAL TRAINING

The next day

"The first thing we want you to do, Kwon, is to grow a beard and shave your head," Nam informed him. "We want to radically change you appearance, to have you look like some offbeat kind of monk by the end of the month. It's part of our deception."

"Don't worry, we won't make you wear an orange robe," Nam added, breaking from his usual formal behavior after noting Kwon's blank stare.

Actually, Nam was being sarcastic. He wanted to shoot this spy, but the CIA had convinced him otherwise, to go with the master plan of converting him into a double agent. But Nam didn't bother to hide his contempt. No matter, Kwon appeared either spaced out or wary and in either case, missed the veiled attempt at humor.

Kwon said nothing. He knew Nam was deadly serious and Nam hated him. And, as the NIS Director had emphasized on prior occasions, they 'had him by the balls.' He didn't need a reminder. Kwon reconciled himself to jump through the hoops. He wanted to live and not further jeopardize his family by screwing up NIS' generous protective custody arrangement for them. They owned him. He knew it, they knew it.

Nam waited patiently for a response while he observed Kwon go into a trance, humming quietly to himself. Nam decided to back off and give him a chance to regroup. They needed to complete his training this month and move on with their plan.

Kwon replayed the events of the past week in his mind while Nam stared at him scornfully. Nam did that a lot to intimidate him. Kwon ignored him and drifted off into recent memories that were quite painful. He quietly hummed his personal mantra, resorting to a form of transcendental meditation he'd mastered to reduce stress, and to achieve a state of awareness and tranquility.

While incarcerated, he had started to believe Nam reneged on the deal. With no contact for five days after the trial and scheduled to be shot the coming weekend in the public square, his anxiety had mounted.

He had been losing hope, fearing they had changed their minds. Then suddenly NIS sprung him from jail where he awaited execution. The stunning jailbreak surprised him as much as every prisoner in the yard. The sudden explosion dazed him. But if they hadn't snatched him, he'd have made a break for freedom like the others.

But he wondered why they organized such a dramatic method of rescuing him from jail? The reasoning for it eluded him like so much else since his capture. Nam was also an enigma. Why not inform him of the details of their master plan? He had an analytic mind, why not explain the overall plan to him so him so he'd have some perspective? Why all the cloak and dagger maneuvers?

After his trial and swift conviction for espionage last week by a kangaroo court, one he suspected NIS had rigged, the verdict was followed by a swift death sentence handed down the same day, unheard of in Korean due process procedures. Since then, Kwon had no contact with NIS. His family had been forbidden to visit, and he felt abandoned. He still smarted from an incident the morning after his arrival in jail. A gnarly guard had delivered a newspaper to his cell without fanfare, poking it through the bars and spitting at him. He'd never forget the gut wrenching headline of *The Korean Times*: *KWON CONVICTED OF ESPIONAGE—TO FACE FIRING SQUAD NEXT WEEK.*

All of Korea read that headline, including his family. He'd shamed them, made them outcasts. Overwhelmed by guilt, he'd broken down and sobbed.

He hoped the other prisoners inside Andong didn't know who he was; he didn't want to test the notion of "honor among thieves."

He'd worried the NIS deal was off. Despite being near exhaustion, he'd become so apprehensive he couldn't sleep. He paced the ten by twelve jail cell with no window, and a straw mattress on the dirty wooden bunk, for hours on end, like a caged tiger. He'd had bigger closets in his family home in Seoul suburbs. And the stench of the toilet nauseated him. They never cleaned it or provided him the means to clean it himself.

He was a nervous wreck, degraded beyond anything he could ever imagine. Misery and depression overwhelmed him. His only respite was the exercise yard twice daily, a lull every prisoner considered a reprieve. Jail was no place to live, or die for that matter. He had been starting to look forward to execution rather than spending a lifetime confined to his cramped, foul-smelling cell.

NIS obviously had a plan, which he vaguely grasped, but they never let him in on the big picture. He'd overheard oblique references, snippets of information to analyze. Why was Cho involved? Why did they drug him last night? He was mafia, not a spy. Surely they weren't planning to infiltrate him into North Korea to run a crime ring or spy for them? No way.

All this clandestine action puzzled Kwon, and he had so many unanswered questions. He gained the impression the Americans played a big role in this conspiracy, but what was the endgame? He found his circumstances baffling, the whole picture unclear, but knew he was a key piece of the puzzle.

But last night he'd slept in a comfortable bed with clean sheets in an air-conditioned hideout. He could now enjoy showers and three good meals a day. The round the clock guards bugged him, and there was no privacy, TV, or computer, but it beat the hell out of jail.

Nam noticed Kwon was in a prolonged trance and broke his trend of thought. "Snap out of it," Nam said. "Are you daydreaming or what?"

"Sorry. Just thinking about what's going on. No one has explained it fully to me."

"We have a visitor coming tomorrow who'll give you a better idea. He'll prepare you for the interrogation by the DPRK. We anticipate that an intense session will take place upon your arrival, and he'll prep you for that encounter. He goes by the name of Reza. He's a pro, served as a double agent for the CIA in Tehran for fifteen years. Reza knows the deep dark stuff inside out, how to survive in a hostile environment, how not tip your hand. So listen carefully to what he has to say. Read his dossier so you will appreciate his expertise in this field, he's one of the world's best operatives."

Kwon nodded. "I intend to listen very carefully."

"Good, your life, your family's lives, and our mission depend on your performance, understand? This morning my team ran through what we've taught you so far. Another training team will test you this afternoon. Repetition will ingrain the essential information and techniques required for success as a double agent. It's of the upmost importance that you conduct yourself naturally as an IT cybersecurity specialist, a returning spy who served his country for twenty years who has something valuable to offer. Remember, you only have one task, but you must execute it flawlessly."

"I understand, Director."

"Good." After a final disgusted glare, Nam left abruptly.

Kwon had no idea how this would all play out, but he was certain of one thing — he was only a pawn in the bigger game.

CHAPTER TWENTY-ONE

REZA

The next day

"**H**ow do we know you're our spy, not theirs?" Reza asked, scowling. "You only returned to North Korea to spy on us, didn't you? Prove to us that you're not a double agent, Kwon, turned by the South Koreans."

Reza astounded Kwon with his tough questions, all this before Nam had even introduced them.

Whose side is he on? Kwon wondered. Reza was supposed to train him, not harass him. Kwon decided this Reza was as bad as Nam, another hard ass; it seemed they had an endless supply.

Reza noted Kwon's surprise, seeing his jaw drop at the abrupt verbal attack.

Kwon stared nervously at the heavily bearded person who didn't look like an American. The middle aged, weather-beaten man had a strange Middle Eastern accent like those in movies. Kwon had expected someone to tutor him in the fine art of deception, not this sudden onslaught of accusations.

Reza's challenge had its desired effect, part of his design to gauge Kwon's reaction. Reza's accusatory style immediately put Kwon on the defensive, indicated by his expression and loss for words. His spontaneous response indicated a glaring admission of guilt to even an average experienced interrogator, a vulnerability they could not risk with this cyber spy. Obviously Kwon would be a challenging work in progress. And it would take considerable time, Reza decided on first impression, to train him to safely infiltrate into North Korea.

"If those had been the opening questions in your interrogation upon arrival in North Korea," Reza told him, "you'd have been shot before sundown the same day. No further questions asked. They're highly suspicious, and you immediately demonstrated your guilt by your reaction. You must do better than that, Kwon, much better. Learn how to handle contentious encounters."

"I'll try my best," Kwon replied. Being chastised by an absolute stranger was rare in Asia and would take getting used to.

"My name is Reza. I'll train you to avoid a firing squad up there and not spill the beans in the process. You have only one simple task to perform, don't blow it," Reza added sternly. "This is serious business."

"I will do better. Sorry," Kwon said, feeling intimidated.

"You can do this. You're intelligent and pulled off a successful spy role in South Korea for twenty years before NIS apprehended you. Instead of execution, now you have a shot at redemption. NIS has been very benevolent to you and your family with the deal they offered. You must prove yourself. It's time to prepare to meet the conditions of your end of the bargain."

"I understand my commitment," Kwon said, regaining his composure. "You caught me by surprise with your questions in this safe setting, my guard was down."

"That's precisely what the North Koreans will do. Expect the unexpected. Be aware. What I did is a basic part of interrogation technique. It's important you grasp the principles I intend to teach you. I've experienced both sides of interrogations. Passing the drill involves certain skills and preparation. Foremost, anticipate their crafty moves, know the routine. They will try to trick you. Your behavior is as important as the words you choose. You must practice deception until it becomes second nature. You must be convincing in your performance or you will die, a simple equation for survival, get it?"

"I understand," Kwon said, worried he might not meet their expectations. Kwon studied Reza, quickly deciding he could be a ruthless taskmaster, so he'd better step it up. This large, imposing man had an unusual appearance for an American, and nothing like what he expected a CIA operative to look like. His attire didn't fit with Kwon's concept of a CIA operative. Reza dressed in jeans, a tattered UCLA pullover with a faded Bruin logo, and weathered Nike jogging shoes.

Then Kwon recalled Nam had mentioned Reza's bloodline and background yesterday. Reza Tehrani had been an Iranian spy trained in Tehran, sent to be educated at UCLA. He'd been caught by the CIA, turned, and recruited as a double agent to return to Iran to spy for them. He rose to the rank of Colonel inside the Revolutionary Guard over fifteen years. That capsule summary explained a lot about the man standing before him. Kwon's history as a cyber spy paled in comparison to this man's dangerous experience as a double agent.

Reza had a military, no-nonsense bearing. Kwon soon discovered Reza didn't mess around. He got down to business with no social niceties or chitchat. Reza was indeed a taskmaster.

"Let me run through the pattern of vetting you can expect to encounter," Reza began.

Over the next five hours, Reza carefully led Kwon through various scenarios and variations involved in interrogation. He quizzed Kwon until he got it right, inculcating the methods of deception. Then Reza shifted to an overview of polygraphs.

"Okay, now let's talk about lie detector tests. If you get this far fooling them, then there're a few tricks you must know to pass the polygraph. It's not an exact science, only ninety percent accurate at best, so it's possible to game the system. I'm not sure how sophisticated they are, but I suspect they're pretty good at recognizing physiological signs of stress, like increased heart rate and blood pressure, sweating, those sorts of things. You must learn how to modify those predictable responses."

"I'm following you. How do I do that?" Kwon asked.

"I doubt they use MRIs to track brain blood flow, that's more difficult to beat. But by playing mind games you can make interpretation difficult for them in both forms of polygraphs. For example, anticipate what they are looking for, like the challenging questions I asked you when I arrived today. Probing, invasive, insulting questions designed to set you off. Some are based on assumptions with no good answer, like 'How long has it been since you stopped beating your wife?'" Reza noted Kwon's astonishment at that remark.

"You never beat your wife so the question is absurd and it upsets you," Reza said. "That reaction moves the needle on the graph and they learn something about you. It's a standard trick, so heads up. They are out to dupe you. Don't be hoodwinked."

"Okay, that's good to know," Kwon answered, impressed by Reza's street smarts as he launched right into explaining a complex subject.

"They hope to catch you in a lie. They ask you things like, 'How'd you get here? Why did you come back? Where's your family? What information did you divulge to NIS? How did NIS know the location of your handler? Did you know Hwan was tortured and they retrieved his computer and cell phone?'"

Reza continued, "Then they'll quickly switch subjects, like, 'How much did Nam pay you to spy on us?' Expect those sort of questions for starters."

"I see."

Reza wondered if Kwon really did, he looked overwhelmed.

"All these questions are designed to shake you up. Don't get rattled. We'll make a list of every conceivable trick of the trade. We plan to have you practice lying on a polygraph until you can master the technique, barely budge the needle. I'll change the questions around so you can't out guess me. Anticipation is fundamental, try to develop the tactic. Practice makes perfect."

"Sounds like a good idea, but ..." Kwon was verging on information overload. Before he could express this feeling, Reza pressed on like he was sending him to North Korea tomorrow.

"Also, they'll toss you some softball questions like 'Who's the President of South Korea?' They probably will ask your wife and children's names and birth dates. You can fake them out by thinking of something stressful and breathing faster in answering those routine questions. Try biting your lip. These are simple control questions that establish a baseline for comparison to relative, probing questions that they expect to stress you. You need to throw them off with unpredictable responses to the non-stressful questions. And fake them out in response to stressful questions, called relevant questions. Try to do just the opposite by envisioning a happy experience. Do everything you can to screw them up."

"Also, be aware that hidden cameras and observers on the other side of the one-way mirror will be gauging your reactions and recording your answers. You'll need to practice your poise under pressure. They will measure your anxiety by evaluating your micro expressions, and performing voice stress analysis, equating both as signs of measured anxiety with telling untruths. A lie detector test is a psychological and physiological test to determine deception. You must master the art of deception."

"I didn't realize this. It seems very complex to cheat the detector."

"Not after you are properly trained. Listen up, there's more. You also must be alert to pretest tricks by your examiner designed to instill fear of the polygraph, create apprehension, intending to cause you to fear failure. He's just setting the stage, trying to psych you out. Ignore it."

"How do I do that?"

"We'll show you how, don't worry. Here's another situation to lookout for. Later on during the exam someone else will dramatically enter the room and announce that your early answers came back 'NDI.'"

Kwon frowned. "What's NDI?"

"Actually, that's the correct response, indicating you didn't know what NDI meant. NDI means 'No deception indicated.'"

"Okay."

"If you'd answered otherwise they'd know you'd practiced passing a lie detector test. So be forewarned. Act like you have no knowledge whatsoever of the exam. Give the impression it's your first go round."

"Okay." Kwon paused. "I was surprised NIS didn't submit me to a polygraph."

"They didn't need to with all the incriminating evidence they had on you. You really bungled that CENTCOM hack job."

"I guess that makes sense."

"It does. Back to how to pass a lie detector test. Stay focused. Keep your answers simply yes or no. No explaining, no elaboration. Keep information minimal, and never offer it."

"Will you write all this down for me to memorize?"

"Certainly, and you must also memorize these caveats, I'm not through yet. Never confess anything. Don't admit anything relevant. Don't hesitate. Answer questions promptly. No levity, be serious. Understand?"

"I do."

"Breathe normally, control your emotions." Reza rattled on with his overview. "I suggest you breathe at a comfortable rate, not like you're breathing now, indicating to me you're nervous."

"I am nervous that I won't remember all this."

"You will learn through repetition, positive reinforcement. Breathe somewhere between fifteen to thirty times a minute, your natural pace that you probably never think about. Vary your rate between their control and relevant questions to screw up their interpretation. Occasionally throw out an off-the-wall answer to a control question. For example, to 'What year is it?' say, 'Year of the snake.' That'll throw them off and make it difficult to interpret the polygraph. We'll practice multiple scenarios real time on a polygraph to prepare you. Just like a flight simulator teaches pilots how to fly, we'll teach you how to lie."

"Good, I'll need a lot of practice."

"Think of the lie detector test as a job interview. Be as relaxed as you can. You must convince them you are not deceitful. That you have valuable information to offer, and you're on their side."

"Like what information?"

"We'll brief you on that. It's a deal maker, your ace in the hole. Later this week, after we determine if you are up to the task, only then will we fill you in on the details. If we can't train you adequately, we'll abort the mission."

"Then what happens to me and my family if we abort?"

"I don't think you want to go there," Reza said. "Don't even think about failing. NIS plays hardball. We bailed you out, so you better learn how to do this job."

Chapter Twenty-Two

MEANWHILE ACROSS TOWN

U.S. Embassy – Seoul

Later the same day

"Reza called earlier to say it may be a long haul prepping Kwon," Tyler said. "Says he's smart as hell when it comes to computers, but he's one-dimensional, not blessed with mental versatility or emotional fortitude."

Biff smiled. "That's a colorful way to put it."

Biff, Tyler, and Gunner sat at a conference table in the CIA quarters of the embassy. Biff referred to that part of the building, the rear of the top floor, as the "attaché suites," an allusion to the not-well-kept secret regarding diplomatic cover for coverts in consulates and embassies worldwide under an "attaché" label.

"Yeah, broke me up," Tyler said. "Reza has a funny way of putting things. He said he'll be over soon for the meeting."

"There's a big difference between being a cyber spy hacking away in a cozy office and being out in the field, Tyler," Biff responded. "Reza's very critical. Not many can meet his espionage standards. It may simply be a case of Reza not settling for less than perfect in coaching Kwon to become a double agent."

"Yeah," Tyler said, nodding, "may be the case."

"Hope so," Biff said. "No need for Kwon to be perfect, just proficient long enough to retrieve and relay the one essential piece of information we need. We're not talking years. Our intelligence estimate indicates it's just a matter of months before North Korea sets their plan in motion. Our satellite photos show a lot of activity at Sohae, where they're building a taller rocket gantry."

"Good point, Reza's probably being hypercritical," Gunner said. "But if Kwon turns out to be a one trick pony we may be in for big trouble."

"We'll see how it goes. If Reza can't train him, no one can," Biff declared.

"Reza said he built a fire under Kwon," Tyler said, "reminding him of the consequences of failing to meet our expectations."

"That ought to do it," Biff commented. "Never underestimate a strong incentive. Kwon fears his family's fate more than his own life."

Biff respected Reza's opinion, his reservations, but everything was at stake in Kwon's case. Biff knew they had to press on. There was no going back at this point. But they were training Kwon as a double agent to complete one simple task, not to assassinate Kim Jong-un.

"Look fellows," Biff said, "it's up to us to vet Kwon. Prep him until we're sure he's ready for the job. Ensure that he has no vulnerabilities their interrogators can detect. No loose ends exposed that we can't fix by intensive training. We can't afford to be caught in a 'no go' situation. We must teach him to become adept at his role. He needs to sell his loyalty to DPRK—how he escaped, why he returned to Pyongyang. Offer his cybersecurity expertise gained by his twenty years with Samsung as an enticement for DPRK to hire him. Convince them he's still a valuable asset as a spy despite his cover being blown in South Korea. They'll obviously know he returned to avoid being executed, but if he can convince them he can offer additional benefits, his chances of getting a job inside their command structure are enhanced. And so are ours."

"Agree," Tyler said. "He's got to get them to take the bait. We're short on options. Agree, Gunner?"

Gunner nodded. "You bet. He has to step up to the plate. Like Biff said, if anyone can teach him deception, Reza will."

"Everyone has a dog in this fight—us, ROK, NIS, and Kwon all have high-stakes bets on the outcome. If we can get him inside North Korea command as a cybersecurity specialist, Rokman has a backup plan that will come into play in case he fails his mission, or his cover is blown. Rokman will go over the final plans for that part of our scheme with us before dinner." Biff glanced at the clock on his iPad. "I expect him to arrive shortly."

"Where is he?" Gunner asked. "Not a good idea to wander around Seoul after our recent experience with that hit squad. They may mount a second wave."

"He's over at NIS coordinating our plans with their cyber division," Biff replied. "Nam has a high-tech setup, sort of like our NSA cipher arrangement at Langley. They have a direct satellite uplink to Langley."

"Good to know we have immediate secure sat communication over there as well as here to coordinate ops," Tyler commented.

"That's the idea," Biff said. "When the time comes for intervention, we're all on the same page. By the way, I invited Colonel Logan Scott, our military liaison, to sit in on our strategy session while we review our game plan. He expressed some reservations earlier when I ran a prelim by him. I figured he should be in the loop in case we start WW III." Biff chuckled at his joke.

Tyler and Gunner looked at each other and rolled their eyes at his dark humor.

"It's a CYA move," Biff admitted. "I know you guys see through my invitation, but I have to follow protocol. Logan's the top military intel officer in Korea, goes by the book. He's in the need to know category, so I'm obligated to consult him." Biff smiled at the thought of the uptight colonel's reaction when they revealed the master plan to him. "Our plan will blow him away."

Tyler and Gunner laughed.

"Did you notice when he takes his colonel's cap off he looks like that TV anchor on channel five?" Gunner said.

"Don't be rude, guys," Biff cautioned. "The man's just doing his job, doesn't enjoy the latitude we do. He's wound a little tight and following military regs. It's West Point deportment. Logan's a ringknocker, an academy grad without combat experience."

A ring from the in-house phone interrupted their exchange.

"The three guests you expected are here," the Marine guard announced on the line.

"Okay, send them up," Biff instructed. He looked to Tyler and Gunner. "Everyone arrived at the same time. Hope it's a good omen."

Moments later Colonel Scott, Reza, and Rokman entered the conference room.

"Okay, gentlemen, let's get down to business," Biff announced. "We've got a lot of ground to cover. Everyone take a seat and get a cold drink from the bar. We'll have a late dinner. Our Embassy chef is preparing a Bulgogi BBQ with his special marinade, his specialty."

Tyler's eyes lit up. Gunner laughed at him, "You chow hound."

"We've successfully launched phase one of our plan," Biff said once they were all seated. "Retrieved Kwon from jail, disseminated the false narratives in the media, hyped the manhunt, and started phase two, training Kwon to be comfortable in his role as a double agent while the disinformation campaign gains momentum."

Before Biff could elaborate, Colonel Scott interrupted, clearly agitated. "Did you guys blow that big hole in the Andong jail wall to spring him? Think maybe that was a bit over the top?"

"I read in the papers that the local mafia did that slick bit of demolition to rescue their Godfather, Cho," Biff answered, putting on his innocent face, not cracking a smile. "Quite clever of them, I'd say," Biff added.

"I'll take that as a no," Colonel Scott replied, frowning, his feathers ruffled.

Biff ignored his comment. He considered it par for the course, overt versus covert objectives. Logan's ROK territory opposed to CIA's foreign mission, a turf thing.

"Our next operative phases are a little trickier," Biff said. "Let's discuss them and work out the kinks. It's a complicated scheme. Here's how I see it coming down. Kwon's jailbreak was a successful ruse, using Cho as a decoy for the manhunt, promoting the notion Kwon happened to be an incidental escapee, but one that must be recaptured quickly, considered a national security threat. Nam has the media in his pocket and will keep the disinformation campaign in full swing. We plan a daily barrage of updates. Next, I'll outline Kwon's escape plan."

"Once he's trained," Biff continued, "we plan to sneak him out of the country on a fishing boat, one accidently straying into North Korean waters. That innocent mistake will be attributed to the boat's faulty

Doppler navigation system. The violation will trigger a boarding by a North Korean border patrol to examine the crews' papers, a routine occurrence, I understand. The crew's documents will be in order, but not Kwon's. In fact, he will have no docs, no ID. He will identify himself to the patrol as their fugitive spy on the run and request safe haven in his country of origin. They will predictably take him in for interrogation by NSA, the North Korean security agency, to check out his story."

Biff paused to take a sip of water before continuing. "Then they'll release the other fishermen with a stern warning. This will be the first time the crew becomes aware of the stranger's notoriety as the wanted fugitive they'd seen on TV. Since his appearance will have been drastically altered and he will have kept to himself, they won't have an inkling of his identity before then."

"Ambitious plan, but sounds plausible," Colonel Scott commented. "But how's he going to land the job aboard the vessel while an APB is alerting everyone to be on the outlook for him? That's quite a stretch."

Biff nodded. "Good question, very perceptive. Simply by disguising his appearance and having Nam pull some strings. Nam will bribe the harbormaster through a third party to get the captain to hire Kwon, under an assumed name of course, posing as an 'out of a job' fisherman. The intermediary will present it as a temporary hire, just for the night, on a trial basis, even getting the harbormaster to vouch for him."

"That'll cost a pretty penny," Colonel Scott commented. "You're confident it will work?"

"Yep, it will cost us a few won, but it'll work. We'll make it work. Now comes some interesting twists to the plan. Kwon will arrive with only the clothes on his back and a USB flash drive. After his capture comes the inflection point in the development of our strategy."

"And, that is?" Colonel Scott couldn't believe what he was hearing. It was an incredible scheme.

"Kwon must convince North Korea's security agency, NSA, and OGD, the old boys' organization and guidance department, that he's one of them, a loyal patriot who managed to escape back home after a long productive service of spying. We anticipate he'll need to pass intensive interrogations and a polygraph up the ladder with RGB, North Korea's Reconnaissance Guidance

Bureau. RGB trained him twenty years ago. They are in charge of clandestine activities including cyber warfare. If he passes their vetting, he's in."

"That's a monumental task!" the colonel said.

"Relax," Biff said. "Reza is preparing him. It's predictable that NSA or RGB will examine his memory stick with a fine-tooth comb. I guarantee you the storage device will validate his credentials, and pique their interest that he could continue to be of considerable value to them. Rokman has tinkered with the flash drive to ensure it."

That elicited a few atta boys in Rokman's direction.

"That ought to do it," Tyler added.

"Here's the clincher," Biff said. "Kwon will offer them something significant. A sweet deal they can't refuse. Something that's essential to our plot."

Colonel Scott continued to look skeptical. "Like what? These guys are very suspicious, believe me. Even with his long history of spying for them, they'll be wary. Not likely to fall for any flimsy deception, even after they vetted him. What could he offer them to avoid skepticism?"

"The latest high-tech cybersecurity and networking equipment," Biff countered. "Kwon must convince them he has an inside track with his Samsung connections. His flash drive will confirm his valuable business links independently."

"Ah, the bait," the Colonel said, suddenly more interested. "That could get their attention. Very crafty move."

"Exactly. Kwon will also offer to include personnel software screening programs through his industry contacts in Malaysia. North Korea has diplomatic relations with Malaysia, so international trade is business as usual. Bottom line, he'll offer to update their antiquated cybersecurity systems. DPRK obsesses about safety measures, so they should take the bait."

"Can he deliver?"

"Yes, he'll make good on his offer through our shell companies and dummy corporations set up in Malaysia and Singapore for that purpose. All firewalled to resist DPRK's anticipated hacking attempts to confirm Kwan's story and verify the planted information on his flash drive."

"Very clever, Biff. 'Elegant' as you Ivy Leaguers say." Colonel Scott finally cracked a smile.

"Thanks, but that's a Harvard expression, I'm a Yale man. Good try." Biff grinned and pressed on.

"Kwon will entice them to streamline their operations, encourage them to upgrade their systems, long overdue. Persuade them he has key connections to incorporate secure modern technology into their scientific programs and military endeavors, affording ultimate protection of their vital secrets. Sway them by asserting he's got the right tickets to obtain deep discounts, including installment payments."

"They should jump at the offer."

"That's the plan. To corroborate the story, we'll transfer his Samsung computer's critical information to his flash drive and plant some classified disinformation on the memory stick. We'll dress it up with glowing letters of commendation from Malaysia business associates in our bogus companies who are linked only to his secure coded password on the Internet. We'll include significant IT information documenting he's an expert in cybersecurity. We'll throw in some non-critical South Korean intelligence intercepts to spice it up, make 'em believe they're on to something with this fugitive spy of theirs who might well fit into their future plans."

"Interesting gambit, maybe they'll fall for it," Colonel Scott commented after a moment of deep thought. He was less pessimistic but still hesitant.

"I bet if we chum the water, they'll bite," Biff said. "Even though they may question his loyalty, they won't pass up the opportunity he'll offer. They'll put it to the test."

"That plan may fly," the colonel replied, "if presented convincingly."

"I anticipate suspicion may creep in, so they'll proceed cautiously to see if Kwon delivers the goods. That'll be the litmus test of whether he's a returning hero or a planted agent. Once he provides the security upgrades, gains their trust, and is good to go, then we're inside their system. We'll make that happen. Suspicion takes a natural course in this business 'til the person under suspicion produces something positive. I can attest to that."

Biff glanced at Reza and smiled. "Over a year ago I extracted a double agent from Tehran," Biff said. "Despite CIA's extensive vetting, I questioned his authenticity for over a year suspecting he might be a triple agent. A remarkable feat finally convinced me of his allegiance to the CIA.

Suspicion comes with the territory, why would it be any different with them? Reza's been through it, knows how to play the double agent game well. He'll show Kwon how to pull it off."

Reza smiled, acknowledging Biff's praise. Their recent close call with terrorists in San Francisco had solidified their mutual trust.

"I still have serious reservations about the plan," Colonel Scott said. "Kwon's mysterious escape and return may be a hard sell under intense interrogation. It requires a flawless performance, and they distrust even their own. One slip up will blow his cover, I'm sure everyone would agree."

The colonel played the role of Devil's Advocate well, Biff reflected. Biff was glad he invited him even though he was a pain in the ass.

"That's the essence of our job to prep him properly," Biff said. "We'll fabricate Kwon's authenticity and embellish his credentials. It will be effective when they discover our planted information while sorting through his flash drive, I guarantee you. When he delivers the goods from Malaysia that should cinch it."

"I concede that the information from the storage devise would lend credibility to his story. Entice them to at least check out his offer, surely. If he delivers, that's your ace in the hole, and a very clever ploy. I compliment your team on that one, but it's a risky venture."

Biff nodded. "Glad you agree on the flash drive ruse. Here's the next step … As I mentioned, North Korea and Malaysia have established relations. Kwon will arrange for rapid delivery of Juniper and Cisco hardware networking systems as well as PeopleSoft software login and human resource software at bargain basement pricing. Arrange to throw in installment payments without interest."

"I'm following you, another enticement," Colonel Scott said.

"Here's the game changer. Unknown to Kwon or Malaysian authorities, the hard drives and software of the newly acquired computer gear will be infected with the Heartbleed virus. We'll introduce a Trojan horse into their computers giving us an inside picture of what's going on up there. We have the critical assets in Malaysia to carry out the cyberespionage—shell companies, undercover NSA and CIA personnel stationed there, the whole nine yards. The viral program should suffice if Kwon becomes compromised. A key feature of our plot centers on the fact Kwon will be unaware of our encoded malware plan, so his answers won't move the needle if they ask him any related questions on a polygraph. He can't lie about something he has no knowledge of. That should further prove his authenticity."

"An ingenious plan, but with all due respect, what assurance do we have that we're not giving Kwon a 'get out of jail free' pass? Once he's up north he's free to renege on the deal isn't he? Expose the deception to embarrass us internationally and cause a brouhaha? What leverage do we have over him once he's out of the country?"

"All strong considerations we anticipated," Biff said. "We have tremendous leverage. NIS has moved his family to Busan under protective custody with assumed identities. Effectively they're hostages under constant surveillance. And under the threat of death if Kwon double crosses us, bolts, or doesn't deliver. NIS plays hardball and made their intentions crystal clear to him. NIS is convinced his family means more to him than his allegiance to North Korea. Our action is based on Nam's belief that Kwon's a family man first, a spy second. That he's highly unlikely to go back on the arrangement with that ominous threat hanging over him."

Colonel Scott frowned. "That's heavy even for a hardball organization like NIS. I find it worrisome if we're disclosed as accomplices. What's the arrangement?"

"We have cover, plausible deniability, don't worry. NIS augmented the deal by promising extraction and reunion with his family in protective custody and a new life under an assumed name, once he accomplishes his task. That will further motivate him to do his job."

"And what is his job?"

"His task is to obtain the target date for the proposed EMP attack on South Korea and/or the U.S. That's all we ask of him, one simple task, confirmation of the time and date of the proposed launch. We have KH-12 recon satellites observing their launch pads. We monitor the coordinates of their nuclear test sites and pads. But that's not definitive intel. He's to relay the coded message to a Pyongyang asset as soon as he knows the specifics. It's a limited mission, but key to our master plan."

"What if you miscalculate?" the colonel asked. "Suppose he's so committed to the regime that he turns his back on his family?"

"We plan to sweeten the deal with a special offer when he's done. His reward will be spending the rest of his life exonerated, a free man with an annual stipend. That should be a strong incentive to get the job done. Not only dodging the firing squad, but a chance for a second life with his family, free, and off the hook for his espionage crimes."

"All sounds good except for the family consideration, holding them hostage under threat of death. Isn't that excessive hardball for the CIA? It's liable to cause a lot of flak if word gets out, maybe even trigger a congressional enquiry. Could get a bunch of folks fired, even jailed. I could get court marshaled."

"I understand your concern. I wouldn't go there if the stakes in this case weren't so high. As I said, we have plausible deniability. It's NIS' operation in name only, their idea and execution. We can't dictate their actions. Is it hardball? Yes. Pragmatic? Absolutely. We're making no-nonsense calculations to accomplish the mission. We're just consultants to an ally, a sovereign nation acting independently, got the picture?"

Biff noted that Colonel Scott looked pale, clearly worried about the potential repercussions.

"Look," Biff added, "if we pull this off, I'll recommend you for a star, and I also promise you won't be court marshaled if we fail. I'll be honest that inviting you here was a courtesy. We're going ahead with this plan. You have no say in this matter. D.C. sanctioned the operation top down. You are absolved of any responsibility, and I take sole accountability if this goes down poorly."

Colonel Scott's eyes narrowed. He stood. "Is that star offer a bribe?" he asked, clearly insulted.

"No," Biff said evenly, "simply a promise. This is an operation sanctioned by those well above our pay grade after due diligence of the risk-reward equation. Keep what you've heard under your hood, not a peep to anyone. This is a very complex and top-secret operation. There's more at stake than I can tell you, but you can probably imagine from your military intelligence background."

The colonel stared at Biff, looking conflicted.

"I understand your qualms," Biff added, "but this is what we do, covert interventions when our national security is threatened. Sometimes it gets really ugly. We have to take chances after weighing the odds of success and finding them even slightly in our favor. If you feel uncomfortable, you may leave. We'll all deny you ever were here. Otherwise, I'd like you to hear Rokman's contribution to our plot. It's ingenious, something worth your time."

"I want to see where this is going," Colonel Scott said. He was clearly a man not used to being dressed down. But he sat back down.

"Fine, we understand each other," Biff said in the tone of a teacher speaking to student. Biff's message wasn't lost on the staff.

Tyler glanced at Gunner, who rolled his eyes. Biff rarely got crusty, but they knew he was intolerant of naysayers. Biff's eyes never left his target, and his mission came first. No one who knew him dared to get in the way.

Reza sat quietly, understanding the potential difficulties, especially the extraction, if it got that far. His escape from Tehran had been hairy. For something like that to work, everything had to go as planned. But Biff's plan seemed feasible in his view. He knew he could train Kwon. He just didn't know yet how long it would take, and time was of the essence.

Rokman glanced at Colonel Scott, who was still stewing, and leaned forward, trying to diplomatically defuse the tension. "Biff's plan should work, Colonel," Rokman said. "It's very doable. Bottom line consideration is this … If we access their computers, it won't matter if they expose Kwon, torture him, shoot him, whatever. He has no knowledge of our viral exploit or master plan. We can still get a jump on them by cyber espionage, pilfer critical information with our spiders, and analyze it."

"Spiders?" Logan asked, clearly unfamiliar with the hacking jargon.

"Robotic programs planted in the Heartbleed malware designed to scrape specifically targeted documents related to their military operations, tactics, and procedures," Rokman said. "We call it 'targeted stealth.' No need to steal everything off their computers and sort through it. That risks raising suspicions of a viral infection and discovery of the malware. Our objective is to keep it simple and specific using spiders. These programs will be incorporated in the cybersecurity equipment imported from Malaysia.

"Once we have a Trojan horse in the system," Rokman continued, "we own them, no matter what happens with Kwon. He's just as messenger delivering the goods. As Biff mentioned, Kwon doesn't know about this, so he'll pass a polygraph if questioned about malware. If they eventually stumble onto our viral penetration, it will take considerable time and effort for them to sort out the exploit and take remedial action. Believe me. It's difficult to purge. It's a complex virus embedded in the hardware and software. Not easy to detect, diagnose, scrub, or decontaminate unless they know the specific targeting schemes of the spiders and the identity and code for the virus. And they won't discover the malware unless they have a Cal Tech trained genius in their ranks."

Biff added, "Cyber espionage diminishes the risks of Kwon's discovery. He'll not be required to snoop around, hack, or send periodic encrypted messages to us. Those tactics risk his exposure as a double agent. He's only required to send one message. Kwon is simply our courier innocently delivering the malware integrated in the Cisco, Juniper, and PeopleSoft gear. Our backup plan goes into action once the virus is incorporated into their command and control systems. At that point Kwon's task has been essentially accomplished, the mission a resounding success in that respect. His covert role should remain secure. We'll extract him a suitable period after we have confirmation of the launch date and have completed the final phase of our mission."

"Ironic that by upgrading their security system, they expose their operations to the Heartbleed virus," Biff added. He looked at Colonel Scott. "How's that scheme grab you?"

The colonel sighed. "Very impressive, I'll admit. I hate to rain on your parade, but I still worry about the downside if the master plan implodes. I don't want us to get burned."

"We won't get burned," Biff said confidently. "The beauty of the scheme is the entrée, offering them computer upgrades they truly need, and providing us a wedge to get inside their operations."

"I admit it's an ingenious plan and may work if Kwon performs well," Colonel Scott said. "If he pulls it off, you deserve a commendation medal. But, the family stuff, it's a sticky wicket."

"We're not into medals," Biff said, "but after Reza grooms him, Kwon may get an Academy Award for his performance."

The Colonel, impressed as he was in many ways by the plan, was still dubious. The potential for a negative outcome was high. Too many "ifs" were involved in this intricate counterterrorism plan for his comfort.

"It's a long shot, Biff," Colonel Scott said. Shaking his head, he rose to leave. He couldn't take anymore. It was too stressful to contemplate failure.

Biff stood. "Long shots are my specialty." Biff grinned and patted the colonel on his back reassuringly. "Hang with me, pal. We'll make it happen."

On his way out, Logan began to understand why Biff had become the CIA's Counterterrorism Director. Dauntless, he seemed to thrive on adversity. No task seemed to faze him, even one that could get him over thirty years in a federal prison. Maybe even trigger World War III.

But to Colonel Logan, the plan seemed way too fast, too risky, and too likely to end in catastrophe.

CHAPTER TWENTY-THREE

FISHING EXPEDITION

Six weeks later

I n mid-September *The Korean Herald* ran the headline *CHO AND KWON STILL AT LARGE, 40 RECAPTURED.*
The Korean Times went with *WHERE ARE THEY? CHO AND KWON STILL MISSING, 40 OTHER ESCAPEES APPREHENDED.*

The headline stories paraded the mystery of how two fugitives could elude authorities for six weeks. There had never been such a spectacular jailbreak in South Korean history. The reports detailed that several jail administrators had been fired for incompetency. A top law official was also sacked for lack of proper supervision of the Andong prison. Six other officials were reprimanded after a lengthy investigation by the government-appointed commission. Other scapegoats would soon fall from grace.

On TV Nam highlighted the punitive actions NIS had instituted and predicted a resolution soon, insisting on accountability. His statements resonated with the public since responsibility constituted a big part of Korean society. Nam was a master at high drama, feeding the frenzy. His reputation soared as the story grew, and he loved every minute of the CIA's scheme. Biff Roberts had engineered a classic disinformation ruse. It fell right in Nam's wheelhouse.

The media fanned public furor over the incident. How could the Kkangpae mafia get away with blowing a massive hole in the prison wall, allowing so many prisoners to escape? Seeking the public's help, authorities released photos from the jail's surveillance cameras showing the perpetrator's van, the scooter bomber, and the suspects wearing ski masks, four disguised in prison uniforms.

The lone suspect filmed on the scooter who had planted the explosive on the jail wall got top billing. His outrageous Halloween mask captivated the public. His photo was shown over and over in the media. The public loved his bizarre disguise ripping Kim Jong-un with its circus clown caricature. The bold act was astonishing, humorous, but also a cause for alarm. Everyone kept talking about the incident, fascinated at its audacity. This was Hollywood cinema becoming real life in Korea, and the public couldn't get enough of the coverage, Nam saw to that.

Nam gave frequent updates on TV promising to close the noose on the two most wanted fugitives, Cho and Kwon. He affirmed his vast NIS security agency resources were assisting local authorities. He reminded the public that they'd captured forty escapees in record time. He emphasized ongoing screenings at seaports and airports, assuring the public no one could flee the country. It was just a matter of time before they apprehended Cho and Kwon, Nam said, urging everyone to be on the lookout for them and to trust him.

Most did. Nam was revered, considered a candidate for the next Presidency of the Republic of Korea. His staunch supporters referred to him affectionately as a "ROK star."

***

U.S. Embassy – Seoul
The same day

"Nam's doing a good job with his disinformation campaign. They're looking all over the country for them," Tyler said after looking over the local news coverage. Cho and Kwon were still safely holed up in the NIS safe house.

Tyler, Gunner, and Biff sat in the U.S. embassy briefing room.

"Yeah, Nam's got his act together," Biff said. "He plans to release Cho soon and report his sighting in Seoul. Then it'll be fox and hound time, until he tips the police about the GPS chip through an anonymous source. That will narrow and intensify the search for Cho, and stir up more headlines to divert public attention while we sneak Kwon out of the country. By the way, how far along is our budding double agent? It's been well over a month."

"Reza says he'll probably be ready next week," Tyler said. "He's finally starting to get the hang of it." Kwon had been enduring daily twelve-hour repetitive vetting sessions. "He's reached the positive reinforcement stage of training. Reza's grilling him hard, going over and over every conceivable debriefing scenario, practicing stuff they may pull on him trying to trick him up. Reza reminds him every day how much he has at stake. Nam comes by daily to give Kwon a menacing glare and whispers to Reza to intimidate and motivate Kwon, but never says a word to him."

Biff nodded. "All part of the plan. Kwon knows Nam despises him, wants to shoot him. That alone should motivate him."

"Seems to be working," Tyler said.

Biff looked to Gunner. "How's your part going in all this?"

"On standby," Gunner said. "We're just waiting for the call. Nam's deputy, Kim, is coordinating it. Says everything's set at dock. Just needs a heads up to swing into action on short notice."

"Good show," Biff said. "On another subject, made any progress uncovering a mole at NIS or at our Embassy? Nam has me convinced we're compromised. Someone penetrated our security and probably at NIS also."

"Got some substantial leads from Kwon's handler's computer," Tyler said. "Kim told me to fill you in today on what they've learned so far."

"Bet you're going to inform me this North Korean agent Hwan Hyon-Hui, Kwon's handler, turned out to be a valuable lead, right?"

Tyler nodded. "Right, big time source, in fact. Hwan never confessed anything under intense pressure but provided significant information indirectly. Nam's team retrieved valuable information from his hideout."

"By intense pressure you mean torture?" Biff asked.

"Maybe more like strong arm stuff, who knows?" Tyler shrugged. "They recognized right off Hwan was a well-trained, hardcore agent, not enough time to break him. Feared he may have armed backup and wanted no part of another shoot out like the one last month downtown. They'd found what they came for, so didn't want to stick around. They killed him, dumped his body in a remote rice paddy, and moved out. They retrieved Hwan's computer and cell phone, plus a flash drive and a few SIM cards. That's all they needed. The records from those sources were partially decrypted, revealing a connection to another North Korean spy, one higher up the chain."

Biff smiled. "This is getting interesting."

"This spy is embedded in the South Korean military intelligence unit, somewhere undetermined. His code name is Jin-Ju. We're working on that connection. Some indication he might be the DPRK's kingpin running their South Korean espionage show. He's deep dark so I expect the search to identify him might take some time."

"That's a major intelligence break for NIS," Biff said. "I suspect Jin-Ju will be extra cautious, lay low for a while after he finds out about Hwan's takedown."

"You bet. It's a huge breakthrough. And get this interesting angle. A few of Hwan's coded cell calls went not only to Jin-Ju but also to the cell number of the ringleader of the hit squad who tried to assassinate you last month."

Biff shook his head. "Damn these agents are tightly networked. How'd NIS make that connection?"

"NIS recovered that hit man's cell at the shootout scene last month and started tracing the calls, comparing incoming and outgoing. This week, after reviewing Hwan's phone records, their computer correlated the corresponding numbers received on that cell phone with Hwan's calls to him. It appears Hwan hired the criminal street gang to do the job."

"Now that's an interesting connection, confirmed?"

"No doubts," Tyler said, "absolutely confirmed. NIS is also ferreting through some of Hwan's other incoming calls from Pyongyang in that same timeframe. Those numbers traced back to DPRK's national security agency, NSA, and appear to correspond indirectly with Kwan's calls back and forth with Jin-Ju."

"That's a major revelation," Biff said. "You're telling me that NIS found a significant connection to North Korea's security agency messaging Hwan as an intermediary and tied that in with an association with Jin-Ju?"

Tyler nodded. "Precisely."

"If so," Biff said, "I suspect one more link."

"And that is?"

"An association between Pyongyang and Tehran. DPRK has no reason to go after me. Iran set it up." Biff frowned. "Weren't the messages encoded? How'd NIS determine all this vital information so quickly?"

"The North Korean security agency, NSA, encoded the communiqués in one of their standard cryptograms. NIS had no difficulty breaking the code. Not that complex to decipher." Tyler added, "And I agree Tehran had a hand in last month's attack on us. NIS tied two of the numbers specifically to a NSA special ops unit in the 850-38 North Korean country-city prefix for Pyongyang. That unit is noted for mischief in South Korea."

"Good to know Nam's team is on top of it," Biff answered, "and has the decipher capability."

"You bet," Tyler said. "NIS is monitoring all incoming calls from up there, hoping NSA will attempt to contact Hwan again before they discover he has been eliminated. Also they anticipate Jin-Ju will try to contact him and they can trace that call either directly or by voice print."

"Okay, smart tactic, but good only for a limited time until they discover Hwan's gone and of no further value. No shocker there, right fellows?" Biff asked.

Tyler and Gunner nodded in agreement.

"Want to give 'em a call in Pyongyang and tell them we've got their number?" Gunner joked. "Ask them 'What's up?'" They laughed, but Gunner wouldn't put it past Biff to jerk DPRK's chain.

"So, it appears Jin-Ju orchestrated last month's assassination attempt," Biff said, "and NIS' investigation reveals the shooters were contractors, not DPRK agents, hired by Jin-Ju through Hwan. Have I got it right?"

"You do," Tyler said. "Good detective work by NIS. Jin-Ju's obviously the man pulling the strings. Interesting ring to his name, kind of like a jingle, you think? Jin-Ju …"

"Yeah, now that you mention it, has a certain chime quality," Gunner concurred.

"Get our local intelligence unit on it and brief our military liaison, Colonel Scott," Biff ordered. "Be sure he's in the loop, checking it out. That'll keep him occupied and out of our business. Keep me posted."

***

NIS Headquarters Seoul
The same day

"We're getting close to the next stage, Kim," Nam said. "Are you and Gunner on the same page? When we move, it will require a quick execution after dark. Have you made a practice run and all the necessary arrangements?"

Kim nodded. "Several runs, Director, I know the area well. Gunner and I are coordinating our plans with our intermediary, Chin Myung-Bak, the harbormaster at the new Inchon commercial fishing dock at the southern tip of Songdo. It's located well away from the heavy cargo ship area, so less conspicuous. He's trustworthy. Asks no questions, just took the money and made the arrangements we requested."

"You're certain of that? No leaks? Traces to us?"

"Confident," Kim said. "Chin's my brother-in-law, knows I'm NIS. He knows it's a classified operation. He'll come through with his end of the deal, and his lips are sealed. I don't anticipate any hitches even with increased seaport surveillance."

"Always anticipate hitches," Nam said. "Assume nothing in our business, even if it's all in the family, Kim."

"Chin's reliable, I promise. When's this part of the operation coming down?"

"As soon as Reza says it's a go, when he's confident Kwon can manage the task. He's been training him for almost two months, so likely soon."

"Think Kwon's capable?" Kim asked.

Nam hesitated but then nodded. "Reza and Biff are optimistic, and Kwon's made significant progress in the last week. Reza said he's started to get it."

***

NIS Safe house – Seoul suburb
Two weeks later

"Okay, Kwon," Reza said. "Let's go through some more test scenarios again. I'll give the interrogation some different twists today. I'll come at you from all angles attempting to trip you up just like they will."

Kwon sat in a wooden chair in the mockup of an interrogation room in the safe house. Reza sat across the table from him.

"They'll look for inconsistencies in your story," Reza continued, "so know your story rote, forward and backward. Be able to recite it in your sleep. Don't deviate. How you respond to their questions is the key to establishing your credibility, so they'll continue to debrief you. You know they'll be highly suspicious. You must shift that perception not only by your answers but your demeanor, so stay cool. Your body language will speak volumes. They'll observe your every response for tension, deception, and plausibility."

"I understand. I must deliver my answers in a natural fashion and stay relaxed, confident." Kwon spoke with much more assurance than he had only days before. Reza was pleased with his progress. But they weren't quite there yet.

"Correct. I'll play the role of their NSA interrogator, as usual. I'll be rough on you, nothing personal, but under a security interrogation they'll be relentless. You're guilty until proven innocent, understand? Just because you spied for them for years won't guarantee they'll cut you any slack. Think of your performance as a tightrope walker balancing on a high wire, a dangerous act with no net under you, got it? Don't look down or you'll slip and fall. Carefully navigate your way. Choose your words carefully, but speak with conviction and without hesitation."

Reza stopped before Kwon. "Ready?"

"Yes."

"How did you happen to arrive at our port, Nampo harbor, in custody of our patrol boat crew with only the fishing clothes on your back?" The compound question quickly followed by another was designed to throw him off guard before he even answered the first enquiry.

"Why didn't you have proper documents in your possession?" Reza continued without giving him a chance to respond. "How do we know you are the person you claim to be? Explain why a USB flash drive was discovered in a waterproof pocket of your shorts? Discovered underneath your wet clothes when our officials strip searched you?"

When Reza finally gave him the opportunity to respond, Kwon answered the barrage of questions without hesitation. He responded confidently to each question he'd memorized in the order Reza asked, all plausibly without any perceptible change in behavior. He answered in the convincing and matter-of-fact manner that Reza had trained him to adopt.

"I was lucky to escape disguised as a fisherman," Kwon said evenly. "I grew a beard and shaved my head to change my appearance. I'd been hiding out in Inchon warehouses and docks after I slipped out of Seoul, laying low until I finally landed a job on a boat. They were one short on their night crew."

Reza noted with approval that Kwon was keeping his cool.

"Regarding my ID," Kwon continued, "I'd escaped from jail, naturally I had no documents. I'm lucky to be alive and to have escaped back here to my homeland. They planned to execute me last month. Regarding the flash drive you discovered, I purposely smuggled out the device. It contains some critical information that NSA or RGB will be interested in studying. It was the only thing I still had of any intelligence value after being captured."

"Why did you maintain this storage device?" Reza asked quickly.

"As a backup for my handler in case I was ever captured."

"Where did you secure it while you were in jail?"

Kwon replied calmly, "In a lockup at the Guui-Dong bus station, 546-1."

"Locker number?"

"1033."

"Key or combination lock?"

"Key."

"Where did you keep the key?"

"I hid it in a special place that only I and my handler knew."

Reza ignored this admission and abruptly switched topics, trying to throw him off. "How did you get to Inchon with so many authorities looking for you?"

"I stole a bike in Seoul and pedaled there in the crowds."

"Which road did you take?"

"Route 6006, the old Gung Dom Gu bus route."

"That's a long way."

"Only about forty kilometers, not a difficult ride for me."

"What time of day?"

"I arrived at dusk." Again, Kwon spoke without hesitation.

Reza kept firing questions.

"Your clothes, where did you get them?"

"Thrift shop." Kwon was purposely not elaborating, not volunteering information, as Reza had trained him. Kwon felt he'd given up too much already.

"The Beautiful Store? The one specializing in secondhand garments?"

Kwon shook his head. "Couldn't afford that store."

"So how'd you get the fishing outfit?" Reza followed up quickly, trying to trip him up.

"Salvation Army."

"Which one?"

"The old store off subway line three near Hongu station." Kwon was being specific, anticipating the next question, and lending veracity to his tale with his accurate responses.

"How'd you pay for them?" Reza asked.

"My American Express card," Kwon said sarcastically, a trick to throw the interrogator off, showing he was confident in his role.

Reza had taught him the maneuver as a diversionary tactic—the surprise answer, one so ludicrous that the interrogator would pause and be thrown off pace. No one being suspected of lying would chance such a defiant response during an intense interrogation. Certainly not in North Korea. The ballsy joke would almost certainly be convincing and accepted by the interrogator. It would infer this man likely was who he claimed to be. At the very least, it would compel the interrogator to give pause.

Even Reza was impressed with Kwon's poise and almost smiled at his spontaneity. Kwon was finally getting the knack of deception.

"This is not a joking matter," Reza said quickly, spoken harshly to admonish him. Reza wasn't letting on that he thought Kwon was actually doing a good job.

"I stole the clothes from the sports section," Kwon said, "trying them on in the stall, and walking out wearing them."

"Tell me what you did with the clothes you wore into the store."

"I left the rags in the changing room stall."

"Where did you get the rags in the first place, after your escape from jail?" Reza asked rapidly.

"I got them from a neighborhood trash bin after I escaped."

"No one noticed you left them in the changing room?"

"The store was crowded with a lot of poor-looking people like me," Kwon said, still poised. "I blended in and no one noticed as I walked out. The old fishing outfit was wrinkled and had holes in it, didn't look new at all, so didn't attract attention."

"That brings up another question. How did you get the bike?" Reza kept pressing him, slipping around from topic to topic.

"I told you that I stole it."

"Correct, you did. But where exactly?"

"From the bike rack outside Salvation Army store. I jimmied the lock."

This routine went on for hours until Reza sensed Kwon's fatigue, and saw signs that he was starting to lose his edge.

"Okay, that's enough for today," Reza said. "You're getting tired. They'll try to do this sort of thing to you, so be aware of the rapid-fire technique, shifting topics, backtracking, always double-checking details. They intend to catch you in an inconsistency. You're getter better at this, much better, Kwon. Take a break for dinner, have some tea, then I'll critique your performance."

Kwon nodded, clearly relieved.

After Kwon left the mockup of a DPRK interrogation room, Reza leaned back in his chair and lit a Marlboro. He inhaled deeply, and blew a puff of smoke over his head, letting out a sigh as he reflected on the past. He still smoked occasionally despite having a lung cancer removed in San Francisco over a year ago. The carcinoma had not spread fortunately. Despite being a chain smoker for years, he'd survived. He still enjoyed smoking, and he felt invincible. He ignored his doctor's admonishment to quit and Biff's concerned plea to let it go and chew gum.

Reza contemplated Kwon's past two months of intensive training. Progress had been slow. Reza had been pessimistic at first, but now he had to admit the cyber spy was coming around. Kwon was almost ready to be released in the field on the critical mission. Kwon had seemingly experienced sudden insight into his role, and had actually started to accept the challenge it entailed. Kwon had taken a quantum leap in the past week in developing the special skill set required for this mission. He was almost primed for his final exam—infiltration into North Korea as a double agent.

Infiltrating him would be tricky, but not as hazardous as extracting him. Once Kwon completed his task, signaling North Korea's proposed missile launch date, they'd address that complicated issue. Reza predicted after the CIA executed their mission to thwart the rocket launch, Kwon would become a prime suspect. North Korean state security would run through the list of those in a position to leak the vital intelligence. Kwon, the newcomer in cybersecurity, naturally would be high on their list of suspects, singled out as one who might have compromised DPRK's mission. If they failed to extract Kwon, the aftermath for him would be ugly.

Reza recalled his own extraction two years ago from Tehran to avoid his discovery in the Revolutionary Guard command post. It had required elaborate collaboration between CIA and Mossad to pull it off through Iranian Green Party underground connections. Well-planned teamwork allowed Reza's escape to Azerbaijan by seaplane, a hairy experience even for a seasoned spy aided by experienced covert agents. Reza wondered how an amateur, a mere hacker, could handle the task with no experience in the field. Could they conceivably keep that part of NIS' promise, to get him back out of North Korea?

Biff described the Kwon scheme as a "Cat's Cradle." Biff used a lot of metaphors, and Reza still fought a bit of a language barrier when it came to American colloquial phrases. He'd looked up the meaning. He was certain Biff was not referring to the child's string game, but to something intricate and complex, a search for truth of sorts. There was no equivalent phrase for it in Farsi. This mission fit the metaphor's meaning in many respects, he supposed.

He admired Biff's audacity designing the complicated operation which was, as Biff had put it, "for all the marbles." Another metaphor that had confused Reza, necessitating another trip to his dictionary of American slang.

One thing he understood for certain. After last year's mission in San Francisco, Biff was now his trusted friend. Reza's role in the San Francisco counterterror op had dispelled Biff's suspicions that he might be a triple agent.

Since escaping Tehran, Reza's life was reinvigorated with his new CIA role under an assumed identity and his marriage to Leila, an Iranian Green Party member who escaped with him two years ago. Biff had set both those circumstances up too, giving Reza a fresh start. Reza felt indebted to the man, and he couldn't let him down. He would see that Kwon's training came to fruition. Everything was riding on his performance.

Reza lit another cigarette.

He was almost there. Soon Kwon would be trained well enough to get him into North Korea to accomplish his mission. But getting him out was another matter entirely, a "cat's cradle."

CHAPTER TWENTY-FOUR

TROUBLED WATERS

The next week

CHO SIGHTED IN SEOUL — AUTHORITIES CLOSING IN AFTER TIP

The *Seoul Times* headline created the diversion Nam intended. The NIS Director figured it was just a matter of time before the police apprehended Cho. He planned for everyone to focus on the Mafia fugitive's capture, providing time to move on with Kwon's escape plan. Nam put the newspaper down on his desk and texted his deputy director a cryptogram:

<KIM-Set our plan in motion, it's a go for tonight>

He did not sign the message. Kim would recognize his incoming code.

***

Safe house

Early evening

"Put on your Salvation Army fishing clothes, Kwon," Reza said. "We're leaving in about three hours. Don't forget to wear your special Nike running shorts underneath."

Kwon's eyes widened. "Where are we going?"

"Fishing, of course." Reza smiled. "Where else would you go in that outfit?"

The rare joke by Reza surprised Kwon. "I guess the mission is a go?"

"You got it. You're good to go. I certified your status."

Reza was pleased with Kwon's progress under his rigorous training. Amazing how much one could learn if his life and family depended on it. Especially impressive was Kwon's performance down the homestretch.

He'd come a long way in just over two months of intensive indoctrination. Reza was sure his coaching would enable Kwon to hold up under pressure in North Korea.

Kwon looked pensive. He missed Reza's attempt at humor, failing to notice that Reza was messing with him. But Kwon was focused. He seemed to know the moment had finally arrived. No more practice sessions, this time it would be for real. A one shot deal. Literally do or die.

Reza judged his chances as decent. He believed Kwon was now capable of pulling it off, especially with Rokman's backup plan. Kwon had proved to be a better student than anticipated. He was very smart. He just needed to develop a knack for the deception required of a double agent.

Kwon, for his part, was still uncertain of his chances. If the Americans and NIS succeeded with their plan to infiltrate him into North Korea, the success of the plan hinged on him first passing grueling interrogation in Pyongyang, and then getting inside DPRK's command as a cybersecurity expert. He could do the cyber part, no problem. But could he deceive the naturally suspicious North Koreans?' He was raised in North Korea and understood their paranoia all too well. Would they believe his story?

The reality of his demanding task hit him like a brick.

Reza noticed Kwon was tense. "Loosen up," Reza said. "You're very well prepared. I'm confident you'll pull it off, Kwon. I've trained you for every eventuality. There will be no big surprises up there. You're good to go."

***

U.S. Embassy, 7:00 p.m.

"Phone call for you, Gunner," Tim said, flipping him the phone.

"Hello."

"I'll pick you up at the Embassy in forty minutes." It was Kim.

"Where are we going?" Gunner asked.

"Fishing. Reza gave Biff the go sign for Kwon, Nam just texted me. Biff's over at the NIS command post with Nam to honcho our plan with him."

"So it's finally show time."

"Is that a question or a comment?" Kim asked.

"Could be either, or both, Kim, that's the beauty of our language."

There was silence at the other end of the line.

"Show time, it's a L.A. term, man," Gunner said. "I'll be ready. Meet you on the Embassy circle," he joshed him. Gunner laughed, wondering if Kim got it.

"Okay, got it. This will be the test," Kim predicted. "Kwon better hold up."

***

Inchon docks

Two hours later – 10 p.m.

"May be a hitch in our plans, Gunner," Kim said. "Look over there."

From where they sat in their NIS vehicle, they had a good view of the nearby docks. They could see a platoon of military police armed with Daewoo K11 assault rifles going dock to dock, warehouse to warehouse, and boat to boat looking for Cho despite the tip he was sighted in Seoul over twenty miles away.

"Better notify Tim and Reza," Gunner said. "They're on the way with Kwon."

The bright young MP captain obviously thought the broadcast news may have been a diversion and decided to scout out the docks. It was a likely place for the fugitive to hide out while looking for an escape route, maybe by sea. The captain likely hoped to make a name for himself by catching the Godfather on the run.

The MP captain looked in their direction. Fortunately he appeared to determine they were sitting in a NIS vehicle and assumed they were on business. He and his men resumed their search.

"I'll call Tim after I alert Nam," Kim said. They were supposed to meet their contact, Chin, near here soon, at eleven. He was organizing a fishing vessel to pull into an empty slip fifty yards to their left to pick up Kwon as a crew member at 11:15. "We've got to move on this swiftly. We've got an hour. Hope those guys move out soon or this could ruin their plans." Kim picked up his cell phone and punched in the scrambled code.

"Director, Kim here. Got a problem... The hitch you warned me about." He quickly explained the situation, and then paused. "Okay, sounds good. We'll go with that plan."

Moments later an APB blared on the car's communication channel: "Alert: Rumored sighting of Cho at Inchon International Airport disguised as a peasant woman. All units in that vicinity please proceed to the ICN airport to assist in Cho's arrest. He may be trying to escape to the Philippines where he has contacts who hid him years ago. Repeat, emergency assistance requested ASAP at ICN."

The All-Points Bulletin elicited the response Nam desired when he put out the disinformation. The MP captain heard the same message on his jeep's APB channel.

Actually, NIS agents tailing Cho through his GPS chip had informed Nam earlier that Cho was hiding in a restroom stall at a Seoul train station waiting to flee on the next train to a Kkangpae safe house in Daegu. NIS agents had the residence under surveillance and lines of communication tapped. Nam planned to have Cho captured in Daegu following an anonymous tip to authorities there, another NIS ruse by his agents tailing Cho's GPS chip. By the time they closed in on Cho, Nam calculated Kwon would be out in the middle of the Yellow Sea, safely out of the country.

"The APB ploy worked, Gunner. Look, they're moving out."

The captain swiftly rounded up his troops. They jumped in four ROK jeeps and sped off, tires squealing on the asphalt, on their way to ICN ten miles to the southwest.

Gunner smiled, impressed. "Nam really gets things done."

"He does indeed command the situation. Let's pull over by that warehouse to wait for our contact." Kim added, pointing to their right.

Kim turned around to face the back seat. "It's safe to sit up now, Kwon. You'll be shipping out in a half hour. Chin is the harbormaster at this dock who arranged your trip across the Yellow Sea to Korea Bay ostensibly to fish. Stay quiet onboard and keep to yourself, understand? This is not a corporation boondoggle. You're on a mission."

"I will. Reza briefed me," Kwon replied confidently.

"Do you get sea sick?"

"No. my father was a fisherman in North Korea. I grew up working on a boat until university."

"Make sure you get those clothes and your body dirty, like you've been knocking around the docks for two months. Look the part," Kim ordered him as a last reminder.

"I will give it my best shot, or be shot," Kwon replied, upbeat, feeling prepared for his assignment.

Gunner appraised him admiringly. Kwon appeared steeled for his task. He knew what he had to do. Kwon was a vastly different man than the one they broke out of jail in late July, only two months ago, Gunner thought to himself. Kwon was altered, not only in appearance, but in his mannerisms. Reza did one hell of a job prepping him.

***

The next morning the *Seoul Times* headline read: *CHO CAPTURED IN DAEGU. KWON STILL AT LARGE.* The *Seoul Herald* ran: *ONE TO GO. CHO IN CUSTODY. KWON STILL LOOSE.*

At NIS headquarters, Biff and Nam reviewed the news coverage with satisfaction.

Nam smiled. "Another cup of tea, Biff?"

"Sure, thanks. Now the ultimate reality show begins."

"Let's hope it's not in troubled waters."

"It won't be. They'll buy into the ruse."

CHAPTER TWENTY-FIVE

YELLOW SEA INCURSION

Late that night

Wearing the slicker the captain issued the crew, Kwon huddled near a lifeboat to keep warm. Most of the crew had gone below, leaving him and a few weathered fishermen on the deck of the sixty-five foot ship. That was fine with him. He needed a few last moments to rehearse his script in his mind. He was well aware he'd only have one shot at this deception, and everything hung in the balance.

The eerie, turbulent seas added to his apprehension. The Yellow Sea derived its name from the sand particles covering its surface, which were blown westward from frequent Gobi Desert sandstorms. The distinctive tint was absent tonight. It was pitch black except for the boat's green and red running lights, port and starboard, flickering on the water's surface and mingling with the foam of the boat's wake. The stars were covered by cumulous clouds, indicating an imminent storm. Thunder rumbled in the distance. The rising swells and wind confirmed an impending squall.

The summer swelter had started to subside as autumn moved in. An inversion layer often associated with an approaching storm swept over the Korean commercial fishing sea craft, known as a 'drifter' in this part of Asia. The temperature rapidly dropped ten degrees. Kwon shivered, hoping it was the weather and not nervousness causing his chill.

The drifter cut through the heavy chop, making its way northwest through the numerous offshore islands west of Inchon. The boat bounced through the rising sea, occasionally pitching sideways. The breeze continued to pick up with periodic gusts rattling the commercial fishing nets and cables hanging from outriggers off the stern, the sound competing with the noise of the engine.

Inside the wheelhouse, the captain switched the boat's heading to north-northwest on autopilot, following his Doppler navigation. The boat was headed to an offshore destination, near the captain's favored fishing shoal. It lay near one of many islands located off Inchon and the western coast of Korea.

In fact, the spot lay very close to the 38th parallel dividing North from South Korea. The demarcation was tricky to determine. South Korean maritime traffic had to avoid straying into the hostile waters of Korea Bay at the northern line of "no man's land." Many rival fishermen shunned this spot for that very reason, wanting to avoid a confrontation. But this captain always had good luck fishing there, so far without mishap. At this speed they'd arrive before dawn, perfect for an early sweep of amberjack tuna, cod, or mackerel, a commercial fisherman's dream.

He was making good time. He glanced at his first mate and took another sip of coffee. "We'll arrive at high tide."

The first mate nodded. "Good timing, Captain."

Arriving at high tide in a sea known for twenty to thirty-foot tidal floods was indeed a good thing. An ebb tide could land the unwary sailor aground on a shoal's sandbar or stuck in the mud around these islands. The captain had learned from experience that navigation and timing were not only important for safety but contributed to the likelihood of a good catch. He planned to hit the special spot right at flood tide and have his sonar pick up a big school of fish. He hoped the brewing storm would hold off and not ruin their chances for a good haul.

To the captain, it was worth the risks netting up here with no competition. The area wasn't overfished by the Japanese and Chinese like other spots around these islands. Other fishermen didn't want to risk tangling with North Korean patrol boats, but he'd always had good luck up there. And he knew the area well.

He'd heard from those who had strayed into North Korean waters and engaged one of their patrol boats that some of the DPRK captains could get testy and overzealous in their duties. These waters had been involved in many disputes by both sides since the end of the military conflict sixty years ago.

A light rain began to fall and the wind continued to pick up along with the boat's pitch and spray over the bow. The drifter continued to pound through the increasing swell with seaworthy ease. Down below, little chatter was exchanged among the fishermen. They napped or smoked, resting up for the arduous work ahead.

The approaching storm forced the remaining hardy sailors below the deck, but Kwon remained up top. The conditions suited him fine. He had kept to himself so far on the journey, appreciating that the others respected his space. He huddled in the spray, wondering if he ever would return to South Korea and his family. He vowed to follow Reza's advice to the letter, convinced the crusty Iranian's instructions offered his best chance for survival.

His musings were suddenly interrupted by a searchlight piercing the darkness in the distance. The small beam was getting larger by the minute as a boat closed in on them from the north rapidly. A wave of tension swept over Kwon as lightning flashed and thunder cracked in the distance.

***

"We've picked up an intruder on our radar, Captain." The lieutenant handed the North Korean PG-T class patrol boat captain the coordinates of the sighting and a photo of the radar blip.

"Looks suspicious," the captain said. "We have no craft in that area?"

"No, sir. It's just a few miles above the parallel. Looks like a sixty-plus footer, non- military profile though."

"Alter course, comrade. It appears someone has strayed into our waters. Let's check it out, probably fishermen poaching our fishing grounds, but we must rule out spies. Never trust South Korea."

"Yes sir."

Ten minutes later the lieutenant reported, "Got her spotted through my binoculars. It's a South Korean drifter, Captain."

"I see that. A commercial vessel, but we must board her according to our regulations. Hit our other spotlights and close in," he ordered, laying down his infrared night vision binoculars. He strapped on his Soviet Tokarev TT pistol. He anticipated a routine evaluation of documents not an incursion, but took no chances. "Ready our boarding squad."

"Yes, sir."

Fifteen minutes later the patrol boat pulled alongside the drifter, now stopped and rocking in the waves. The bright spotlights blinded the drifter's crew as they huddled on deck, looking apprehensive.

"You have intruded into North Korean waters, standby for boarding," the patrol boat captain blared the order through the bullhorn, adding to the tension among the fishing boat crew. "Have your documents and identification papers ready for our examination."

The patrol boat crew threw lines and bumpers alongside the drifter's starboard and secured them as armed marines prepared to board. They carried Type 58 assault rifles, patterned after Russian AK-47s. And they looked intent, ready to engage.

Kwon forced himself to remain calm. His moment of truth had arrived.

* * *

Kwon watched as four marines searched the craft while the others stood guard. The patrol boat captain questioned him briefly, his face stern as Kwon recited his prepared answers and asked to be returned to North Korea with him. The North Korean captain said little and returned to speak with the fishing boat captain. Kwon listened as the two captains conversed. They seemed to be sorting out the incursion amicably.

"Your documents are in order," the patrol boat captain said, "except for one, the bald man with the scruffy beard over there." He pointed at Kwon.

Kwon watched the exchange closely. How this situation resolved was critical to the plan.

"He has no identification," the patrol captain continued. "Is he a stowaway? Do you know him? He claims he's a North Korean, told me he's a fugitive hiding from the law. Know anything about that?"

"I just signed him on tonight as a last minute replacement," the fishing boat captain replied. "I was one short on my crew. Don't know anything about him, or the story he gave you. Our harbormaster vouched for him, so I brought him along to help haul the nets. He's kept to himself tonight, so I know really nothing about him, whether he's a fugitive or not. I took the harbormaster's recommendation, known that man for years, I trust him."

"I see." The patrol boat captain thought it all sounded plausible. The man appeared a wet, harmless soul down on his luck. Not a threat. The bizarre story fit. Maybe.

Kwon waited. Now it was just a matter of time before phase two of his infiltration plan kicked in. The North Korean captain appeared an experienced, older seaman and not upset about their incursion into foreign territory. His professional, calm reaction surprised Kwon, who'd expected hostility. All the better for him if there was no testy confrontation.

The patrol's armed guards boarding the drifter also observed the captains' amicable conversation, and they relaxed, looking bored as they leaned against the gunwales.

The drifter crew stood in line on the deck, documents in hand as instructed. Rain pelted everyone as a cloudburst hit. The drifter crewmembers were relieved the discussion going on between the two captains involved him, the newcomer, not them. Still, the conversation seemed to be going well. They anticipated this would soon be over and they would be on their way to fish.

Since there seemed to be little tension involved, Kwon figured these incursions must occur frequently and were generally settled without gunfire. The drifter captain handled the matter smoothly.

"My Nav Aid must be off and I strayed too far north," he said evenly. "It's poorly demarcated. I regret the intrusion." His intrusion into North Korean waters was not a mistake. His Doppler navigation system functioned dead on. The headings were the specific instructions he followed to the precise coordinates into these highly patrolled waters. The drifter captain recognized he was lucky to be dealing with a seasoned, professional North Korean officer and not some uptight young communist zealot with a hard-on about a sixty-year-old border dispute established years before he was born. Indoctrinated during childhood to follow DPRK dogma and prolong the hostility, those sailors could be difficult to deal with.

His simple excuse was exactly the line the harbormaster handsomely paid him to recite. Now he knew why he was instructed to fish at this well-patrolled spot. Evidently this was a well-planned, deliberate incursion to disputed waters to deliver this newcomer crewman to the North Koreans.

For the kind of money the harbormaster offered, the fishing captain asked no questions. Maybe he was transporting a fugitive, maybe a North Korean, maybe a South Korean spy. It wasn't his concern.

He had no idea what this murky scheme was all about, but he'd accomplished his assignment. When he returned to report the mission was successful, an additional bonus awaited him that would dwarf the money from the day's catch. As soon as he settled this matter, he planned to head for his usual fishing spot twenty miles southwest of their present location, well away from the 38th parallel. He hoped to beat the worst of the storm. Things were working out just as the harbormaster assured him they would.

The fishing boat captain maintained his poker face as he announced, "He's all yours. Sorry again about this intrusion."

"We'll take him in for interrogation, Captain. You may leave the area with your crew and return to your waters. I'd suggest you get your Doppler navigation system checked out. It's obvious you made an innocent mistake by straying into our waters. But some of the younger patrol boat captains are sticklers for regulations and can make a lot of trouble for you. Carry on with that warning in mind."

"I will heed your warning. I didn't realize he lacked proper papers. He came highly recommended."

"I understand. We'll determine if his confusing story plays out." The patrol captain motioned for Kwon to come with him and his men.

As they led Kwon to board the patrol boat, he thought that everything appeared to be going according to plan, just like the Americans said it would.

Chapter Twenty-Six

NAMPO, NORTH KOREA

Later that morning

"**S**o you claim to be one of our spies fleeing home?" The seaport authority officer glared across his desk at Kwon. "You have no documents to establish your identity, so why should we believe your preposterous story?"

The officer believed the intruder was wasting his time with some poppycock story about being a fugitive spy. Most likely he was a South Korean agent caught attempting to sneak into the country to spy on them.

The officer's CZ75 firearm lay on his desk in plain view, an act of intimidation. "Do you think we are fools?" he continued. "Who are you and what are you doing here? Tell me why I shouldn't just shoot you now and get this charade over with?" He fingered his gun, contemplating carrying out his threat to dispatch this charlatan.

Kwon sat in an uncomfortable metal chair, dripping wet and shivering, in the same clothes he'd worn since he departed Inchon, still drenched from the storm at sea. Kwon knew he must endure the man's antagonism if he planned to succeed in his mission.

He closely assessed the wizened officer in his olive drab uniform, predicting this bureaucrat would die behind that same desk without distinction, one of thousands like him in a country obsessed with layers of bureaucratic authority. This officer might quite possibly die before he completed his preliminary screening questions directed at him. He looked appallingly ill. His eyes were sunken and jaundiced, filled with blatant enmity.

Kwon read his military nametag: *Major Kang Soo-Hee.* Knowing DPRK, the major was a mid-level career officer assigned to this humdrum post for life. His opening accusations indicated a contentious interview awaited Kwon.

Kwon did not respond immediately. He glanced around the austere office where the patrol boat marines had escorted him. Reza recommended he employ the stalling tactic to appear self-assured but also to allow him to regroup.

He found the irony of his present circumstances inescapable. His life had come full circle by returning to Nampo, the North Korean seaport where he grew up and the city where he graduated with honors from Sohae University in computer engineering. It was a quirk of fate that it was here, the 225th bureau of the RGB, the Reconnaissance General Bureau of the National Intelligence Service, had recruited and trained him for espionage with a master plan to infiltrate him into South Korea.

He'd departed from this seaport over twenty years ago, entering South Korea under the guise of an oppressed refugee seeking asylum. Now, again a refugee of sorts, he was engaged in the paradox of selling another story. He must convince them that he was indeed that same loyal spy returning home after his cover was blown. Everything hinged on his persuasive performance convincing this hostile officer sitting across the desk.

He surveyed the drab surroundings as he mulled his current situation, not rushing to answer the interrogator's question, making him wonder what was going on.

The office lacked any redeeming virtues, reflecting the officer's low level in the North Korean bureaucratic hierarchy. He occupied a small, stuffy space with no window, one desk, three wooden chairs, and an old North Korean flag in the far corner. The obligatory photograph of Kim Jong-un, the supreme leader of the Democratic People's Republic of Korea, hung crooked on a wall. The wall itself had peeling paint and numerous cracks begging to be repaired. Kwon had forgotten the how severely the government cut corners to bolster its military budget.

It must be depressing to work here every day, he supposed. But then again, this major would likely not have to endure this cramped space much longer, considering his apparent poor state of health.

The interrogator continued to stare at him from behind his littered desk, tapping his finger, not hiding his annoyance at his captive's delay in answering. A disinterested armed guard stood by the door, clearly not considering Kwon a threat.

"Are you listening?" the officer said. "Is there something wrong with your hearing? Tell me why we should believe your outlandish story."

Kang sighed impatiently, accustomed to quick responses, especially from someone in subordinate circumstances. The officer was annoyed at Kwon's impertinence and for wasting his time with his obviously concocted excuse for lacking proper ID.

Reza had prepared Kwon for this intimidating reception and these very questions. Kwon gathered his thoughts and gave a capsule summary of his journey.

"Sorry, I've been up all night and my mind wandered. Here's what happened, and why I have no identification. I spied successfully for North Korea for twenty years posing as a cybersecurity specialist with Samsung Electronics in Seoul. RGB records will confirm that fact. NIS, the South Korean Intelligence Service, exposed me last July after intercepting an encrypted message that had a flawed code. NIS quickly tried me for espionage and sentenced me to death. While in jail last July awaiting the firing squad an extraordinary event occurred that saved my life."

"What happened?" Major Kang asked, the statement capturing his attention.

"The Kkangpae, the South Korean mafia, blew a hole in the Andong jail wall outside the exercise yard to rescue their Godfather, Cho Yang-Eun, a notorious criminal. I escaped with others through the gap during the confusion. I've been on the run ever since, trying to figure out how to get back here. I landed a job on a commercial fishing boat that strayed into your waters last night. Your patrol boat solved my problem of finding my way back here, another stroke of luck when they arrested me for lacking identification."

The major narrowed his eyes at Kwon, still suspicious, but listening with interest now. He moved his hand away from his gun. "I recall reading about that jailbreak two months ago, a spectacular episode. How did you manage to avoid apprehension?"

This bizarre tale was far more colorful than a typical screening of an intruder captured at sea. Kang decided to listen to what he had to say after all. The adventure was so bizarre it almost had to be true.

Kwon noted the major's interest was piqued.

"I shaved my head and grew a beard as a disguise," Kwon continued.

"I can see that. How did you survive for two months?"

"I wore rags I salvaged from trash bins. I hid out on the Inchon wharfs looking for a job on a fishing boat. Everyone was searching for me and Cho. The Godfather split after the jailbreak, I never saw him again. Finally, last night I landed a job on a fishing boat short a crew member."

"You've already told me about the job," Kang interrupted.

"Sorry. As I said, last night your patrol boat boarded the drifter for straying above the 38th parallel. The marines searched the boat and examined everyone's documents. When they came to me, I had no documents, only the clothes on my back. They got upset. I told your patrol boat captain I was a North Korean spy on the run. I requested he bring me home and let the authorities sort it out."

"Home? He told me he didn't believe you. Where are your documents? How did you hope to prove you were North Korean?" Kang's voice rose again. "You must have possessed South Korean identification if you lived there."

"My South Korean documents were confiscated by NIS in July when they arrested me and put me in jail."

"I see." Plausible, the major thought. "But how did you live for two months? You do not look malnourished.

"I kept money in a security box for an emergency in case my cover was ever blown. So I was able to purchase food and water from wharf cafes."

"Location of this box?" the major asked. He picked up a pen and yellow legal pad and began to take notes.

"In a security box in a Seoul bus station."

"Which one?"

"Guui-Dong 546-1."

"Locker number?"

"1033."

"Combination lock?"

"Key."

"Where did you keep the key?"

"In the rose garden of Grand Park."

"Anyone else know about the key in case something happened to you?"

"Only my handler."

"His name?"

"Hwan Hyon-Hui," Kwon admitted without hesitation.

"Hmm … Did you speak with him after the jailbreak?"

"No."

Kang noted that divulging his handler's name lent authenticity to his story. It was something they could easily verify. He began thinking this interrogation might be leading somewhere. This man sitting across from him answered quickly, concisely. He had an answer for everything he asked, and he remained composed. Maybe he wasn't lying. Maybe.

"Do you expect me to believe that you never spoke with your handler?" Kang asked. "He would have helped you hide out. It's his responsibility to protect the network."

"We communicated only by encrypted computer messaging to pass intelligence over the past twenty years. I had no computer access to contact him after my escape."

"Are you telling me you never actually spoke with him, never met him once during that entire length of time?" the major asked incredulously. "Hadn't arranged an emergency number to call?"

"I am. We never met or spoke once, and we had no emergency number to contact each other."

Kang scowled. "Never once, in over twenty years?"

"Never," Kwon said firmly. "Hwan considered direct contact a needless risk. Said we had a good thing going, not to blow it, demanded I stay covert using our encryption programs."

The major considered a moment and then said in a calmer tone, "Smart advice, obviously that practice worked until last July."

"We passed valuable intelligence information for twenty years without a slipup."

"Then what happened?"

"I got greedy. I got caught hacking into South Korean CENTCOM's security system. NIS traced the attempt to me at my Samsung office when I used a flawed code."

"Unfortunate. Who did your handler answer to in the chain of command after you got caught? Who would he notify him of your exposure?"

"I don't know."

Kwon did know, but planned to save this information for the next level of interrogation he anticipated. He wouldn't waste it on this yahoo's preliminary screening. He planned to divulge critical information in bits and dribbles. Chum the waters as Reza instructed, lead them on to take the bait.

Kang narrowed his eyes. "Are you telling me the truth?"

"I am. My handler played it close to the vest. Said I couldn't divulge what I didn't know under torture if I was ever caught spying. He said I didn't need to know who he answered to in the chain of command."

"Sounds like he went by the book, very disciplined," the major acknowledged.

"Hwan was all business. He must have told me a hundred times to stay under the radar. He never asked me about my family or anything personal in our electronic communiqués over all those years."

"Your family?"

"Wife and three young boys."

"What happened to your family when they jailed you?"

"I have no idea. They didn't allow visitors while I was in jail. I worry ..." Kwon let his voice trail off. The question was truly painful.

Kang saw Kwon's anguish as genuine.

"We all make sacrifices for the Fatherland and our dear leader," Kang said, his tone less hostile.

"I worry about them. What will happen to them after all the bad news about me in the media?" Kwon said.

"Of course, that's natural to worry," the major said before moving on. The family topic would lead nowhere but to further distress. "Did NSA torture you?"

"Yes."

"Did you give them Hwan's name?"

"Yes," Kwon said, "only under duress."

"What kind of coercion?"

"They tried to drown me."

"You were water boarded?" Kang asked.

"I suppose you could call it that."

"So what did you tell them about Hwan?"

"That I only knew how to reach him by our encryption codes over the Internet. That he changed codes frequently on no set schedule for security reasons. Hwan also changed our passwords often. He was extremely cautious. For all I know he may not have resided in South Korea and may have handled my case from up here."

"Did you give NIS the code, the password?"

"I did. I feared they would drown me. They threatened my family with torture as well."

The major slid a pad of paper and pen toward Kwon. "Write down the password and code for your last communication with Hwan and the date of that transaction on this pad. I presume that was just before NIS captured you."

"It was."

Kwon did as requested. The questioning went on for two more hours. Kang took careful notes, and tried repeatedly to trip him up to no avail. Finally the major asked, "Can you pass a lie detector test to verify everything that you've told me?"

Kwon nodded. "I can."

"You're aware that if you are lying, you will be shot?"

"I am quite aware. I'm a North Korean, I know the consequences." He spoke confidently.

Major Kang concluded that this was an educated man who told a plausible story, one deserving a follow-up interrogation at the next level.

Kang excused himself. As the major stood, Kwon noticed a campaign ribbon with oak clusters on his uniform from the Korean War, the Fatherland Liberation War. Other ribbons indicated he received decorations for Hero of the Republic and the Order of Soldier's Honor. The man had fought with valor sixty years ago in a conflict that was still going on, but now without gunfire. Kwon knew the major would soon be buried without fanfare despite his outstanding service to North Korea. The major was yesterday's news, insignificant and uncelebrated.

Kang limped toward the door, paused, and turned back. "I need to make a phone call. I'll send in some tea for you. Write down your family history, education, and résumé on my legal pad so we can confirm it. Write legibly." His tone was not harsh this time, more like a schoolteacher instructing a student.

In all his years behind the Seaport Authority desk managing mundane problems and investigations, Kang had never encountered a set of circumstances like this. This strange man's story seemed credible to him. It merited further scrutiny.

Either he's one of us returning home after a harrowing adventure, or a clever spy, a very clever spy indeed, he thought as he headed for a private phone in an adjoining office to call RGB command.

CHAPTER TWENTY-SEVEN

THE NEXT LEVEL – RGB INTERROGATION

Pyongyang, North Korea

"**H**e's either one of ours or a very clever spy, one of the best I ever seen," Major Kang said into the phone moments later. "He tells an intriguing story, Colonel."

"Really?" Colonel Kyung Min-Jae said. "Give me a brief synopsis. This line is secure."

"He claims RGB trained him here twenty years ago, then infiltrated him into South Korea posing as a refugee to spy for us. While in Seoul he spied under the guise of a cybersecurity specialist with Samsung. He obtained a degree in computer engineering from our university, he claims, so he fit right into their program. Said he worked as one of our undercover agents and passed valuable information for years through covert channels to his handler, something he claims he can prove. Says NIS caught him hacking about three months ago, threw him in jail, sentenced him to death, but he escaped by a fluke."

"Interesting claims, we need to verify them. We had a spy program like that back then, but it's common knowledge. All this could be a cover story to take advantage of an opportunity." The colonel paused briefly. "I do recall NIS capturing one of our spies last July and news reports of a spectacular jailbreak around that time. So maybe … How'd he arrive in Nampo and end up in your office?"

"One of our patrol boats brought him in after a border intrusion by a South Korean fishing boat last night." The major went on to tell the colonel in detail about Kwon's discovery by the patrol, him being brought in for questioning, and his claims about his identity.

"Interesting," the colonel said when Kang paused. "You say he claims to be Kwon do-Hyun? Name doesn't ring a bell, but that was a long time ago. If it's true we'll still have records and fingerprints on him. We were not using DNA identification back then on recruits, only on senior officers in sensitive positions. Do you believe his story?"

"He is convincing," Kang said. "He had no holes in his story. He seems self-assured with quick replies, concise answers, all responses on target. His body language shows confidence, no signs of deception in his behavior. Don't let his weird appearance deceive you, he's intelligent; knows our spy jargon, methods, and sources. Told me he could pass a polygraph. We'll see, right?"

"Interesting," the colonel said, "sounds very self-confident."

"Or legitimate. His statements surprised me. Most don't even know what a polygraph is."

"That's unusual to offer a challenge like that. Maybe he's genuine."

"I'm inclined to believe him," Kang said. "I'll send him up the road to you for a formal interrogation. His story certainly deserves to be checked out by your team to determine whether he's telling the truth. He may be a valuable asset to us in the long run if he's authentic."

"Why is that?"

"Said he worked in cybersecurity for Samsung, learned a lot about advanced IT technology over the years. Claims to know everything about firewalls, malware exploits, advanced computer hacking, and cybersecurity systems. Claims he has overseas access to items we need to shore up in our outdated security system. He had a good run spying for us in South Korea, only slipped up once in twenty years, if he's not lying."

"What was he doing when they caught him?"

"Hacking into South Korea's CENTCOM. NIS nabbed him red-handed, traced his computer ID."

"Okay. We can find out easily enough if his story is true or not with our interrogation and polygraph."

"One other thing, listen to this. It may also be critical information to double-check."

"I'm listening, Major." The colonel sensed the officer's excitement at this intrigue as one layer of mystery after another unfolded.

"Kwon also related his handler's name, Hwan Hyon-Hui. He had to be one of your best agents to run a covert operation down there for that extensive period. That name should be easily traceable in your records. He insisted that they never met, never spoke, and that they only communicated by computer-coded messages relaying pilfered bits of South Korean intelligence, mostly military."

There was a long pause on the end of the colonel's line before he responded. "Tell me the handler's name again," he said in an anxious tone. The colonel wondered, could it be the same person? Was there a link?

"Hwan Hyon-Hui."

"Hmm … Name sounds familiar. But I find it remarkable that they had no contact for twenty years other than encrypted Internet messaging."

The colonel suddenly made the connection. Hwan was the same spy that had been missing in action, presumed eliminated by NIS in South Korea. The two spies may be linked. Colonel Kyung had assigned the Dragon Lady to get her network to investigate Hwan's unexplained disappearance. So far the case remained a mystery.

"It's difficult to believe," Kang said, "but Kwon said his handler was 'very cautious, secretive, risk adverse, absolutely not willing to take a chance.' Those are his very words."

"I'll take your word for it, Major. We'll check it all out," Colonel Kyung Min-Jae replied. "Quite a story, I must say."

"Almost unbelievable."

"It may be fiction. He could be a well-coached spy posing as Kwon. Good work, comrade, commendable, in fact. You have good instincts," the colonel added, impressed with the major's due diligence and referral up the chain of command.

"Thank you, sir. We'll deliver Kwon to your Pyongyang facility within an hour. I took extensive notes for you to review, plus I had Kwon write out his family history and résumé. Something else your team can verify."

"Good, that will be helpful. Save us some time getting to the bottom of this mystery. If this information pans out, I'll see that you get an office at the Port Authority with a view of the sea." The colonel paused. "By the way, how's the chemotherapy going? You sound fatigued."

"I am very tired. The doctor said the CT scan last week showed the tumor has spread to my liver." Kang kept his voice even. "Not a good prognosis, the doctor said to get my affairs in order."

"Sorry to hear that, Major. Take the rest of the week off, my orders. I promise you'll have the office by the first of the week. Let me know if I can do anything else for you. You've served the Republic well. You're a good man."

The empathy, so rare in Kang's experience, surprised him. "Thank you, Colonel. I fear I won't be a long-term tenant, but I appreciate it. I've always wanted an office with a window." Kang managed to speak with a stiff upper lip, an ingrained military response.

* * *

Pyongyang, three hours later

"How do we know you are our spy, as you claim, not theirs? Could it be that you are impersonating Kwon? If you are Kwon, not an imposter, convince me. How do you explain yourself?" With no introductions, no prelude, Colonel Kyung Min-Jae had marched into the interrogation room and began firing questions to intimidate Kwon. Kwon knew he was presumed guilty until proven innocent in North Korea. Reza had prepared him for this.

The colonel glared at him like he'd gladly shoot him at the slightest provocation. A semi-automatic military issue CZ75 pistol lay on the table between them, in plain sight for Kwon to notice, just like Major Kang's gun a few hours before. *Must be a standard form of intimidation,* Kwon reflected.

The interrogation started almost verbatim with the first round of questions that Reza had trained him to expect in his rigorous mock preparations at the safe house in Seoul. The colonel used the predicted questions designed to shock him and throw him off guard immediately. But they failed to rattle him. Forewarned, Kwon stayed cool, aware four hidden cameras recorded his reaction. He smiled at the surveillance camera behind the North Korean flag before he replied respectfully.

"Colonel, your RGB unit 225 recruited and trained me over twenty years ago as a cyber spy following my graduation from Sohae University in Nampo. Surely that is a matter of record at the intelligence bureau. No one in their right mind would risk impersonating me."

"And why is that?" the colonel asked, taken aback by Kwon's defiant, confident reply.

"There's an APB 'shoot on sight' BOLO issued for me in South Korea. And, no South Korean spy of sound mind would dare arrive the way I did. He'd sneak in undercover somehow in a carefully planned operation, not chancing a providential intrusion on a fishing boat. I was desperately trying to avoid execution, hiding out on fishing boats. Only by chance did I end up here. You can't plan an act of serendipity."

"Serendipity? That's a big word for a spy," the colonel retorted. He planned to put this man who claimed to be their agent in his place. "Any clever spy organization could fake your unit 225 credentials and get you on that boat," he added, hoping to throw Kwon off guard. "How do I know you're not actually a South Korean agent, not one of ours?" the colonel continued.

This man professing to be one of their spies returning home had the slight build of a North Korean, and had subtle features atypical in the South. He talked a good game, his appearance fit, maybe ... But he would continue evaluating him until he was certain.

"Such a scheme would require an ingenious deception," Kwon fired back, "A plot way too complicated that leaves too much to chance. I suggest you check my fingerprints. I can't fake those. Your sergeant took mine before this session. You can compare them to those in my file from twenty years ago. The sergeant also took a sample of my blood for DNA identification, although I have none on file. That procedure wasn't routine back then."

The colonel noted that Kang was correct. This man was sharp, and may be telling the truth. He would see if he could answer more probing questions as well, the colonel thought.

"Who is or was your handler in South Korea?"

"Hwan Hyon-Hui."

"Where did he live?"

"I don't know."

"Didn't you frequently communicate?" The colonel knew the answer, but tried to find an inconsistency from Major's Kang's report.

"No, not frequently, only periodically. Only when I had some useful intelligence to relay or he had a specific request or task for me to perform, and then only over the Internet using encryption messaging."

"Never met in person? Never spoke over the phone?"

Kwon shook his head. "Never. Not once over twenty years."

"Isn't that quite unusual?"

"It seemed odd at first, but we had no personal relationship." Kwon shrugged. "That's how he wanted it, just business. I answered to him, strictly followed his orders and his protocol. Hwan took absolutely no risks."

"Where is Hwan now?" It was a trick question. The colonel knew Hwan had been missing since about the same time NIS busted Kwon, well over two months ago. When the major had mentioned Hwan's name earlier on the phone it caught the colonel off guard, but now he'd put two and two together.

Was there a connection to this man sitting before him? The spy seemed puzzled by this question about Hwan. Did he know where he was or not?

News from Seoul was meticulously monitored and analyzed daily in the colonel's intelligence briefings. The North watched the South like hawks, predators looking for circumstances to exploit. There was some Internet chatter in South Korea suggesting Hwan was eliminated but nothing verifiable. RGB assumed NIS either took him out or Hwan went deep dark following Kwon's arrest. That was the standard operating procedure. But Hwan should have emerged by now and contacted Jin-Ju, his superior, following DPRK standard protocol.

Colonel Kyung closely studied this man claiming to be Kwon, the possible link. He found it uncanny that the weird-looking man sitting across from him professed to be the spy involved in the spectacular news story captivating South Korea and much of East Asia over the past two months.

This peculiar situation and strange coincidences baffled him. Was this man pretending to be Kwon? Could it be possible that the little man in the chair staring at him expectantly, patiently waiting for his next question, actually was the same spy mentioned in those reports? This man only vaguely resembled the photos of the escaped spy in the media. And if this man was the sleuth who eluded the authorities like a veteran field operative, then he had mastered clandestine skills not associated with the new generation cyber spy. Kwon had a reputation as a hacker, not a covert operative. Something didn't quite fit the story. The colonel became more suspicious.

Colonel Kyung had spent a lifetime in the espionage field and he found these circumstances mindboggling. He tried to put the big picture together and assess the extent of compromise to their intelligence network in South Korea, the impact resulting from Kwon's exposure. How much damage control was in order? Hwan, Kwon's handler, one of their best agents, was missing along with his computer and satellite phone, confirmed when Jin-Ju's agents checked out his premises. Everything else had been in order, with no sign of a break-in or a struggle. His safe house was intact reportedly with no surveillance devices implanted. Hwan had simply disappeared without a trace three months ago, presumably eliminated by NIS. There had to be a connection with these events and Kwon. But was this man telling the truth?

Colonel Kyung wanted to observe this man's response to two key questions. Did this man claiming to be Kwon know what happened to Hwan? More importantly, did he know about Jin-Ju, their top agent running the Seoul network down there? If so, RGB was in big trouble if the Dragon Lady found out her network had been compromised. Heads would roll, hopefully not his.

"I repeat," the colonel said, "where is Hwan?"

"I have no idea where Hwan is," Kwon answered truthfully. "In fact, I never knew where he was. Our relationship involved only encryption messaging carrying out business, as I said."

Kwon seemed genuinely to have no idea of his handler's whereabouts. The colonel decided to shift direction in his interrogation.

"Major Kang told me you claimed to have escaped from Andong prison when the Kkangpae mafia blew a hole in the exercise yard wall. Didn't you try to contact your handler to hide you and help you escape the country after that episode?" the colonel asked, taking another tack to gain information about Hwan.

"As I've stated, we communicated only by computer. Mine was confiscated. I had no idea where he lived. We shared no phone number that I could call. Nor did we set up any drop box arrangement or other method of backup communication. For all I know he managed my case all those years over the Internet from Pyongyang, or someplace else, not from Seoul. For all I know, you could have posed as Hwan. That's how well disguised his cover was."

"You could have gone to a chat room, or a library," the colonel replied, watching him carefully. "Seoul has an abundance of public computers you might use, so why not try?"

"I thought about that option, but they had a huge dragnet out for me and Cho, as I said, an APB. I cased several prospective locations off the beaten path, but found all the Internet places were too well guarded. They obviously anticipated I might try that."

"What did you do then?" The colonel could not argue that the man had a plausible answer for everything, at least so far.

"I hid out on the Inchon wharfs posing as a down and out, unemployed seaman. I hoped to land a crew job and get out to sea, up north away from the search teams. I shaved my head and grew a beard so I wouldn't look like my photo in the news. I blended in with a crowd of other men seeking work on the docks."

The colonel nodded. "I can see that your appearance would not remotely suggest you're a computer expert or the spy they sought. But how do I know you're not lying about your computer skills too?"

"Test me."

He was a confident fellow, Kang got that right, the colonel mused.

"How'd you survive? Eat, drink, sleep?"

"I explained all that to Major Kang this morning. He took a lot of notes. I can go over it all again if you want."

"Give me a brief rundown. Try not to be overly verbose or repetitious." The colonel would check inconsistencies in his testimony by recording the man, taking notes, and then comparing the details with the major's report.

"I had the foresight to stash a supply of wons in a security box in case my cover was blown and I happened to be on the run. That got me through the last two months, but I was running low on cash, needed a job."

The colonel fingered through Major Kang's copious notes. "Yes, I see the major's reference right here, a bus station. Can you tell me which one?" the colonel asked, double-checking his accuracy.

"Guui-Dong 546-1."

"Box number?"

"1033."

"Okay, tell me this. Who did Hwan answer to in the chain of command?" he asked, trying a quick switch in topics.

"Jin-Ju." No hesitation.

"Did you ever meet or communicate with him by any method?" The colonel hid his alarm that this man knew of Jin-Ju; it was a troublesome complication.

"No."

"How did you know his name?"

"Twice Hwan let his name slip in his communication, something to the effect that 'I must notify Jin-Ju at once about this, I'll get back to you.' And then he broke off our communication abruptly."

"Nothing more than that?"

"Nothing more."

"Did you divulge Jin-Ju's name to NIS under harsh interrogation?"

"No, I only identified Hwan as my handler when they were drowning me, choking me to death."

"Did you realize NIS could trace Jin-Ju with your confession of Hwan's name?"

"How could they? Even I couldn't even identify Hwan after twenty years, much less Jin-Ju whom I'd never had contact with, no knowledge of his code. I tried to trace Hwan, curious to challenge my computer skills, see how good a spy I was. For all I knew Hwan was just a code name. The man had no pattern to his codes, passwords, or our cryptogram methodology, nothing predictable or traceable. I never knew if he was a real person or a consortium of spy managers somewhere afar in some backroom, or operating from an intricate clandestine cloud somewhere. Hwan was like a ghost, passing in and out of my espionage life with tasks, relaying intelligence."

"So you gave Hwan up not fearing they'd identify him?"

"Sure, I gave him up under duress, thinking they'd never find him anyway. They were drowning me, and I knew they'd stop if I gave them his name. I figured he'd immediately go to ground when he heard of my arrest for spying anyway, that's standard practice. My arrest was all over TV and the newspapers. Hwan would have to reside on another planet not to know about my capture and take proper precautions, knowing they'd try and break me to get to the next level."

The colonel paused. He was forced to admit this man talked a good game. He was either one of them, or a very knowledgeable enemy spy. He understood the intricacies of their operation, knew far too much for this to be made up. He also appeared not to be hiding anything, answering every question without hesitation with plausible explanations. But what were the odds of his escape through the hole blown in a jail wall a week before his scheduled execution? And skillfully eluding the authorities for two months? Or a fortuitous fishing incursion landing him on their doorstep?

Could it all be contrived? The bizarre happenings leading to his arrival made Colonel Kyung suspicious of an ingenious conspiracy. But what were the chances of someone pulling off such a convoluted scheme? Who would even attempt such a risky plot?

The colonel decided more questioning was needed. They would move onto to the next step with this strange man. A step that would almost certainly reveal whether he told the truth.

CHAPTER TWENTY-EIGHT

THE POLYGRAPH

RGB – The next day

"Have you undergone a lie detector test before?" Major Myung-Sook asked. "You answered all of our routine questions without hesitation or nervousness, implying that you've had some experience."

"No," Kwon said.

"Didn't NIS subject you to one?"

"No."

"Why not?"

"I guess they had plenty of evidence against me, so went directly to sleep deprivation, harassment, then to waterboarding to break me."

"What did they want?"

"My handler's name."

The major continued questioning Kwon about his handler, how much he knew of him, and how they communicated. Remaining calm, Kwon answered all the questions consistently, with no deviations from his previous accounts.

About a half an hour into the test, Kwon told his interrogator about having no idea where his handler was even located. Major Myung-Sook paused and glanced at his polygraph technician for verification, finding this admission astonishing.

The tech nodded an affirmative; the lie detector's needle never wavered from earlier baseline, routine questions where Kwon had no reason to lie. The subject was telling the truth.

The major resumed his list of questions RGB command had given him to verify from yesterday's grilling session.

"Did you know NIS eliminated Hwan after your capture, presumably based on your confession? The information you divulged allowed them to trace him."

Kwon shook his head. "No, I didn't until you just informed me. I assumed he'd go deep dark when the news of my capture broke."

Up to this point the polygraph needle had remained in the normal range of the earlier routine baseline questions, ones about family names, his workplace, and the capital of South Korea. But with this question Kwon's pulse rate, blood pressure, and respiratory rate flew out of normal range. The needle shot up as his vital signs showed his surprise at the news.

"I'm sorry to hear that," Kwon said. "But they were drowning me. And I figured they'd never find him if I couldn't locate him over all those years. I didn't intend to get him killed, believe me."

The needle went back to normal range as he settled down with this truthful reply.

"Who are you?" The major shifted topics abruptly, a tactic designed to rattle him.

"Kwon do-Hyun."

"Not a spy?"

"I'm a North Korean spy, like you."

"Are you telling me the truth?"

"Yes, didn't my fingerprints match your records?"

"We'll soon know," the major said. "Who is Jin-Ju?"

"I presume Hwan's handler."

"Ever meet him or communicate in any way?"

"No, never."

"How'd you learn his name?"

"By two casual comments Hwan made when he suddenly broke off our Internet messaging to contact him with some important news that I'd just given him, a slipup in his strict protocol, very uncharacteristic of him."

The interrogation went on for another two hours, covering many of the previous day's questions for clarification, cross-checking purposes, or just to try to irritate Kwon or trip him up.

Suddenly the side door opened. Without stepping into the room, a captain announced, "NDI, Major." Then he closed the door again, not waiting for a reply.

"NDI?" Kwon asked, faking confusion. The surveillance cameras recorded his feigned response, and the major bought into it. Thanks to Reza's training, the "NDI" ruse failed.

"NDI means 'no deception indicated,'" the major informed him. "If your prints match and there are no more surprises, I must conclude you are one of us. Welcome home," he added unenthusiastically. The major ordered the technician to take off Kwon's monitoring wires.

The major was still distrustful, however, and still confounded by the turn of events. He shuffled through his notes to see if he had missed anything.

Kwon sunk back in his chair and sighed quietly as the technician removed all the polygraph monitoring wires. He had on new, dry clothes after showering and shaving earlier. They even had fed him a decent meal. He felt a strong sense of relief.

He was "in."

The hall door opened. Another officer rushed in and handed the major a paper and a small object.

Kwon tensed.

"Looks like your prints match, Kwon," the major said. "But what is this object they discovered in a waterproof pocket in your shorts? It looks like some type of data storage device. A model I've never seen."

"It is, Major. It's the latest USB Flash Drive. Came out last year, holds one terabyte of information."

"That's an incredible amount."

"This storage device includes flash memory with an integrated universal serial bus interface. It holds a backup of my computer files, and some vital contacts in Singapore and Malaysia that RGB could use to update DPRK's cybersecurity systems."

"Interesting," the major said. "How did you keep it out of NIS' hands when they captured you and confiscated your computer?" The major sensed this might be his last chance to trip him up.

"I kept it in my security box with my emergency supply of wons. I updated the information periodically. My handler knew of my precaution and the security box location."

"At the same bus station in Seoul."

"Yes."

The major was impressed with Kwon; any lingering doubts about his truthfulness were fading. "Tremendous foresight."

"Thank you, Major," Kwon said, his relief growing at the major's warmer tone. He believed him.

"We can't be too careful in this business, Kwon. The South Koreans are clever spies. I need to notify Colonel Kyung that you passed the test and request he call General Pak, the man in charge of RGB. I'm certain he'd like to meet you. Help yourself to some tea while I phone him."

* * *

Soon after, the major returned.

"Colonel Kyung has invited you to dinner tonight at RGB headquarters," the major told Kwon. "He wants you to meet our Director, General Pak. I'll arrange for some finer attire for you. Not many get such an invitation, Kwon. You should be honored."

"I am honored to be in the service of my country."

Kwon smiled. He had made it; he was truly inside now. All he had to do now was be himself, only talk about his area of expertise, and wait for the revelation of the date the Americans wanted him to discover. Just like Reza instructed.

CHAPTER TWENTY-NINE

THE GENERAL'S DINNER PARTY

Pyongyang

That evening

Kwon sat in General Pak Jin-Se's office at RGB headquarters. Kwon faced the general across his large, imposing desk. Colonel Kyung sat to Kwon's right.

The general stubbed out a cigarette in the ashtray before him, already close to overflowing. "You've had a remarkable journey, Kwon." General Pak paused, examining the strange-looking little man who claimed to be one of their veteran covert agents. One who had successfully operated in South Korea for the past twenty years until he got caught spying, jailed, and sentenced to death over three months ago.

Now supposedly this same man sat before him, a fugitive returning home under astonishing circumstances. With his beard and shaved head, he did not remotely resemble the photographs the media had released during the manhunt following his escape from jail. The vetting reports mentioned he'd altered his appearance to avoid recapture.

The general wondered if his story could be a clever disguise.

"Perhaps that's an understatement," the general said, his tone derisive. "Your travels have been nothing short of extraordinary. As I understand it from reading the transcript of your interrogation by Colonel Kyung, you've faced one challenge after another. Somehow you've managed to prevail over each adversity." General Pak Jin-Se assessed him critically through steel-rimmed, thick bifocals.

Kwon met his stare. The general's olive drab uniform displayed a chest full of ribbons and medals expected of every high ranking North Korean general whether he'd faced battle or not. General Pak had an imposing presence for such an elderly, small man. The general's dark eyes bored through Kwon, his expression signaling clear disbelief of his story, despite the debriefing results.

But the general's intimidating manner failed to shake Kwon. He had been trained by Reza to anticipate such threats.

This general had almost as many decorations as North Korea's "dear leader." Kim Jong-un had never fought a war, much less undergone military training. He was a stage-managed dictator for the old school communists cabal.

Kwon thought with disdain how much pomp and circumstance played into controlling the North Korean psyche. The masses had never been exposed to a free society like he experienced in South Korea over the past twenty years. While he'd loyally spied for the North for an extended period, he'd come to appreciate the other side's worldview. He grasped the scope of the sixty-year struggle for hegemony between totalitarian and democratic governments. His musings were interrupted as General Pak resumed his rant.

The general scowled at him. "Pay attention, young man."

"Sorry. I was pondering what you said, leading me to think you don't believe me, sir."

"Let's say I'm dubious at this point despite our vetting. You've beaten long odds by arriving here. You might say describing your story as 'preposterous' is a masterful understatement." The general eyed him closely, waiting for his response.

Kwon did not even blink. He said nothing, remaining composed.

It wasn't the response the general expected. He had to admit the man maintained his composure well. He didn't fawn either but appeared to take his hostile reception in stride. Still, the general wondered if there was more to this man than met the eye.

"But Colonel Kyung assures me you passed our polygraph and your fingerprints matched those in our file," the general continued, "so presumably you are who you claim to be." He paused and added, "I suppose." He couldn't help adding the qualification, to register his disbelief despite all the objective evidence to the contrary. Intuitively, he rejected the story.

Still Kwon appeared unshakeable, inscrutable. The man's poise surprised General Pak. He didn't seem intimidated even in his presence, the general in charge of the feared RGB. He could order his swift execution on a whim by a snap of his fingers. He'd never encountered such a response. It puzzled him.

Colonel Kyung noted the general's perplexed reaction to Kwon's demeanor. The colonel nodded to his superior officer, indicating, "I told you he was a tough nut to crack."

The general nodded acknowledgment to him and resumed his caustic comments.

"So … it's clear to me you are Kwon, the spy we trained years ago. However, a lot can change over twenty years."

That statement unnerved Kwon a bit, but he hid his emotion well.

"My question is … Are you the same person we trained? Perhaps. Or perhaps not." The general paused for effect again, watching Kwon's reaction. "Alliances can evolve with time and other influences. Loyalties can wane."

Kwon anticipated where this was going. He tensed, on the verge of losing his composure.

"How do I know the NIS didn't turn you? Why should I not suspect you're a well-coached double agent attempting to infiltrate our intelligence operation? That would be a clever ploy, now wouldn't it, Kwon? Clever, but not an unusual maneuver in clandestine organizations. Is history repeating itself in your case? Hoping we didn't learn its lessons?"

The general was a cagy character, Kwon thought, trying to trap him. He regained his poise, aware of this ageless trick. He must play the cat and mouse game.

He was a hard ass general who had likely arrived at his exalted position by stepping over the bodies of his predecessors. He was clever, leading with a shrewd premise, one that Reza prepared Kwon for, thankfully. Reza had warned him that you don't rise to the top to run the RGB by trusting people, becoming complacent, and not maintaining a high index of suspicion. Despite his vetting, he was clearing taking no one's word for Kwon's authenticity. The general's private evaluation of him was the ultimate test.

Kwon reevaluated his circumstances. He wasn't "in" yet. What Reza referred to as "the game changer moment" had arrived, and he must not blow his cover by wavering.

He carefully crafted his answer, knowing his demeanor must be as convincing as the words he chose. He'd practiced his response to this anticipated challenge over and over at the Seoul safe house until he had it down pat.

The general snuffed out another cigarette, blowing smoke in Kwon's direction. Kwon interpreted the gesture's symbolic overtones—that the general intended to blow all the smoke in this exchange. The general's glare conveyed the message as well, "Don't even think about blowing smoke up my ass."

Kwon assumed a humble attitude. "Your skepticism is justified, General, but I respectfully submit that your premise is flawed. I've maintained my loyalty to our regime. In fact, I've brought back valuable information to fortify our cybersecurity systems. I'm sure you would acknowledge your current system is outdated. Your firewalls are vulnerable to penetration by the enemy's newer cyber tactics. They will gain the upper hand by hacking into your systems and stealing our secrets.

"Knowledge is power," Kwon continued. "The latest cybersecurity data is contained in my flash drive, which should allay any suspicions of my allegiance. I can understand your cynicism. My journey is an incredible story of survival. I understand your reluctance to accept the long odds it required for me to return home. But the fact remains, I'm here."

"I'm glad you understand my reluctance to believe your adventurous tale. We are in the process of reviewing your flash drive. That may settle some issues we have with your story."

"General, I couldn't make this saga up. I have been very lucky. But I have nothing to hide. I'm telling the truth."

It was apparent to the general that Kwon was an intelligent, capable man. Still, his story required leaps of conviction the general was hesitant to take. He lit another cigarette.

"The colonel said you sequestered that memory device in a waterproof pocket. We discovered it going through your clothes. Unfortunately, it's a new type of storage device our technicians are experiencing difficulty deciphering."

Kwon nodded. "It's an encrypted, hi-tech USB flash drive that I'll gladly decode with your intel technicians."

"Then that leaves what's on the storage device up to your interpretation," the general said, scowling. "Do you think we're fools?"

"No, the information becomes self-evident once deciphered, no way that I could deceive anyone by decoding it in their presence. It's a computer-driven cipher."

The general took a drag of his cigarette before replying. "What's on it?"

"My complete computer files, limited recent military intelligence, but most importantly my contact information with cybersecurity companies in Malaysia and Singapore. IT specialists I recently worked with while at Samsung's security division. We contracted with the South Korean military intelligence to build new firewalls. My contacts supplied the latest electronic gear at reasonable prices. I had a top secret clearance to manage the transactions."

"Interesting line of work you had at Samsung. Would that enable us to penetrate their firewalls you installed?"

"Once I was exposed I'm certain they changed all access codes, IP protocols, passwords, anything vulnerable to a viral exploit. But you could try."

"I understand. They certainly would undertake damage control. Did you contract with NIS also?"

"No, they worked only with the American consultants from NSA, using their complicated electronic cybersecurity systems."

"Why complicated?" the general asked.

"They use arcane mathematical algorithms, computerized cryptography, unpredictable rotating schemes. Way too esoteric."

"I see your point. Tell me, why did you have the flash drive with you?"

"To get the information it contained to RGB, to protect our national security against a cyberattack," Kwon said. "I kept it updated and in a security box in case my cover was ever blown. The files were classified and encrypted. I was concerned if NIS ever captured me they would suspect that the flash drive existed after they deciphered my computer's hard drive and traced its transfers."

"What if you failed to escape and retrieve the flash drive?"

"We had a backup plan. My handler, Hwan, knew how to retrieve the memory stick and how to decode it. He also knew where I hid the key to the security box and its location. That was our fall back plan, in case my cover was blown and I was arrested. He couldn't have missed the news of my capture. So naturally, I was surprised to find the flash drive was still in the security box after I escaped from jail."

"How do you explain that?"

"The jailbreak or why the flash drive was still in the security box?"

"The flash drive."

"I checked the security box to retrieve my emergency stash of wons after the jailbreak. I was surprised when I discovered the flash drive still there. I assumed Hwan must have gone to ground and didn't want to run the risk of retrieving it, suspecting a NIS surveillance trap. I retrieved it with my cash and took off to hide."

"It appears Hwan's backup plan wasn't possible. We suspect NIS took him out shortly after you blew his cover," the general said angrily.

"They were torturing me; that's how they got his name out of me," Kwon said, following his rehearsed script once again. "But I don't see how NIS could trace him by only knowing just his name. That's all I knew about him over twenty years of sharing South Korean secrets with him, only his name. And, I assume it was a code name. I tried tracing him to test my espionage skills several times and couldn't find a clue. Not a shred of evidence he existed."

Not exactly a warm welcome home, Kwon thought. He didn't like where the conversation was going. But he knew he must continue to artfully dodge the General's questions.

"Did you expose Jin-Ju?" General Pak asked.

"Absolutely not. Fortunately, they never asked me about him, leading me to conclude NIS had no knowledge of his existence."

The general's eyes narrowed. "So you knew Jin-Ju was Hwan's handler in the network, but they didn't? Is that what you're telling me?"

"I assumed so, but I didn't know for certain. I told the colonel that Hwan let his name slip on two occasions; that he needed to break off communication with me to notify Jin-Ju about our communiqué immediately.

That's how I picked up on the connection between them. I can't attest to what NIS knew or didn't know about him."

"You may have exposed the heart of our covert Seoul network," the general said menacingly, staring at Kwon, "do you realize that?"

"Only under duress did I surrender Hwan's name and not Jin-Ju's. But I couldn't confess knowledge that I was not privy to regarding Hwan, much less Jin-Ju. I had no need to know, so wasn't in that loop. NIS finally figured that out, and let that line of questioning go."

"So you never mentioned Jin-Ju's name?"

"Never."

"Just Hwan's name?"

"Yes."

"And you don't think your confession of his name would lead to NIS taking him out?"

"I figured Hwan would go to ground while I was in jail, as I stated. I never expected him to be eliminated. He was extremely cautious. It's a great mystery how they would have ever discovered him."

"NIS did discover him. He's gone. Plus his computer and satellite and cell phone were missing when Jin-Ju's agents went to check on him after your arrest. He went missing despite our rapid attempts at damage control. There are only two logical assumptions to explain his disappearance, and the favorable one, going deep dark, seems highly unlikely since he's failed to establish contact with Jin-Ju over the past three months through back channels. We assume NIS assassinated Hwan."

"My assumption differed at that time, General. I doubted NIS eliminated Hwan because he never took chances. As I said, I assumed he went deep dark, explaining why the flash drive was still in the security box when I checked the day after I escaped from jail. After twenty years of working with him I naturally predicted he took adequate precautions and went to ground. When it came to security, he was a control freak."

A plausible explanation, the general mused. Kwon was unquestionably quick on his feet. "So you retrieved the storage device," the general said. "Have you carried it with you ever since?"

"It has never left my possession until I arrived here. I bought the shorts with a waterproof compartment at a thrift shop. The USB drive is also waterproof, but I didn't want to test it if I got a job on a commercial fishing boat. I desperately needed to figure out how to get the information on the device to RGB. NIS cut off my Internet avenues of communication, so I was running short on options. I hoped to connect somehow with another North Korean agent to pass it on, but I knew none."

The general's attitude suddenly mellowed. He stood from his desk and stamped out his cigarette. "I accept your explanations despite their extraordinary nature. I suppose there are some things in life that are inexplicable. I plan to assign you to our cipher unit to work with Colonel Kyung's team to decode your files. I'm interested in your claim of having valuable foreign contacts for cybersecurity equipment. We could use an upgrade. The Japanese and ROK hackers try daily to penetrate our computers."

"I can make the necessary security upgrade arrangements for you, General," Kwon said. They kept double-checking him, he realized. He would be closely monitored, so he must produce results. Once the new systems were acquired, they would likely fully accept him.

"When was the last time you had a full meal with rice wine, Kwon?" the general asked, his tone suddenly cordial.

"It's been a long time," Kwon said.

"Then enjoy dinner now. Welcome back." The general motioned for him to go with him. Kwon rose, quickly following the general and colonel into the hallway.

As they walked to the dining room, the general conversed privately with Colonel Kyung. "Keep a close eye on him," the general said quietly. "I sense a serious disconnect in his story. We don't want to get burned. He's either one of us retuning home with an incredible explanation, or he's a well-coached double agent."

The colonel nodded. "I understand, General."

"I'm glad you do. He's clever, as you said, perhaps too clever. We couldn't trip him up. If NIS turned him, I predict he'll try to hack into our command and control systems sooner or later. Set traps for him. Fly periodic false flags to see if he'll take the bait. Dangle tantalizing intelligence within earshot to snare him. Keep trying to contact Jin-Ju through multiple channels to alert the Dragon Lady that Kwon turned up here.

They should meet to reorganize, proceed cautiously to assure damage control. See if they know anything about the circumstances of his convoluted journey. Ask them to investigate the possibility that NIS set up a clever disinformation scheme to delude us, allowing him to infiltrate back here as a double agent."

"Yes, sir. That would be a mind-boggling set of circumstances, sir."

"Never underestimate our enemy's ingenuity. Also, check out Kwon's contact claims regarding his sources in Singapore and Malaysia for cyber-security equipment. Make sure it's not a bogus offer, shell companies. Go over his flash drive with a fine-toothed comb, understand?"

"Yes, sir. If he's genuine, we could really use a cybersecurity upgrade."

"I agree, but be very careful. His story is over the top. If it's too good to be true, it probably is."

On second thought perhaps he should contact the Dragon Lady himself, the general thought. He would warn her about his misgivings about Kwon and see what her take was.

CHAPTER THIRTY

DRAGON LADY IN THE LOOP

Pyongyang – RGB Headquarters

"**M**ajor Lee, please encrypt this message to the Dragon Lady. I want her in the loop. I need her feedback regarding a potential threat."

"Immediately, General Pak. She'll receive the coded message within the hour."

***

< *DL - I have concerns Kwon may be a very clever double agent in a position to spoil our master plan of a surprise nuclear/EMP attack on the USA. We are nearing completion of the project and believe they have no knowledge of our plans. We've invested too much time and effort to get to this critical point to have it ruined by a spy in our midst. Kwon talks a good game, and we can't trip him up. Although he's passed our intense vetting, I still have lingering suspicions. Do you have any hard evidence he is not on our side? If not, we may accept his offer to upgrade our cybersecurity systems. It's too good a deal to pass up if he's legitimate. He showed up with a USB drive documenting his credentials with Samsung and well-placed connections with high-tech companies in Malaysia and Singapore. I need to make a decision soon -P >*

Two hours later the reply came from South Korea:

< *P- I share your concerns, but have no evidence against Kwon. He was a reliable cyber spy for twenty years, although now he's performing like an expert field agent, which is quite out of character. The coincidences surrounding*

his escape from jail to Pyongyang also raise my suspicion that NIS may have turned him into a clever double agent and infiltrated him back into RGB. Despite your interrogations and polygraphs indicating otherwise, I recommend you proceed with caution, set traps to snare him, bug his computer, and tail him day and night. We cannot afford to have him spoil our EMP scheme. We must teach the Americans a vital lesson not to thwart North Korea's ambitions. We've managed Kwon's exposure down here, only his handler was compromised. My network is intact, codes changed, and our damage control protocol followed to the letter. We're secure; are you, General? Be careful DL >

General Pak read her cryptogram closely, not finding it reassuring. The Dragon Lady's spy career was legendary, and she was second only to him in the North Korean intelligence and security agency hierarchy. Her opinion carried weight with him.

At the same time, DPRK units in RGB seriously needed the cybersecurity upgrades Kwon offered. Their old computers were vulnerable to NIS and CIA penetration using sophisticated modern malware. It would be foolish to pass up the chance to strengthen their security with no evidence of Kwon's disloyalty. However, Pak would take due precautions as she suggested. RGB would watch Kwon like a hawk.

Chapter Thirty-One

"HE'S IN"

CIA Headquarters Langley
One month later, Early November

"He's in," Rokman said as he took a seat in Biff's office.

"How do you know?" Biff asked.

"We just received some feedback from our Pyongyang hack job on their computers. Our Heartbleed virus has penetrated the RGB cyber network. The Cisco and Juniper gear we bugged is relaying targeted intelligence from our spiders infiltrated into their command and control systems, not only in Pyongyang, but with their affiliated communication systems in North Korea. It gives us a picture of their network. But not much valuable info yet, nothing we can connect to their launch plans."

"Anything back from the PeopleSoft virus yet that would enable us to tap in on their intranet communications? Be nice to monitor that chatter."

"Not yet. But eventually that'll kick in. Our red team designed some freshly minted zero-days to exploit vulnerabilities in that software. Maybe we'll get some passwords, hopefully worm into their backup system. That's where most of the critical information is kept."

Biff smiled. "How sweet it is." Biff credited Reza's intensive training for allowing Kwon to sell his story to RGB, enabling them to compromise their computers' vulnerabilities. RGB clearly had bought his story lock, stock, and barrel.

"Fill me in on how it all came down," Biff said. "This cyber espionage stuff blows me away." He grinned. "You NSA guys are changing the parameters of the spy game. No more cloak and dagger stuff. You're putting the old guys out of business. Better get rid of my raincoat and fedora."

"Ha! You'll never go out of style, Biff."

"The facts, give me just the facts," Biff said, doing his best *Dragnet* impersonation.

"Okay, here's the rundown. Kwon's flash drive documented his Southeast Asian business contacts and transactions at Samsung. Kwon convinced RGB to upgrade their security systems. They purchased the cybersecurity equipment last month, mid-October, from our shell companies in Malaysia and Singapore. Before reaching that decision, RGB techs tried to hack into the computers of our dummy companies in Southeast Asia on numerous occasions to no avail; our firewalls blocked them."

"Trying to check out the legitimacy of Kwon's contacts, no doubt. Naturally they expected shell companies as a trap and did their due diligence."

"Correct," Rokman said. "They're paranoid about security. To fake them out we allied with two established brick and mortar electronic companies over there, both owned by our assets, both in operation for over thirty years."

"Smart move. They'd definitely check that aspect out first off to rule out a shell company."

"So now we now have covert oversea NSA signal offices manned by our specialists in Singapore Security Systems and Malaysian Electronic Specialists in Kuala Lumpur. Both properly registered in the host countries. We used separate cover names in those offices in case North Korean agents or assets come to check out the premises. We lease space and have no ostensible interaction with the parent companies. Remaining under the radar is a mutually beneficial arrangement. They have no clue about our operation, and frankly don't care considering the exorbitant lease agreement we're paying them."

Biff nodded. "Good way to corroborate Kwon's contacts' legitimacy."

"Precisely our objective, to deceive the due diligence we expected RGB to exercise once they deciphered Kwon's flash drive and evaluated the disinformation we planted on the device. We leased a back office in each location using our influence with our intelligence agency colleagues over there. A favor here, a favor there, you know the procedure. We manned the setup with one of our NSA signals teams to sell cybersecurity systems only through our classified Internet website requiring a series of limited passwords to establish a link. No business is transacted without an authentic introduction, vetting process, and password. It's impossible to reach the website directly, or through the main office by mail or phone."

"So walk-ins would be required to go on the Internet, access the site, avoiding face-to-face interaction."

"Precisely, and no contracts go forward for business considerations without bona fide introductions."

"In other words, it's 'No ticket, no laundry.' You took elaborate security precautions to avoid exposure of the subterfuge."

"You got, Biff." Rokman laughed at the old quip about Chinese laundries. Biff wasn't into PC. "We expected North Korea to come calling, hacking, whatever it took to check us out. Any direct enquiries through the front office had to jump through the hoops, referred automatically to another website that had sophisticated caller ID tracer systems. We detected and deflected numerous attempts by RGB to make conventional enquiries as well as multiple attempts to hack into our system."

"Clever job. Well planned, Rokman."

"Thanks. We enhanced our deception with fake registrations, credentials, and resources. You name it, the whole nine yards of pretext. That lent credibility when the North Koreans attempted their due diligence to check out these two electronic companies and found them impenetrable. Finally, after frustrated efforts, RGB allowed Kwon to access the site with his passwords. He answered the list of questions to verify his identity, questions that only he would know how to answer. Kwon sealed the deal in one lengthy communication, navigating the gatekeepers' complicated procedures."

"That really must have impressed them."

"I'm sure it did. The cybersecurity transaction processes were shrouded in secrecy with convoluted transaction arrangements designed to obfuscate any investigation of them. RGB didn't have a clue they were dealing with shell companies, much less ours. Kwon built up his credibility, pulling off this deal as we predicted."

"Another crafty move, Rokman."

Rokman nodded. "Thanks. As I mentioned, the requirement for certified referral credentials before doing business with these two electronic merchants blocked North Korea from directly dealing with them, putting the responsibility squarely on Kwon's shoulders. The restriction forced RGB to use Kwon as the intermediary for any purchases since North Korea was on the published international restricted list, and their efforts had failed. North Korea has diplomatic relations with these two countries, but in general, corporations in Asia are reluctant to do business with DPRK. It's a matter of timely payments, bad faith reputation, and governmental restrictions."

"I'm impressed how you set that scheme up. That deal enhanced Kwon's standing, no doubt."

"I'm sure it did. RGB was forced to have Kwon arrange the deal, one they couldn't vet in advance. That definitely boosted his cover story, instilled some confidence in his boast of having well-placed connections, those links we planted on his flash drive. Our companies refused to work with RGB's techs, or its officers. They made it clear that they would only work with Kwon for security reasons."

"Find that ironic?"

"I do, as a matter of fact." Rokman smiled proudly.

"Another well thought out ploy by your team. You guys are good." Biff slapped Rokman on the back, grinning. "You're becoming an urban legend, man."

Rokman laughed. "Okay, listen to this. As instructed, Kwon sweetened the deal by arranging a heavy discount and installment payments for the North Koreans."

"They must think he's a big shot now."

"That's why he's in. He's down to only one task now, to determine the launch date in case our spiders fail to pick up that critical info from our viral exploit of the RGB computers."

Rokman reported the viral penetration of the North Korean intelligence agency with glee. His cyber exploit, Heartbleed, was working, just as he predicted. The spiders hidden in the Cisco and Juniper hard drives were performing. The targeted virus already was electronically pilfering selected data critical to formulate CIA intelligence estimates to present to the Joint Chiefs of Staff and the National Security Council. They predicted that it was only a matter of time before they'd learn details about a planned sneak EMP attack by the North Koreans. Not much intelligence yet, but they'd had received a few pieces of the puzzle they hoped eventually would reveal the big picture when they put them all together.

Biff grinned. "I really love this cyber spy stuff. Any clue how far they are along with their program?"

"Nothing vital yet, too early. Appears they have a capability to launch a satellite but lack the reentry technology for an ICBM attack."

"We knew that. What about a warhead?"

"No specs yet. We think they've overcome the miniaturization hurdle. We know they have low kiloton capacity from Japanese intel monitoring their underground testing. Something in the eight kiloton nuclear range."

"Again, nothing new. It seems Dr. Vincent's scenario is in play. A 'weather satellite' launch to disguise the plan for a low megaton nuclear explosion one hundred fifty miles above the U.S. The explosion would release devastating gamma rays, a crippling EMP storm knocking out all of our electronics."

"And all of our defense systems that depend on it," Rokman added.

"No margin for error. This is it."

Neither of them was grinning now. The stakes couldn't get much higher.

CHAPTER THIRTY-TWO

THE DRAGON LADY

Pusan, South Korea
Early November

"I find his odyssey highly improbable," the Dragon Lady said. She stood with her back to Jin-Ju, looking south out the window of her apartment. She gazed at the magnificent view of Gwangalli beach twenty stories below. The diamond spires of the Gwangan Bridge spanning the seaport's harbor a mile to the east glistened in the morning sunlight. She was desperately trying to control her rage.

Weekend beachgoers thronged the white sand cove despite the chilly forty-five degree autumn weather, taking advantage of a rare sunny day at this time of the year. Few ventured into the cold, churning waters of the Sea of Japan here at the southern tip of the Korean peninsula. Only a dozen or so hardy children waded and happily frolicked in the shallow waves as if it was a summer day. She envied their joy.

The Dragon Lady, also known as Madam Bae Doo, wished she could have experienced such a pleasant childhood. Raised in a harsh North Korean reeducation facility, she'd never really known happiness. When she was seven years old her family became reclassified in North Korea's songbun category of "wavering." The pitiful designation followed her father's single unfortunate remark alluding to the merits of democratic, free markets while teaching a class in economics at Pyongyang University. His ill-fated observation wasn't tolerated in their totalitarian social order, and seriously disrupted her family's life.

They became marked for life, her family status reduced by a harsh, discriminating caste system. The family suffered humiliation, going from a professional level lifestyle in a small but comfortable home to a dreary future overnight. They were assigned to a reeducation camp as punishment. Her parents died destitute, starving, and heartbroken a few years later in the Hudan Gulag, Camp 22. Meanwhile, she survived by guile and grit. Her strength and resiliency were noted at an early age by guards and reported to higher ups. These favorable traits were rewarded by her selection and transfer to an elite spy and military training camp in remote mountains near Sunchon.

After five years of intense indoctrination and preparation at the training camp, the RGB recognized her exceptional skills. They moved her to the Kumsong political-military university in Pyongyang known for special training of secret agents to run covert operations in South Korea. Following indoctrination, in her late teens, RGB infiltrated her into South Korea to spy under the tutelage of the elderly Ri Son-Sil, the legendary agent who ran the vast network of North Korean spies at that time. Noting her natural talent and figuring a female spy would be less suspect, he took the time to groom her well.

She succeeded Ri in 1986, running a tight ship until the recent fiasco appeared about to run it aground. The Dragon Lady ran the entire South Korean clandestine operation. Now she feared her tight knit covert network was at risk of coming apart at the seams.

Her daily ritual of gazing out the window at the lovely view failed to bring her tranquility today.

Jin-Ju could see that the Dragon Lady was upset. And when upset, she could be a real bitch, ready to unload on him.

"I agree, his odyssey seems improbable," Jin-Ju said, "but it's a small world. Some say only six degrees of separation between us." He spoke politely, knowing he'd still suffer her wrath.

"I'm not interested in discussing philosophical theories." She turned away from the window, fixing her gaze on him. "But, I'm glad you finally showed up. I might say you were 180 degrees out of phase for months, if you insist on that particular analogy. Why didn't you contact me sooner?" She did not smile or show any indication of being the least bit glad to see him after more than a three-month lapse in communication. He sensed her displeasure, knowing he must explain his actions, carefully outlining his rationale for not contacting her sooner.

The Dragon Lady had a reputation for being as tough as nails. She was a force to be reckoned with. Even in her late fifties, she was his superior physically and intellectually. She was woman who took no prisoners, literally or figuratively. Trained in martial arts, she could swiftly deliver a karate shot that collapsed the victim's trachea, causing asphyxia. He'd also witnessed her impressive skill with firearms and explosives, on par with the best. He knew she kept a Glock 18C in her desk drawer. Not many men could match the lethal skills of the Dragon Lady. He dared not test her. She could react like a trapped tigress to protect her territory, one that was currently threatened.

Jin-Ju hesitated, figuring out the best way to justify his absence. He glanced around her Spartan apartment, absent any hint of femininity. It reflected her ascetic personality that required only the basics in life, a life that had been unkind to her. He'd anticipated this contentious reception, in fact, dreaded it.

"I went deep dark after Kwon's exposure, Madam Bae Doo. I figured my best course of action was to go to ground, remain incommunicado. I feared Kwon may have blown my cover like he did Hwan's under enhanced interrogation. I'm certain the NIS tortured him."

"Naturally NIS worked him over and broke him. Not a monumental task in his case, I suspect," she added sarcastically. "He was a mere office spy dedicated to cyber hacking, not an experienced field operative like you. My concern was with your status, Jin-Ju. Kwon and Hwan were valuable agents, but low level compared to you, my second in command. How did I know whether or not they had captured or killed you? I received no message through any of our back channels indicating you were safe."

"Let me explain further," he said, trying to hide his anxiety. "I assumed Hwan didn't escape capture since he had strict orders to contact me in an emergency by a preset code. Too much time had lapsed to believe he fled with his communication gear and failed to get in touch with me. We presume NIS took him out a week after they broke Kwon, although we couldn't find his body. NIS apparently retrieved his computer and phones before we could get to his safe house to sanitize it. My agents checked his safe house from top to bottom and found it intact and tidy except for those missing items. No sign of a struggle or ransacking. My agents were surprised NIS posted no lookouts, no bugs, or booby traps at his safe house anticipating we'd show up once we got word of Kwon's capture."

"You don't know that for certain in this age of modern surveillance cameras and miniaturized chip technology," the Dragon Lady said. "Have you heard of micro dots? The South Koreans are very tech savvy. I'm certain they set up some form of hidden surveillance. Never mind, move on," she said impatiently. "Continue your explanation for not contacting me sooner."

He put his hands up in mock surrender, admitting she was right. No argument there. He'd forgotten about microdots. She was at the top of her game. He was not. He struggled to maintain composure.

The Dragon Lady noted Jin-Ju's embarrassment. When he raised his arms, she also noted that the small Hanji Chinese character inked on his right wrist had faded over the years. She recalled he'd confessed the tattoo had resulted from a drunken teenage fling in Hong Kong. The tattoo indicated he was born in the Year of the Snake. Tattoos were uncommon in Korea and usually associated with gangsters. She knew that Jin-Ju had a Chinese mother and North Korean father, a DPRK envoy living in Kowloon. He had been born in Hong Kong and went under the birth name of Choi Sang Kyo until he received his code name, Jin-Ju, later in life in North Korea. Tattoos were not shunned in the cosmopolitan city where he was raised. But she wondered why he'd not removed it. Why call attention to himself? Maybe it was a cover of sorts, indicating he was Chinese, not Korean?

His response broke her train of thought.

"I understand your point, Madam, but I needed to know about the status of Hwan's safe house. I took a calculated risk with my agents' search of the premises. I intended to get there before NIS. My team confirmed the absence of his computer, smart phone, and our satellite encryption phone, as I mentioned. That worried me. After that, I took all precautions to avoid discovery of me and any evidence that might lead indirectly to you."

No one in their network even knew the Dragon Lady existed, except Jin-Ju and a few generals running the operation from RGB headquarters in Pyongyang. Their South Korean organization took orders directly from Jin-Ju.

"I answer to you and am obliged to protect your identity," he continued. "Kwon and Hwan never knew about you, so they couldn't divulge your identity, and in Kwon's case, probably not mine either, unless Hwan had inadvertently let something slip."

"I'm following your line of reasoning so far," she said. "Your point is?"

"I figured if NIS broke Hwan's computer code, they might trace me to you by tracking any future communications through the compromised channels. I anticipated NIS would be closely monitoring our network communications from that point on, laying fatal traps for us as we scrambled for damage control. So I chose not to contact you over the past three months. That's why I showed up here in person today by a roundabout route. I drove all night. I took precautions to shake any possible tails. I hesitated to visit you in your bookstore for fear of someone seeing us together. Your store has been a valuable cover for you for many years; I felt there was no need to take any risk, no matter how small."

"Judicious decision," she acknowledged. The store was good cover for her as well as a steady source of income.

"I know that's not our protocol for me to show up here, but we must assess damage control together and formulate a plan for moving forward, to establish new channels and codes of communication since the Kwon-Hwan part of our network is blown."

She felt her anger recede. His good judgment was why she respected Jin-Ju and was satisfied with him as her second in command. Most of the time at least, she thought, until this situation with Hwan and Kwon.

He watched, nervous, waiting her response.

He wasn't just an ordinary hit man, and she knew she should likely cut him some slack under these circumstances. Her mood toward him lightened, but she still seethed over the recent breach of protocol in her covert network that had performed so well over the past thirty-five years. She feared a domino effect, with a toppling of lower level agents leading to Jin-Ju's discovery and ultimately to her. That must not happen. She had to probe further into the matter, test his perspective, his discretion.

"Don't you find it implausible that Kwon, a mere cyber spy," she said, "virtually chained to an office computer for the last twenty years at Samsung, could suddenly function like veteran field operative? Escaping from jail, expertly eluding a manhunt, and returning safely to Pyongyang after an uncanny encounter with one of our patrol boats?"

Jin-Ju nodded. "It's very difficult to explain, Madam."

"Kwon lacked proper training to accomplish such a feat. Think about it!" She scowled, frustrated that Jin-Ju lacked skepticism or a realistic explanation of Kwon's journey.

He shrugged. "I'm at a loss for how he pulled it off."

"Something is fishy."

She waited to see if he was insightful enough to pick up on the inconsistencies, the contrived nature of Kwon's story.

To her cynical mind, the explanation of Kwon's odyssey seemed professionally manufactured. The plot had to involve an elaborate disinformation scheme, another spy agency orchestrating a very clever ploy dedicated to bring them down. The ups and downs of her long, successful clandestine career had jaded her perspective, sharpened her intellect, and honed her survival instincts. She viewed the world through a lens of suspicion. Few things were what they seemed to be at first appraisal. First impressions could deceive you, positively or negatively. Missing either interpretation could end in disaster. She'd come close to getting burned and vowed she never would. She understood the nuance, the contrast between reality and what one perceives in the real world.

Jin-Ju watched her ruminate, wondering where was she going with this.

After squirming a few moments, searching for an explanation, he finally mustered a response.

"The strange coincidences certainly raise suspicion, Madam Bae Doo. He defied enormous odds with his escape through a chain of timely, fortuitous events. But, he survived through circumstances he could not possibly control, much less engineer. Consider the spectacular jailbreak at Andong. It appears solely a matter of fate the Korean mafia broke Cho out by blowing a hole in the jail wall. He simply lucked out escaping with other prisoners from the exercise yard."

"Your explanation strikes me more like fiction, very imaginative, but missing the point, Jin-Ju. Did it ever occur to you someone else controlled him and engineered all those uncanny events? That someone very experienced in spy craft turned Kwon and cleverly trained him as a double agent? An outside intelligence agency might have influenced and carefully stage-managed all those mysterious, if not supernatural events. Didn't it cross your mind that the 'mystique' you attribute to fate that facilitated Kwon showing up in Pyongyang was ingeniously contrived by a very smart intelligence unit?"

The Dragon Lady deplored events she could not explain. To her nothing happened by chance. Every effect must have a cause. She became livid that Jin-Ju failed to think of this subterfuge, which was so obvious to her. She expected him to be more circumspect in the art of deception.

Jin-Ju's jaw dropped at this improbable premise. Her idea seemed far-fetched to him, a wild conspiracy theory.

"Nam and the NIS are clever, but not that smart," he blurted. "And who would they conspire with?"

"There must be more to this preposterous story. Think hard about who the co-conspirator might be." She looked like a bird of prey about to pounce on him. Cheating, betrayal, and trickery defined the art of spying. He should have learned that fundamental by now.

"Someone has an end game using Kwon as a pawn. And now we are in the middle of it, whether we like it or not." Her frown deepened, the wrinkles on her weathered face more pronounced. Her exasperation was palpable; she looked about to explode.

She left the window and walked toward her desk, contemplating shooting him. The Glock had a silencer, but how would she dispose of his body? She quickly decided it wasn't a practical solution and resumed her tirade.

"The big question is … What is the end game in this ploy?"

Jin-Ju braced for an unrelenting dressing down. He had no inkling of the end game, much less the wild conspiracy theory she'd proposed. But he had enough sense to realize the Dragon Lady might be correct, envisioning the scenario of a foreign intelligence agency pulling Kwon's strings like a puppet. That idea had never occurred to him. He was no match for her intellect. She was always a step ahead, a master of conspiracy and spy craft. They may well be involved in a high-stakes game with an unknown opponent. He had no notion of the next move to make.

His shoulders slumped, his body language indicating his profound loss of face. He avoided Madam Bae Doo's glare, not daring to challenge the alpha female. She'd earned the appellation "Dragon Lady" out of respect in a country dominated by heartless, misogynous men who were impressed by her superior acumen and performance. They were forced to respect her ability in spite of her gender. While Jin-Ju was a match for most men, he was no match for her. Not wishing to further enrage her, he dared not argue and decided to take the heat.

She resumed her tirade in a quieter, professorial tone, but she was no less critical of him.

"Those involved in clandestine life should obey protocols to avoid errors, uncertainty, and failure. I thought we'd learned those basic facts of human nature from past tragic mistakes, Jin-Ju. Protocols were breached in this case. Kwon should not have attempted hacking into South Korean CENTCOM allowing NIS to trace him. That was a foolish, bold move not called for. Our covert program with him had worked well for over the past twenty years, providing a steady stream of vital foreign intelligence operating below ROK's radar. The potential reward did not justify the risk of hacking into CENTCOM."

She began to pace the room. "That event had a domino effect," she continued. "Now Kwon's gone, Hwan is dead, and you may have been exposed if NIS deciphers critical information from his computer linking him to you. This misfortune results from the unintended consequences of not following our protocols. And, if they discover you, Jin-Ju, think about it..."

She stopped pacing and glared at him. She briefly reconsidered shooting him, eliminating a potential weak link in the chain.

"They may trace me on up the chain of command," she said. "Do you realize the implications to our spy network here in South Korea?" The furrow of her brow deepened, displeasure written all over her face.

"Unfortunately, I do, Madam. I regret the breakdown. I had no idea Kwon would do something so imprudent. I accept full responsibility for my complacency as supervisor of Kwon's handler. Kwon blundered without my knowledge, but I'll take the blame for that also."

The Dragon Lady's code name had been bestowed upon her following the successful North Korean terror attack that blew up a KAL 707 en route to the 1988 Seoul Olympics, causing a huge international uproar. Acting as the handler, she set the operation up and managed the two North Korean operatives who placed the timed explosive device in an overhead compartment of the ill-fated, inbound flight 858 to Seoul. The objective was to panic travelers to the Seoul Olympics and deprive South Korea of its moment in the spotlight. The episode had led to North Korea's branding as a terrorist state and launched her notorious career as DPRK's top undercover agent, one of the world's best. She had been the top spy in South Korea for almost over forty years. A North Korean disinformation scheme successfully hid her identity for all these years. Everyone thought she was either dead or sequestered in China under an assumed identity after the KAL airliner terror attack in 1987.

Jin-Ju was her most reliable operative with a career almost rivaling hers, paying careful attention to details, performing covert activities professionally and effectively up to now. It was now clear he was less cerebral than she was, and lacked the ability to envision the big picture.

For years, she harbored resentment over his far easier path to becoming a spy. She'd arrived at her position by a far more rigorous path.

Born into the highest social tier, Jin-Ju's family's songbun designated them as "Loyal." His father was a former envoy to Hong Kong where he met his Chinese mother, both factors conferring prestige. Privilege was a relative term in impoverished North Korea. His family enjoyed it in a gated Pyongyang enclave while her family wasted away and died in a concentration camp, supposedly for reeducation, but in reality for punishment.

Jin-Ju's groomed pathway to a covert career was well planned, as he spoke three dialects of Chinese plus Japanese. He had been fast tracked along the way, all instrumented by DPRK, not attained in the hardscrabble survival mode like hers. She'd tried to get over this resentment, but it lingered.

Nevertheless he'd always been respectful and obedient to her command, knowing how she arrived at the pinnacle of DPRK's foreign operation in South Korea. She knew he admired her perseverance and knew her merits got her there.

Perhaps she was evaluating him too harshly, she decided. This was his first mismanaged operation, although it involved a serious breach. She felt she should forgive him, but compassion is not a dominant North Korean trait. Only results counted.

"I'm deeply disappointed in this breach of protocol and your lack of depth in your analysis," she said. "I fear the worst for our future operations. This will not sit well with our generals, particularly Pak. There may be hell to pay."

"I take full responsibility," he offered meekly, his spirits sinking at the rebuke.

"You may accept the blame, but nevertheless, Kwon committed a grave error leading to our current predicament. Our network may be seriously compromised beyond repair."

"I suggest we lay low for a while until we see how this pans out," he said plaintively.

"Do we have a viable alternative?"

"I suppose not."

"Of course not!"

She shifted the topic abruptly.

"General Pak notified me in a recent cryptogram that he's concerned Kwon may be a double agent, turned by NIS, but he can't prove it. I'd already arrived at that notion. Kwon passed all their tests, but the general is setting traps for him. I suspect a grand conspiracy. How else do you explain such an incredulous turn of events?"

"Respectfully, Madam," Jin-Ju said, "I submit that may be another stretch. Kwon's been lucky; he's computer smart, but no way he's a double agent. That requires a level of cleverness he lacks. He was accomplished in cyber espionage, but deficient in the cunning skill and ingenuity required in that role. Nam has a bag of tricks, but not the capacity to turn Kwon and train him."

That statement took all the courage he could muster; he feared her reaction. He was surprised she accepted his take on Kwon's limited ability without another stern rebuttal.

"Perhaps," she said. "In any case, the general is very cautious, despite the RGB vetting Kwon with an intense debriefing including a polygraph."

"Forgive me, no disrespect, but I don't share the general's concerns because I worked with this man for twenty years. Believe me, it's simply not in Kwon's character. He couldn't possibly pull it off."

"I'll hold you to that statement. I still suspect some clever meddling." She returned to her desk and sat down.

"We'll see," he said politely. "Again, I apologize, Madam Bae Doo. Incidentally, I've heard through back channels that Kwon's working in RGB's command and control system headquarters in Pyongyang."

"Another big surprise," she said. "Is there no end to his mystery? Care to divulge your source of this information?" she added sarcastically.

"One of my agents just back from Pyongyang informed me two days ago that Kwon arranged delivery of the latest cybersecurity equipment last month from Singapore and Kuala Lumpur."

"How'd that deal come about?"

"Kwon arranged the transaction through his Samsung connections in Southeast Asia to update their programs. Why would he do that for them if he's not one of ours?"

The Dragon Lady shook her head. "The annals of spy craft are full of stories of deceit, disinformation, and betrayal, Jin-Ju. In our line of work there is no such thing as random events. I'll reserve my judgment whether or not Kwon is a very clever double agent, but I find it inconceivable that his story can be attributed to serendipity. This episode has CIA's fingerprints all over it."

Chapter Thirty-Three

SHARING INTEL

"**S**o what do we know about this Jin-Ju?" the senior U.S. intel officer, Colonel Scott, asked. He sat with the NIS Director in Nam's office.

"His name popped up several times on Hwan's computer," the NIS Director answered. "Took a while, but our forensics department has partially deciphered his hard drive and gleaned some key tidbits about him."

"Hwan's computer? Refresh my memory, Director."

"Hwan was Kwon's handler."

"Okay, got it, the spy you tracked from information you pieced together from Kwon's interrogation. The guy you eliminated?"

"Yes, that same spy, Hwan, the guy running Kwon," Nam said, ignoring Colonel Scott's inference about Hwan being "eliminated."

"We raided his safe house and retrieved all of his personal communication gear," Nam continued. "We left his TV and lights on, making it look like he took off in a hurry taking only his basic communication equipment. It's standard procedure to go to ground to protect the network. We figured he'd go deep dark, fearing Kwon might expose him, so we closed in fast, captured him and his equipment before he could take off running. By making him vanish, we hoped to create confusion about whether he was hiding out incommunicado, captured, or dead. We bugged his house with microdots rather than manning a stakeout or employing listening devices. We planned to closely monitor Hwan's incoming communications to uncover other agents in his DPRK network, maybe catch some bigger fish in the pond."

"Good moves, but let's talk about Jin-Ju. Where does the suspected 'bigger fish' fit in? You may be on to something."

"Our technicians went over Hwan's gear with a fine-tooth comb. The code was tricky, but our techs figured a partial pattern from prior North Korean decipher experience. My techs are still trying to figure out the device encryption. The limited information they retrieved indicated Hwan answered to someone named Jin-Ju, but revealed no specifics to indicate the location of his operation, or his precise position in the hierarchy of the DPRK espionage network here in South Korea. We extrapolated from the sparse intelligence we gathered that Jin-Ju ranked much higher than Hwan in the network, but forensics could not retrieve definitive details to document that assumption, clues that would enable us to trace him or higher ups, except for one oblique reference to the 'Dragon Lady.'"

"Dragon Lady?" Colonel Scott said. "Sounds like a character in a spy novel."

"My first impression also. However, decades ago a person with that code name existed, but it's thought she's dead or living in China under cover. Real life is often stranger than fiction."

"The reference on Hwan's hard drive infers she runs the show from a bookstore," Nam added.

"A bookstore? Here or North Korea? China? Where?"

"No clue yet, still delving into that interesting link based on Hwan's allusions to her role. We don't know how big her tent is, the number of players. As I mentioned, we left microdots to stake out Hwan's safe house. We figured a stakeout would spook them."

Colonel Scott nodded. "Good move."

"We also are monitoring the communication channels on his equipment we recovered. We hope to uncover any of their agents that might visit the premises or attempt to contact him. That may add pieces to the puzzle, and create some additional leads.

"As I said," Nam continued, "we weren't able to crack all of their covert system's intricate setup, unfortunately. Their ciphers are improving. That means it will take more time to decode the hard drive's encryption. These North Korean spies are clever at covering their tracks, changing codes and contact tactics frequently."

"Cell or satellite phone links checked out?"

"Both, they use encryption on their cell phones that hide call connections to mobile phone towers. That prevents us from locating the connection and bread-crumbing past GPS signals."

"So how'd you catch Kwon? Overcome those obstacles?" Colonel Scott asked.

"Kwon just screwed up by not following protocol. He tried to hack into ROK CENTCOM, that's how we caught him. He operated for twenty years right under our noses at Samsung's security systems. One slip up doomed him. We lucked out."

"But it seems you've hit a wall in tracking this guy, Jin-Ju."

"Maybe we have, maybe not. Just by chance, one of our alert Internet techs discovered an interesting correlation with Jin-Ju's cell phone number, linking it to another dramatic incident that occurred last spring. A connection you'd be very interested in pursuing since it involves a high-ranking American in an alarming encounter I'm certain you'll recall. That's why I invited you over for a chat. The rest I told you was just background information."

"And, that is?"

"We linked Jin-Ju's name to Park Hyo Wook."

"Who the hell is he?"

"Park is, or was, the street gangster who led the assassination squad that attacked our NIS limo last May outside the U.S. embassy and attempted to assassinate Biff Roberts."

"There's no way I could ever forget that stunning incident. But how's the assassination attempt tie in? What's Jin-Ju's connection to the gangster?"

"We recovered the street gang leader's cell phone on his dead body during the investigation of the shootout scene. Fortunately, it was not encrypted like Hwan's, enabling us to trace incoming and outgoing calls as well as GPS locations. Forensics cross referenced information and numbers from Park's phone, and compared them with Jin-Ju's phone numbers and computer information we'd deciphered months ago containing Jin-Ju's contacts."

"That involves a lot of man hours, labor intensive."

"Not really. We run a computerized software program for retrieving, tracing, and correlating information in cases like this. So here's the bottom line. Coincidentally the phone numbers showed the hit man received two calls from Jin-Ju the day prior to the attempted assassination. The time sequence of the calls matched perfectly when we correlated the incoming and outgoing calls between them. Seems it was a rush job. It became apparent Jin-Ju organized the hit on short notice targeting Roberts. We believe Jin-Ju was the intermediary in the plot, setting it up from the get go."

"Interesting, I'm sure there's more to the story."

"There is," Nam said, nodding. "Jin-Ju must be high up in the organization for that assignment."

"Hmm … Now that's really a sensational revelation. But why would the North Koreans want to knock off Biff Roberts?" Colonel Scott leaned back in the plush leather chair, pondering the alarming implications of this revelation, one with enormous repercussions. Could there be a connection between those two bad guys?

"Obviously DPRK was doing the Iranian Revolutionary Guards a big favor, carrying out a contract hit job on Roberts," Nam said, getting right to the point. "Sound logical?"

Nam had no difficulty with the conspiracy theory. In contrast, the colonel appeared flabbergasted, absorbing this shocking news. But he quickly realized Nam had hit the nail on the head. Why didn't he immediately perceive that link?

"I believe you're right, Director. Iran's been assisting their nuclear ballistic program. Why not reciprocate by giving them a hand in their *fatwa*? I congratulate you, great detective work by your forensics department."

"Thank you. Evil minds like those two think alike. Never underestimate our enemies."

"But tell me, how did they know Roberts was here? Any ideas how we can snare this spy, Jin-Ju, and squeeze him to find out the connection? Maybe lead us to snaring the Dragon Lady?"

"Not at this point; that's a tall order. We suspect a mole, maybe two or more. We're investigating. Perhaps you could alert your military intelligence unit to the connection and notify Director Roberts to have the CIA check out the leads, consider the possible collaboration between the two enemies. We need to delve deeper into why they would join forces to kill him. We should coordinate our intelligence and investigation of this matter. We share a mutual interest."

"You'll have our full cooperation. I appreciate your bringing me into the loop."

Colonel Scott stood to go. Nam signaled him not to rush off.

"One other thing, Colonel, before you leave. You raised the question of how DPRK knew Roberts was visiting us. That's a pivotal question. After the attack, both Roberts and I suspected a mole in your embassy and possibly one here in NIS who tipped them off. Someone who knew the Americans' plans, someone who relayed the precise time our NIS limo boarded Roberts and his staff outside the embassy. The attack was too well coordinated to explain it otherwise. Although we think, and hope, that they didn't discover the primary reason for his visit. To have full knowledge of his visit's purpose, the EMP threat, would implicate a high-ranking mole with insider access to sensitive classified information. So far there's no indication of that compromising circumstance."

"I understand your concerns. So, how did you detect the mole?"

"Once again by associating and correlating phone calls and GPS locations to the hit man's cell phone. Park's cell led us to the critical connection. As I mentioned, his phone was not encrypted. Park received a call ten minutes prior to our limo's departure from your embassy and the surprise attack. The GPS signal indicated the call originated from inside the U.S. embassy lobby. We checked the log, at that time only three guards and a janitor were present in the lobby. We checked all their cell phones. The janitor's number matched with Park's incoming call, tipping him off they were leaving the embassy grounds. We arrested the janitor, and he talked. He said DPRK paid him handsomely to keep a close eye on the American visitor's moves. He didn't know Roberts' position or the purpose of his visit, nothing classified, just that he was an American target to keep an eye on. He confessed to his role as a spotter in the assassination attempt."

"Confessed?"

"With a little persuasion." The NIS director gave an innocent smile and shrugged.

**

CIA Headquarters – Langley

"Colonel Scott's holding on a secure line, calling from Seoul, sir," the captain told Biff. "Says it's important, must speak directly with you."

"Got it, Captain," Biff said. Whatever the colonel had to tell him, it must be really important to call at this hour. It was late in the day in Seoul.

"Hello, Colonel," Biff said as he leaned back in his chair. "What's up?"

Colonel Scott proceeded to update Biff on the most recent developments in South Korea. Biff was shocked to learn that the mole Nam had nabbed was a janitor in the U.S. embassy. For a second he wondered if Colonel Scott wasn't putting him on, but he knew that wasn't the colonel's style.

When Colonel Scott continued to tell him that the janitor had confessed under torture that North Korea paid him to act as a lookout, the colonel made it clear he was concerned about Nam's methods.

"Yes, I understand your concern," Biff said, "but Nam plays hardball. It's just his unconstrained style of interrogation."

"I think he gets a kick out of," Colonel Scott said, his disdain clear through the phone.

"He's not a whack job," Biff said. "The man gets outstanding results. That's what makes big-leaguers, big-leaguers." Biff sighed. "Look, I know it's a touchy subject, but let it go. Nam doesn't give a rat's ass about a janitor when it comes to protecting national security. It's not our problem."

Colonel Scott was silent for a moment, likely deliberating whether he would let the subject go. Fortunately, he did.

"Nam's tracking a possible mole in NIS also," the colonel told Biff. "No details yet, but they're setting a trap for six possible suspects."

"Good," Biff said, nodding. "I suspected that."

"Nam also discovered a reference to a higher command structure of North Korean spies in ROK," Colonel Scott said. "It involves a guy named Jin-Ju. Nam suspects he's a well-placed spy in a legitimate enterprise, the disguise giving him access to classified material."

"A classic tactic," Biff said, "having a spook placed in a high station, above suspicion, maybe embedded in an OGA."

"Exactly what Nam said," the colonel replied. "Nam's forensic crew also found a reference to a 'Dragon Lady'. He suspects she may be running the show, possibly operating from a bookstore somewhere."

"A bookstore?" Biff said.

"Yes, and we think this guy Jin-Ju may be her second in command."

"Is his name spelled like it sounds?" Biff asked. He leaned forward and jotted it down on a pad of paper.

Biff listened carefully as the colonel shared more details. It was clear they couldn't verify this Jin-Ju was the top dog, but they suspected he was high up the DPRK food chain answering operationally to the Dragon Lady. Neither character was on the colonel's military intel radar. He'd apparently already checked that out and found no trace of him or her in their current military spy database in ROK.

"Maybe NSA should run a background check," the colonel suggested.

Biff nodded. "Good idea, Colonel."

"So far it's a dead end street," the colonel said.

"We'll check old NSA archives."

"You might want to go way back," Colonel Scott said. "We're also having trouble breaking the encryption on Hwan's hard drive."

"We can try to help with that."

The colonel paused before adding, "There's something else. A tie-in to the assassination attempt on you last May."

"You're kidding."

"Nam's forensic department in NIS correlated Jin-Ju's cell phone numbers to this gangbanger, Park Wook, who attacked you.

"So this Jin-Ju, which is probably just a code name," the colonel said, "we think Jin-Ju orchestrated the Seoul hit job on you and your staff last May. Forensics correlated his calls with Park setting it up, and NIS linked the mole to the lobby janitor in our Seoul embassy. We think it was a contract job to return the Revolutionary Guards a favor."

"Based on what evidence?" Biff asked.

"We've traced a record of calls exchanged between Tehran, Pyongyang, and Jin-Ju in same time frame. It's circumstantial, but highly suggestive evidence."

"Let me tell you," Biff said, "it doesn't surprise me. That premise is so far out that I believe it! They're conspiratorial bastards." After last year's assassination attempt while he was skiing in Italy, Biff wouldn't put anything past them. They would apparently try to carry out the mullahs' *fatwa* on him anywhere, anytime.

As they wrapped up their conversation, Biff thanked the colonel for his effort to keep him in the loop. Biff promised to get the CIA and NSA investigating the leads, skimpy as they were, and help with deciphering Hwan's hard drive.

"And give my regards to Nam and his forensics department," Biff added. "Tell 'em they did a great job, appreciate it. Hope the canary trap traces the NIS mole. Thanks for the call."

After the call, Biff sat at his desk contemplating the implications of the information Colonel Scott had shared. He stared at the family photos on his desk, regrouping his emotions over the persistent attempts on his life. The *fatwa* just would not go away; it always seemed to be hanging over him like a dark, ominous cloud about to deliver a thunderbolt. He tried to escape the inescapable, the entanglement of his personal involvement in the international plot involving Iran and North Korea in their quest to develop and deliver a nuclear EMP bomb to cripple America in a surprise modern day 'Pearl Harbor' attack. It seemed the Revolutionary Guards threw in the mullahs' *fatwa* on him as a twisted reminder they were tracking him to the ends of the earth, involving DPRK just to complicate matters. He had gone to Seoul to deal with the imminent North Korean threat, not Iran's obsessive, adventurous attempt to kill him.

Whether he liked it or not, he was deeply involved in a high-stakes game of chess involving shrewd enemy clandestine agencies with formidable adversaries. It was a contest he must win.

He thought about his next counter move. He'd already had infiltrated a pawn into North Korea. Kwon now functioned as a double agent. They were close to a two-move, Fool's Mate—a task Colonel Scott claimed impossible, but that pawn now posed a valuable preemptive stopgap to DPRK's imminent threat. NSA had also added another cagey backup move by penetrating RGB's cybersecurity system with the malware program through Kwon. Kwon was inside and operational, but they had insurance built into their plan. The Heart Bleed virus was already feeding them targeted intelligence from North Korean military and security computers. It was just a matter of time to obtain the critical intelligence they sought. Biff's next move must lead to a checkmate, game over. He pondered the strategy. The pressure was on.

CHAPTER THIRTY-FOUR

NSA ARCHIVES

Langley, the next day

"**D**oes KAL Flight 858 ring a bell?" Rokman asked.

Biff shook his head. "Not right off."

They were seated at the conference table in Biff's office. Rokman had called Biff early that morning to arrange the meeting, saying he had updated info on his archive search at NSA.

"Would the date 29 November, 1987 refresh your memory?" Rokman said. "A sensational world event occurred that day involving that particular Korean airline flight."

"Given that time frame, it rings a loud bell," Biff said. "That event caused an international ruckus. Two North Korean agents time-bombed an inbound flight to Seoul Olympics filled with South Koreans. They'd been working in Germany and Baghdad, and were returning home on that date. The agents committed the heinous act to intimidate visitors to South Korea planning to attend the games." The episode had led to labeling North Korea a state sponsor of terrorism. The act of terror was on the news everywhere for days on end. Biff had been in Central America fighting communist insurgents at the time, and the event had even made headlines there.

"Right on target, Biff, the sabotage killed all 115 aboard." Rokman opened his laptop and brought up a file.

"So how's this nasty bombing of KAL 858 tie in with your research yesterday?" Biff asked. "Connect any dots to Jin-Ju and the Dragon Lady?" Biff knew there must be a connection, since Rokman brought up the episode. "Fill me in."

"Very intuitive," Rokman said. "I couldn't tie it in with Jin-Ju, but the Dragon Lady is implicated as the mastermind of the KAL plot. Our records indicate she handled the two North Korean agents involved, Kim Hyun-Hee and Kim Sun-Il."

"Related?"

"No relation between them. Kim's a common surname over there." Rokman glanced at the document on his screen. "They traveled as father and daughter under the name Hachiya on fake Japanese passports. The big difference in age lent credence to the ruse."

"Interesting, please brief me on the details."

"The two agents travelled to Europe and the Middle East on forged documents. Pyongyang to Moscow to Budapest to Vienna to Abu Dhabi. Both were fluent in Japanese and well trained in espionage, pulling off the father-daughter guise well, posing as Japanese tourists. The female spy, Hyun-Hee, twenty-three, traveled under the name Myumi Hachiya. She was young, Sun-Il's protégé. She followed the sixty-seven-year-old man's orders. Sun-Il was a legendary spy experienced in subterfuge. Well known to ROK intelligence. He also assumed the same surname, Hachiya, of course. He knew the game, called the shots. He coordinated the operations with European assets and agents, aiding the plot along the circuitous route. It appears each step was carefully orchestrated."

"Got the picture," Biff said. "I'm starting to recall some of this, their attention to details. Sun-Il was a smooth operator."

"They took roundabout routes to carry out the scheme, arriving in Abu Dhabi with the ostensive purpose to catch the second leg of KAL 858 from Baghdad. They'd reserved seats well ahead of time. But their sole objective was to plant the time bomb on the plane, and not take the flight to Bangkok, then on to Seoul."

Rokman turned his laptop around so Biff could see a graphic of the explosive device believed to have been used.

"Disguised inside a Panasonic transistor radio," Rokman continued, "the device was rigged with plastic explosives, a detonator, and a timer. They placed it in an overhead bin of their reserved seats, 7B and C of KAL 858, when they boarded in Abu Dhabi. A liquid explosive disguised in a liquor bottle contained in a duty-free bag was placed next to the radio to increase the explosive impact."

"Not big on screening in those days obviously."

"Lax security, especially in the Middle East back then, terrorism hadn't kicked in like today," Rokman said, nodding. "But back to my story ... the North Korean agents arrived from Belgrade via Vienna to Abu Dhabi on Austrian Air to connect with this KAL flight. They'd obtained the radio bomb device from other agents in Belgrade. As I said, planning well ahead, they'd reserved seats on KAL flight 858 in Abu Dhabi, allowing them time to plant the device in the overhead. But they both deplaned the Boeing 707 without anyone noticing before it took off on its second leg to Thailand, full of South Koreans, businessmen, and tourists."

Biff frowned. "Deplaning? Isn't that unusual?"

"At that time, evidently not, fifteen got off. The records showed two of them traveled under Japanese passports, one fake. After the 707 exploded nine hours into the flight, over the Andaman Sea west of Burma en route to Bangkok, authorities sent out an alert, suspecting sabotage."

"Too little, too late."

"The North Korean agents caught another flight to Bahrain three hours later."

"Devious plot," Biff said. "Before the days of suicide bombers, they chickened out."

"Got that right, but they were atheists, not fervent Islamists who believe they are awarded in heaven for suicide bombing."

"Good point."

"Things went south for them in Bahrain," Rokman continued. "Authorities there got the Abu Dhabi memo, and they were arrested for carrying fake passports. The male, Sun-Il, bit into a cigarette containing an ampoule of cyanide to avoid harsh interrogation and died on the spot. The young woman, Kim Hyun-Hee, tried the same suicide maneuver, but an alert Bahraini agent snatched away the cigarette before she could swallow a lethal dose of the cyanide. She was treated for poisoning, and in a coma for three days in a hospital there, but she recovered. They extradited her to Seoul for prosecution."

"Some story. First generation airline terrorists on a designed North Korean mission to terrorize foreigners from visiting the Seoul Olympics."

"Correct, that was their main objective, to introduce fear into travel to Seoul. North Korea aimed to rob the South of international acclaim for hosting an Olympics."

"Didn't work out that way."

"Correct. But, it gets more interesting, Biff. South Korean intelligence managed to turn her while she awaited a death sentence. They used her for a propaganda campaign, turning the tables on DPRK. She was given a reprieve and is living in protective custody under an assumed name somewhere in ROK. She was an impressionable twenty-three-year-old back then, brainwashed about life in South Korea, indoctrinated in a strict DPRK mindset. NIS showed her around, treated her nicely, and convinced her otherwise. She became more valuable to them alive as a propaganda tool. Given a second lease on life, she performed well for them."

"So she's in her early fifties now?" Biff asked. "Are you thinking what I'm thinking?"

Rokman smiled. "As a matter of fact, I am."

CHAPTER THIRTY-FIVE

QUICK TRIP

Langley

The same day in mid-November

Later that day, Biff called his bodyguard. "Tim, tell my pilots to tank up the G-550 to capacity with G-8."

"Where we going, boss?"

"We're making a nonstop trip to Seoul with our cipher whiz, Rokman, to sort out a problem that's cropped up over there. Pack your bag, we've got a fire to put out, need to move out quickly. Also, round up Tyler. Tell him we're shooting for wheels in the well at 1600 at Andrews. Call Gunderson, our Embassy station manager there, to set up our security and BOQ arrangements, give him a heads up to set up our DIPSEC."

"That's six hours from now, check," Tim calmly replied. "I'll take care of it, Biff. I'll notify Gunner and Tyler right away. I assume Rokman's with you and knows your plan so it's not necessary for me to contact him? Confirm it's just the four of us."

"Right, Rokman's with me, we're discussing our plans right now. It's just the four of us making the trip. The reason we've got to hustle is we're dealing with Pacific time zone changes. If we're in the air six hours from now, we'll arrive in South Korea around 0600 their time tomorrow. We can eat and sleep on the jet. That will give us a full day to get things rolling. We'll gain almost a day across the international dateline. I'll contact Nam myself regarding arranging a brainstorming session at NIS. Got some big problems to solve."

***

NIS Headquarters, Seoul – Noon, the same day

"Sorry to interrupt your lunch, Director," Kim said, "but a crypto-gram just arrived from Langley, sounds urgent. I took the liberty of having it decrypted since I know that's not your bag."

"Not a problem, Kim." Nam had expected to hear from Roberts soon after Colonel Scott relayed his message to him. Nam took the message and thanked Kim. Kim nodded and left the office, shutting the door behind him.

He appreciated his assistant director's courtesy, especially having the NIS code unit decipher the CIA transmission with their NIS key to the Langley encryption. Nam kept a carefully guarded Fortezza crypto card under lock and key, but complicated coding and ciphers weren't "his bag," just as his deputy said. Nam smiled at Kim's use of the American collo-quial phrase, one of the few he recognized. Kim used a lot of American expressions he'd picked up while studying at UCLA.

Encryption was not Nam's field of interest, and his skills were in strategic planning and keeping a close eye on North Korea. Kim and the younger agents were hotshots at ciphers. Even if Nam lagged behind in that category, he excelled in eliminating threats to national security.

The Director of the ROK intelligence service, an agency patterned after the CIA, read the decoded communiqué from the CIA Director of Counterterrorism. The message was permeated with code words despite being sent encrypted. Roberts took no chances in communications. Like Nam he was "old school" in that regard.

< NAM - WE PLAN TO DEPART ANDREWS AT 1600. ETA 0600 YOUR TIME/ BRINGING ROKMAN AND SMALL STAFF TO TACKLE ENCRYPTION PROBLEMS. SERIOUS TRAFFIC ANALYSIS REQUIRED / NEED TO TRAP SOME MOLES / TRACE BIRDWATCHERS' GRAY MAIL / PRIORITY-TRACKING DOWN D.L. – SUSPECT SHE'S A SLEEPER WITH IMPRESSIVE LEGEND / YOU ARE COMPROMISED. NEED TO PUT OUT SOME FIRES ASAP / GUNNER WILL PICK US UP AT GIMPO INTERNATIONAL. PLAN TO STAY AT STATION. – BCR V >

"DL? Really?" Nam said. "*Guseju*! Oh my God!"

If Roberts was referring to who Nam thought he was, they'd be chasing the ultimate deep dark sleeper, a North Korean covert agent lost in time and space—the Dragon Lady.

Nam frowned. But how could you trace a forty-year legend without a starting point? For decades she'd been believed to be either dead or sequestered in China. Not one verifiable espionage factor to deal with, just clues, nothing substantial. There was no confirmation of the oblique "bookstore" mention discovered on Hwan's computer. Would they be chasing a ghost?

Roberts must have something up his sleeve to arrange such a hasty visit. Probably intended to help Nam get his "ducks in a row," he thought and smiled. Nam had come to like the man's dynamic personality. Not disposed to Asian reserve and protocol, Roberts came right to the point. No "beating about the bushes," as Kim had characterized Roberts.

Nam had learned that catchy "ducks in a row" phrase when Roberts last visited. It aptly described the present circumstances bedeviling the NIS. His intelligence agency could use CIA assistance in tracking the suspected mole in their midst, and in ferreting out North Korean clandestine cells residing in ROK. Foreign agents critically positioned, like Jin-Ju, could torpedo their intricate plans, conceivably discover their carefully crafted Kwon deception, blow his cover and the entire operation.

Though it came as a surprise that Roberts seriously suspected the Dragon Lady's existence. Everyone else considered her a specter from the past, a long gone character of historical interest only as the notorious ringleader who engineered the infamous '87 KAL terror attack. She had been off the NIS grid for well over three decades, a glacial age in the espionage game. No one could remain deep dark that long.

NIS forensics had hit a dead end in deciphering Hwan's computer hard drive. They needed the definitive information suspected to be contained on that drive. A lot was riding on its discovery. What was Hwan's connection to Jin-Ju? And what was Jin-Ju's relationship to the Dragon Lady? All they knew for certain at this point was that Hwan skillfully managed Kwon for twenty years without an instance of personal contact. The North Korean handler defined covert in his performance.

In retrospect, Nam fretted that maybe NIS should not have eliminated Hwan. But welcome help was about to arrive. He sighed, feeling the stress. He was reacting to events, not controlling them, an unfamiliar role.

But Nam knew the unknown information buried deep on Hwan's computer disk was required to get his ducks in a row.

* * *

Late afternoon the next day
NIS Headquarters, Seoul

"I've spent all day with your computer forensics experts reviewing their deciphering methods," Rokman said, "and I've examined their limited findings contained on Hwan's computer hard drive you recovered. Here's my take, Director, preliminary, of course, just an overview accompanied with a few assumptions and educated guesses."

Nam, Kim, and Biff sat with Rokman in the SNIF conference room just outside of Nam's office. Rokman had their full attention.

"Of course, we appreciate your input," Director Nam politely responded. "Please share your thoughts and recommendations with us."

"It's technical," Rokman said, "a lot of geek IT jargon, but I'll try to keep it simple."

"We would appreciate that." Nam was an old school 'cloak and dagger' intelligence officer, not up to speed in the fast moving developments in cyber technology, the new wave in espionage. His strengths lay elsewhere.

"It appears that Hwan used two different encryption systems," Rokman began, "one program for simple communications, another for transmitting classified intelligence using a more complex system of encryption. Your forensics unit broke the simpler code for the first system but failed to decipher the complicated second encryption program containing classified information, intel critical to your pursuit of the spies."

"Classic slips of tongue decoded on the simple communications explain how you retrieved tidbits of tantalizing information," he continued, "like the oblique mention of Jin-Ju and reference to the Dragon Lady, but not supplying enough information to form the big picture, to connect the dots. Without deciphering the second program, your forensics unit failed to retrieve any definitive or specific details hidden in the encryption on the hard drive. Once that's deciphered, you'll have a record of Hwan's spy activity, his connection to Jin-Ju, his assumed case officer, and possibly you'll retrieve file data linking Jin-Ju to the Dragon Lady. But at this point, you lack actionable intelligence. With no leads to follow, you've reached an impasse."

"Interesting," Nam responded, "please elaborate."

"In the first case, Hwan used a random substitution encryption which provides excellent security for general communiqués between spies. It's simple and reliable, breaking the message into four-byte blocks. Your techs discovered Hwan added pseudorandom numbers to each block. It's a clever technique that requires the person receiving the encrypted message to backtrack through the same series of pseudorandom numbers from the cipher text to recover the plain text—the message the sender wishes to convey."

"I see," Nam commented.

Biff wondered if Nam really understood. But Rokman continued his dissertation assuming Nam was following him, attempting to "keep it simple."

"Overall, it was nice work by your techs. This program will defeat all but the most skilled and determined hackers. When we catch one this good, we recruit him for NSA rather than send him to jail. However, your forensics team just revealed the tip of the iceberg by deciphering the simple communication code. The second series of algorithm encryptions on Hwan's hard drive stymied them, with good reason."

"How's that?" Biff asked, fascinated with Rokman's skill with cyber codes and ciphers, and his flair for anything that involved a computer. Biff saw Nam and Kim were taking notes on their iPads, appreciating the expert instruction by his NSA super geek. "Rokman nuggets," they called them at Langley.

NIS had hit the wall in their investigation, and Biff knew Rokman would bail them out, breaking the code by sharing his vast experience and NSA expertise. Otherwise, there was no good reason to fly seven thousand miles for hands-on consultation with NIS. Face to face discussion allowed give and take, Q and A exchanges, and formation of a cogent game plan.

Rokman continued his briefing to his attentive audience.

"In the second case it appears the North Korean agents communicated using a DES or AES symmetric cryptogram for classified messaging. This system provides a high level of security using complex blocks of cyber text with sequences of arithmetic operations and/or substitutions. It's called symmetrical because following the same algorithm sequence, the recipient converts the cyber text into plain text. This system was secure until the development of supercomputers or Beowulf clusters, high performance parallel computing.

"It appears the North Koreans used an older program. AES has largely replaced DES by using larger keys, 128 to 256 bits. My gut feeling is they've not advanced that far technically. My bet is they may be using the Japanese Camellia cipher as an alternative to AES. The program is popular in Asia, relatively easy to learn. This encryption has one security weakness—both sender and receiver must share this key and keep it a secret from everybody else. Discover one, find the other. Got the picture?"

"So what do we do next?" Nam sounded uncharacteristically nervous, Biff noted. Clearly, Nam needed a way out of this dilemma, sooner rather than later. National security was at stake.

"Here's my recommendation," Rokman said. "Let me shadow scan the disk and send it to my Fort Meade colleagues at NSA for supercomputer analysis of the encryption algorithm."

Nam frowned. "Shadow scan?"

"It's an efficient and cost-effective forensic tool developed by SnapCopy to examine file differences, eliminating hours or days of man hour analysis. Let's say your suspect tries to hide his tracks by changing or deleting a file. The Shadow Scanner will quickly recover those changed or deleted files on the disk. It has a 64-bit app, so it's a good tool for DES or AES cryptograms, moment-in-time snapshots of files on a computer. Shadows are created anytime the restore point is triggered. Nothing's lost in cyber space, it's all retrievable."

"You have our permission," Nam said. "When can we anticipate some answers?"

"All disk encryption programs seem to contain a security hole. Perhaps we'll find a backdoor, maybe hit upon another software or hardware vulnerability in their cipher program to exploit that speeds up the process. Or discover other possibilities to link the spies. For example, reverse engineering that may lead to Jin-Ju's digital signature, presenting a potential lead to track him, and possibly reveal any communications between him and your mole. If it's a symmetrical encryption, the supercomputer should break it in forty-eight to seventy-two hours. If it's an asymmetrical encryption, it becomes more complicated, but NSA has workarounds for that eventuality. Don't worry; we'll have an answer soon."

"You lost me on that last bit, too technical," Nam said. "Please break it down into simpler terms."

"Sorry," Rokman answered. "Let me summarize … We always go after temp files first. We have Hwan's encrypted files on his computer so we can scan his computer for any signatures of the program that the person used to encrypt the program's message. Encryption is not done by hand, that's what software programs are for. So Hwan's computer has to have an app of some type on it. And that program will leave breadcrumbs on the computer that you can search for and trace. That quickly narrows down which app, which encryption was used. When it comes to tracking encryption, it's wise to go after the guy who wrote it, the North Korean cryptographer."

"Why is that?" Nam asked, starting to get it.

"Why?" Rokman said. "Because the guy who wrote the program has the backdoor. Most encryption programs have a distinctive style to them. This enables you to back track to the creator of the cipher. This is a shortcut that our supercomputer will decipher. We'll know a whole lot more in a few days, Director."

"We'll help you get your ducks in a row, Director," Biff added, grinning. "Don't worry."

There he goes again, Nam reflected.

Chapter Thirty-Six

CANARY TRAP

NIS-3

One week later

"It's difficult to believe it's her," Nam said. "Minsuh has been with us fifteen years. There must be some mistake, Kim. She has a top-secret clearance, has been exceedingly well vetted. I've never questioned her loyalty."

Kim wasn't surprised to see that Nam was clearly shaken by the revelation that his private secretary was the mole inside NIS. Kim had been just as shocked when he'd first realized it was Minsuh.

"Are you certain of this?" Nam added. "Possess ironclad evidence of her treachery? This is a very serious charge."

"I know it's difficult to accept, Director. Lee Minsuh would be last on my list of suspects, but we set traps for those with access to knowledge that Biff Roberts was here last May, someone in a position to tip off Jin-Ju, enabling him to set up the hit job on the CIA director. We narrowed the suspects to six, and we've been closely monitoring them in a sting operation, a canary trap."

Nam frowned, clearly not wanting to believe the news. "How did you conclude she was the mole?"

"She was in the office when Roberts and his staff first arrived, had the most exposure to him, and overheard our conversation before we went into the sensitive compartmental information facility to discuss highly classified intelligence." Kim paused. "Since she and the others were not allowed in the SCIF, I am certain that our detailed discussion of the North Korean EMP threat remains secure."

"I certainly hope so," Director Nam commented. "If not, we're in for a huge disappointment, to put it mildly. But, get back to my question."

"I understand the dire implications of a leak of that nature, sir. Let me explain the situation further, and you'll follow my line of reasoning in bagging her. Over three months ago, we set traps for her and the five others, but nothing happened to implicate anyone during that time period. So we set up another deception to snare anyone privy to Roberts' planned arrival on this trip, figuring they wouldn't miss the opportunity to pass on that bit of private information. We gave different versions of sensitive details of his trip to each suspected leaker to see which version got leaked."

Nam nodded approvingly. "A classic canary trap, MI6 would be proud of your plan." It was an old bit of spy craft, popularized in Clancy novels, but highly effective. His deputy was on the ball.

"Thank you, sir. The other five were cleared, not her. She's clever, but we nabbed her this time. She obviously leaks information sparingly, not even on a monthly basis. Only divulges information when something big is brewing, like the CIA's CT Director's present visit."

"And?"

"Look at this, Director," Kim said, handing him a transcript.

<JOE-HE'S BACK>

"You got this off her computer? An intercept?"

"Yes, we hacked the message she emailed to a deep cover agent. I suspect 'Joe' is code for Jin-Ju, the block cutout for the North Korean spy network operating in ROK. She's the letterbox, a chain cutout, merely a courier to pass information—a mole, not an operative. That's my theory at this point. She sent the message to a Dropbox address."

"Dropbox?"

"A computer site on the cloud to maintain privacy, store data, park information, you know, a cyberspace location, suited for modern spy stuff not requiring cryptography."

"I don't know," Nam admitted, "but go on."

"The method does not necessarily provide high security to prevent tracing, however it acts as an effective interface. She posts the message there. Joe picks it up. It's a simple, convenient form of communication between them. The transaction is not shrouded in secrecy, so it's counterintuitive that someone would suspect a nefarious motive, think to look for it there."

"Interesting concept, perhaps that's the case. I agree, she's just an asset, not an agent, so she keeps it simple, no cryptograms. So you're telling me you've tapped into her computer?"

"Yes, hers and the other five suspects are hacked, being monitored."

"Think she's wise to this maneuver? Suspect we're watching her?"

"Doubt it. Shall I arrest her for treason before she does any more damage?"

Nam contemplated Kim's question at length. Which course of action should he pursue? He considered the risks and benefits involved in managing her case. This dilemma was sticky, personal. He decided to take a pragmatic approach.

"I think we have other options, solutions more practical in nature, Kim. If we arrest her and put her on trial for treason, we risk a graymail defense exposing our sources and methods. And, we'd be subjected to bad publicity, worst case scenario, alerting our adversaries we're on to them, sending them to ground." Nam paused. "After consideration, I favor either a forced disappearance—have her simply vanish from public view without a trace—or confronting her with the incriminating evidence and convince her to participate in a honeypot operation rather than face elimination. That should be an easy choice."

"She's an attractive woman," Kim said, nodding. "I'm sure she'd choose to cooperate in trying to lure Jin-Ju, her Joe, to a meeting, enabling us to capture him. After working here fifteen years, she understands the implications of a forced disappearance, Director. Doubt she'd go that route."

"Surely she'll recognize we've caught her red-handed and will seek a way out. We'll offer her one she can't refuse. When confronted, I'm certain she'll cooperate. She's a one-dimensional asset, not an operative willing to die spying for North Korea. I assume she has limited knowledge of their network, so nothing would be gained by enhanced interrogation. You said she just passes snippets of information right under our nose to some cyberspace dead drop in coded, ambiguous language?"

"Yes, she's a birdwatcher."

"I imagine she could summon him to a personal get together, hinting that NIS is searching for a mole, and they need to change their method of communication. Suggest rotating the site on a prearranged pattern.

Request a personal discussion, then have her show up in a sexy outfit. Like you said, she's just a letterbox, a go-between, but she'd be attractive bait. I'm still curious she never used cryptograms."

"She'd established credibility here. The cloud has worked well for years probably. No reason to change the game plan. When Roberts' NSA cipher expert, Rokman, breaks the encryption on Hwan's hard drive, we'll have a better insight into their network's communication scheme. Minsuh probably didn't want to risk arousing our suspicions by sending cryptograms directly to Jin-Ju. She definitely worked off the cloud drop box and he retrieved it from there. Forensics is tracing the address of her last communication. We're all over it."

"Okay. We'll convince her to set up a rendezvous with Jin-Ju. Train her to memorize a convincing script. Let's go with the honeypot scheme, Kim."

"Consider it done."

CHAPTER THIRTY-SEVEN

FLOATING BOX

Two nights later

Downtown Seoul

Kim's ear bud crackled as an agent reported in. "She's executing a brush pass. Guy in the leather jacket and baseball hat just gently bumped her and slipped her a note. See him? Look at the curb, up the street thirty meters on your right."

"Too crowded," Kim said, "can't spot him." He studied the intersection through his tinted glasses as he stood casually in front of an upscale restaurant, the crowds bustling around him. Anyone passing by could easily mistake him for a movie star, he was so handsome and well groomed, or at least someone patiently waiting for a date to arrive. It was just the image he intended to project. His Burberry raincoat disguised his shoulder holster and Daewoo K5, a .9 mm semi-automatic pistol. The NIS' Deputy Director maintained a rep as a crack shot. He might have a live fire opportunity tonight to demonstrate his skill.

Kim returned to the back seat of his black, unmarked chase car.

"Track him," he said over the wire to the other agents. "I doubt that's Jin-Ju, more likely just a courier setting up the rendezvous. You others continue to closely observe her movements, shadow her from all directions. Communicate with each other over your wireless, and keep me in the loop, got the plan?"

NIS agents were executing a floating box, a surveillance of Lee Minsuh from all angles to see where the honey pot operation led. Hopefully it would take them to Jin-Ju, their target.

The crisp night air in late November did not discourage hundreds of pedestrians from negotiating the heavy traffic in the busy Jung-Gu district of Seoul. Jin-Ju likely chose this congested area as the designated site for Minsuh to receive further instructions for their rendezvous because she'd be difficult to track in this crowd.

Jin-Ju took no chances, setting up an intermediary to lessen his chances of getting burned, Kim reflected. Clearly this Jin-Ju was no amateur.

Kim got a rush out of these close encounters. It beat the hell out cyber espionage as far as he was concerned. This was what he signed on for.

Neon lights from billboards and businesses flashed an eerie glow over the bustling throngs, some heading home, many going to a restaurant for dinner, others shopping. Horns blared and brakes squealed, but no one yelled or cursed. Asian society observed certain decorum despite the aggravation. The smoky scent of BBQ beef from the hibachis of nearby street vendors pleasantly covered the smell of exhaust fumes. Periodic wind gusts wafted the aroma through Kim's open car window, reminding him he was hungry. Dinner could wait; important business required his attention. Maybe he could catch a snack.

Kim sat back in the car, waiting for the action to unfold. He offered a cigarette to his driver. "Smoke, Lieutenant?"

The driver shook his head.

Before Kim could light his own cigarette, his earpiece buzzed.

"She seems confused about which direction to take," the agent reported. "Starts and stops, looks around … She's getting jostled in the evening crush."

"It may be a ploy to see if anyone is following her, be cautious." Kim directed the order to his floating box crew, all listening into the conversation's wave band. "Don't lose her in the crowd," he added. "I don't know if she has the skills to shake a tail. Remain inconspicuous so Jin-Ju won't bolt. I'm sure his agents are observing her and checking for tails, so be careful. Don't tip your hand. We may not get another opportunity like this one."

Two minutes later another wireless report came in. "The brush pass guy went up the street and ducked into a bar," the agent said. "Now he's placing a call on his cell."

"Probably giving Jin-Ju a heads up that the exchange went as planned and notifying him she's on her way to meet him. Detail someone to stay on him."

"Okay, boss."

Another communication quickly followed. "She's reading the note under a streetlight. Now she's backtracking down the avenue."

"Stay in front and back of her," Kim said. "Doubt she's trained in evasion tactics, but assume nothing. Take adequate precautions in case she decides to double cross us."

Moments later the message came in, "She's entering the Lotte Hotel lobby. We're on it."

"So, they're meeting at a five-star hotel. Didn't realize that Jin-Ju and Minsuh had expensive tastes," Kim quipped. "I'll saunter on over and stage from the hotel bar to see what develops. Be there in five minutes. I won't enter if she's waiting in the lobby. Give me a heads up."

"Okay, boss."

"She's nervous," Kim said. "Acting kind of dumb, but maybe she's kind of smart and playing a game... But being placed in this situation, her behavior may become erratic, understand? I don't want to spook her. Keep me apprised... I'm on my way over there."

"Roger that. She's probably just following instructions on the note from the brush by, boss. Minsuh never impressed me as a high flyer able to pull a stunt like this."

One of his best agents, Moon, defended her. "I still can't believe she betrayed us."

"Life is full of surprises," Kim said. Her betrayal still stung him, too, though he refused to show it. "There's no question Minsuh's a traitor... I was just joking about their expensive tastes, Moon. I'm sure they chose the hotel because there'll be a lot of activity in the lobby to provide cover. Not exactly an underworld hideout."

Kim felt a growing uneasiness about the operation. Angry as he was at her for being a traitor, he had worked with her for years. He worried she might not be up for what could happen... He quickly pushed away those fears. She was the enemy, and he had a job to do.

"Keep a keen eye out," Kim added, "she could quickly duck into an elevator and disappear. So guard all the elevators alcoves. If she gets on one, have one of our female surveillance agents get on with her, check where she gets off and see where she's heading. I doubt they plan to meet in the bar, too conspicuous. Post an agent on each floor for forward surveillance."

* * *

In the lobby of the exclusive hotel, Minsuh paused to reread her instructions. Her hands trembled. She crumbled the note and put it her purse after confirming the type written message:

<MEET AT 1930 / LOTTE HOTEL> ROOM 320. KNOCK THREE TIMES.>

She checked her watch. It was now 7:20. Ten minutes until she met her handler. She took the next elevator, hoping to control her anxiety on the ride up to the third floor. She was a low-level birdwatcher, not an agent. How'd she arrive in this predicament? When she'd first been contacted about passing along information, the risks had seemed low. She needed the extra cash, and she was above suspicion. Or so she'd believed.

She knew now that she'd made a huge mistake. But Nam had made it very clear that she had no choice but to go along with their scheme to trap Jin-Ju.

She'd never met Jin-Ju, never even spoken with him. She was surprised he'd agreed to meet with her. Strict DGSE protocol dictated otherwise. She didn't know what to expect from this encounter. Resigned to her fate, Minsuh pressed the elevator button for floor three.

A well-dressed woman hurried into the elevator after her. The woman glanced at her, her gaze skimming over the revealing outfit she wore. Judging from the woman's smug expression, she dismissed her as a call girl.

Minsuh felt her face flush. The woman ignored her now, texting the whole time until Minsuh exited the elevator at the third floor.

Kim received the woman's text message one minutes later < GETTING OFF ON 3rd FLOOR>.

As the elevator doors closed silently behind her, Minsuh felt her heart begin to race. She was scared to death of what faced her.

After she walked only a few steps along dimly lit hallway, her emotions overwhelmed her. She staggered, feeling faint. She leaned against the wall and took some deep breaths, trying to regain her self-control. She'd never done anything like this. They called it a "honeypot" operation. Explained to her if she accepted this task she would avoid a "mysterious disappearance." She understood. NIS played for keeps. They'd prepared her with a carefully scripted explanation for requesting this impromptu meeting. She only hoped she didn't stumble.

Her anxiety and hesitation was noted by an agent down the hall, pretending to read a newspaper on a sofa surrounded by potted plants. Kim had hastily posted an agent on each floor to observe the elevators. This operation required a lot of manpower, but NIS pursued big game tonight and they were taking no chances. The agent maintained a low profile to see which room she entered. He carried a special device in his briefcase for the occasion.

"She looks nervous," he observed.

She was indeed very nervous. Minsuh had reconciled to prostitute herself for Nam and NIS. She was desperate. She did not want to die. She told herself once more that she could do this.

The next hundred steps were the longest in her life; she only hoped it wouldn't turn out to be a death march.

When she reached the door, her trembling had subsided. Instead, a numb fear took over. She knocked three times, as instructed, on door number 320.

Chapter Thirty-Eight

LOTTE HOTEL MYSTERY

Seated in a back corner with his lieutenant, Kim admired the exotic ambience of the luxury bar. Their leather booth overlooked a pool that spilled onto an expansive terrace tastefully decorated with artwork. Other than potted tropical plants more suited to Southeast Asia, the establishment definitely rated five stars, Kim thought. The bar seemed full of movers and shakers tonight. The animated scene reminded him of L.A., absent the aroma of cannabis smoke from the reefer crowd.

He surveyed the crowd. Affluent Asian businessmen were still making deals over cocktails before enjoying an expensed dinner. They'd soon retreat to either the Korean or the Japanese restaurants flanking the terrace, constructed with sliding pocket glass doors for outdoor dining in warmer weather.

Kim admired the western-influenced lifestyle. He'd been missing out by not taking advantage of this vibrant nightlife more, he decided.

He and his lieutenant had decided to grab a quick snack while waiting for the surveillance plan to deliver their prey. Kim had received a text that Minsuh, their enticing bait, had gotten off the elevator on the third floor. He had seen her earlier. She was a knockout in just about any outfit, but in the sexy, stylish dress she wore tonight, few men could resist her unspoken invitation. His agents reported that she'd turned a lot of heads in the hotel lobby. Soon, if everything went according to plan, she'd seduce Jin-Ju and they'd capture him in bed with her, defenseless.

They were enjoying *makgeolli*, a Korean rice wine, accompanied with *pageon*, a form of pancake, when his ear bud sounded the alarm. Moon was on the line and he sounded excited.

"Getting worried, boss."

"What's up?"

"Minsuh entered room 320 twenty minutes ago," Moon reported. "I put one of our new listening devices outside to monitor and record their conversation through the wall."

"And?"

"They exchanged cordial small talk, then Minsuh mentioned the need for a new communication system because NIS suspected a mole. She said she feared exposure. She followed our script to the letter, sounding genuinely concerned about this development, explaining why she requested this sudden meeting."

"Was he buying it?"

"Hard to tell, he wasn't saying much, just seemed to be listening to her story. She sounded very convincing, by the way."

"That's good to know. Could you confirm that he's Jin-Ju?"

"Not at first. There was no introduction. She got down to business right off. As I said, it was one-sided exchange with her relating the story she'd rehearsed. Early on, I could only tell she was talking with an unidentified Korean male. Nothing about his speech suggested an affiliation with the North. He was very reserved."

"When did you determine that it was Jin-Ju?" Kim asked impatiently.

"Not until the end of her explanation, maybe twenty minutes after she'd entered the room, when she finally addressed him as Jin-Ju."

"Tell me exactly what happened."

"She called him by that name, Jin-Ju, for the first time. Then he suddenly interrupted and asked her in a harsh tone, 'Did you know you were followed to our rendezvous tonight?'"

Kim felt his unease growing. "Not a good sign, Moon."

"His exact words, inferring someone tipped him off, that his spies were watching her and us all the time and he knew it was a trap. Then the conversation ended abruptly."

"Ended? She didn't reply?" Kim's voice raised an octave in alarm. "How long ago was this?"

"Less than one minute before I called you. It became way too quiet— Not another peep, no sound of a struggle, but I'm very concerned."

"Do you have anyone to cover your six?"

"Two backups just arrived."

"Break and enter the room immediately. She's likely in big trouble. Take Jin-Ju alive if you can, otherwise shoot him."

***

Kim threw a fistful of wons on the table. "Got a situation, let's roll."

"What's up?" his lieutenant asked.

"We have to deal with a serious problem, room 320."

They rushed out to the lobby and caught the first elevator up to third floor. They ran down the hall to room 320. The lock was busted and the door wide open, practically hanging off its hinges.

Inside, Moon and two other NIS agents stood over Minsuh, fully clothed, lying face up in the middle of the room. The white carpet around her was dark with blood. Her lifeless eyes were wide open. There was no sign of a struggle.

She had been expertly garroted.

Jin-Ju had vanished.

A curtain rustled in the far corner of the room. Kim lifted his .9mm and rushed over, followed by his agents. He quickly pulled the curtain back, his gun ready.

The window was wide open. A fire escape led down to a back alley three stories below. The alley was empty and silent. They had foolishly neglected to think of covering the alley.

"He's gone," Kim said. He turned back to the other agents. "We have a problem, gentlemen. Our target escaped, we have a high profile situation to deal with, and a body to dispose of."

"What's the plan?" Moon asked.

"We'll chalk it off as a 'mysterious disappearance.' There will be no public investigation, no police report, no notification of kin, or any mention of this to anyone, understand? This is a national security problem. Get our forensics over here to check for Jin-Ju's prints, repair the door, and clean up the blood before management gets wind of this. Post a guard outside the room to dissuade curiosity seekers until we clean up the mess. Pass the damage off as a domestic argument that got out of hand. I'm certain Jin-Ju paid in cash for the room under an alias, or someone else did, but discreetly check out that lead while I regroup."

"We're dealing with a mean son of a bitch," Kim said under his breath as he left the grisly murder scene. "Nam will go ballistic over this screw up."

CHAPTER THIRTY-NINE

C3I

The next day

"I'm sorry to hear about that nastiness," Biff said after Nam had called and related the details of the disaster at the Hotel Lotte. "It's a Whisky Tango Foxtrot situation, Nam. Shake it off. That kind of stuff happens. Jin-Ju's obviously a seasoned spy, not easily burned. He'd seen that honeypot movie before, took out your mole expertly to blur the trail, and sent a message he plays for keeps. But we have other resources to track him, rest assured."

"Did Rokman's NSA analysts break the encryption?" Nam asked, his mood picking up. Embarrassed by their failure to trap Jin-Ju, he held out hope that the CIA would bail them out by deciphering Hwan's hard drive. Biff Roberts appeared upbeat, and not the least bit judgmental about their failure. Nam felt he'd lost face with his CIA counterpart, but the Americans seemed undisturbed by the NIS bungling the operation. Their CIA colleagues just kept moving on to their objective, apparently chalking it up to the vicissitudes of spy craft.

"As Rokman predicted," Biff said, "Hwan used the Japanese Camillia cipher, a symmetrical 64-bit complex block cryptogram used widely in Asia as an alternative to AES. It has a weakness. The sender and recipient must share the key and keep it secret. That characteristic should allow some clever sleuthing to breadcrumb back to Jin-Ju's encryption signature. Rokman's working with your computer forensics team on that lead as we speak."

"Good to know," Nam said.

"It gets better. Preliminary indications lead us to suspect Jin-Ju is deeply embedded in ROK's military intelligence unit, C3I."

Nam frowned. "C3I? We don't use that designation here."

"An acronym we use for a unit's command, control, communications, and intelligence."

"My God!" Nam said. "That leaves us precariously exposed if that's the case. Jin-Ju is in a position to do some serious damage."

"Precisely the problem we face. If we initiate our proposed counter-measures to abort North Korea's EMP launch, once we know the date, ROK military must be informed in time to take defensive action. But that action would provide time for a critical leak by Jin-Ju to occur if he intercepts our warning to ROK command. We must make certain that doesn't happen."

"Absolutely, we can't risk exposure of our plan."

"We must disable his computer."

"How do you propose to accomplish that?" Nam asked.

"With a RAT."

"A RAT?"

"A remote access tool," Biff said, "a sophisticated virus to hack into and take over his computer. We'll spook him, make him act irrationally and tip his hand."

"How's that work?"

"Once Rokman obtains Jin-Ju's signature, he'll make it happen. That's what he does. Don't sweat the details, I don't. While we're trying to identify and capture Jin-Ju, we'll take him out of operation by cutting off his communications. He's in a critical position inside ROK's infrastructure. It's imperative we find him and eliminate the threat to our master plan."

"ROK intel has three divisions: surveillance, target acquisition, and reconnaissance," Nam said. "All very large units, he'll be tough to trace."

"Undoubtedly, it won't be a piece of cake, but it's doable."

"It's essential we do it expediently."

"We have another option," Biff said. "Track him from the top down."

"Top down?" Nam wondered where Roberts was going with this. He was difficult to keep up with, always plotting.

"Leapfrog to the Dragon Lady, his commander. Catch her, catch him."

He must be joking, Nam thought. But he kept his tone even. "We've had no contact with her for four decades," Nam responded. "She disappeared off our grid following the KAL sabotage in the 1980s. She's either dead or sequestered somewhere in protective custody in China or North Korea."

"She must be pushing sixty by now, maybe dead."

"Not according to our deciphering of some of Hwan's encrypted communications with Jin-Ju. She's very much alive and running the show somewhere in South Korea. Jin-Ju's her top lieutenant. Multiple references to a bookstore on the South Korean peninsula further verify her existence. Apparently it's been a clever cover for her and an adequate source of income for many years."

"Okay. Given that as fact, where do we start? We have a very literate society, with probably thousands of bookstores. And we have no idea what she looks like."

"Here's my suggestion," Biff replied. "This master spy mentored a very young female North Korean spy years ago. As I recall, she was a coconspirator in that KAL terror incident you mentioned. Your NIS predecessors caught her, turned her, and cleverly used her as a propaganda tool against the North. Then NIS retired her under an assumed name in protective custody. She knows what the Dragon Lady looked like. Contact her to cooperate. With our artists and facial recognition software, we can age her description of the Dragon Lady's features to about age sixty for starters."

"Then what?"

"Then you'll instruct your NIS field operatives to visit every damn bookstore in South Korea searching for a person matching that description. We have a lot at stake here, Director. We have to crank it up."

Nam wondered how Roberts came up with these ideas. But it was a sound suggestion.

"Okay," Nam said, "let's get on it."

CHAPTER FORTY

BLACKSHADES

Two weeks later – C3I

Jin-Ju almost fainted as he stared at his computer screen at C3I head-quarters. He swore under his breath as he broke out in a cold sweat. "How could this possibly happen?"

"*Geseki!* Son of a bitch! … *Shibal!* Fuck!"

He looked around the office to make sure no one heard him cuss or caught a glimpse of his computer. Fortunately, no one else was nearby. His screen showed in no uncertain terms that he'd been discovered in cyberspace. Hacked.

< YOUR COMPUTER HAS BEEN HIJACKED. YOUR PRIVATE FILES HAVE BEEN ENCRYPTED INTO OUR ASYMMETRIC 128 BIT BLOCK CIPHER CODE. YOU MAY NO LONGER ACCESS YOUR FILES OR COMMUNICATE WITHOUT OUR KNOWLEDGE. WE ARE INSIDE YOUR COMPUTER AND INSIDE YOUR HEAD. YOUR FILES CAN ONLY BE DECRYPTED AND RESTORED BY US. GOOD LUCK ATTEMPTING TO RESTORE THE SHADOW SCAN INFORMATION ON YOUR HARD DRIVE. WE HAVE DISABLED THAT ALSO. WE PLAN TO KEEP IN CONTACT WITH YOU. HAVE A NICE DAY, ASSHOLE >

"*Sheeba!* Shit! … *Jotgatne!* Fucked up!"

He sat back in his swivel chair, shocked. The significance of the message didn't take long to sink in. The message threatened to abruptly end his long covert career inside ROK military intelligence, the C3I division. He'd been badly compromised. And the result could be the end of their North Korean spy network.

He was a pivotal link in their DPRK spy program. He knew it was just a matter of time before they'd breadcrumb his cyberspace signature back to him personally, identifying him as the owner of the computer exchanging cryptograms divulging ROK intelligence. They'd already traced his existence, identified him as a North Korean agent by somehow breaking his encryption code, an astronomical feat.

Next, they'd track and capture him. He knew the game. And NIS didn't treat spies lightly. ROK had granted him refugee citizenship twenty years ago. Being guilty of treason guaranteed he'd face a firing squad after a summary trial—in the best-case scenario. More likely they'd keep his discovery quiet, torture him, then eliminate him without fanfare after they squeezed some information out of him about his network's sources and methods.

The threat was palpable, creating a level of anxiety he'd rarely experienced. He felt lightheaded and queasy. He struggled not to panic and bolt. He couldn't begin to contemplate the blowback to the DPRK network, the fallout of being exposed as a spy. And, most of all, he feared the Dragon Lady's recriminations.

He read the message over again. No mistaking its incredulous claims or implications.

"Who the fuck are these guys?" he muttered. "How the hell did they find me?"

He pondered the sophistication of the cyber-attack. *Not your ordinary hacker,* he deduced. It must be a state-sponsored activity conducted by pros to pull off something of this magnitude.

It was late afternoon, not leaving him much time to organize damage control, especially without his computer's encryption program to warn others to go to ground, destroy evidence, switch codes.

NIS must have broken their code. But he suspected they used outside help, just as the Dragon Lady suggested last month. She had been right all along. CIA's fingerprints were all over it.

And when he informed her, she would kill him.

***

U.S. Embassy, Seoul

"Jin-Ju" had guessed correctly. NSA's supercomputer at Fort Meade broke his Camellia cipher encryption in just three days. Biff and Rokman had crafted the threatening message that NIS sent to Jin-Ju an hour ago. They were getting a good laugh out of the viral exploit. Now they had Jin-Ju by the balls, and it was just a matter of time before they'd take him down.

Biff and Rokman were at the top of their spy game, enjoying cocktails and cigars back in their suite at the U.S. embassy, celebrating the cyber-attack's success. They toasted and laughed. As Biff and Rokman clinked glasses, Tim and Tyler looked up from their chess match at the gleeful exchange.

"What's so funny over there, guys?" Tyler asked from the corner of the living area.

"We just checkmated our opponent," Biff said, grinning.

"So you nailed, Jin-Ju?" Tyler asked.

"Just about," Biff said. "We left him with no way out following Rokman's infection of his computer with a nifty malware program."

"Blackshades," Rokman clarified. "We fucking disabled his computer."

"Good show!" Tim shouted. "He's toast. Bet he crapped his pants."

"Just a matter of time to take him down," Biff said. "I can't wait to inform Nam about all this in the morning. It will blow him away."

"Maybe we should let him know tonight," Tyler suggested. "He's been sweating it since their honey pot operation failed. He could use some good news."

Biff shook his head. "It's almost midnight. Nam wouldn't be able to sleep or might act precipitously. I want Jin-Ju to stew a bit, figure out his plan for damage control before he bolts. Let's see if he has any accomplices in C3I. When we finish enhancing the digital images tonight from his computer's screen shots we'll know what he looks like, so Nam can easily identify and apprehend him tomorrow morning over at ROK military command."

"Sounds like a plan," Tim commented.

"And," Biff added, "Rokman's team has to finish analyzing Jin-Ju's encrypted communications with the Dragon Lady tonight. They were using the same type Camellia encryption program as Hwan with different passwords, so they shared a key that we can backtrack. Plus, we can breadcrumb back to her computer by tracing her encryption signature like we did with Jin-Ju. We'll have a fuller picture by early morning. Let's not jump the gun."

"Makes sense," Tyler agreed. "No rush, he's cornered, his computer out of order."

"I'll bet Jin-Ju's in a state of shock," Tim said, "assessing his options, his escape plans. He may not have a solid contingency plan set up yet."

Biff marveled at Rokman's ingenuity. He'd infected Jin-Ju's computer with a RAT, a remote access tool to access and view the victim's files, documents, and photos. The Blackshades virus could record keystrokes, steal passwords, and even use the machine's cameras to spy on users. The spy's Camellia encryption program shared the same key between sender and recipient of the encrypted communiqué. That key was used to translate cipher text to plain text, the message they wished to convey. Biff knew Rokman would soon discover that critical key. Not only were they closing the noose on Jin-Ju, but they were on the verge of a significant lead to expose the Dragon Lady, DPRK's ringleader of spies in South Korea. Jin-Ju would connect them to her, giving NIS a good shot at bringing down the major North Korean spy network.

Biff smiled. He couldn't wait to see malware photos of Jin-Ju's shocked expression upon receiving the email they'd sent him earlier today. He knew Jin-Ju wouldn't dare contact anyone on his computer's encryption program for fear of exposing them. He'd make his move to alert the network soon through back channels, Biff surmised. Maybe they would discover those also.

Biff took a sip of his whiskey and swirled the ice around in the glass as he contemplated their next steps.

Once identified, should they set up surveillance on Jin-Ju or arrest him? Biff decided that would be Nam's call. They'd compromised him, so he was temporarily out of the loop, unable to cause further harm until he regrouped.

CHAPTER FORTY-ONE

GWANGAN BRIDGE

The next day, 8:00 a.m.

C3I Headquarters – Seoul

"He's gone?" Nam asked. "You're telling me he didn't show up this morning?"

"Yes, Director," Major Lee said, "his first no show ever in over twenty years. Choi Sang Kyo, the man you call Jin-Ju, has an unblemished record with our intelligence unit, one of our best and most reliable analysts. We called his home phone and cell, but both were reported as 'service disconnected.' His office has been sanitized, his computer and personal effects missing, but there's no sign of foul play. He requested my permission to stay late last night to complete some unfinished business. I saw no problem, so I consented."

Major Lee shook his head and added, "Your revelation he was a covert DPRK agent comes as a great shock. He's the last person in my unit that I'd suspect as a foreign agent."

"Do you have his home address?" Nam asked.

"He has a downtown apartment near the Lotte Hotel. I'll have my secretary get the address for you."

Nam turned to Kim and said, "Take a few men over there. Summon forensics to join you. Check out the premises with a fine-toothed comb. Captain Park and I will examine his office." Nam turned back to Major Lee. "Lead the way, Major." Nam was all business, furious that Jin-Ju had escaped again.

Biff miscalculated, Nam thought. Biff should have awakened him at midnight. Jin-Ju has fled, no doubt setting damage control in motion, and the manhunt is on. Nam reflected that even the most experienced operatives dropped the ball sometimes.

***

Pusan – Same morning

Jin-Ju knocked three times on door 2005 with his distinctive cadence. He heard no noise inside and hoped she'd not left for her bookstore. It was nine o'clock, and the store opened at ten.

Inside the twentieth-floor suite, the Dragon Lady looked up from her tea, recognizing the characteristic rap on the door. *Him again,* she thought. And arriving this early, unannounced, spelled trouble. He'd broken protocol twice in the last month despite her reprimand, and here he was again. She sighed and went to the door, resigned to the fact that they must be in danger.

A glance through the security peephole confirmed it was Jin-Ju. She unlatched the double locks and ushered him inside without a greeting.

From his haggard expression she immediately knew something had gone wrong. Very wrong. He looked awful, his eyes sunken, his color pallid. He fidgeted nervously.

"I drove all night from Seoul," he blurted out and flopped on the sofa, looking drained. "We're in big trouble."

"Why didn't you send me a cryptogram?" The Dragon Lady scowled. "You can't keep showing up here unannounced, risking my exposure."

"I'm burned, Madam Bae Doo. Late yesterday NIS hacked my computer. They'll soon have the cipher key we share. They broke our Camellia code, got my signature, and traced me to C3I. Soon they'll trace my encryptions to you. You must flee immediately and notify our network of the compromised circumstances through back channels. Avoid using your computer. They may have already tapped into your communications with a malware virus."

"By 'they' you refer to NIS?"

"Yes, NIS, with the assistance of the CIA, as you suggested last month. Deciphering our encryptions required a supercomputer, so CIA must be deeply involved in taking us down. They're closing in fast."

"NSA collaborated obviously if that's the case. And yes, we're in big trouble. I fear there's not enough time to control the damage to our network. This will not go down well in Pyongyang. General Pak will be livid. RGB will go ballistic."

She stepped closer to him, glaring down at him on the sofa. "I warned you that the CIA had their fingerprints all over this last month," she continued. "First Kwon's captured, then Hwan's eliminated, now you're burned. So you finally got the big picture? A carefully crafted series of very methodical, expedient takedowns occurred, all in a matter of months under your command." Nam was clever, but he lacked CIA's enormous resources and clandestine experience. It would require vast malware experience to have penetrated their supposedly invulnerable security systems. CIA was collaborating with NIS, no question.

"If you are burned," she said quietly, "I won't be far behind, Jin-Ju."

She had a quick solution to the problem. Without ceremony, she went to her desk and pulled out her Glock with the silencer attached. She chambered a bullet.

Jin-Ju heard the telltale click and his eyes widened. He didn't move but looked up at her from the couch, his expression pleading.

"No Madam," he said hoarsely, "we can manage this problem together. I'm very sorry …"

"I hate to do this, Jin-Ju," she said, stepping closer to him, "but you've become a liability. You know our rules."

"But, Madam, please don't—"

Dispassionately, she shot him between the eyes in mid-sentence.

She had hoped this day would never come, but she had a contingency plan to dismantle her operation. And she had no remorse about dispatching her second in command. He had it coming for screwing up. She had warned him last month.

Now it was all about survival. She put a few personal belongings, her desktop computer, and other incriminating evidence into a large canvas shopping bag. From the wall safe, well hidden behind a painting of a tranquil, pastoral scene of a rice harvest, she retrieved her passport and a quarter million dollars in cash.

Then she hastily packed a small duffel bag with some clothes. She grabbed her coat, turned on some classical music, and locked her apartment, leaving Jin-Ju dead, sprawled askew on the blood-soaked sofa, his face obliterated by the .9mm bullet.

She took the elevator to the underground garage. After locking the bags in the trunk, she drove her small Mazda straight to her bookstore. She must recover any incriminating evidence there, and it was getting near opening time. She wanted to avoid any early customers. Time was of the essence, but she remained cool, calm, and collected.

Just as she was unlocking the front door, a gentleman in a suit and tie approached the bookstore. She quickly decided that she had no choice but to let him in if she didn't want to arouse suspicion.

It soon became evident he had no intention of browsing for a good read. She noted the slight bulge under his suit jacket. He looked at her intently, before glancing down at a piece of paper with a photograph on it — one of her, she surmised. But where would they have obtained a photo of her?

At any rate, they knew and were closing in fast. She maintained her innocent composure as the man sent a brief text, then approached her.

"Madam," he said pleasantly, "do you have any identification papers, any work permits? Just a routine inspection of businesses operating in this vicinity. It's a simple tax matter, it won't take long."

Not the least bit ruffled, she replied, "Not a problem. I keep them locked in my desk in the back office. Please follow me," she added politely, not showing signs of tension, which the agent fully noted.

The agent wanted a closer look at her features. His instructions ordered him to proceed with caution to avoid mistaken identity. Many years had transpired and NIS couldn't be certain how accurate the picture was.

As they entered the back office he got a closer look at her. He decided she vaguely fit the facial recognition photo he held. The artist's rendition had been reconstructed into a photo by the CIA based on descriptions from a former agent of hers, one turned by NIS years ago, now in protective custody. He felt this woman could be the person they were seeking.

The computer-generated photo of the Dragon Lady had been dispatched to all NIS agents to conduct a countrywide search of all bookstores, based on an intel intercept suggesting she ran a bookstore as a cover. It was a long shot, but the Dragon Lady was a high value target worth the effort. Now it looked as though it might pay off. He hid his excitement. He'd get a promotion out of this if he was right. But he had to be sure.

"Please have a seat while I find the right key to the drawer," she said. She pretended to fumble with a key ring while trying to find the right key. She noted the gentleman surveyed her office suspiciously, obviously looking for clues.

"Here we go," she said. "Thank you for your patience." She opened the drawer, not the least bit flustered.

He admired her composure, deciding he might be wrong about her. She seemed like a nice lady.

"Sorry to be a bother so early in the day," he apologized—the last words he would ever utter.

In one deft move the Dragon Lady blew off the top of his skull with a hollow point .9mm fired from her Glock semi-automatic, the backup pistol that she kept locked in the drawer for threatening occasions like this. The impact blew him over backward in his chair, sending both crashing to the floor. His bone, blood, and brain splattered the wall and floor. He never knew what hit him.

The Dragon Lady played for keeps without constraint. She had no hang-ups about killing anyone who threatened her or got in the way of her mission, and she felt no remorse about killing a stranger in cold blood. Or for having made a second kill in less than an hour.

Besides, she reflected dryly, *he never even introduced himself, a serious breach of etiquette.*

She left him sprawled on the floor, not bothering to check his ID. She knew he represented NIS, packed iron, and had come to scout her out. In case he'd texted his backup, she needed to move out. She briefly stooped to glance at the bloodstained photo of her that he still grasped in a death grip.

"A reasonable facsimile," she said to herself, smirking, "but not flattering, too many wrinkles. I'm much too fit to look that old."

She quickly and calmly gathered her personal belongings in a sturdy book bag, adding her laptop computer and the Glock pistol. She placed the "CLOSED" sign in the window and left her bookstore forever without the slightest twinge of nostalgia. After a lifetime of adversity, she assumed survival mode naturally. She possessed the instincts of a wild animal, one that refused to be captured and caged.

***

Pusan Airport
Two hours later

"I'd like one-way ticket for this evening's early flight to Beijing. First class, please."

"It's much cheaper to purchase a round trip ticket, madam," the ticket agent said, "especially first class. Don't you plan to return soon?"

"Not for some time. I plan to visit friends in Tokyo after attending to some business in Beijing. I prefer to keep the dates open. Expense poses no problem." The Dragon Lady smiled at the surveillance camera behind the Air China desk at Pusan's International terminal, knowing NIS would be checking the footage sometime in the next twenty-four hours, looking for her.

"Credit or debit card?" the agent asked.

"I'll pay cash in dollars."

The agent nodded. "That will be $3,000 for a one-way ticket, first class. Do you prefer a window seat or aisle?"

"Window."

"Number of bags?"

"Carry on only."

She was traveling light for such a long trip, the agent thought, but she didn't comment. The woman seemed to know what she wanted and could obviously afford it. She must be very wealthy to pay in U.S. dollars.

"Passport?" the agent asked.

The Dragon Lady handed the forged passport to the Air China agent. The perfect fake, made by an expert North Korean cobbler, had a photo that flattered her alias, "Bong Cha."

"Here's your ticket, Madam Bong. Your 737 flight boards at 1940 hours, gate four. It's a three-hour flight depending on the prevailing winds."

***

At 1800 hours it had been dark for over a half hour. That suited her plan. The Dragon Lady pulled her Mazda 3 over into the bike lane in the middle of Gwangan Bridge. She put on the car's hazard lights. She got out, unlocked the trunk, and removed its contents. She peered over the railing at the murky sea churning two hundred feet below. The current was swift, the wind whipping up white caps. She could see her favorite Gwangalli beach a mile to the west, near her apartment. She knew this would be the last time she viewed the white sand. Her small car sheltered her from the traffic whizzing by, and no one seemed to notice her activity. Many passing drivers no doubt assumed she had a flat tire, but no one bothered to stop to assist her. Asian society was changing, she had felt for some time, becoming more like other parts of the world with people increasingly self-absorbed.

First she dropped the canvas shopping bag, watching it splash and sink rapidly in the swift current. The book bag followed. She hated to abandon her Glock pistols, but she had no choice. They'd served their purpose.

Then came the moment of truth. She had two options: jump or flee the country. She contemplated the dark water for a moment.

It was a long way down, she decided, and damn cold.

Besides, despite her network crumbling, not everything she had worked for was lost. The planned attack on the U.S. could still go ahead. And would go ahead. Soon. That was a victory she would like to live to savor.

Walking briskly against traffic in the bike lane, carrying her duffle bag, she backtracked a quarter of a mile to where she'd entered the bridge. When she looked back, her car's lights were still blinking. Still no one was curious enough to stop.

Two blocks away she hopped into a cab.

"Pusan International terminal please," she told the driver. "I must board in one hour."

CHAPTER FORTY-TWO

MOPPING UP

The next morning

BELOVED PUSAN BOOKSELLER FEARED SUICIDE VICTIM OFF GWANGAN BRIDGE

The front-page story in the local newspaper, *Kookje Shinmun*, included a photo of her abandoned car parked in the middle of the bridge in the bike lane, caution lights blinking.

It is believed she jumped to her death ... the story continued, the report speculating on the reasons she might take her own life. But no photos of the bookseller were published. The article speculated her body would not be recovered from the swift currents of the deep-sea inlet and predicted the city would mourn her unexpected loss, especially the university students.

All the news was carefully managed by Nam, a master at disinformation, experienced at damage control in matters of national security. Nam moved quickly after receiving his agent's text message alerting NIS to the Dragon Lady's presence in Pusan. The bookstore was popular with university students in the port city of 3.5 million, and the Dragon Lady had carefully managed her covert persona for over forty years. The truth could be very damaging to NIS if it ever got out, so Nam took elaborate precautions to ensure that fact did not become public knowledge. The editor of the paper was a personal friend and political supporter.

NIS forensics mopped up her apartment, suspecting the corpse with the shattered face was Jin-Ju. DNA and fingerprint confirmation by the C3I unit he'd infiltrated would soon clarify that issue. They'd also quietly removed their dead NIS agent out the backdoor of the bookstore and cleaned up the premises. He would have a private funeral without any mention of the circumstances of his death in the line of duty—closed casket, of course.

Chagrined at the outcome, Nam commiserated with Biff Roberts later that day at the U.S. embassy before Biff's flight back to Langley.

"She was a pro, utterly ruthless," Nam said. "She cunningly faked her suicide, but she predicted we'd be suspicious of her deception." Nam told Biff how she had smiled derisively at the surveillance camera behind the China Air desk as she booked her one-way flight to Beijing last night. "It was as if to say, 'Catch me if you can.' She was taunting us." Nam scowled. "She can easily book a flight to Pyongyang from there."

"I suspect she can and will," Biff said. "Sorry she escaped, Director, but you dismantled her network, and her mission is irreversibly compromised. In retrospect, it would not have made any difference if I'd notified you of Jin-Ju's identity inside C3I at midnight. He probably stayed late at work that last night to find a way to alert her through back channels, but couldn't find a safe route. He feared compounding a bad situation by exposing other agents. So Jin-Ju drove all night to warn her, his last act of devotion, which he paid for with his life."

Brutal acts like this were common in the spy game. The Dragon Lady was clearly a survivor, Biff thought, and dispassionate in her role as a master spy.

"Jin-Ju became a risky liability," Biff added, "so she took him out. Look at the bright side. It'll take DPRK years to recover."

"I hope so," Nam said, not sounding completely convinced. "How could something that seemed so right turn out so wrong? We were closing in on both of them."

"In a perverse way you have to admire the ingenuity of her escape," Biff said, "the way she handled adversity, managed the personal threat to her and her network."

"She was a cunning operative, I must say," Nam reluctantly admitted.

"Her spy ring was good, but yours is better. As things turned out, we're still on top of the situation unless she somehow manages to expose Kwon before he delivers the target date. Hopefully our spiders monitoring their computers as a backup won't fail to confirm DPRK's launch plans."

"She's shrewd, but has no credible evidence to expose him, just suspicions," Nam responded. "He's built up trust by now."

"Suspicion is the key word," Biff agreed. "But in North Korea it carries a lot of weight."

"Here's my take, Biff," Nam said. "RGB would have eliminated Kwon by now if they had a shred of convincing evidence of him being a double agent. Reza trained him well. He's been up there in covert status since September, almost three months without detection. He procured the latest cybersecurity equipment for them, building confidence. The Dragon Lady can only introduce her suspicions. I view our risk as limited." Nam sounded as if he was trying to convince himself as well as Biff.

"In paranoid North Korea suspicion is usually sufficient," Biff observed. "The Dragon Lady could turn out to be the fly in the ointment."

Nam didn't find his candid remark reassuring. He knew Biff was correct in his assessment of the Hermit Kingdom's brutal nature and their pervasive paranoia. Their collective mindset was one obsessed with mistrust. The surprise return of the Dragon Lady to Pyongyang might change their calculus. Kwon and their plans may indeed be at risk if she heightened RGB's suspicion or convinced them Kwon was masquerading as a double agent inside their intelligence unit.

And Nam knew he could do nothing to prevent it. She'd cunningly slipped their noose and now jeopardized their well-laid plans.

Chapter Forty-Three

CONFRONTATION

RGB, Pyongyang

Three days later

"**I**'ve read all the transcripts of his interrogation and studied his polygraph, General," the Dragon Lady said. "I concur that he's either one of us, or one of the most talented, determined double agents I've ever encountered in my career. But would you grant me the opportunity to speak with him? Directly confront him?"

General Pak leaned back in his chair, considering.

"I still have a sneaking suspicion he's not really who he says he is," she added. "He's Kwon, certainly, one of our agents, but no longer on our side. I maintain NIS and the CIA turned him, intensely trained him, and cleverly infiltrated him into our midst to spy on us. There are too many coincidences and multiple inconsistencies in his epic story for me to accept. His journey defies logic. It's almost laughable if the consequences weren't so monumental."

"I understand your concern. Those were my initial impressions." The general recognized she was pissed, despite her calm demeanor. He'd let her vent. She'd earned it as RGB's best operative who just came in from the cold. He'd also learned long ago not to discount anything she said.

"Kwon's capture last spring by NIS started the problems for my network, and a series of mishaps and setbacks followed. Hwan's elimination, our moles inside the U.S. embassy and NIS exposed, a honeypot trap set for Jin-Ju. After that, Jin-Ju's encryption cipher was broken, leading to an encryption key and signature to trace me. I had remained deep dark for over forty years until NIS captured Kwon. Then shit started hitting the fan. You must understand my suspicion that he's part of a NIS/CIA conspiracy to bring us down. How else can you explain it, if Kwon's not a traitor turned into a double agent?"

The general nodded. "As I said, I shared your opinion initially. I dealt with those same reservations and fears, but we've intensely vetted him, watched him like a hawk, set traps, followed him everywhere, bugged his computer and apartment, dangled sensitive information in front of him and have not discovered one iota of espionage activity. Not a single questionable instance, mind you. I've been very skeptical from day one, but his behavior and performance have been exemplary. He's clean, madam, squeaky clean by all accounts. In fact, Kwon's one of our brightest analysts. He facilitated the installation of a state of the art cybersecurity system. After months of scrutiny, our intelligence unit director and his top officers now sing his praises. That many experienced intelligence agents couldn't be wrong about him. Wouldn't you agree?"

"I'd like personally to confront him, General. Please grant me my wish."

General Pak understood her reluctance to accept Kwon. The Dragon Lady had been badly burned, forced to flee South Korea on the spur of the moment, killing two men in the process, one of hers, one of theirs. She managed her escape deftly, professionally, but clearly aggravation gnawed at her. She wanted someone to blame — a natural instinct. Normally the conversation would have ended there, but out of respect for her long, distinguished service, he indulged her. She'd earned universal respect at RGB as a legendary field operative, one without peer.

"You may arrange an appointment to interview him in a room where we can record the conversation and his reactions. You understand the conditions, of course?"

"I do, sir. Thank you for granting me the opportunity. I've learned the hard way that nothing stays the same. You have to be willing to play the game. In Kwon's case, we must separate perception from reality."

Profound statement, the general thought as he dismissed her. She was not an ordinary spy, but one of a kind. He knew her life story, one of tenacity, the adversity she'd overcome, and the enormous contribution she'd made to North Korea for over forty years. He had no problem granting her an interview with Kwon. In her distrust of Kwon he felt she was likely wrong—a rare event for her—but her interviewing him could do no harm. The general had long admired her suspicious nature and her perseverance.

Someday he planned to make her a general and have her succeed him running RGB as its first female commander. She'd more than earned it.

***

The next day

Kwon had been waiting alone in the interrogation room for almost half an hour before a woman suddenly strode in. She stopped across the table from where he sat, but she did not sit.

"Do you know who I am?" she spoke contentiously, placing her hands on the table and leaning forward.

"No. Should I?" he answered politely, not fazed by her aggressiveness and hostility.

"Madam Bae Doo. Does that name mean anything to you?"

"Sorry, it does not." Kwon straightened in his chair. "Should I be acquainted with that name? Does it belong to you?"

"Does the appellation 'Dragon Lady' ring a bell?" she said, her scowl deepening.

She closely watched his reaction. Not a twinge of recognition showed in his face. He only appeared puzzled, but not rattled.

Kwon wondered why he was suddenly faced with a surprise interrogation after three months of building RGB's confidence in him. Who was this wiry, old woman and where was this going?

She hurled another question at him. "Who was Hwan?"

"He was my handler."

"What did he look like?"

"No idea. Never met him or saw a photograph of him."

She pushed away from the table and crossed her arms. "You worked with him for twenty years and you never met your case officer?"

"That's correct. He preferred it that way. He called the shots. Hwan was all business, not a guy who'd ask you to go out for a drink."

"How'd you communicate?"

"Online, using cryptograms."

"Didn't you find that strange that you never met?"

"At first, but I got over it. Our communiqués constituted the vast majority of our contact. Hwan didn't chitchat. He was my handler and that was that the extent of our relationship." He spoke in a matter of fact manner.

"Jin-Ju … Does that name mean anything to you?" she pressed on. She remained inscrutable, her frown the same, not showing any reaction to his answers.

"Everyone keeps asking me that. I told them his name only came up twice in twenty years in a conversational setting, like a slip of tongue."

"Remember the situation?"

"Yes, both times Hwan abruptly broke off saying he had to contact Jin-Ju immediately."

She had carefully reviewed all the notes from previous interrogations. His story was tight, natural and consistent, but perhaps too consistent.

"What was Hwan's connection, relationship to Jin-Ju?" she asked.

"I supposed he answered to Jin-Ju since both times he quickly broke off our communication to contact him and relay important information."

"Who in the CIA trained you to be such a proficient double agent?" she asked out of the blue, hoping to catch him off guard.

"Dick Tracy," he fired back, not showing emotion.

Reza had prepared him for blind shots like this, training him to quickly give an outrageous response to swiftly turn the tables on the interrogator, throw them off, and allow time for him to regroup his thoughts when caught off guard.

Surprise flickered in her eyes. "Please be serious. This is not a joking matter," she sternly admonished him.

"I apologize. I thought you were kidding." He smiled politely. "No one ever asked me anything that far out."

She raised an eyebrow but let it go. Either he was a world-class actor, or the best damn double agent on the planet. So far, the man was unflappable.

"I hope I didn't offend you, madam," he offered apologetically while she was regrouping. He knew he'd stumped her.

She chose to ignore his apology and move on, dismayed at not being able to get inside his head. She wondered how he'd dreamed up an answer like 'Dick Tracy' on the spur of the moment.

"Did any reference to the 'Dragon Lady' ever come up in your communications with your case officer, Hwan?" she asked, quickly switching topics again to blindside him. "Did Hwan ever mention that name?"

Kwon shook his head. "Never, not once." He was at loss where this was going. He was telling the truth; he'd never heard of the Dragon Lady, so his response very convincing.

"Any idea of who the Dragon Lady might be?" she pressed. "What her role is?"

"No idea." He kept his answers short, on point, no more joking around. This woman clearly lacked a sense of humor. Reza warned him never to elaborate and to limit attempts at levity. The "Dragon Lady" sounded like a fictional character to him, but he refrained from expressing this view.

He watched her reactions; she watched his even more closely. They both engaged in a cat-and-mouse interaction, and the contest appeared to be a draw.

Behind the one-way mirror, General Pak watched both of them. She was clearly frustrated at Kwon's calm, confident demeanor. While he remained collected, he was obviously puzzled at this impromptu interrogation and curious what role this woman played. The general couldn't wait to tell her that he'd told her so—Kwon was imperturbable.

Kwon remained a riddle. Maybe she was correct and Kwon might be playing a game, but the general had no clue what kind of game. And if so, what was the endgame? Whatever the truth, Kwon was a master at the game if it involved deception.

But the fact that the Dragon Lady failed to trap him only reinforced General Pak's assessment that Kwon was trustworthy. No double agent could be that good under pressure, so Kwon must be legitimate. The Dragon Lady based her claims on suspicion, and she lacked evidence. Meanwhile, Kwon was providing valuable cybersecurity upgrades.

The general decided he would tell her to let it go.

But he knew deep down she could not let it go. Trust was simply not in her nature.

Chapter Forty-Four

THE CALL

Pyongyang, December 15th

The sleet pounded Kwon's face, making his eyes water as he walked briskly away from his small apartment in Pyeongcheon. The tears quickly froze as he hurried through the storm. A block away, in one of the city's nicer downtown districts, he passed the ruins of a twenty-three story apartment building that had collapsed in May due to poor construction. The fiasco at Ansan 1 Dong had caused considerable embarrassment to the government's central planning committee. Nothing had been done to rectify the situation, other than the project's chief contractor had been shot—a popular form of saving face in the DPRK. Someone must always be blamed, punished, or reeducated to set an example in order to keep the masses in line.

None of these events would ever happen in South Korea, Kwon thought. North Korea diverted its limited resources to the military, not public housing projects, so tragedies like this happened too often. He shook his head in dismay, surveying the rubble, thinking of all the lives lost.

He'd almost forgotten how harsh life was in North Korea. His twenty years in South Korea had opened his eyes to the appeal of capitalism and democracy. The contrast was inescapable. Most North Koreans knew no better, they just struggled to survive while South Koreans thrived in a nation rich with modern amenities.

Now here he was, living a life of deception, trapped between the two conflicting systems. He was pretending to be one of them, "a spy returning from the cold," as his trainer and case manager, Reza, portrayed his convoluted journey to Pyongyang. NIS had offered him a way out if he served as a double agent for them, tasked with one single mission. He'd accepted the offer after considering the alternative of facing a ROK firing squad for committing espionage.

The time had come to execute that mission. Tonight was the culmination of Reza's intensive training. Kwon knew he could do it, so much depended on it. He was on his way despite the miserable weather.

He paused on the sidewalk to look back at the broken piles of concrete from the disaster, blocked off by yellow tape.

"Those people never had a chance," he muttered.

He lived a block away from the rubble, thankfully in a small, low-profile complex. RGB recently awarded him an apartment for his "good work." He swore he'd never live in a high-rise anywhere.

He shivered, wishing for a heavier coat and a scarf, but he had neither here. It was bitterly cold. Usually busy at this time of the evening, few braved the cold and wet streets tonight. For those who had ventured out, the wind whipped umbrellas inside out, and traffic snarled on the poorly lit street. Kwon glanced at his watch; it read 7:00.

Another block to go to honor his pledge, he thought, then he was off the hook. He privately rejoiced. Soon they would extract him and he'd be a free man.

A few minutes later he saw it, a public phone booth without the usual long line because of the foul weather. Communications bordered on the primitive, like many services in North Korea. Only a few special citizens owned a cell phone, fewer had a landline. Others bought or rented a SIM card if they wished to place calls. He dared not use his for relaying this cryptic message.

Kwon entered the booth, took out three ten chon coins, enough for two minutes of a local call. He wouldn't talk that long unless the connection was bad. He dialed the number he'd committed to memory months ago: 850-2-381-1234. He knew all calls were monitored, so he'd follow his instructions to the letter, sticking to the script he'd practiced for this moment.

A Chinese voice answered on the third ring. The man spoke fluent Cantonese, intelligible to Kwon, who'd studied the language at university.

"Fuk Yu Chinese Palace ..."

Kwon smiled at the chosen name of the restaurant. Obviously the man had been expecting his call to answer with a joke. Kwon assumed it had to be a designated line to receive this single message from him since public phone booths lacked caller ID.

Kwon replied in perfect Cantonese in a Guangzhou dialect, the lingua franca of the Chinese province neighboring Hong Kong. "I'd like to make reservations for the 25th at two p.m., a small private table."

"Your reservation is confirmed for Sunday, December the 25th at two p.m.," the man replied.

"That's correct," Kwon affirmed.

The line immediately went dead. There were no further questions regarding name, or number in the party. Time elapsed was less than thirty seconds, so difficult to trace. That was it. Task completed.

Kwon felt a tremendous weight lifted from him. He contemplated grabbing a bite since he was already out. He couldn't get any wetter or colder. Maybe some hot rice wine to knock off the chill, a celebration of sorts. Relief filled him at having completed the call, making him feel almost giddy.

"Fuk Yu!" he said, laughing out loud, recalling the witty greeting by the agent receiving his call. He realized it was his first laugh in over half a year.

As he exited the phone booth he glimpsed an elderly, wiry little woman studying him from a bus stop shelter thirty meters away. He tensed. Dressed in a raincoat, collar up, she peered out from under her rain hat and dripping umbrella. Kwon immediately sensed that she was a spook, and he was the target. She never looked away, staring at him intently.

He knew RGB had kept him under surveillance for months, but they had backed off recently. Was she out on a hit job? A wave of apprehension swept over him.

He carefully looked around. They were the only two people in the block. No surveillance team seemed to be operating, so she must be working alone. But he'd exercise a "dry clean" maneuver to evade surveillance on the way to the restaurant as a precaution, and hopefully lose her tail. He knew the neighborhood and hoped she didn't. He doubted she would stand outside very long in this miserable weather. He bet she'd abandon her task when he lingered inside the café if she happened to find him there.

After walking a half block, he looked back over his shoulder. She was gone. She wasn't tailing him.

Confused, he ruled out a forward spotter; there was no one in sight. No cars where someone might be observing him from the dimly lit street. The worsening storm had driven everyone inside. Even the traffic was letting up as the sleet blew by horizontally. The freezing wind bit him to the bone.

He turned around and started back, curious where she'd gone. He knew he shouldn't be pursuing her, snooping, but he couldn't help himself. He had to be certain. Then he spotted her, in the same phone booth he'd used, talking on the phone, her hat off. He squinted to make out her features through the sleet and the booth's sleet-spattered windows from this distance. She seemed too involved in talking to notice him.

He gasped and stopped walking abruptly. It was her. There was no mistaking the wiry little woman who'd harshly interrogated him two days ago, Madam Bae Doo.

Who the hell was she, and why was she tracking him?

He turned and took off while the opportunity presented itself, maintaining a fast pace directly to the restaurant.

***

"This is Commander Bae Doo, RGB," the Dragon Lady said from inside the phone booth. "I want you to trace that last call from this booth, number 1964, immediately. I assume you monitored the call as we require, so retrieve it."

"Yes, Commander," the reply came, "right away."

Two minutes passed, and she became impatient. "Please hurry, this involves national security."

A moment later the answer came. "A short call was placed to the 'Fuk Yu Chinese Palace' restaurant, a local number."

"Check your directory for an address," she said.

It seemed as though an eternity passed. "What's happening, operator?" she asked impatiently. "What seems to be the problem?"

"Sorry. Something's wrong. There is no listing for a Chinese restaurant under that name. Not in Pyongyang or in North Korea. We've double-checked and cross-referenced all Chinese restaurants on our computer. We found nothing even close to that name. The number dialed was 850-2-381-1234. That's a local phone number. I had my supervisor trace that number, and there is no such number locally or in North Korea. When we dialed it, we reached a dead line three times. It simply doesn't exist."

"Neither exist?" she asked, incredulous. "No restaurant? No phone line?"

"That's correct, no listings, Commander."

Frustrated, she took another tack. "Did you record the conversation?"

"We did. They spoke for less than thirty seconds."

"What did they say?"

"They spoke in Chinese, a Cantonese dialect, we believe. It sounded like a simple, brief request for a dinner reservation."

She slammed her hand against the wall of the phone booth. "*Shibal!* Fuck!"

"Pardon me, Commander?"

"Nothing … Sorry." She slammed the phone back into its rest.

They had used a one-time pad, not traceable.

The irony of the name, "Fuk Yu," was not lost on her. They were mocking her, adding insult to injury, knowing RGB would trace the call at some point.

This episode convinced her that Kwon was intricately involved in a very clever plot of some sort. He'd been setting something up with a prearranged code, a doublespeak message in Cantonese.

Now she was convinced more than ever that Kwon was a double agent. She vowed to unravel the riddle.

CHAPTER FORTY-FIVE

BINGO

Langley, December 16th

Rokman was smiling as he strode into Biff's office.

"Kwon came through big time, Biff," Rokman said. "Nam wired the target date we've been waiting for. Cryptogram came in late last night, relayed from our Chinese operative in Pyongyang. I deciphered it."

"Good news. When do they plan the launch?" Biff asked.

"Get this, December the 25th at 1400 hours, two p.m. their time. A few hours later, early this morning, our spiders' malware inside their computer system confirmed their plan."

"So we can bank on the intel since it's been confirmed by both sources?"

"Right on, DPRK set the date late yesterday. Kwon contacted our covert agent last night who notified Nam. Our SIGINT confirmed the HUMINT twelve hours later. Sweet, huh?"

"Bingo! Impressive when both human and signal intelligence come together. How'd Kwon establish contact with our embedded Hong Kong operative? Follow our plan?"

"To the letter, from a public phone booth to the number he memorized, as we instructed."

"Traceable?" Biff asked.

"Nope, they used a one-time pad. They communicated for only about thirty seconds in a Cantonese dialect. Something Reza set up to add complexity to confuse anyone trying to trace the brief call. Kwon stuck to the script verbatim, but our operative adlibbed the name of the Chinese restaurant when he answered Kwon's call."

"How's that?"

"Jimmy answered the call with, 'Fuk Yu Chinese Palace.'"

They shared a good laugh at the riff.

"Sounds like Jimmy Wong," Biff said, smiling. "He's a character. You have to let Reza know about this," Biff added. "He'll get a kick out of it."

"Will do. Good show, huh? Kwon kept his commitment, nailed it, and our malware spiders established DPRK's plan beyond a doubt."

"Which is?"

"Same as last year's, they plan to launch their satellite from Sohae out over the Yellow Sea, coursing south over the South China Sea. Plan to announce to the world it's another routine space launch of a weather satellite."

"They've chosen the predictable route they've used before, using a proven guise, not surprisingly. Obviously they haven't perfected ICBM reentry technology, so they'll go the satellite route for deception to explode their nuclear EMP device above our stratosphere. So the date's Christmas day."

"Right, and Christmas falls on a Sunday this year."

"It looks like they're taking a page out of Hitler's book, trying to catch everyone off guard by launching a major offensive on a holiday or weekend. The Fuehrer loved that tactic to unleash an attack. That's only nine days from now." Biff stood from his chair. "I'll go visit the admiral to get the ball rolling on our counteraction plan. Everyone's been briefed on the contingency plans, so it'll be just a formality to fire it through the levels of command."

***

Joint Chiefs of Staff

"Great job of counter intelligence, Admiral Delaney," General Abrams said. "I commend you and your staff."

"I must give credit to my Counterterrorism Director, Biff Roberts, for coming up this scheme," Admiral Delaney said. "He's worked closely with NIS in ROK the past seven months. If I told you our sources and methods you'd never believe it possible, but Roberts made it happen, General."

"If Roberts was involved, I'd believe anything. He's got a knack for pulling off the spectacular." The general added, "We'll move the Seventh Fleet up north from the South China Sea to a position off the tip of South Korea and Japan as soon as the DOD authorizes it. Our contingency plan is solid and tested under spontaneous action scenarios. Our Navy's good to go under all circumstances should Plan A fail."

***

U.S. Department of Defense

"Solid strategy, General Abrams," the Secretary of Defense said. "All options have been considered. We'll get it signed off with POTUS within an hour. He's on board with the proposed plan. You have our permission to start moving the Seventh Fleet northward out of the South China Sea under the guise of conducting a routine exercise in the East China Sea off the southern tips of Japan and South Korea. We'll announce it publically as a prearranged joint maneuver with Japan."

"Thank you, sir."

***

Seventh Fleet Carrier Task Force – South China Sea

"Got our orders for operation 'Santa Claus', Admiral," the captain said.

Admiral Ross Thompson carefully examined the orders out of D.C. and smiled.

"Captain Turner," the admiral said, "give the order to start moving our carrier task force north out of the South China Sea. Hold our position off the south coast of South Korea in the East China Sea, coordinates 31 degrees 00 N/ 128 degrees 20 E, our rendezvous point with the Japanese Fleet."

Admiral Thompson continued, "Instruct our fleet admirals and captains to rehearse our anti-ballistic missile protocols with respective personnel while en route. I want all of our BMD systems battle ready in case Plan A fails. Instruct our fleet cruisers and destroyers to double check their Aegis, RIM, and FTM intercept missile defense systems, including

MERV capabilities, in case our North Korean intel turns out to be disinformation. Not taking any chances, a lot at stake, Understand?"

"Yes, sir."

"Be certain our missile terminal guidance jamming systems have the critical Sohae launch site coordinates locked in to include the anticipated missile flight path. Also, contact our destroyer commanders that have the new electromagnetic rail guns and tell them to be ready for a live exercise. We may need to employ the full array of our missile defense systems."

"Yes, sir, right away. Anything else, sir?"

"Yes, Captain, contact Captain Sorensen of SSGN Shark to call me on my private line in my quarters at 1800 hours," he added. "We need to go over Plan A."

Within a half an hour, the aircraft carriers U.S.S. *Shiloh* and *George Washington* with their Seventh Fleet strike task force of 160 aircraft, 60 escort ships, and 7,500 Navy and Marine personnel, steamed north. The fleet was outfitted with sixty-eight of the latest, cutting-edge intercept missiles, a defensive arsenal tested for threatening scenarios like the one they anticipated loomed ahead. They understood they were Plan B, the strategic fallback plan for America's national defense.

***

Aboard the SSGN Shark, 1800 hours

"Captain Sorenson here, Admiral."

"Line secure," Admiral Thompson said. "Just want to make certain we're on the same page, Captain. We're heading north as we speak. Operation 'Santa Claus' has been cleared. I received the task force orders not long ago and ordered my carrier strike force to head on up to the East China Sea air defense identification zone. Those coordinates are 31 degrees 00 N/ 128 degrees 20 E. Got 'em?"

"Yes, sir," Sorenson said, "I'm quite familiar with the waters there." As captain of the Ohio class SSGN nuclear attack sub, nicknamed "Shark," Alf Sorenson was looking forward to this newest mission. He knew of its importance for U.S. and global security, and was eager to be a part of it.

"Good," the admiral said. "We'll meet up with our Japanese allies there, ostensibly to conduct joint exercises. The DOD will announce this operational plan publically tomorrow. Where are you presently?"

"In sushi heaven," Sorenson said, "residing in port at Yokosuka, just awaiting your call, sir. Plan to head out in the a.m. to meet up with you at the rendezvous point. We're double-checking our vertical launching systems retrofits. Our top sub engineers here like our VLS modifications. We'll be good to go."

"You're certain of your new toy's range and the VLS functional modifications?" the admiral asked.

"Yes, sir, got six hundred miles range, but won't need that much, maybe 200 at most. VLS modification's a good fit, houses our toys that have about the same specs as a Tomahawk missile. I foresee no problems, sir."

"Okay, sounds good. We'll create the diversion with our mock exercises in the East China Sea while you cruise up into the Yellow Sea. We're your backup anti-ballistic missile defense, Plan B. Advise you to stay out of North Korea territorial waters, stay well off shore. You're on your own up there by the 38th parallel."

"I fully understand, Admiral. I'm fortunate in having the same crew as on my two prior critical missions. You can count on us, sir. I don't think you'll need to expend your BMD arsenal."

"I'm sure your crew will perform well, Captain. That's why I requested your transfer to the Seventh Fleet. This is, as you mentioned, a very critical mission. A lot is riding on your performance."

"Thank you for the opportunity, sir. We'll get the job done."

Captain Sorenson was a rising star in the SSGN attack fleet. In the past two years he'd conducted successful missions with distinction in the Gulf of Mexico and the Mediterranean to thwart enemy plots considered existential threats. CINCPAC picked up on those accomplishments and granted Admiral Thompson's request for Sorenson's transfer with his intact crew to the Pacific theater.

"You'll make Rear Admiral if operation 'Santa Claus' goes as planned," Admiral Thompson assured him before he signed off. "Carry on, sailor."

"Aye, sir."

***

RGB Headquarters – Pyongyang, North Korea

The Dragon Lady stood before General Pak's desk, her eyes narrowed. "This is so over the top, General. Kwon went out in that storm last night and walked three blocks in sleet to make a thirty-second phone call from a public booth to a nonexistent Chinese restaurant using a phone number that doesn't exist either. They spoke in a Cantonese dialect, ostensibly to make a dinner reservation nine days from now. It's bizarre; why would anyone do that?" The Dragon Lady was livid, her usual calm gone. "I'm convinced he's a spy, General. There's no other explanation for his outlandish behavior."

"How can you be certain? Maybe he has a lady friend who's married and is simply arranging a rendezvous," he said, trying to calm her tirade.

She shook her head. "He called a man, not a woman. They spoke in a code. The reservation date he requested coincides with the date of our rocket launch on the twenty fifth of December. That can't possibly be another of his strange coincidences. Kwon relayed a message. He's up to no good."

"Even if he did this," the general said, "I don't see that relaying a date is a threat, Madam. We'd planned to announce our satellite launch publicly tomorrow, for the twenty-fifth of December. We'll simply change our announcement to a January first launch date, but go ahead with our original plans on the twenty-fifth. That disinformation should throw off any plans they might have. I agree that is suspicious behavior by Kwon, but there's no way our adversaries can prevent what we bill publically as an innocent weather satellite launch. They didn't interfere last year. No reason to interfere on this occasion. The EMP warhead is a closely guarded secret among a dozen of us. Kwon had no access to that classified information. Only the director in his intel unit and a few generals and top leaders know our plan. Nothing can stop us now."

"Possibly not, General," she said, "but the Seventh Fleet is planning a joint exercise with Japan next week before our launch. Is that also a coincidence?" She was clearly frustrated he didn't share her sense of alarm.

"They don't have the technology to shoot down our UNHA-3 rocket, or they would have demonstrated that capability by now," General Pak countered. He could tell by her expression she was disappointed in his response, so he added, "I promise to look into the situation personally." He hoped that would calm her down. No one had been vetted as thoroughly as Kwon. "But I am certain Kwon is no double agent, he's passed every test."

"I hope you are correct in your appraisal, sir. If not …"

"We've watched him like a hawk. Your information is the first and only incident of anything remotely suspicious in his behavior since his mysterious arrival here. He's upgraded our cybersecurity systems, and given us valuable intelligence regarding ROK capabilities. Why should he do that unless he's on our side?"

"How do you know he wasn't disseminating disinformation," she said, "cooked intelligence?"

He didn't answer, just stared at her. She was certainly persistent in her skepticism, not retreating an inch.

"General Pak, Kwon's a spy. We've each had forty years in this business and should recognize a clever operative when we see one. Kwon's an expert double agent in a position to compromise our mission," she warned. "We must act now before it's too late."

This woman just wouldn't let go of her preoccupation with Kwon as a double agent. Although the general conceded there were some uncanny coincidences she cited with Kwon, he had already concluded Kwon was no double agent, and now he had bigger matters to deal with. Their EMP-missile master plan took priority. Perhaps later he would revisit her ideas about Kwon, but not now.

The Dragon Lady was the only officer in RGB he considered his peer. He respected her judgment, but he was convinced he was right on this one. No one could be so accomplished as to delude everyone but the Dragon Lady.

Or was he missing a part to the puzzle? Could the Dragon Lady's intuition be on target?

"Let me think about this, Madam," General Pak finally said. "I'll take your reservations under consideration, and I'll get back to you."

"Soon, I hope, General." She turned without being dismissed and marched off in a huff. Only she could get away with such an act of insubordination.

CHAPTER FORTY-SIX

OPERATION SANTA CLAUS

Yellow Sea
December 25th

"**A**re coordinates for the Sohae launch site programmed into our computers from our present GPS location, Commander?" Captain Sorenson asked.

"Affirmative, sir, DMS Latitude 39 degrees 39'70N / Longitude 124 degrees 42' 5E punched in our computers. Also double-checked for correlation with our satellite GPS uplink," his XO, Commander 'Jock' Williams, replied.

"Accuracy is paramount in this operation. No room for error."

"Those numbers are right on the bull's eye for the Sohae, North Korean rocket pad, Captain."

Captain Sorenson glanced at his Luminox tactical watch. "Ten hundred now, they should be well into the process of fueling their UNHA-3 rocket booster for the 1400 launch."

"Our ELF antenna is relaying sat images that confirm your observation, sir. Affirmative, they are in that fueling process. You can see the liquid fuel trucks pulled up alongside the booster rocket. DPRK is definitely set to launch today, the date our CIA intel indicated. The January 1 launch date DPRK announced last week was disinformation by North Korea designed to throw us off. The CIA intelligence estimates nailed it this time, right on the 25th of December.

"By the way," the XO added, "Merry Christmas, Captain."

"And a very Merry Christmas to you, Jock, can you believe it? Some way to spend the holiday, out here in the middle of the Yellow Sea."

"War games never take a holiday, sir."

"Got that right, XO, and this is big game time … Okay then, if fueling is underway, our mission is set to go. We have no Christmas tree, but let's open our special packages anyway."

"Yes, sir." The commander smiled. "This will be a big time celebration no one will ever forget."

"Alert the launch crew in fire control to ready our VLSs for live fire at those coordinates at exactly 1030, one half hour from now," Sorenson said. "Order them to start fully pressurizing the compartments. I'll instruct CACC to acquire our target and lock it in on our command computers and fire command."

"Firing sequence, sir?"

"Sequence all six CHAMP cruise missiles to strike targets two seconds apart. Follow our protocol to alternately fire the canisters from starboard to port VLS compartments. Six missiles may be a bit of overkill, but we only get one shot at this."

"Aye, sir, orders will be relayed immediately." The XO scurried off aft from the CACC, the submarine's command and control center, to personally communicate with fire control officers. His excitement wasn't lost on the sub's captain.

"Why not use the sub's intercom? Oh, well …"

The nuclear attack sub SSGN Shark lay submerged in quiet mode twenty fathoms beneath the Yellow Sea, two hundred miles southwest of North Korea's satellite launch site at Sohae. The remote rocket site was located 130 miles north of the capital city of Pyongyang on the country's west coast. They'd launched a weather satellite from this seaside location the prior year. Sohae presented an ideal over-the-sea surface target from the Shark's vantage position. Captain Sorenson was assured they were undetected in international waters below the 38th parallel. His sensitive radar array could practically spot a whale fifty miles away. No maritime activity noted. Tactically he sat in the cat bird's seat.

He smiled in contentment. They enjoyed a stealth factor to launch their modified cruise missiles in six different low trajectory courses to avoid early radar detection and countermeasures. Even after spending almost half his adult years underwater as a submariner, he still experienced a thrill with every new mission.

Captain Sorenson checked his watch again — fifteen minutes to go. His XO returned from delivering his orders.

Obviously Jock wanted to brief the fire crew in person, Sorenson thought. This XO left nothing to chance or misunderstanding, an admirable trait, he noted.

"One final question, commander," the captain said, "have you double-checked that all six missiles are programmed to self-destruct after our mission is accomplished? We dare not leave a signature, not a trace."

"Yes, sir, after accomplishing their mission, they're set to explode ten miles past our target in an unpopulated area inland northeast of the Sohae launch pad. Our TERCOM guidance technology will ensure that happens. Nothing will remain of the missiles for DPRK to reconstruct, not enough fragments to track the weapons' source, or even begin to figure out anything technical about our latest weapon. They will not document who delivered the attack, no way."

"Good. They won't know what hit them. They'll suffer no loss of personnel or infrastructure, just experience all their electronics suddenly fried, totally out of commission. Their EMP rocket mission will be interdicted by our EMP missiles leaving their UNHA-3 rocket impotent, resting limp on the pad. Find that ironic, Edwards?"

"Ultimate one-upmanship, sir. Incredible."

Sorenson nodded. "I must say it's a fascinating weapon, this CHAMP missile. Our counter-electronic, high-powered, microwave advanced missile project delivered a drone-missile hybrid, an ingenious bit of engineering, to cripple an enemy without loss of life. This will set them back awhile, having to replace their electronics, repair the site, and rethink their strategy, realizing we have an effective countermeasure."

"Our satellite overhead and our logs will record this for Navy history books, Captain."

"Won't be surprised, Jock." Sorenson checked the time again. "It's almost 1030, time to commence firing." A minute later he gave the order. Then he pushed back in his console chair to await the satellite feed of the results of the attack.

Swiftly, on his command, six CHAMP missiles sequentially broke the surface of the Yellow Sea from their pressurized VLS compartments, heading skyward, each missile two seconds apart. Solid fuel propellant kicked in, driven by an F-415 turbo-fan engine powered by an Arc MK 135 rocket motor similar to those used to thrust a Tomahawk cruise missile into flight. Stabilizing fins automatically deployed, propelling the missiles in a subsonic 600-mph trajectory to target acquisition. Sophisticated guidance systems assured precision accuracy. GPS and inertial systems would guide the CHAMP missiles in six different low trajectories to reach the programmed target in Sohae about twenty minutes from launch. Aeronautical engineering built-in guidance systems—TERCOM, terrain contour matching; DSMAC, digital scene matching area correlation; and ATR, an algorithm for automatic target recognition—would determine each missile's pinpoint terminal accuracy. The low-trajectory course would evade enemy radar, making it highly unlikely defensive radar and SAM missiles would detect and intercept the incoming self-propelled missiles. The missiles also were equipped with jam-resistant GPS receivers, enhancing efficacy. Finally, the submarine launch conferred a stealth factor over a land or air launch. The Shark enjoyed the element of surprise with this bold operation.

Captain Sorenson smiled. "This is what we live for, Jock. This is what we do, young man."

***

The Annapolis Naval Academy archives would later record that at precisely 1030 hours on December the 25th Captain Alf Sorenson, class of '76, commanding an Ohio class nuclear attack submarine, gave the order that introduced a new era of modern warfare by initiating a successful EMP cruise missile attack on a hostile North Korean rocket site. The bold attack aborted a nefarious enemy plot with the intention of a sneak, nuclear-triggered EMP attack from their space satellite over the USA. The SSGN Shark averted a twenty-first century Pearl Harbor, thanks to actionable CIA and South Korean intelligence.

***

Sohae Launch Site

"*Shibal!*" General Pak cursed. "What happened?"

The refueling of the UNHA-3 booster rocket had just abruptly stopped. All of the lights in the entire area flickered out. Sunlight still reached the control room through the large observation window that faced the launch pad.

"We've lost power," Pak realized. "Contact the launch pad engineering control immediately, this is a serious complication! A liquid oxygen or hydrogen leak, or slightest spark may ignite the kerosene-nitric acid liquid propellant in the stage one booster rocket, causing an explosion."

"I can't contact anyone, General!" the chief engineer cried. "All of our electronics have suddenly shut down. We have no electricity!"

"Our propane back-up system should have kicked in. What's going on?"

"The automatic relay shut down. Nothing requiring electricity is functioning. We're blacked out, General. No computers, no communications, lights—nothing's working. We have lost control. We must abort the mission. The Galaxy-3 rocket booster might explode at any time if there's a leak in the tank." The panic in the chief engineer's voice alarmed General Pak.

"It appears that our rocket just aborted itself on the pad. Clear out our gantry personnel for their safety," General Pak dourly said, stunned at this catastrophe.

"Send someone to run over to contact fire control immediately!" he hastily added. "Get them hopping! This is an emergency!"

A wave of anxiety swept over the dozen or so rocket engineers, high-ranking military, and intelligence officers who filled the control room, all cleared for this top-secret mission. Mass confusion reigned. General Pak struggled to regain his composure. He knew he had to take charge of the perilous situation to avert a disaster.

Stunned, he sank back in his chair in utter disbelief. "What the hell happened?" he said.

In a state of shock, everyone awaited his command, exchanging theories for the sudden total loss of electricity. The general was at loss as to what he should do.

A moment later a colonel rushed into the room. "We were just attacked by missiles coming in from the sea," he announced, "traveling undetected at very low altitudes at high speed. They just missed us. I saw them whiz by overhead. They exploded ten miles northeast of here after passing directly over our launch site."

"You say they missed us? They exploded ten miles away?" General Pak shouted, exasperated. "How do you explain the entire shutdown of all our electronics? Account for the absence of any loss of personnel? Or explain that no destruction of infrastructure occurred at our launch pad?" What was this officer telling him? "What kind of a missile attack is that, Colonel?"

The colonel shook his head, wide-eyed. "I can't tell you, General. I have no explanation for what just happened."

"I do." It was a woman's voice, clear and strong from the back of the room. Everyone turned to see who was speaking with such a crisp, commanding attitude.

"The explanation should be obvious to you," the Dragon Lady said, stepping forward out of the shadows. "We were just hit by a cruise missile EMP attack that irreparably destroyed all of our electronics. Forget our hopes of a surprise satellite attack of a similar nature on them. It's been preempted. Our mission is over. Our rocket satellite plans have been aborted by a clever enemy countermeasure. To accomplish this attack they had to know our plans all along. How else could they successfully foil our launch during the fueling process, just hours before liftoff? Someone divulged our plan."

Everyone in the room listened intently. You could have heard a pin drop in the command post. A few in the know recognized her, but most did not. But all recognized that this imperious woman knew what she was talking about from the conviction in her tone. The plausibility of her explanation for this catastrophe convinced them of her intellect. Her swift grasp of the enormity of the situation swayed them. And clearly, she must be a powerful, high-ranking official to address generals in that lecturing tone. Women rarely reached this level of influence and command, but it became evident that she was taking charge while General Pak wavered in indecision. She commanded everyone's attention.

"Our classified master plan was compromised," she continued, "and our intelligence circle penetrated to allow this to occur. Witness the massive sabotage by an electromagnetic pulse emitted from a pinpoint missile flyby. This timely event preempted a similar scenario we intended to inflict upon the USA on a grand scale under the guise of a weather satellite. They aborted our lift-off. What just happened is a well-calculated and executed plan by our enemies using inside information to thwart us. And they used a high-tech weapon we never even knew existed."

General Pak had immediately recognized the Dragon Lady's shrill voice. As she delivered her accurate interpretation of events, she glared at him with contempt. He averted his gaze from her scowling face. As stark reality sunk in, his spirits deflated. He broke out in a cold sweat.

Madam Bae Doo-Na was correct all along. He had been badly mistaken and would be held responsible for this disaster. He must accept the consequences—the blame, the shame, and loss of face that came with it.

She knew it, others would soon know it, and he would soon be a pariah, having fallen from grace in North Korea's insular, unforgiving society. It had taken him forty years to reach the pinnacle of his career, but now it was all dashed in a moment, just like their launch plans. The Dragon Lady was correct. Kwon must be a double agent who had exposed their secret plans, leading to this foreign military interdiction, and destroying their grand strategy to cripple the USA. The general had not a shred of evidence to prove it, but he sensed the Dragon Lady's suspicions would prevail when he was pressed to answer for this calamity. He would have to explain why he accepted Kwon into their inner circle of RGB intelligence.

As if the rocket failure was not a monumental enough of a problem, moments later the Galaxy-3 first stage rocket booster being fueled on the space launch vehicle tower exploded. The ground shook. Windows were blown out from the concussion. Flames leaped high into the sky; acrid smoke billowed. The thirty-meter gantry teetered and then collapsed into rubble on its launch pad.

Recovery of the rocket's nuclear warhead inside the weather satellite atop the rocket would pose a critical problem, General Pak realized, with the threat of nuclear contamination. And culpability lay at his doorstep.

A bad situation had just deteriorated into a much worse state of affairs for the respected commanding general of the RGB. General Pak had personally convinced Kim Jong-un that the plan would succeed in defeating America. Kim bought into the scheme; the bold concept fit Kim's ego-driven quest for recognition and respect. Kim had none of his father's military insight or restraint. He trusted General Pak to punish America.

Once the great leader had been convinced, Pak became caught up in an Abilene paradox of management of the classified mission. Despite its risks, quirks, and tactical challenges, everyone went along with the reckless plan. If the supreme leader endorsed it, no one questioned its feasibility. So the foolhardy, dangerous project had lurched ahead.

The stratagem represented a madman's quest, Kim Jong-un's pursuit of identity on the world's stage as a powerful national leader, one to be respected. He viewed himself as an emperor, but he was just another loose-cannon dictator bent on a wicked mission. The annals of history were filled with stories of ill-advised conquest attempts to fulfill the delusions of grandeur of men like him.

Next to Kim Jong-un, Pak was considered the most important man in the nation. No more.

Only the Dragon Lady had rocked the boat with her suspicions of Kwon. She'd expressed her disbelief for Kwon's story in no uncertain terms to General Pak, but he'd dismissed her accusations. The soundness of her suspicions was clearly evident in retrospect. He should have listened and possibly avoided this calamity. Now his fate lay in her hands.

CHAPTER FORTY-SEVEN

THE FALLOUT

Moments later

Aboard the Shark

"**H**oly shit!" Jock said. "Look at the live satellite feed, Captain. You won't believe it."

Sorenson immediately realized what had happened. "Their rocket just exploded on the pad. Our EMP missiles knocked out everything connected with electricity, but something or someone must have accidently ignited the rocket booster's liquid fuel … Maybe a leak, a last minute spark, what do you think, Jock? Now they have a critical warhead recovery problem."

"Got that right, they're in deep kimchi. Don't have a clue what ignited the fuel, but you bet there'll be serious repercussions. A lot of explaining to do."

"Unexplained mishaps with liquid rocket propellants are not uncommon. They may never discover the cause of the explosion. But I'll tell you this — the incident will really screw up their rocket program. Heads will roll."

His XO shook his head. "Hate to be the one in charge of that project."

"Whoever he is, he'll pay dearly. Let's get out of here and reunite with our Seventh Fleet in the East China Sea. We've done our job. Time to move on, not leaving a trace," Captain Sorenson ordered.

Jock was still shaking his head as he prepared to move the sub out. "I didn't see that coming, Captain. Wow! What an explosion."

***

NIS Headquarters – Seoul

The American spy satellite, the eye in the sky, documented the episode occurring just 250 miles north of South Korea's capital city of Seoul.

Director Nam and his deputy, Kim, stared at the enhanced screen relaying the photos of the spectacular explosion. Moments later, they watched the remains of the North Korean space rocket and its gantry collapse on its Sohae launch pad. Stunned, their jaws dropped. The uplink to the U.S. satellite photos left no room for confusion, the cameras' clarity dispelling any doubt of what just transpired.

"If they had a nuclear warhead concealed in that satellite," Nam said, "they're in seriously deep shit. We should contact Biff Roberts at Langley, Kim. I'm anxious to hear his reaction to this unexpected dividend. I can't wait to see how the North Koreans try to squirm out of this."

"I'm certain they'll manufacture a lie, mask the failure, and not breathe a word of sabotage, Director, much less allude to an EMP attack."

***

CIA – Langley

"Director Nam on secure line from Seoul," Biff's Marine attaché said.

Biff picked up the phone quickly, eager to hear Nam's reaction.

"I assume you just saw that?" Nam asked, getting right to the point.

"I did, can you believe it? The UNHA-3 uses flammable liquid fuel in their rocket booster. It's based on old Scud technology, driving four clustered Nodong motors in the phase one booster. That fuel powered their weather satellite payload into space successfully last year, so I suppose they saw no problem using it again. But it blew sky high this year, a risk inherent when using liquid fuel. Kerosene mixtures will burn hot and long; it'll be a mess to recover the warhead."

"That explosion was incredible. What happened? Related in any way to the EMP attack?"

"Doubt it, suspect it was coincidental, but we're trying to figure that one out. No explanation at this point. We've lost some of our rockets without a clue despite all of our experience."

"You know they will never divulge what happened, will deny everything," Nam said. "That's their modus operandi."

"I won't hold my breath waiting for them to explain the launch failure. I do know there will be serious repercussion behind the scenes and a lot of hog wash denials. Not to mention difficulty recovering the nuclear warhead. It will not end well for whoever honchoed the project."

"You bet. Your sub EMP missile attack was a resounding success. This could turn out to be a bonus for us."

"Indeed. Our SSGN did a number on them with the CHAMP missiles, fabulous technology. The operation came off without a hitch, and the surprise detonation of the rocket on the pad may be a windfall in setting back their space program. It'll make it difficult for DPRK to cover up the incident with disinformation."

"I agree. It will be more than an embarrassment for RGB's General Pak. Our spies inform us that he spearheaded the project from day one. He'll take the rap."

"His role may cost him his head," Biff said. "Political legitimacy is the coin of the realm in North Korea, and Pak has spent his capital."

"This will certainly not end well for him," Nam agreed. "He's the number two man up there. It's more than loss of face. As you Americans say, he's toast."

Both intelligence directors shared a laugh, pleased over North Korea's misfortune. Schadenfreude thrived among intelligence agencies when an enemy plot cratered, especially if they covertly contributed to its failure.

"I'm certain they will seek a culprit," Biff said, "but lacking one, someone will definitely be the scapegoat. Pak may be the first to go. Kwon did a great job as a double agent, accomplished his task. He's earned reparation as a free man in South Korea as we promised. Let's get him out of there."

"We plan to extract him. It will pose a challenge not to lose any of our embedded agents in the process. It will require skillful execution."

"Successful extraction is never a foregone conclusion in my experience. It's a tricky business, just like infiltrating a double agent."

"Speaking of infiltrating Kwon," Nam said, "initially I was skeptical of your elaborate plan, but your team pulled it off. Getting Kwon inside the RGB along with infecting their security system with malware was a masterful ploy. Your submarine operation, 'Santa Claus', was another resounding success. My congratulations."

"Thank you, the breaks went our way."

"The freak explosion was a windfall complicating their rocket program," Nam said. "They'll need to rethink their agenda. We owe you. Kwon deserves our gratitude, also. We need to reward him and quickly get him out of there, as you say."

"The sooner the better," Biff replied, "he'll be under suspicion for sure. Time is of essence. They'll look to place the blame, and lack of evidence will not dissuade them. They need to hold someone responsible. Let's pull him out of there as soon as possible."

"As I said, extraction might be easier said than done, but we'll get on it right away," Nam agreed. "I hope to come up with a plan to bring him home to his family soon. It's a dicey business as you well know. Let's touch base next week and I'll run our plan by you."

"Okay," Biff said, "I'll call you for an update."

***

The next day
Pyongyang, North Korea

THE *Daily Times* headline read: *FREAK EXPLOSION DESTROYS SPACE WEATHER SATELLITE ROCKET ON PAD IN SOHAE.*

The story that followed explained the fueling risks of rockets with liquid propellant, citing numerous space rocket accidents worldwide, downplaying the incident. But the article made no mention of the sudden electronic failures at the Sohae launch site. Those who witnessed the blackout were sworn to secrecy, no personal accounts were allowed. The editor emphasized that no one was killed, and there was no evidence of sabotage. And no blame was placed, although an investigation into the incident was underway. The supreme leader, Kim Jong-un, expressed his regrets and assured the public that DPRK's space program would continue unabated, reminding them last year's space launch of a weather satellite had been successful.

General Pak desperately hoped the news release would put the issue to rest. He had carefully crafted the article for the editor.

***

RGB Intel Unit – The same day

Kwon read the newspaper article with trepidation, knowing General Pak had crafted the disinformation. That was the general's forte. No one in the unit suspected Kwon's role, but he knew the woman who interrogated him last week harbored misgivings about him. She'd followed him in the storm, saw him make the phone call. That could raise a cloud of suspicion, which might put him at risk. The senior officers treated her with deference and respect to her face, but scornfully called her the Dragon Lady behind her back. They clearly feared her, and so did Kwon. He worried she might expose him or use him as a scapegoat for the rocket disaster.

He needed a way out. He'd communicated with his handler last week using a one- time pad call to prevent tracing, but that left him no bailout number to call for help. He was stranded. If the Dragon Lady accused him of being a double agent, under these frenzied circumstances, they would likely believe her. Kwon felt a sense of impending doom. He could only hope and pray Nam and the NIS would keep their end of the bargain and extract him in time.

Kwon missed his family, and almost as intensely, he missed South Korea. He'd forgotten the brutal nature of everyday life in North Korea. He'd grown to appreciate the freedom and opportunity in South Korea. It had taken a journey back north for him to realize how deeply he had changed.

He wanted out. He wanted to return home.

***

One week later, Seoul

"Langley on secure direct line, Director. Biff Roberts calling."

NIS Director Nam reluctantly picked up the phone, dreading this anticipated call from D.C. They'd arranged to touch base today to discuss Kwon's extraction.

"How's your extraction plan going?" Biff asked.

"Not well. Shit hit the fan up in North Korea this week, Biff," Nam said, frustration clear in his voice.

Biff didn't like the sound of that. "Fill me in," he said.

Nam took a deep breath, choosing his words carefully. His message was painful to relate.

"As we predicted, a big shakeup followed the Sohae rocket launch failure. Madam Bae Doo, the Dragon Lady, conducted a coup d'état, forcing General Pak to step down. She's now running the RGB show for DPRK."

"Pak got sacked, as we anticipated," Biff commented.

"The fallout doesn't end there…" Nam continued reluctantly. "Kim Jong-un got involved."

"And?" Biff asked, anxious for the details, certain Nam's story didn't have a happy ending.

"The supreme leader had Pak shot the next day in the public square."

"An act of vengeance to set an example for the other generals to demonstrate his power, I assume?" Biff said.

"Precisely, Kim made an example of Pak. North Korea's version of harsh, swift justice. No trial or tribunals."

"What's Kwon's status? Will you be able to extract him?"

"That won't be necessary, I'm sorry to say. They moved too quickly to administer punishment. Kim had Kwon eliminated the next day based on the Dragon Lady's accusations he was a South Korean double agent. They had no evidence but used him to settle the score. He went down following the summary judgment of the dictator, with no day in court."

"Good Lord!" Biff said. "They shot him too?"

"I wish he'd been so fortunate," Nam said quietly. "Kwon died from a barbaric act."

"Don't tell me…" Nothing that brutal regime did would likely surprise him, but it didn't make their atrocities any less disturbing to hear.

"I have to … It's horrible, Biff, unthinkable cruelty … That savage, Kim Jong-un, viciously ordered Kwon burned to death with a flamethrower!"

***

One week later – January
Mossad – Kidon Headquarters, Tel Aviv

"Langley calling on a secure line for you, Philippe."

It's got to be Biff Roberts, Philippe thought. Philippe Andros, Kidon's Director, knew Biff only called when something big was brewing.

"Haven't heard from you in a while, what's up, Biff?" Philippe said.

"I need to get away, Philippe, it's been a tough year. Thought Patricia and I would fly over next week for a short vacation at her Herzliya beach house, have her kids fly down from Europe for a family visit."

"No ski trip this year?" Philippe asked. He figured Biff might not want to go back to Cortina, where he'd been shot last New Year's, but maybe a different ski spot.

"After last year's incident, I decided on a change of scenery this winter. Patricia may go ski with the kids in Italy following our Tel Aviv vacation. We're looking forward to kicking back on the beach. Enjoying the Mediterranean sun and surf. Your security is far better than Cortina's. I doubt my *fatwa* has expired. It has a long shelf life, I understand. I'm safer in Tel Aviv."

"Not many would say that after all those Hamas rocket attacks on us six months ago."

"You guys survived, you always do," Biff said. "Besides, we need to conduct some business."

Philippe should have known there was more to it. Biff wasn't a man to stop working for long, even while on vacation. "What have you got in mind?"

"Got a new toy, great technology; one that may offer an interim solution to your Iranian problem."

"So that Sohae explosion wasn't just an accident?" Philippe asked, sensing Biff's drift immediately.

"Not entirely," Biff said. He always admired what a quick study Philippe was. "I'll fill you in after my arrival; go over the toy's specs with you. If you like the technology, we could finance the plan out of my black vault. Politics in D.C. are a mess presently with our nations' relationships strained."

"That's putting it mildly. Bibi's still fuming."

"So you understand that I can't run the operation though the normal chain of command. I have a certain amount of autonomy as CT Director with funding for global counterterror operations. The covert funds are dispersed at my discretion, circumventing the politics. My plan would be 'committeed' to death, I don't want to deal with going through normal chains."

"Tell me about it."

"I'm supposed to be apolitical," Biff said.

"Yeah, right, you're reluctant to express an opinion. But I understand where you are going with this covert op, acting within your prerogative as CIA's CT director."

Biff ignored Philippe's comment about his conservative politics.

"Until the next election we need to play the clandestine game," Biff said. "We have a mutual responsibility to address existential threats like Iran. You catch my drift?"

"All too well," Philippe replied. "We're on the same page. We share a common threat. We'll talk at length. Send me your ETA and my security detail will pick you up at Ben Gurion and escort you to Patricia's beach house. I guarantee to provide a safe sanctuary for your vacation."

Biff smiled. "Okay, you got it. Thanks. See you next week, Philippe."

www.ingramcontent.com/pod-product-compliance
Lightning Source LLC
Chambersburg PA
CBHW031254170626
46807CB00001B/137